UNDER FIRE

**Books by *New York Times* Bestselling Author
Lindsay McKenna**

SILVER CREEK series
Silver Creek Fire
Courage Under Fire

WIND RIVER VALLEY series
Wind River Wrangler
Wind River Rancher
Wind River Cowboy
Wrangler's Challenge
Kassie's Cowboy (novella included in
CHRISTMAS WITH MY COWBOY)
Lone Rider
Wind River Lawman
Home to Wind River
Wind River Wedding (novella included in
MARRYING MY COWBOY)
Wind River Protector
Wind River Undercover

Published by Kensington Publishing Corp.

COURAGE UNDER FIRE

LINDSAY McKENNA

ZEBRA BOOKS
KENSINGTON PUBLISHING CORP.
www.kensingtonbooks.com

ZEBRA BOOKS are published by

Kensington Publishing Corp.
119 West 40th Street
New York, NY 10018

All Kensington titles, imprints, and distributed lines are available at special quantity discounts for bulk purchases for sales promotion, premiums, fund-raising, educational, or institutional use.

Special book excerpts or customized printings can also be created to fit specific needs. For details, write or phone the office of the Kensington Sales Manager: Attn.: Sales Department. Kensington Publishing Corp., 119 West 40th Street, New York, NY 10018. Phone: 1-800-221-2647.

Zebra and the Z logo Reg. U.S. Pat. & TM Off.

First Printing: March 2021
ISBN-13: 978-1-4201-5083-4
ISBN-10: 1-4201-5083-9

ISBN-13: 978-1-4201-5087-2 (eBook)
ISBN-10: 1-4201-5087-1 (eBook)

10 9 8 7 6 5 4 3 2 1

Printed in the United States of America

Chapter One

"No . . . no, don't murder the bees!" Cari Taylor turned in her sleep, reliving a moment in her life when she was five years old. Moaning, she cried out, "Don't hurt them! They won't sting us!"

Mrs. Johnson, their day care teacher, was horrified. There, near the rear gate of their playground in back of the house, was a huge hive of honeybees, the size of a basketball, in the apple tree.

Frantic, Cari saw her teacher's face go from shock to horror. Her own heart bounced in fear for the bees. Her father and uncle had beehives and she had grown up with the beekeepers and dearly loved her little friends. "No!" she cried. "They're harmless, Mrs. Johnson!" she squeaked, putting herself between the twenty other children who surrounded the teacher, who were all staring at the ball of bees in the fruit tree, fear in their faces.

"All of you," Mrs. Johnson said, her voice hoarse with near hysteria, "in the house! Get in the house! The bees will sting you!"

Tears jammed into Cari's eyes as she stubbornly stood her ground between her teacher and the fruit tree. She could hear the soft, gentle buzzing of twenty thousand honeybees all in a ball, protecting the queen, in the center of it, who had flown from someone's beehive to find a new home. The hive had become crowded with too many bees and the queen had taken half of her female worker bees and perhaps some of her drones who attended her, on a flight from the hive in order to find a less crowded place to start a new hive. Cari knew this, but it was obvious blond-haired Mrs. Johnson, who was only twenty-two years old, did not. She was frantically gathering all her five- and six-year-old charges to her, pushing them gently toward the rear door of the house.

"I'll call the fire department," she told the kids, continuing to herd them inside. "They'll kill the bees and you'll be safe. Then, you can go outside and play on the swings, slides, and monkey bars."

Cari followed dejectedly, hearing the teacher's words. *Oh, no!* She turned on her small heel, looking longingly at the ball of bees. They wouldn't hurt anyone. How could she get the teacher to believe her?

"Cari! Get in here!" Mrs. Johnson ordered, gesturing frantically. "Hurry up! The bees could come and sting you to death! Run!"

Grudgingly, she came, a pout on her lips. She shook her head as she approached her teacher. "They won't hurt anyone!" she cried out. "Don't kill them! They'll leave in a bit. They're just resting. They're trying to find a new home, is all!"

Frustration appeared on Lucy Johnson's face. She

grabbed Cari's pink T-shirt by the shoulder, pulling her forward. "Get in the house! You must be kept safe!"

Cari entered the house. All the kids were in the large sleeping area where they took naps, looking at one another, some afraid, some upset, some curious, and others stressed. A few were crying. Mrs. Johnson had never been in such a dramatic and emotional state like this before and it scared all of them. She was afraid of bees. Dodging to the right, Cari ran out of the room, down the hall, and into another room that led to the rear door out to the backyard playground. As she quietly, like a shadow, edged toward that hallway, she saw Mrs. Johnson pick up the phone, dial 911, her voice cracking with fear as she told the dispatcher that the fire department had to get over here right now. They had to kill the bees in order to protect her children.

Cari slipped away when Mrs. Johnson turned her back on the nap room. On tiptoes, she ran to the rear exit. Heart pumping with terror for her bee friends, she leaped down the steps, ran across the yard to the fruit tree. Just above her, the group of bees were surrounding a fork in a large branch. Terror filled her as she looked back at the door, making sure Mrs. Johnson didn't discover her out here. Would she find her missing?

Pursing her small mouth, Cari closed her eyes and sent a mental message to the queen bee she knew was at the center of this swarm of honeybees. She had been taught that she could "talk" to the bees with her mind. "Let me find you, queen. Guide me to you. I need to carry you out of here or they will come and murder all of you! I'll take you down the alley. There's a nice fruit tree orchard at the other end. I'll find a safe place for you!"

She opened her eyes, struggled up the trunk, grabbing branches to hoist herself up to the mass of bees.

Without hesitation, Cari gently placed her small fingers into the mass. The bees were humming, but were not upset by her nearness. They felt like warm, living, soft velvet enclosing her as she eased her fingers down, down, down toward the center. The edge of the bee swarm was almost up to her armpit as she slowly, gently, felt around for the large queen. There! She'd found her!

The bees continued to hum, not at all perturbed by Cari's arm stuck into their swarm ball.

Mentally, Cari told the queen that she would ease her into her palm, close her fingers carefully around her, and slowly draw her out of the center. She felt the queen, who had a much larger, longer body, and cupped her palm beneath her. In a moment, she had the queen and began to ease her hand back, bringing her out of the swarm.

The bees continued to hum, undisturbed by her human presence.

Once her hand drew free, Cari struggled down to the ground, carefully holding the queen, ensuring she would not accidentally squeeze her and kill her. Running for the gate, she unlatched it, moved outside of it, closed it, turned right, and dug her toes into the dirt of the alleyway, running as hard as she could. The wind tore past her, her mouth open, gasping for air as she passed the alleyway and headed into the huge stand of apple trees in the nearby farm orchard. Spotting an easy-to-climb fruit tree, Cari raced over to it, nearly tripping on a small rise of dirt in her path.

Climbing awkwardly, with one hand only, she wriggled up into the tree, spotting a low-hanging Y-shaped branch.

Cari was sobbing for breath, tired and worried. What if Mrs. Johnson did a head count and found her missing? That would be very, very bad for Cari. But she had to rescue her bees! They couldn't be murdered by the firefighters! And the fire department was not that far away from the day care house.

Gasping, her lungs burning with exertion from her run, she twisted a look over her shoulder. There, behind her, was a dark cloud of honeybees flying toward her, following the pheromone scent of their queen, heading directly to where Cari was standing.

She told the queen that she'd be safe here with her family, that no one would find or hurt them. Gently placing the queen on the fork of the branches, Cari pushed off and fell to the ground, landing on her hands and knees. Quickly leaping up, brushing off the knees of her jeans, she raced back toward the alley, opened the gate and slipped in, latching it behind her.

Once inside, Cari hurriedly tiptoed through the supply room, cracked the door to the hall and peered out. She could hear the teacher talking loudly to the firefighters who had just arrived. Her heart felt like it was going to burst out of her chest, and she walked quietly down the hall, edging silently toward the nap room. All the children were gathered together, frightened, some clinging to Mrs. Johnson's slacks. There were three firefighters standing there, listening to her.

Cari tried to slow down her heart, still breathing through her mouth, trying to remain undetected and quiet. She pressed her back to the hall wall and listened intently.

"Well," the lieutenant was saying, "we have foam, Mrs. Johnson. We can use that to get rid of the bees. We'll go look at that fruit tree and assess the situation. We could also call a beekeeper to come and get them. That way, they wouldn't be killed."

"I want them killed!" Mrs. Johnson said, her voice high-pitched with fear. Her arms weren't long enough to hold all the children who were now fully frightened and watching the firefighters with trepidation.

Cari knew the bees would be gone. They followed the queen, no matter where she flew. Leaning down, she made sure her knees weren't dusty looking, or sharp-eyed Mrs. Johnson would see the patches on her jeans and ask a lot of questions that Cari didn't want to answer. She straightened and saw the children dispersing from around the teacher, wandering about, not knowing what to do.

Mrs. Johnson had left them and went to the back door to watch the firefighters as they tramped through the house and out the rear door. It was then that Cari silently slipped back among them, no one having missed her presence under the circumstances.

Just as Cari got comfortable on her little bed in the corner of the nap room, she heard the door open and close, the clomping of heavy boots, the firefighters moving back near the front door and the nap room.

"Well?" Mrs. Johnson demanded. "Did you see them?"

"No, ma'am," the lieutenant said. "They're gone."

"What? No! That's impossible!" she said, hurrying past them, disappearing as she headed for the rear door.

Cari held her breath for a moment. The bees were gone! Relief made her sag, her small back against the corner of the two walls. She heard the click-clack of

Mrs. Johnson's low-heeled shoes echoing and coming closer and closer.

"They are gone!" she exclaimed to the firefighters. "Where did they go? Are they hanging around? Will they come back?"

"No, ma'am, they're gone and we don't know where they flew. That's a swarm. In the spring, honeybees will swarm if their hive is too crowded. They're harmless, really. When they're swarming, they don't sting anyone. They're following their queen to a new home, is all."

"So? They won't return to harm the children?"

"They would never harm anyone," the lieutenant said. "Now, it's safe to let the kids out into the playground."

"Heck," one of the other firefighters said, "you might even use this as a teachable moment for the kids, ma'am. Let the children learn about bee swarms and why they happen?"

Mrs. Johnson curled her lip, glaring at the younger man. "Never! This was a dangerous situation to my children! I'm charged with their safety and welfare. I hate insects!"

The lieutenant shrugged and lifted his hand. "Come on," he told his team, "we're done here. You and your children are safe now, Mrs. Johnson."

And so were her bees, Cari thought, staying silent, remaining the shadow that she was. When she got home this afternoon? She'd tell her parents what happened. They'd be proud of her for helping the queen and her worker bees to safety. But she could never tell the teacher what really happened. Not ever. Mrs. Johnson would not be happy, and Cari knew she'd get five minutes of detention staring at a corner if she was found out. Secrets were good.

When the dream ended, Cari opened her eyes, awake in the darkness of her bedroom in her San Francisco loft. Looking at a digital clock, the red numbers said 3:13 a.m. *Ugh.* Why did she have such a rich dream life? Most nights, she had happy dreams. Flights of fancy. But tonight? This one was different.

Sitting up in bed, she rubbed her face, pushing back strands of her black hair away from her face. At twenty-nine years old, her life was like a dream come true. She was a beekeeping consultant with an MBA and worked with countries around the world, showing them how to make beekeeping and the honey they made in their hives a commercial venture.

Because the bee populations around the world were nosediving thanks to pesticides, hive collapses, and loss of rural land for the bees to gather pollen from local flowers, they were in a crisis. A global one.

Cari worked for the state of California as their bee expert and was always busy with the farmers from the Imperial Valley, where so many crops grew. The many almond orchards thrived and all were dependent upon bee pollinators. That was where she came in, giving them sound, healthy advice on what beehives need in order to pollinate the crops successfully. No cutting corners, no use of bee-killing pesticides, she tried to get farmers to work with more organic and sustainable ways to grow their crops, as well as to protect the sagging honey-bee population.

She saw herself as a Don Quixote tilting at windmills at times, because agriculture wanted to use pesticides. Now there was a global clash on using them, and billions of bees were dying off at such a swift rate, it would take a toll on how many crops would not be pollinated. No pollination? No food. Starvation could occur. Combine that with a horrifying loss of birds—another pollinator— every year, Mother Earth was in a real crisis, thanks to man.

She felt like a frontline warrior trying to help both types to not only survive, but thrive. There were many raptor rehabilitator activists and bird sanctuaries around the world fighting right alongside of her to protect all bird species, just as she was fighting to save bees.

Sighing, she got up, knowing that she'd never go back to sleep.

The phone rang. Frowning, she picked it up.

"Hello?" Who would be calling at this time in the morning?

"This is the sheriff, ma'am. Am I speaking to Ms. Cari Taylor?"

"Yes?" A frown creased her brow as she sat down on the edge of her bed. "Why are you calling me? What's wrong?"

"Ma'am, your stepbrother, Dirk Bannock, just escaped from the prison. The officials from that prison called us about it. We've already contacted your parents, and now we're letting you know."

Gasping, Cari shot to her feet. "What? Dirk broke out? He's on the loose?" Instantly her heart thundered in her chest, and she felt suddenly dizzy, abruptly sitting down, her one hand wrapping into the quilt cover across her bed.

Was she still dreaming? This was a nightmare! It couldn't be true!

Oh, God, if it was?

Dirk had entered her life when her mother married Blake Bannock, a civil engineer. He had a son from his former marriage, Dirk, when he married her mother, Nalani,

Terror ripped through her. She suddenly felt faint from the shock. "B-but, he was in for twenty-five years for murder!"

"Yes, ma'am, we know. We have an all-points bulletin out to all law enforcement, and we're working with the prison directly to find and apprehend him."

Pressing her hand to her chest, feeling the pounding of her heart, adrenaline racing through her, she whispered frantically, "But he promised to come after me! He threatened me in open court. He'll kill me!"

"Yes, ma'am, we're very well aware of that. We are sending a police unit over to your home. They will be on watch twenty-four hours a day."

Her throat ached, and she squeezed her eyes shut, hot tears streaming out of them. "H-he said he'd kill me. You have to find him!"

"We're doing our best."

"What about my parents?" Dirk hated her mother and her. He was competitive and wanted all the attention of his father, who now shared it with his second wife and Cari, a product of Nalani's first marriage. Dirk had hated her the moment he met her. He saw her as direct competition.

"They also have police protection."

"But for how long?" Though Dirk had threatened her

mother, the biggest part of his hatred was reserved for Cari. She'd seen him fire the handgun at his girlfriend, Denise, and murder her. He was a cold-blooded killer. In court, a psychiatrist had labeled him as sociopathic. His world consisted of his rules and regulations. He defied the laws of society at every turn.

By age twelve, he was selling drugs at his school. And that was when he became an addict. By age fifteen, Dirk had amassed a group of boys who sold the drugs over an even larger area where they had lived. And by the time she was sixteen years old, and saw him murder Denise, he was a regional drug lord. And as much as law enforcement tried to indict him for drug running, Dirk was incredibly intelligent and was able to avoid being caught.

Until Denise. She felt sorry for the girl then, as she did now. Dirk was a law unto himself. Cari wondered during the trial if he'd murdered other kids. If so, it had never been found out. But her intuition, which was very strong, told her that Denise had not been his first victim. Or his last.

"How long can you give us protection?" she demanded.

"Ma'am, we can't do it forever, but we will make sure while we try and hunt him down, that you are protected twenty-four hours a day."

That wasn't much consolation because Cari knew how smart Dirk was. He hadn't graduated high school, disappearing into the massive suburbs around their home with his gang. She'd seen it all happen with her own eyes, never interested in taking drugs or selling them, which he'd wanted her to do. She'd told her parents about his illegal activities, and they had talked with law enforcement, spent tons of money with psychiatrists and social workers, to try and "save" Dirk.

But none of that type of support had worked. Dirk was out of control with a fierce, focused need to have his own "army," as he'd referred to his drug gang. And, he hated women. Especially her. Dirk had created a tattoo when he was twelve to make the boys around him feel like they were part of something special. Anyone wearing the Nazi swastika on their left forearm, with the word WARRIOR below it, indicated that he was one of Dirk's followers.

Too often, Cari had seen him in school with his gang, bullying other boys and girls, as well as selling drugs anytime he could get away with it. He was always being sent to the principal's office, always getting his hand slapped, but he wouldn't stop. Adults didn't scare him in the least. In fact, Cari wondered if anything scared him. She was sure as hell afraid of him.

She wondered about her parents. Were they still up? It was near four a.m. Should she call them now or wait until a decent hour? And what about herself? She usually took the bus into work, her car left in the garage beneath the townhouse. Was she safe to go out now or not? Was Dirk nearby? Watching where she lived? Waiting to jump her and put a bullet in her head like he had through Denise's head?

A cold wash of terror, so deep and upsetting, flowed through her. Intuitively, Cari knew Dirk would go after her first. He hated her more than anyone else on earth.

Sitting on the bed, she heard herself say into the phone to the sheriff, "What if he jumps me on the way to work?"

"Ma'am, we don't have those kinds of resources. The best we can do is to watch your townhouse."

Her throat closed up with dread, her hand moving against her neck, her fingers tightening around the phone. "What can I do? How do I protect myself? Dirk hated me and he hates my mother. What if he goes to attack her?"

"We've already talked to your parents, ma'am. They know the realities of this. Maybe you should take a vacation and remove yourself from this area for a week or two? We hope to catch him by then."

That was little comfort for something that was life-or-death to Cari. "A vacation?" There was derision in her tone. Disbelief. "That's the best you can do to protect us?"

"We told your parents to hire a trained bodyguard who could provide around-the-clock protection. You could do the same."

That blew her away. "I'm sure a personal bodyguard for hire would cost a fortune."

"Yes, ma'am, it would be a lot of money."

Anger wound through her. "Will you keep me and my parents informed on your search to find Dirk?"

"Yes, we will. Once he's caught, you'll be the first to know."

"Did he escape alone or with others?"

"No. He was alone."

"He had a huge drug ring. Wouldn't it be logical that someone in that group helped him from the outside?"

"The prison is still trying to trace his steps to escape. I don't have those answers yet, but once we do? We'll be in touch with all of you."

Her voice drained. "Okay, thanks for letting me know." And she hung up, sitting there, staring at the window with the blind drawn. A bit of light leaked in around the edges of it. Living in the city meant she couldn't see the stars at night, something she'd loved as a child. But now, having streetlights felt comforting, making her feel less unsafe.

What was she going to do? *What?* Her mind was a clash of questions and no answers. What if they didn't catch Dirk? Prisoners had escaped before and disappeared. Why couldn't he? And she knew he was like a chameleon. He was scarily intelligent, crafty, and strategic in his thinking.

She wiped her cheeks dry. Tears of fear.

The phone rang.

Cari jumped. Her heart took off in a wild staccato beat.

"Hello . . ." she whispered, afraid of who might be on the other end.

"Thank goodness you're there."

Relief plunged through her. It was her mother.

"Mom? Are you and Blake okay?"

"We're fine, Cari. I just wanted to call you to see if you'd heard from the sheriff yet."

"I-I just got off the phone with them. What are we going to do?"

"Not much except wait," Nalani said, sadness in her tone.

"How is Blake taking this?" After all, Dirk was his son.

"Not well at all. He's torn between Dirk maybe getting killed if law enforcement corners him, to Dirk hunting you and me down like he promised he would once he got out."

That cold, icy hand gripped her heart again. "Yes," she whispered faintly, "I've never forgotten, Mom."

"Neither of us have. He's so smart," she said wearily. "A brilliant genius gone astray."

Cari snorted. "He's a cold-blooded murderer, Mom. I don't care how smart he is."

"You're right, of course. We need a plan, Cari. What if they don't capture him? I know in my soul he's going after you first, and I'm tied in knots worrying about it."

Her hand tightened on the phone. "Yes . . . he will. I feel so helpless. What can I do? I hate guns with a passion. I don't want to learn how to carry or shoot one. I couldn't kill anything, you know that. God, I've had such a wonderful life since graduating. I have a dream job, something I love. Everything was going so well . . ."

Nalani sighed loudly. "Blake and I were talking about that just now. If Dirk isn't caught in two weeks, we both think you need to leave the state, get another job where Dirk won't find you. That way, you can at least have some peace. I know how much this is going to affect you daily, Cari. You're not the kind of person to deal with this type of situation long term. If they don't apprehend Dirk, we don't have a hundred thousand dollars a year to pay for one bodyguard, much less two of them, to protect you and me."

"Is that how much it costs?"

"Actually, most bodyguards get around a hundred and fifty thousand dollars and upward, a year. We don't have that kind of money."

"And I don't either," she whispered wearily.

"His hatred is aimed at you, darling girl, and we're sick over this. We'll be fine. Blake is a hunter and we have guns in the house. He also can get both of us a concealed carry permit to have a weapon on us, which would make me feel much safer. I know you would not go that route."

"No, never . . . I saw him fire his gun at Denise . . . it's something I'll never forget, Mom. I-I just can't . . ."

"Which is why we think you should look for another job, Cari. My sense tells me Dirk isn't going to be recaptured very soon, and we need to keep you safe. We need a long-range plan in case he isn't in custody in the next two weeks. Also? We'd like you to vacate your townhouse for now. Blake would like to see you go on vacation. Dirk could wait for you when you leave to go to work, too."

"I've already thought of that . . ."

"Would you do that for us? We don't trust the authorities to know your whereabouts. Computer information gets hacked out of sheriffs' departments, too. We want to wipe your footprints clear of your job and where you live."

"To tell you the truth, I hadn't thought of these things. Yes, I think what I'll do is take my car and go to Muir Woods and the redwoods. I can get an extended motel room rental in nearby Mill Valley. I would feel safe there because I know the area well. I can do a lot of hiking. The redwoods always give me a profound sense of peace, and it's so calming and healing an area for me."

"Plus, you didn't start going there until after Dirk was in prison. He doesn't know your haunts, where you love to go."

"That's what I was thinking. Did you ever mention my love of Muir Woods to him when you visited him in prison?"

"No, he never asked about you and we purposely didn't talk about anything regarding you in any way."

"Dirk never liked Nature. He was a city person. He liked the nightlife, the excitement, noise and lights," Cari murmured, feeling her heart rate begin to slowly stop racing. The adrenaline in her bloodstream made her feel shaky, a reaction to the fight-or-flight response, she supposed.

"I can call the sheriff's department and tell them they don't need to watch your townhouse twenty-four hours a day, then. We aren't going to tell them where you are, as I said."

"Good plan." She looked up at the clock. It was early May, a beautiful month to be in San Francisco, one of her favorite times of the year. "We'll know in two weeks," she said, more to herself than her mother.

"Knowing Dirk? I don't think they'll capture him. He's elusive, like a wild animal."

Animal was right, but Cari wouldn't even want to compare Dirk to any other living thing. "He's a monster without a heart. Soulless. I don't care what anyone says."

"He is all of that," her mother sadly agreed. "You need to get on the computer and look for another job, just in case, Cari. I hate saying that because I know how happy you are with this one."

"I know. But I'm so afraid of him. I know he'll come after me." She rubbed her face, her whole world in a slow motion tumble, being destroyed once more, by Dirk. "Everything Dirk touches dies, Mom. You know that."

"Yes, and I'm afraid you're going to have to disappear until he's caught if we go past this two-week limit we've set for law enforcement to recapture him."

"If only they would!" She could have her life back!

"We'll see," her mother answered hesitantly. "Dirk's mother was a drug addict, as you know. That's why Blake divorced her. Sherry loved her drugs more than anything else and Blake was worried about Dirk as a baby. He's sure that she sexually abused him even though he couldn't prove it."

"It was proven by his behavior as he grew up, Mom. He was angry all the time. I've lost count how many times he flew into a rage if you looked at him wrong, or stood up and confronted him. He hates women in general. All he wanted to do was destroy you if you disagreed with him on anything."

"Then let's move forward with this plan. Muir Woods has always been your healing place. In the morning, pack and get out of there. You call us when you find a suitable motel to hole up in. Take your hiking gear, knapsack, and boots."

She smiled softly, resting her elbows on her knees, phone in her left hand. "You know me so well, Mom. I'll worry about you two, also."

"We'll be fine. It's you we worry about. You have no protection against him."

"I can have it by disappearing. He doesn't know where I live, knows nothing of my life, my likes or dislikes. I'm going to give him a cold trail to follow. I'll use my degree in agriculture, move to my biology major, and take my camera and photograph the creatures that live in Muir Woods. That will make me happy. I'm always at peace when I'm out in the wilds and in rural areas."

"I know you are. Who knows? You might run into a honeybee hive out in the woods," she said.

"Oh, wouldn't that be wonderful? I'd love that! To see a wild hive? Nirvana." She laughed, feeling better, feeling some hope in the darkness embracing her.

"I'll never forget when you were five years old and

told us what you'd done to save the queen and her swarm at the day care. That was just incredible. Blake and I knew then that you would one day work with the bee people."

Cari appreciated her Hawaiian mother. She had grown up on Oahu, outside of Honolulu, where her farm parents had fifty bee hives. Their honey was sold throughout the Hawaiian Islands. Nalani had been taught by her father to become a beekeeper, too. There were five generations of her family who maintained the hives. "Finding wild hives is hard unless you're deep in the woods where few people go," Cari agreed.

"Well, let's get this plan into motion."

"It's not fair one person can upset all our lives," Cari muttered, frowning.

"Nothing in life is fair," Nalani said gently. "Women are adaptable and we'll do just that with Dirk on the loose. If we're lucky? This will be over soon."

"I hope you're right, Mom," she said, no hope in her tone. "My gut tells me my whole life is about to change and I have no idea if that's good or bad . . ."

Chapter Two

May 15

Chase Bishop barely held back a curse. The beekeeper who was supposed to know "everything" about bees had left an email on his home computer, unexpectedly quitting this morning.

Chase then called the Sandoval family, a Hispanic family of beekeepers who had, according to the mother, Theresa Sandoval, three generations of expertise on bees. They were from central Mexico. She was the only one he trusted to help him out of this serious business disaster.

A year ago, he'd tried to persuade her family of five to take over the job of managing the twenty-five hives, but they had refused. Was it because of this supposed beekeeper, Troy Court, that he'd hired to oversee the business? The balding man had been an egotistical bastard, bragging about his ability to create successful commercial beekeeping start-ups. And it had been Theresa Sandoval who had warned him that Court was no beekeeper. She'd seen him out at the area where Chase had the hives and had come to him later that day, warning him about it.

But what the hell did Chase know about bees? This was his fault due to his ignorance about the bee industry. His mother, Mary, had founded Mama's Store, the highly popular organic grocery store in Silver Creek, and had pushed him into creating honey production as an "egg" in the ranch family's financial basket. Mary wanted only raw, unfiltered, organic honey to sell in her store, not trusting other companies or their labels that touted the slogan.

His mother was hell on wheels when it came to details. She'd collected five commercial honey companies from around the USA, regional as well as national, and asked them to send her one jar each of their honey. And then she'd had it run through every test known to mankind to find out if they were telling the truth that their product was raw, unfiltered organic honey—or not.

Unscrupulous companies could put water in with the honey, making it thinner. Another trick was to mix fructose syrup with the honey. A third had no pollen in the honey, so it couldn't legally be called honey. The fourth had filtered out the pollen because it came from China and not the USA, but the company was selling it fraudulently as "Made in the USA." The fifth jar had not only no pollen in it, was from China and had antibiotics in it, of all things. Mary remembered in 2001 that Chinese beekeepers had an epidemic of foulbrood disease that killed millions of honeybee brood eggs. They used chloramphenicol, a carcinogenic antibiotic that had been banned by the FDA, to fight it. That honey couldn't be legally sold in the USA, as a result.

Cheating businesspeople, Mary told him, showing him the results of the lab tests on all five jars. These companies were after money, not caring what they sold to the public. That was when they hired Court to set up and create a commercial honey production on the ranch, instead. Mary always wanted to know where the product came from, and that it had damned well be raw and organic—or else. By putting hives on the ranch, they would know the honey was the real deal. Her consumers could buy their honey with trust.

He called his mother on his cell phone.

"Helllloooooo, good morning . . ." Mary sang.

"Mom, it's me," he said heavily, scowling. "Court has quit."

"Really?"

Chase expected his mother to say anything but that. "Yeah, he sent me an email this morning. You don't sound surprised or unhappy about it."

"Well," she said, "that's good news and bad news, son. The good news is that egotistical idiot is gone. The bad news is what might be wrong with our beehives? He left for a reason. Have you been out to look at the hives this morning?"

"No, it's only seven a.m. And I know next to nothing about beekeeping." His mother got up at five a.m., was at her grocery store by six thirty a.m. "Besides, what would I look for?"

"Well, it's mid-May. Those hives need a lot of care and work at this time of year because they're coming out of winter. I wonder why he suddenly up and left?"

"I don't know and I don't care. One thing is obvious: He's left us high and dry. We don't have a beekeeper."

"Call Theresa Sandoval. She's up at this time of morning. Ask her to come out, bring her three grown children, or whoever is still at home, and carefully check each of those hives, Chase. I don't trust Court any further than I could throw his swelled-headed body."

Mary disliked Court, that was no secret. She'd warned Chase he was a braggart and didn't know half of what he said he knew. Mary knew more about the beekeeping industry and caring for bees than he did, she'd told Chase. But he'd relied on Court to manage the new company. *What the hell!* Sighing, he growled, "I'll call her. But I need a trained professional commercial beekeeping person to run this operation and business for us, Mom. I can't do it and neither can you."

"Right you are," Mary said lightly. "Call Theresa. Have her come over and check out those hives and give us a report. There's a reason why Court suddenly quit. I don't trust him."

"Where do you find a professional commercial bee person?" he wondered out loud.

"Leave it to me to suss out," Mary said archly. "I get beekeeper magazines. They have a classified section. I'll start lookin'. Call me back when Theresa has checked out those hives, okay?"

"Yes, I will." Chase scowled and hung up, fingering through the Rolodex on his desk. He wasn't blazingly fast on a computer, and in fact hated typing in general because he was no good at it. But running the forty-thousand-acre family dynasty, Three Bars Ranch? That he could do and had been doing very well. At thirty years old, he was pretty damned good at managing the different groups of wranglers who did the hard, daily work to keep the ranch not only solvent, but flourishing. Except for the bee-keeping part of it.

He punched in the numbers for Theresa Sandoval, hoping she'd answer.

"Hello?" Theresa said.

"This is Chase," he said, "and I desperately need your beekeeping expertise, Theresa, and any of your kids that can come along to help you."

Mary and Chase sat with Theresa at four p.m. that same day at the kitchen table. Mary had made a pot of coffee and they were grouped around the large, round maple table that had an oil cloth of brightly colored flowers across it.

"To sum it up," Theresa said, opening her hands, "this is very bad news," she warned. "My two daughters, son, and I, opened up every one of those twenty-five hives to inspect them. Twenty of them were in hive collapse." She frowned, her brown eyes flashing. "The reason is because Court fed them corn syrup through the winter, which is not nutritious like honey is. They've starved to death and died. You have anywhere from forty- to eighty thousand bees dead in every one of those hives. Twenty of the twenty-five hives you bought last year, are gone."

Mary gasped, her hands flying to her mouth, her eyes huge with shock and grief.

Chase bit back a curse. He'd spent a *lot* of money buying those hives and stocking them. Each hive cost a thousand dollars, not to mention three hundred dollars for three pounds of live bees that were a nuclear colony or *nuc*, plus a queen bee. In all, each of those hives easily cost over one thousand dollars. And Court had just destroyed twenty thousand dollars of their money and walked off to parts unknown. Chase felt guilty as hell that all those bees were dead. He had no idea of what Court had been doing out there. Dammit!

"I'm sorry," Theresa said, sadness in her tone. "The other five hives are lean and close to collapsing. I would suggest that you let us give the honey stored in your barn to the bees to eat. We'll remove the fructose, which is starving them, and they will have a chance to survive."

"Absolutely!" Mary said, pushing away from the table, getting up and pacing, her face filled with anger. "Can we hire you, Theresa?" she asked the Hispanic woman. "We *need* your help. Just name your price. We'll pay it."

Theresa sat up, surprise in her expression. "Señora Mary, you have helped out our family so much that I could not take a dime. We will work hard to save the other five hives."

"Well, we'll pay you, anyway," Mary muttered, scowling. She turned to her son. "Chase, I'm gonna run down some possible candidates to replace Court. We have to get a *real* expert in here, pronto."

Chase grimly nodded. "Like yesterday . . ."

Mary finished off her last sip of coffee and stood up. "We did not trust Court."

"Wish I'd listened to you, Theresa," Chase said, shaking his head, giving her an apologetic look.

Patting his shoulder, Theresa said, "If you hire some-one who knows what they're doing, me and my family will do the weekly and monthly work to keep your hives healthy, safe, and strong. We will *never* feed your bees anything but their own honey. That way, they will winter successfully. They will live because they are getting the nutrition they need. Honey has many properties, even vitamins and minerals, and the bee people need them in order to survive."

"I'm going to learn a whole lot more about bees," Chase stated flatly, rising. He pinned his gaze on Theresa, who was five-foot-two-inches tall, the same height as his mother. "Would you help us sort through résumés and come work for us temporarily? To care for the beehives?"

Giving him an adamant nod, Theresa said, "We will help you, Señor Chase." She crossed her heart with her hand. "Your family has been more than good to us. We owe you in return."

"Well," he grumbled, "you'll be well paid. All of you."

"Yes, this bee business must take off," Mary agreed. "The most important thing we need to do is hire the right person."

May 25

Cari finished packing. She was still in Mill Valley, having never gone back to her loft for fear that Dirk might be there, waiting for her. A cold feeling overcame her as she zipped up her second suitcase. The last weeks had been unending, brutal stress. Law enforcement had not found Dirk. She knew they wouldn't because he was so cunning and a primal animal with the survival instincts of one.

Her fingers trembled as she closed the zipper. She was a mess. She was hunted. And Dirk would murder her as easily as he had killed his girlfriend. Straightening, she tried to get herself together. She was flying to Silver Creek Airport in Wyoming. Her résumé had been chosen for an in-person interview with Chase Bishop, owner of the

Three Bars Ranch, who wanted to hire someone with her credentials. Nothing in her résumé hinted that Dirk was hunting her. Conscience pricking her, she wondered just how desperate she was to hide from him. Scared enough to involve people who knew nothing of her private life? How could she, if she was hired, put all of them at risk? Dirk would stop at nothing to take her down. He'd kill whoever stood in the way of getting to her. It was plain wrong not to tell her possible new employer.

Why hadn't she said something when she talked to Mrs. Mary Bishop last week? It was a long, exhausting, and searching phone call. And after that, Theresa Sandoval, a third-generation beekeeper, called her, delving deeply into all aspects of beekeeping to the last detail with her. Obviously, the ranching family wanted to make sure she was more than just paper credentials; that she knew the ins and outs of hive management in all four seasons, the health of a hive, and so much more.

Shaking her head, Cari knew she had to tell Mr. Bishop the truth. *The whole truth.* And she was sure when she did, he would scratch her off the list of applicants to hire, in a hurry. No one wanted a murderer endangering the people around their ranch or harming their employees. Turning, she looked at the cell phone. She should call him now. They were, after all, paying for her roundtrip flight.

Torn, she sat on the bed, leaning down, hands hiding her face. Her whole life had been upended. Desperate to disappear, Wyoming seemed the most remote, the last place Dirk would think to look. It was hell to be stalked.

Something told her that Chase Bishop would understand. But what did she expect him to do? She had enjoyed her chat with Mary, a spunky older woman who owned a hugely popular grocery store in Silver Creek. No, she couldn't do it, but what should she do? She'd start out the in-person interview with the truth. And then, the cards of her life would fall where they may. She had enough money saved up to reimburse Mr. Bishop for the round-trip flight and would immediately do so. Honesty had served her all her life and she wasn't about to start by lying or hiding important life-and-death information from him. No one deserved to be blindsided.

May 26

Chase waited impatiently at the small regional airport for the passengers to disembark. Outside the large, clean windows of the airport lounge waiting area, the sky was a light blue, the sun shining brightly. It was a beautiful May morning.

On his cell phone was a photo of Cari Taylor. By anyone's imagination, she was stunningly beautiful, seeming to have more a model's figure to go with her shining black hair that was loose and free around her shoulders. Maybe it was her cinnamon-gold-colored eyes that entranced him so much, or those long, thick black lashes that framed them. She wore absolutely no makeup, but she didn't need any. He'd gone over her very impressive résumé. His mother told him he had to hire her. She was that sure of Cari. Having Theresa Sandoval's thumbs-up approval on this woman made him feel less worried about the possibility that she would be a female version of Court. Theresa swore this woman knew beekeeping inside out, upside down, and right side up. Chase didn't want another twenty-thousand-dollar loss. His ranch was solvent, doing well, but taking hits like that was deadly to his bottom line and to the other up-and-coming growth ideas he wanted to institute to keep Three Bars viable and robust as a company.

"Mr. Bishop?"

Snapping his head up, he saw Cari Taylor standing in front of him. He grinned apologetically, quickly sliding his phone into his pocket. "I think I have nose-glued-to-the-cell-phone disease," he said, holding out his hand toward her. "My mother raised me better than that. Call me Chase. It's nice to meet you, Ms. Taylor," and he shook her long, slender hand. He expected her skin to be soft but firm. Instead, he felt small calluses on the inside of some of her fingers, and it was a bit sandpapery on the heel of her hand, which told him she worked outdoors a lot. "Welcome to Silver Creek," he added. "And thank you for coming. Do you have some luggage with you?"

She shook his hand and smiled tentatively. "Yes, I do, but before we get to that? I'd like to be able to sit down and speak to you about something very important that wasn't on my résumé." Hesitating a moment, she added in a lower tone, "And you may not want to think about hiring me because of a . . . situation in my life . . ."

Surprised, Chase released her hand. "Well," he said, "my ranch is only ten miles away. Would you agree to sit down at the kitchen table over a cup of coffee and talk about it?" He was confused. *What* wasn't on her résumé? She looked stressed, a bit pale, perhaps. It wasn't easy to ignore that she wore a tailored navy-blue pantsuit with a ruffled collar of white silk. The white pearl earrings certainly brought out her femininity.

"Don't you have a restaurant here in the terminal?" she

asked. "I don't want to put you to all that trouble of going out to your ranch."

He gave her an affable look. "No worries. Come on, let's go to the luggage carousel down at the end, over there." He pointed in that direction. "Silver Creek is a small community and we're lucky to have an airport at all, never mind a real carousel." He looked around. "There's no restaurant here, Ms. Taylor."

Managing a slight, nervous smile, she bobbed her head. "Point made. Please call me Cari?" After all, his friendliness and easygoing nature made her shed a lot of her professional modus operandi.

"Fair enough. Let's go. You show me your luggage and I'll carry it for you to my truck that's parked out front."

More surprise. "Nowadays, men don't do that."

"Well," he said, giving her a teasing look, "welcome to the Land of Cowboys, Cari. We aren't called the Knights of the Range for nothing."

He did, after all, wear a black Stetson cowboy hat, a short-sleeved white cowboy shirt that was pressed, and a pair of Levi's. The only thing was that his boots were pretty well scarred up and certainly not new. There was a boneless grace to him. He stood well over six feet tall to her five feet seven inches. His arms were already getting tanned and she guessed it was because cowboys were outdoors all the time. At the carousel, she pointed out two pink bags.

"That's all you have?" he asked, leaning over and picking them up. "They're pretty little."

Grimacing, Cari said, "I wasn't thinking I'd be staying very long."

Chase frowned. "I was hoping you'd stay a couple of

days, see the ranch, see the layout, our clover and alfalfa pastures, our fruit tree orchard, which I understand from Theresa Sandoval, who is going to be working with whomever we choose to run the operation, are essential to honey production."

Cari couldn't avoid the worry she saw in his gray eyes. "I'll wait until we reach your ranch to tell you the rest of the story."

Nodding, he ushered her out the nearest door, pointing to his white ranch pickup that had bright red lettering on the door that said: THREE BARS RANCH. Cari Taylor appeared to be a scared rabbit trying to hold herself together over whatever secret she was hiding until they could talk about it at the ranch house. Worry nibbled at him, but he let it go, placed her bags in the extended cab seat and opened the passenger door for her. Again, he saw her surprise over his gentlemanly ways. He wasn't sure that the world had to destroy everything about respecting a woman, in the name of equality. That was a discussion for another day. What was she going to reveal to him that seemed so awful that she'd already assumed he wouldn't hire her? The mystery deepened.

Cari waited tensely, legs crossed beneath the large, round table as Chase made them coffee. He offered her some donuts to go with it, but honestly? Her stomach was tied in proverbial knots that refused to ease and disappear. She gently declined his offer.

Chase set out the creamer and the sugar, and then retrieved the mugs of coffee. "Here we go," he murmured, sitting down across from her. "Help yourself to whatever you need in it." He pointed to the tray between them.

"I like my coffee black," she said.

Nodding, he said, "I do, too. So? What's this all about? What wasn't in your résumé that you want to tell me?" He placed his elbows on the table, large hands around the white mug.

"I really hesitated in even coming," she said in a low, apologetic tone. "I waffled between making it a phone call instead of spending your money on a plane ticket. But after talking with your mother, Mary, and Theresa, I felt it would be cowardly of me to just do a phone call. I wanted to tell you in person because, frankly, I think your mother and Theresa are wonderful, heart-centered and caring people who only want the best for your ranch and this beekeeping assignment. They deserve to hear directly from me."

Taking a deep breath, she dove into why. Her voice was scratchy at times, low with pain and apology. It rocked her world that Chase Bishop seemed almost unaffected by what she revealed about Dirk and the murder and subsequent incarceration. Even more stunning, the cowboy just didn't seem as upset as she was about not telling him the whole truth of her sordid situation before this. When she finished, the silence stretched between them. If anything, his expression was sympathetic, not angry or upset that she'd duped him.

"I'll also pay you back for the money you spent on the airline ticket," she added. "In no way should you pay for it."

Chase lifted the mug to his lips and took the last sip of coffee. "You're assuming I'm going to send you packing.

Right?" He rose, motioning toward her cup. "Your coffee's cold. Would you like another cup? A hot one?"

Stunned, she stared up at him. "But, aren't you going to find someone else other than me? I'm in a dangerous situation. It's not fair to put that danger over you and your family, your employees, or this town."

He gave her a patient look, reached across and took her cup. "Maybe you want something stronger?"

Blinking, she didn't know what to say, shocked by his reaction to her tale. He stood waiting, cups in hand, watching her. "I—uh . . . no, I don't drink."

"Coffee it is," he murmured, turning and walking casually into the kitchen.

All the air went out of her lungs as she sat there watching the broadness of his shoulders, the long breadth of his back, the quiet power that exuded from him. In some ways, Chase Bishop reminded her of a jaguar: lethal, silent. There hadn't been a bit of recrimination in his eyes or face as she'd told him everything. No worry. No . . . well . . . nothing. How could that be?

Her hands were sweaty, gripped in her lap beneath the table. Her armpits were damp, too. Just telling this stranger about the shame of her family, Dirk's murdering way, and the fact he had targeted her, seemed to go right over Chase's head. He looked totally unconcerned, but he was attentive, didn't interrupt her, and listened with a focus that she'd rarely seen. Except the focus of a jaguar, which he seemed to emulate. The South American cat was her favorite animal and she'd seen them in zoos, as she sat and watched them for hours. And they watched her, too. It was the only species in the cat world that was equally at ease in a river or lake as it was on solid jungle ground. They were exceptional hunters.

Chase came back to the table, offering her a steaming mug of coffee and one for himself, and he sat back down. "My mother and Theresa seem to think you are the one we need to save our honey business," he began quietly, hands around his mug in front of him. "We've had ample opportunity to talk to, phone, and Skype other applicants, Cari. You were the only woman wanting this position." One corner of his mouth barely lifted. "My mother is a force of nature, if you haven't already figured that out."

Cari nodded once, under the spell of his low, slightly roughened voice, his gaze never leaving hers. She had a sense that he was monitoring her on so many levels that it would have scared the hell out of her if it wasn't him assessing her. The one word Chase created for her was *safety*. He was a big man, broad shoulders, thick muscling, but not like a weightlifter. There was a quiet, intriguing sense of danger around him, as well, but it wasn't aimed at her and she knew it. Normally, in her experience, men hid their real feelings, They kept their faces still, no emotions whatsoever, in them. Chase was totally different. Sometimes, as she'd told him about Dirk, she would see a flick of anger, or concern for her, or outright sympathy for the predicament she was in. It was so refreshing to be with a man who she could easily read. Under normal circumstances, she would have been ecstatic. But this circumstance was anything but that. It was life-and-death for her. And for him and his family and employees, too.

"I fell in love with Mary," she admitted hoarsely. "That's why I can't take the job. I want to protect all of you from my miserable situation."

"Well," he drawled, taking a sip of coffee, "when my mom hears directly from you about your situation? She'll pitch a fit the size of Texas if you don't take this job. I'm more scared of *her* reaction than that of your step-brother, Dirk."

Her eyes widened enormously as she allowed that low growl to vibrate through her, seeing the humor and seriousness in his face and the slight downward movement of his black brows to go along with it. "But . . . I'm putting your whole family, this town, in jeopardy," she protested, a catch in her voice, tears jamming into her eyes. "I-I can't do that! I couldn't live with myself if anything happened to any of you." She swallowed several times, blinking away the unshed tears, her emotions raw and helpless.

"Let me tell you a little bit about myself, Cari. Maybe that will help ease some of your worry. I joined the Marine Corps at eighteen. I grew up hunting with my dad, who died years ago. I've always been a pretty good marksman. While in boot camp, they singled me out because of my shooting skills. After graduation, I went to Marine Corps sniper school. By the time I came out of that, I was shipped over to Afghanistan where I worked with recon marines, SEALs, and Army Rangers. My years over there were spent hunting down ISIS and Taliban leaders and taking them out. I was often alone out in the mountains for weeks, sometimes months, finding my target. I know a lot about strategies that keep people safe. I worked in life-and-death environments like that for five years. I can apply what I learned for us, here, as well as for my mother and Theresa's family."

"Your world is foreign to me," she admitted, opening her hands. "But I know my stepbrother."

"Was he a sniper?"

"Not that I know of. He always carried a weapon on him though." Her voice became choked. "And he used it. I saw him murder his girlfriend."

He sighed. "That's a heavy burden for you to carry," he admitted gently. "Look, suspend this idea that I'm going to tell you to do an about-face and leave. I have two women I should have listened to when I hired this guy who has created hive collapse in twenty of my twenty-five hives. They both swore you could do the job and do it brilliantly. I rely on them because I know next to nothing about bees. I need to learn, though, and I was hoping you would educate me after you take the job. But," he said, rising, "let's settle this once and for all, Cari. I hope you brought some down-home-on-the-ranch kind of clothes? That's a nice pantsuit, but where we're going, it won't be ideal to wear. Do you have some jeans, work boots and such to wear, instead? I want you to drive around with me, see a bit of the spread, see where the last of the hives are located, our pastures and so on. I need you to get a feel for the ranch. We are all open to your experience. If you tell us the hives need to be moved, or whatever is needed, we'll do what you guide us to do. Fair enough?"

"Are you *sure*, Chase? Is this really what you want? I'm a target. Your family and employees will become targets."

"Let me worry about your safety, okay? You just stick to your bees and we'll keep you safe and happy. And my family and employees will also be safe. I'm putting no one at risk and I believe the severity of your situation. I'll put my knowledge and experience against that stepbrother of yours."

Cari slowly rose. "I do have one pair of work clothes with me."

"Good," he said. "Come with me and I'll show you your room."

"Here? In your home?"

He walked from the smooth cream-colored tile flooring to the edge of the living room, all of it open concept. The morning sunlight was slanting in through the large picture windows, shining across the cedar flooring, illuminating the gold and crimson colors of the wood. "Sure. You'll live here and your office is located in a nearby building. If you like the job, I anticipate that next spring, we'll build you a house next to the office. You'll have your own, private home at that time."

Rocking with shock over the generosity of the man, she could only say, "That sounds wonderful, but I need to assess your ranch and its qualities for the sake of bee culture and if it's a fit or not."

"Sounds good to me." He walked over to the front door and picked up her luggage. "Follow me?"

Nodding, Cari felt like she had to shake herself. This was like a dream, not a nightmare. In a matter of minutes, Chase had refuted or rebuffed all her fears and concerns. The fact he'd been a marine, a sniper, was not the point. What she did place trust in was the confidence that exuded from Chase, and that made her feel safe. Even more important was that his family, employees, and the town of Silver Creek would be safe, too. She had no idea how he could fulfill such a promise.

"Here it is," he said. "It's a mini-suite, with a nice, large bathroom, a small living room with a TV, small refrigerator, microwave, and your bedroom." He pushed it open. "Go on in. Get changed. I'll be waiting for you in the kitchen."

"Okay," Cari replied faintly, moving into the obviously feminine room. He shut the door quietly and she heard his booted feet against the floor, echoing and growing fainter and fainter.

She couldn't believe what had happened. At least, not yet. She'd thought she'd be sent back to the airport.

What kind of person was Chase? He wasn't like most men she had known. That drew her, and the attraction took her by surprise as she quickly changed out of her good clothes into her work clothes. Luckily, she'd brought two days' worth of tops, and didn't know why. Her intuition was strong, and there was nothing that could deter her from telling this very generous family the truth. Oh, she knew that many people figured that half-truths or telling a person only what they needed to know, and not the whole story, was in vogue. Not with her family or his, and she was grateful for that. She'd been raised to tell the whole, raw, unfiltered truth, not a part of it. At least she wouldn't have any guilt, or perhaps less of it, as a result, because she'd come clean up front with Chase.

Pulling on a white three-quarter tee that was loose and comfortable, a pair of jeans, socks, and boots, she settled her sun hat, which protected her face, neck, and upper shoulders from sunlight, and left the room.

Looking down the hall, she saw Chase on a wall phone talking in a low tone with someone. He wasn't handsome in a conventional way. He was deeply tanned—perhaps by years out in the deserts of Afghanistan? He had an oval face with high cheekbones, and wide-spaced, large gray eyes that seemed to miss nothing. Cari tried to ignore how toned and muscular he was. She'd rarely seen a man in such taut, good shape, and yet not muscle-bound, which turned her off completely. And for whatever piece of luck, Chase Bishop was an approachable human being, not like the patriarchal, sexist males she avoided at all costs. She could read him easily. But he could read her, too, and it didn't make her feel uncomfortable. Her mother, Nalani, had taught her long ago as a child to always tell the whole truth. Don't fudge it, don't manipulate it.

As she walked quietly across the living room, she saw him turn, as if either hearing or sensing her coming toward him, or both. She was still in shock that he wanted her to stay, to potentially hire her, providing she wanted the job. Well, she was going to find out because he hung up the phone, pulled his black Stetson off the wall peg and settled it on his head. She should feel nervous, but for whatever reason she did not. In her left hand she had a black baseball cap and a notebook.

"Ready?" he asked, opening the door for her.

"As ready as I can be," she answered, walking past him and onto the porch.

"I think Mary and Theresa filled you in about the ranch?" he asked as he drove out of the oval gravel driveway in front of the ranch house.

"Yes. But hearing about it and actually seeing it are two different things." She saw the large, flat rectangles of fields. "Tell me about that field," she said as she pointed to it.

"One of our four clover fields," he said, slowing the truck and making a turn to a low hill that had a dirt road running over it. "My family, over the generations, were very concerned about the soil and ensuring that all the nutrients were not leached out of it. This clover field comprises five thousand acres. We cut and bale it three times in a season, selling the bales to local and regional farmers and ranchers."

"Do you use pesticides or herbicides on them?"

Chase chuckled. "My mother would skin me alive if I did. No. The family matriarchs, for the last hundred years, have used only old farm practices. They planted herbs that naturally deterred pests from ruining any crop we have on this ranch. Further, we rotate our crops to keep the soil rich. We have an area near the ranch that has forty compost bins. Annually, every fall, we distribute that enriched soil back into the fields."

He parked the truck and got out. She joined him, notebook open, pen in hand. Pointing to the field, which was flourishing with pink-headed flowers everywhere, he said, "They plant marigolds along the edge, at least ten feet wide, all around it. Over the decades, even though they are annuals, they drop their seeds and reseed the next spring."

"I can see them," she said. "That's wonderful. Are you using marigolds to keep rabbits out of it? Wouldn't they love to eat the clover?"

"Right you are," he praised, giving her a curious look. "Are you steeped in natural ways to keep pests out of a crop?"

"Very much so," she said, writing down the information. "Since you're going to have beehives, you need to stay far, far away from pesticides, herbicides, and no GMOs. You don't have them here anywhere on the ranch, do you?"

"Hell no," he growled. "Everyone in this valley has agreed to never use GMO seeds or anything that has been genetically altered or tampered with. My next-door neighbor, Logan Anderson, has had family in this valley longer than anyone. His ranch is a hundred thousand acres. Ours is forty thousand. They butt up against one another on one boundary. We had a talk about this at the ranchers and farmers meeting when GMOs first came out, and we all agreed never to use them. So far, that pact has held. Besides, my mother is an herbalist, among the many hats she wears."

He pointed to the right, on the other side of the main ranch area. "Over there are a number of gardening plots, vegetables for Mary's grocery store—Mama's Store—in town. She will sell only organic produce with no fertilizers on them except natural ones, like our compost soil. The compost is put into the soil in late fall, after the vegetables have been picked. She uses marigolds, basil, and perennial lavender, around her plots."

"The bees are going to love your clover and alfalfa fields," she said, pleased with his explanation. "If you really want a good year of honey, usually from May to September, and sometimes later, if winter is mild, you need large areas of one type of plant. Then, the bees will go back to the hive and do a waggle dance and tell other bees where it's located. They generally don't like to travel more than a mile to get their pollen."

"Hmmm," Chase said, scowling, "we were never told

that. Court put all twenty-five hives over there"—he pointed to the west—"next to our fruit orchard. That's several miles away from our hay fields."

"Then, what you do, Chase, is put a number of hives outside the clover and alfalfa fields so that they don't have to travel so far. The closer the flowers and pollen, the more trips a honeybee can take and bring it back to the hive. That adds up to a lot more honey. If it has to travel two or three miles, that cuts down on how many runs a day they can make. That limits how much honey you get, too."

He scratched his jaw. "That makes a lot of common sense. Those poor bees over at the fruit tree orchard had four miles to go before they could reach this clover field."

She gave him a sad look. "That might explain why there probably wasn't enough honey, from what Theresa told me. The flowers were too far away, fewer trips, and, according to her, Mr. Court took *all* the comb and honey out of the hives and fed them fructose sugar throughout the winter. That's what killed them. They need the nutrients found in honey. Did you know honey contains vitamins and minerals? Bees are just like us. We need the same things to stay healthy."

"Yes . . . I did know because Theresa told me a few days ago." He gave her a wry look. "I'm feeling a lot of anger toward Court. He never shared anything like this info with me."

"I'm sorry that happened."

"I didn't listen to my mother or Theresa. This is on me."

"It can be turned around," she said quietly, giving him a slight smile. "Are all your clover and alfalfa fields the same size and vicinity?"

"Yes, they are."

"Any other hay crops?"

"We have two of alfalfa fields, the same size. They're north and south of the main ranch area. I have a good map that lays out where all our crops are, the size and where they're located. Would that help you?"

"Very much so. Theresa said the bees starved to death, so that means all the hives you bought can be reused. What I'd have to do is order so many pounds of honeybees for each one, and that's something I can do after I inspect each of them."

"That will save me a lot of money, then. I thought it was all gone."

"No, just buy a new bee colony to restock each hive."

"That's good news." He gave her an admiring look. "You really do know your stuff."

Her lips twitched. "Yes, I should. Can we drive around? We don't need to see all of your ranch, but I would like to get a feel for the general field areas. Plus, the last stop will be the hives. I want to look at them myself. Theresa has been feeding them honey and she said the brood boxes in each of the surviving hives are looking good."

"What's brood mean?" he asked, walking her toward the truck. The sun felt good on his shoulders.

"Brood box is a beekeeping term. When the queen lays her eggs, a honeybee attends. By the way, honeybees are all female. The only males are drones and there's between a hundred to four hundred of them. The only thing they are good for is eating honey and trying to mate with the queen bee when she's ready. They're dead weight."

"Sounds like a good job," he teased.

"No, not really. As soon as the lucky drone catches the

queen in flight, mates with her, she tears out his abdomen along with his male family jewels, eviscerating him on the spot. I don't think you want that job, Chase. The drone, of course, dies."

He opened the door for her. "Oh . . . no, not a job I want. That's pretty harsh treatment of the only males in a hive."

"Females get more done. Males are an inconvenience in the bee world, good for only one thing." She stepped up into the truck.

Chase considered her comment. "Well, I think it's time women step up and lead. We men haven't done a very good job at all lately."

"I don't generally get into politics," she said, grinning, "but I wouldn't argue with your observations." The look on his face was priceless. Cari wished she'd had a camera.

As Chase climbed into the truck, he said, "Smart choice. I want to show you Mary's gardens. They have a lot of blossoms. Maybe bees are interested in them, too?"

"Lead the way," she said, pulling her seat belt across her body.

Chapter Three

May 26

Chase was taken with Cari's quiet authority. Totally unlike Court, who bragged all the time about how good a shape the hives were in, and how much honey was going to be produced for sale at Mama's Store, she was a very welcome change. As they toured four huge rectangle plots of different vegetables that were flourishing, she was making notes. When they were walking to the truck afterward, he said, "You're taking a lot of notes."

"Yes. There have to be enough plants that are flowering to be able to estimate whether it's worth it for the bees to pollinate them or not. Fruits and veggies only bloom once a year. Bees need more than one resource after those bloom, to keep them alive the rest of the year. I like that clover and alfalfa fields are next to Mary's garden areas. That gives bees a chance to thrive and make more honey because your hay crops bloom three times in a season."

"That almost sounds like they are thinking," he said. Cari beat him to the passenger side door, opening it herself.

"If there is a clover or alfalfa field closer with more

blooms, versus these vegetable plots? They will forage the hay fields first and always. Their bottom line is where can the most pollen, which will later be turned into honey, be found. They can make more trips in a day, because of that."

He slid in and shut the door. "So? Mary's vegetable gardens aren't as good a possibility as pollen producers?"

She brought the seat belt across her body. "They would be down on the list. What I would do is put two or three hives nearby, for a given time, during blossoming of the veggies, and let the bees pollinate and gather the pollen. Then, move these hives to the two nearby clover and alfalfa fields for the rest of the season. They should do fine."

"So, you can move hives around?"

"Yes, if need be. You have to go where there's blooms." She pointed far off to a huge orchard. "For example, your fruit trees are usually early bloomers because they have a season to produce a fully formed fruit. Are we going over there?"

He nodded, putting the truck into gear. "Right now."

"I can assess your major bloom areas and then look at how many hives you have. Then, I can figure out how many to put in a given area and create a schedule, if need be, to move them to the next pollinating area."

"The fruit orchard is next to one of our alfalfa fields."

"Which would be a good place to put a lot of your hives because alfalfa, weather conditions cooperating, is going to bloom three times in a season. For a bee? That's wonderful because if the hives are close to the field, they have an incredible pollinating area with a high honey yield. The hives could be placed at the edge of the alfalfa field where the orchard perimeter is, and they can do double duty since both are close to their colonies."

He slid her a glance. "You almost sound like a military strategist, figuring out who, what, where, and when to place hives in the best locations."

She smiled a little. "That's exactly right. So? Did Mr. Court move your hives around at all?"

"Not to my knowledge. They remained where they were for the entire season." He saw her mouth thin for a moment, but she said nothing. They drove along a dirt road that was between the fields.

"After the fruit-tree stop, I'd like to go see the hives, Chase."

"Sure," he said. In another mile, they would be at the beginning of a fifteen-thousand-acre fruit tree area. And that is where the alfalfa field began, parallel to it on the other side of the orchard. When he pulled over and parked, about a mile into the two fields, they got out.

He enjoyed watching her. He stood back, staying out of her way. Clearly, she knew what she was doing, what she was looking at, and calculating the beehive activity potential. Eventually, she turned to him.

"What fruit do you raise here?"

"We have apples, pears, peaches, bing cherries, apricots, plums, and down at the other end is about five thousand acres of almonds. We're very lucky that we have a number of creeks and a river through our property, plus we have an aquifer beneath the land that we access via the wells we've dug."

"Has climate change affected your area yet?"

Chase looked around. "Silver Creek is in what we call a microclimate valley. It's based upon landmasses, a mountain range, and it just happened to get lucky enough to be where it is. On the western boundary of Wyoming, they get nine months of winter and the temperature can dive to thirty or forty below. Here"—he gestured around—"we will get down to about twenty-two degrees Fahrenheit in the worst of winter, and the general temp is around thirty-two degrees Fahrenheit for the four months of snow we get."

"How much snow?"

"On the western boundary, they can get five feet of snow dumped on them all at once. Here, we've never seen more than a foot. We have an actual four seasons here, unlike there on the western boundary, which is winter and summer. They don't have a ninety-day growing season, either, unless they've got a greenhouse. Here, we have from May to the end of October. That's what allows us to have three good crops of alfalfa and clover."

"It's ideal for a bee colony, too. They can winter over, but they need a lot of protection and their own honey stores in combs, to get them through it." She pointed toward the five-foot stone wall that ran the length of the orchard, creating a boundary with the wide dirt road. "I would put hives inside that rock wall, which is ideal protection against westerly winter winds. It will protect the hives and the bees won't freeze. The bees sit around in large groups within the hive, like a ball, keeping warm by being packed in close to one another to survive the winters."

"That sounds like good news."

"It is. I noticed on your other fields, those rock walls are on the longest stretches."

"My great-great-grandfather spent a year building

them. We had a lot of rocks in our soil and he had to remove them, anyway, for planting purposes. My great-great-grandmother was the one that gave him the idea for the rock walls, as well as for planting marigolds next to them."

"Your family is very environmentally minded and wise," Cari said. "After I study your map when we get back to the ranch house, I can identify perfect places for your hives. I'll ensure that we use those rock walls as part of their winterization plan to protect them. Plus, I would also like to see you build hive pads out of concrete. That way, there's a specific place for the hives and the concrete platform where you'll set those hives, which are made of wood. That way, they're protected from wood rot. If you place them on soil, instead, it's just a matter of time before the wood would rot. Concrete platforms are cleaner, no water issues, and have a far longer life, which in the long run saves you money. You won't have to buy wooden hives as often."

"That sounds like a great idea. I can have my wranglers build them for you once you show us where they should go."

"Let's go see your hives?"

"Yeah, what's left of them."

"In my last phone call with Theresa, she said they'd cleaned out the twenty hives that lost their colonies to starvation. She told me they are ready to be recolonized. If you approve that, I think the next chore is building those concrete pads and placing them around your property in strategic locations. Then, ordering the packets of bee colonies for each one."

"Sounds like a plan. Let's go see your bees."

* * *

Cari climbed out of the truck, her gaze on the five hives that had survived massive starvation. All the hives sat up on a slight knoll. She tried to ignore the quiet charisma of Chase Bishop. He was focused entirely on her, what she had to say, and he asked good questions. He cared about the bees and that made her heart swell. There was no question that he really wanted a honey operation here on his ranch, but he wanted it done right, and most important to her was that he wanted his bees protected and well fed. He had everything a bee could want to make honey on his ranch, plus the weather goddesses and gods had given a microclimate blessing to this verdant valley. She now understood why Mary had come up with the idea in the first place. She'd done a lot of reading up on bee operations for honey making and saw the potential on her son's ranch. Talk about an empowered woman!

They climbed the knoll side by side, the grass green and lush. At the top of it were all the empty hives. At the other end, Cari could see a lot of bee activity. She halted and handed him her notebook. "Are you familiar with working around bees?"

"No, not really. Court said I didn't need to be out here with him." Shrugging, Chase said unhappily, "I should have come out, I should have learned."

"Do you have a bee hat with a net?" she wondered.

"No. Nothing. I used to see him from time to time and he wore a white suit with a white hat and net, plus gloves. He was always carrying around something in his hand."

"Probably a smoker," she said. "You use that to squirt

a few gentle puffs into the hive to calm the bees so they don't attack you. The smoke calms them."

"And where's your bee suit?"

"I don't need one."

Alarmed, his brows went up. "You're going to go to those hives without any protection?" He saw her eyes sparkle.

"Me and the bee nation are friends," was all she'd say. "A good beekeeper, who has the trust of the bees, rarely needs anything more than a hat with netting, and a smoker. I'm going to just stand with them, watch them. You can tell a lot that way."

"But won't they sting you?"

"I hope not. Sometimes, when I'm opening a hive, a bee will suddenly slip between the wood and me raising a panel. That can upset them and they can sting. But that's pretty rare. If you watch me, you'll learn." And she walked away. Some people had a fear of bees. She did not.

Walking across the nubby spring grass, she came to within five feet of the hives and just stood watching them. There were hundreds of them flying in and out of the small, round hole at the bottom of the hive. She watched the guard bees, whose job it was to protect the entrance into the hive, behaving as they should: being alert and watchful. That way, no bee, or any other insect, would be allowed into the hive to harm the brood eggs, the queen, or anyone else. They were the ones who would most likely attack someone if they felt threatened by their presence.

A bee landed on her right hand. She smiled, watching it walk around, checking her out. She did not move, rather, remained at ease. Bees could sense fear or tension around a human in a heartbeat. She gave off energy and pheromones, which bees could pick up instantly and react to. Two more guard bees flew over, one on her other hand and one landing on her right shoulder. They were, indeed, checking her out. Soon enough, all three of them flew back to the hive to their respective guard posts outside the entrance.

She did the same "introduction" with the other four hives. Here, she was in her element. She was with her bee people that she loved with a passion. And the bees sensed her love and respect for them. At the last hive, not only did some of the guard bees come out, but about a hundred honeybees came out and landed on her left shoulder and made a soft, velvety gold and brown ball, just sitting there, humming. Her heart soared with such love for these sentient, intelligent beings. Cari hummed softly in return to the cluster of bees. The guard bees joined them and she smiled, looking down at them. After five minutes, the bees all disassembled from their ball and flew back to their hive. They had work to do!

Lifting her chin, she gazed toward Chase, who had a stricken expression on his face. She smiled at him. "I'm all right," she reassured him, and returned her attention to the hives.

Most modern-day hives were of one type and design only, known as Langstroth. There were two other types used in the world: the top-bar hive and the Warre hive. Chase had the Langstroth type, which looked like a bunch of boxes painted different colors so that each resembled a five- or eight-story apartment building made from wood. She walked slowly around each one, noting how it was cared for, the age of the wood, and if the boxes were in good repair or not. After finishing her inspection, she walked toward Chase, who still had a worried expression on his face.

"Relax, I didn't get stung," she said as she came to a halt in front of him.

"That," he rasped, "was amazing."

"Yes, bees are amazing," she agreed, smiling up at him. She could see in his gray eyes that he hadn't quite believed what he had seen just a moment ago. Explaining that the guard bees had come to suss out her intent, and finding her not to be a threat to the hive, they left her alone. And that would enable her to thoroughly check the exterior of the hives without being stung.

"Then," he asked, "what was that ball of bees doing on your shoulder? I thought they were attacking you."

"Oh, no, they weren't," Cari said, turning and standing at his shoulder, gaze on the hives. "I told the bees I was their friend, that you, I, Mary, and Theresa would help them become strong and healthy again."

"You told them that? I didn't see you talking."

"Mental telepathy."

Chase stared down at her. "Who *are* you?"

Laughter spilled from her lips. "I assure you, and as you know already, I'm terribly human."

"But . . . I saw what happened . . ."

She felt him searching for a logical answer and couldn't find one. "I've been around bees since I was a little tot. My family raised bees for five generations in Hawaii. I grew up with them. I found out very quickly that they could read my thoughts, or my intentions toward them. My mother, Nalani, who is Hawaiian, comes from those wonderful generations of beekeepers. She told me one day to 'talk' to them with my mind, that the bees would pick it up and understand."

"These bees don't know English," he said, frowning.

"No, they don't. But humans give off pheromones and bees are acutely sensitive to them. That is one way that they communicate with one another in and outside the hive. Their sense of smell is acute, and they can smell us as well. They know by the odor if we're friend or foe."

"And so, they see you as their friend?"

"Most definitely. I told them I needed to look at their home, to make sure it was in good condition."

"I noticed none of them followed you around the hives when you did investigate them."

"Right. They know I'm there to protect and support them. It was like a group of friends following me around, curious but unthreatened by my presence."

He lifted his Stetson, scratched his hair, and then settled the hat back on his head. "Unbelievable." And then he gave her a teasing look. "Are you sure you aren't fey? A fairy in the disguise of a human, come visiting?"

"I've been accused of that," she assured him with a slight smile, taking her notebook and opening it. "Most beekeepers have a very calm energy around them and bees pick up on that. That's why we can work in the hive and outside of it without upsetting them and making them feel threatened."

"It takes a particular type of personality, I suppose?"

"You could say that," she said, scribbling down notes on each hive's exterior condition.

Chase gave her a humored look. "I feel like I just went

from this world into another dimension or universe. Sort of like that movie *The Matrix*, or *The Twilight Zone*."

She smiled fully. "Do you read science fiction, by any chance?"

He laughed. "Guilty as charged. Not that I have a lot of spare time, but I'm a great sci-fi fan and reader. Usually, I listen to them in audio-book form because I'm out, driving around on the ranch a lot."

She became serious once more as they walked off the knoll and to the truck. Cari opened her own door and climbed in. "Listen, Chase, I'm more than worried Dirk will find me here someday. That puts all of you at risk. I believe, after a number of phone calls with Theresa, that she and her family can handle your hives very well. She's what I call an 'old-fashioned beekeeper,' meaning she has a lineage of wisdom and working with bees, through the generations." She held his darkening gaze as he pulled the seat belt across his body. "I feel guilty about being here. You're wonderful people. I couldn't live with knowing I might have caused any of you harm."

Chase nodded. "I hear you, Cari. But I believe we can surmount these genuine concerns you have. Believe me, I'm not taking this lightly. I know my family could be a target, as well as anyone who works for the ranch." He gave her a pleading look. "Please, stay awhile. At least to get this company of ours up and running properly. Theresa and her family will take care of the hives. My mother is thrilled about that. Finding out that most of our bees starved to death makes me feel guilty as hell. I thought Court knew what he was doing. But he didn't. Just the way you went around the ranch and what you know about bee behavior, shows me everything I want to know. Please, stay?" His voice went low with pleading.

Moving uncomfortably in the seat, she squirmed inwardly, as well. Chase was *very* persuasive. If she hadn't been drawn to him, woman to man, Cari would not have weakened. The image of Dirk shooting his girlfriend flashed before her eyes. "I'll tell you what I'll do. I'll stay long enough to get your operation in working order. I'll have Theresa at my side, and there's many things she needs to know, as well. After I've done all that, we'll call my consulting work with your ranch complete."

"Then where will you go?" he challenged quietly.

"I honestly don't know. I haven't figured this all out. It's just happened. I know I'm still in shock over it, and when a person is in that state, they don't think clearly."

"You're right about that, you are in shock. Anyone would be." He rested the heels of his hands on the top of the steering wheel. Opening his fingers, he said, "Look, let us, the ranch and employees, be a refuge for you. No one's better at this kind of stealth than me. I'll hold a meeting with my employees, tell them what's going on and get a vote from them because they, too, are at risk and it's not right of me to make that decision for them. If they don't want you here? I'll abide by that decision. In the meantime, you can begin teaching me the business of selling honey. You have an MBA, and no one knows this business better than you. None of us around here do, that's for sure. Could you stay long enough to see this through to that stage? I'm pretty good at business, anyway, but I don't know the honey business, the distribution chain or anything else about it. That's where you come in. I'll pay you whatever consulting fee you want." His voice went raspy. "I need you, Cari. Don't walk away from us. We'll keep you safe. I'll also be talking to Sheriff Dan Seabert about the situation very shortly."

Stunned by his emotional plea, she sat feeling it vibrate powerfully through her. Chase was not the kind of guy she'd always run into. He *was* different. Maybe, as some of her girlfriends opined, they needed twenty-first-century matriarchal males who respected a woman as an equal and treated them as such. Did Chase have an ego? Of course he did. But it was well in check and she could tell by driving around with him today, it didn't run him. "I like that you're able to admit when you don't know something. And I like that you respect what I know. There's many good things about you that make me want to be here." She sighed heavily. "Look, I'll stay on for a while. I don't know what that means or how long that will be. I'm relieved you'll talk to the county sheriff and any other law enforcement in your valley about Dirk. They need to know him on sight and that he's dangerous. That's all I can give you, Chase." She saw his expression lighten, and she felt tension leaving the cab of the truck.

"Okay, that's fair. Dan will have a plan after he checks out Dirk. He's an ex–Navy SEAL and we have a SWAT team here as well. He'll make sure the safety net around you is secure. Settle in with us. You'll have a nice little suite in the main ranch house, and let's go look at the office building where you'll be. It's only half a mile from the home. I work out there daily, too, so I'll be around or nearby, sort of like a watchdog."

"That feels good to me. Not that I've ever had something like this come up, where I did need some help."

"Just consider me your friendly next-door-office bodyguard. Okay?"

She responded to his light teasing. "Okay, I can do that. Now, let's go see the office?"

"The map of the place is on my office wall. You will want to look at it. I can get a copy of it made for your purposes."

"Good idea. I do want to see it. We'll need it to strategically place the hives."

Turning over the engine, he took the truck out of park. "I'm going to be interested in your final strategy for our honey business."

Warming to his mellow voice, Cari felt more at ease, less endangered by Dirk's shadow and threat. How refreshing to meet a man who truly wore his heart on his sleeve. As they drove down another road toward a single-story, rectangular stucco building in the distance, she felt more safe than ever. Still, Cari did not want other people hurt or killed when Dirk came after her. And she knew he would. Dirk was always good at keeping his word.

Chase was happy to see his mother show up and have dinner with them that evening. Mary had her own home about a mile down the road from the main ranch house. Living alone, he ate for one. But now, with Cari agreeing to stay for an unknown amount of time, there were two people he had to cook for.

Mary had dropped over and she brought a huge casserole of bread pudding, still warm from the oven, for dessert. He was grateful. As usual, his mother had saved the day. She'd even brought homemade caramel to drip over the dessert. And luckily, when he was ten years old, she'd started teaching him how to cook, and not just open a can and eat out of it, either. Tonight, he'd had some leftovers and made them each a beefsteak salad replete with spinach leaves, European greens, yellow pear and red tomatoes, shredded carrots, celery, and his special homemade Italian dressing. Luckily, he had some leftover biscuits he'd made from a day ago, to add to the meal.

Cari had come out from her suite when the doorbell had rung. He'd caught sight of her, and she was wearing a pair of soft green linen slacks with a pale yellow long-sleeved tee. Her hair had a bluish tint to it as she moved across the living room in a pair of cream-colored shoes. Chase tried to quell his physical and emotional reaction to her. He knew from her résumé she was single. Did she have a man in her life? A woman? Nowadays it wasn't good to assume anything about a person's gender until it became known. He had seen an almost unearthly glow around her face as she stood talking with the bees earlier today. Unable to shake what he saw, he knew he was seeing something . . . well . . . miraculous, sort of . . . He had not had the time he needed to really digest and absorb that incredible, out-of-time moment. Her whole demeanor seemed to change. It wasn't obvious, it was something he sensed more than saw.

Having been a hunter and sniper, Chase had learned to rely on things that weren't in any military manual or, for that matter, anywhere else. He sometimes felt invisible to the man he was hunting, as if in another dimension but able to see into the normal third dimension where everyone else lived.

There had always been a shift when that invisibility cloaked him, when he needed not to be seen or detected, waiting for his quarry. And that same shift of energy happened today, out there on that knoll where Cari stood quietly, unmoving, in front of the beehives. Maybe she was right; he read too much science fiction. Wryly, he smiled to himself. There was something . . . well . . . magical, about Cari. *What* was it? He would dig for that answer until he knew. That glow around her face reminded him of a saint with a halo around their head. *What* had caused that glow? He believed in what he saw. There was this faint, almost golden glow that came to her face as she communicated with the bees.

And he didn't look too hard at *why* he wanted her to stay here. Maybe the bees were an excuse, because the woman was certainly unlike any other woman he had ever known. And Chase had seen and been with his share of women. He'd always seen women as somewhat mysterious, unknowable, and yet, like a proverbial moth to a flame, he was drawn to the opposite sex. It wasn't their physical form or face that drew him first. No, it was something else, something gossamer and unseeable. An energy he felt, maybe? Energy wasn't seen, but one could sure as hell see it in action and motion in this 3D world of theirs. Wind couldn't be seen, but it could wreak havoc, even death, on humans if a tornado or hurricane hit an area. Gravity couldn't be seen, but when an avalanche of fifty tons of rocks exploded when there was an earthquake in Afghanistan, less than a mile from his hide, those bus-sized boulders all rolled down that mountain, because gravity proved its existence in spades.

In his business of being a sniper, he never talked about his "shift," as he referred to it. But one day, when back at the base, another sniper, a friend of his, Jason, had just come in off another mission. They sat in the cantina with cold beers between their roughened hands, trading sniper stories. They were pretty damned drunk at that point, three pitchers of beer shared between them, a "coming down" from the constant danger they were in for weeks at a time, he supposed. And then, Jason told him how something weird had happened when he found his quarry, and he felt like he became invisible to the Afghan tribesmen nearby as he stalked his enemy. He didn't know what it was, or that it had really happened, but it was a strange feeling, as if moving through another veil, as he referred to it, and he couldn't any longer be detected as he set up to take the shot.

Chase had played dumb, but listened raptly to his friend. He wasn't sure he wanted to confirm that shift or feeling to Jason, for fear someone would send him to a psychiatrist and he'd be given a medical discharge from the Marine Corps. Still . . . as they parted to stagger back to their bunks to sleep off the beer, that story Jason shared had never left him.

He nodded in Cari's direction as she came to a halt at the edge of the U-shaped kitchen that had a long island in the center of it. "That's my mother, Mary. Would you get the door?"

"Sure," she said. "Finally, it will be nice to meet her in person."

Chase brought the sheet of biscuits out of the oven that

had warmed them up. So? What had he seen today with Cari? She hadn't disappeared or become invisible. But she had that unearthly glow around her face. Was she aware of it? Did she feel something happening when she talked with the bees? Hopefully, he could gain her trust and she would open up more. His sniper mind was used to ferreting through a lot of debris, and finding proof of what he sought. Mary had always said she thought he'd make a great police detective. And even the sheriff, Dan Seabert, had said the same thing of him. He had to be patient with Cari, gain her trust and allow her to open up to him. Did she have a secret regarding what he saw earlier? Was she really of the fey people? Not really a human, but here for some reason? He liked the mystery she presented. It was a challenge to him, rather exciting and unexpected. Who was Cari Taylor? Really?

"Helloooo," Mary sang, coming through the door.

"Hey, Mom," he called. "Mary, meet Cari. Cari, meet my mother, Mary."

Mary grinned and hugged Cari's shoulder, quickly releasing her. "Oh! I've waited for this moment, Cari! Welcome! We're so glad you came to see us!" She put down a casserole dish on the nearby kitchen counter and then shed her lightweight blue spring coat, hanging it on a wooden peg near the door.

"Wonderful to meet you, Mrs. Bishop."

"Oh, pshaw! Call me Mary." She pointed to the casserole. "Bread pudding for dessert tonight! Made it myself! Would you carry it into the kitchen, slide it into the oven so we can warm it up?"

"Of course," Cari said.

Mary smoothed down her bright red slacks and walked

up to the table where Chase was placing the warmed biscuits into a blue glass bowl. "Mmmmm, smells good, son. What are we having for dinner tonight?"

"Leftovers," he said, and grinned. "Steak salad."

"I was hungry for vegetables today," Mary said, taking the bowl of biscuits that now had a red-and-white striped towel over them to keep them warm, to the table. "You must have been reading my mind again!" Mary turned and looked at Cari, who was closing the stove door. "You know? My son is probably gonna scare the pants off you, Cari. He reads minds. Scares me sometimes!" She chortled, going into the kitchen.

"Oh?" Cari said, raising a brow. "Really? Do you read minds, Chase?"

He could feel his skin burning. Damn, he was blushing! "Well, not exactly . . . just . . . hunches, I guess is what you call them."

Mary gave a good, bullish snort as she poured three cups of coffee. "It comes from him being a sniper for five years, Cari. He lived out in enemy territory for weeks or months at a time, and all he had was his gut instinct and psychic senses." She picked up two cups, taking them to the table.

Cari gave Chase a mirthful look. "Psychic, huh? And you were flummoxed over what you saw with me out there with the bees today?"

"Oh," he protested, picking up the last cup, "don't go there."

"Why not?" Mary demanded, moving to the refrigerator. "You know, Cari, he's a sci-fi nut."

"So he told me today," she said, following him to the fridge. Chase handed her two bowls of salad and took the third one, shutting the fridge door. "Are you holding out on me, Chase? You looked so surprised when I told you I telepathically talked to bees earlier. And if you're a sci-fi kind of guy? You've got to have read fiction books where characters had mental telepathy. Hmmm?"

"Busted," he admitted, giving her a boyish, nervous smile, following her to the table. "Let's eat, huh?"

Mary thanked her son for pulling out the chair at the table for her. Cari seated herself. Chase sat opposite her.

"Have you decided to stay?" Mary asked hopefully, pouring the Italian dressing over her salad.

"Well," Cari hedged, picking up a biscuit, "I'll stay to get everything on the ground for you, Theresa, and Chase." She didn't want to bring up her predicament at dinner. Chase had given her a glance that she took as indicating he would tell his mother about it later.

"Oh, good!" Mary said, pleased as she handed the dressing to Chase.

"And she's going to teach me the business of honey," he said.

"But? We'd want you to stay here and run it for us," Mary protested, giving her a quizzical look.

"Mom, she has a global clientele and works with many companies who process honey."

"Oh," Mary said, saddened.

"That was sweet of you to offer something like that," Cari said, wanting to mollify her.

"She has a life," Chase reminded Mary. "Not everyone is a rancher or rural person." And he saw his mother perk up.

"Well"—Mary sighed, giving her a kind look—"then

we're so blessed to have you here at all. Chase? You did give her the mini-suite here in the house?"

"Sure did," he said, picking up a biscuit himself and handing the blue bowl to Mary.

"It's such a beautiful house," Cari said. "I just love the décor."

"My mother, Chase's grandmother, did all the decorating and choosing of the furniture. The only thing I added was a queen-sized bed that didn't have squeaky springs."

Chase chuckled, digging into his salad, slicing the beef in it. "Mary goes crazy over high-pitched sounds and it drives her to distraction."

"It's my wolf ears," she informed them proudly. "In fact, it's a family trait: We hear things that most humans don't."

"Is that part of your psychic gear?" Cari teased him unmercifully after he'd made such a big deal over hers.

"Well, I don't know I'd call is psychic. Woo-woo isn't my thing. But yes, it seems the whole family has the DNA genetic gift of extraordinary hearing capability."

"Matter of fact," Mary piped in, waving her fork in Chase's direction, "when he went to sniper school in the Marine Corps, the auditory guy couldn't believe his hearing range," and she gave a devilish chuckle, proud of her son.

"Any other family traits I should know about?" Cari wondered, giving him an unmerciful look and taking no prisoners.

"My grandmother—Mom's mother, Polly—was a tarot reader," Chase admitted hesitantly, knowing Mary would tell Cari, anyway.

"And, oh! Polly was the best!" Mary said, enthusiastically. "She was *never* wrong when she laid out those cards. In fact, my mother used the tarot to help me set up Mama's Store in town. I really miss her for all kinds of reasons, but her tarot readings were spot-on. Now we have Poppy Johnson, who owns The Unicorn, a bookstore in town, and she is almost as good as Polly was! If you ever want to know what your future holds? You should go ask her! She won't lead you wrong."

Chase saw the sparkling light that danced in Cari's eyes snuffed out. His mother didn't know the rest of the story, about Dirk. "Well, I think Cari is doing just fine on her own," Chase told his mother, hoping to mollify some of his mother's remarks. "Besides," he said, trying to change the topic, "Cari and I are going to be working on that plan at our offices tomorrow morning."

"Oh, when will I know about them?" Mary asked, excited.

"As soon as we get them done," Cari said. "It's going to take a week or more. I've never worked on a ranch this size before and it's a big consult."

"Good," Chase murmured, his voice a deep purr, "that means you'll be here for a long time . . ."

Chapter Four

May 26

"Have you seen all of the ranch?" Mary wondered, giving Cari a kind look.

"No. Chase was going to show me more of it tomorrow morning."

With a sly smile, Mary said, "I saw in your résumé that you also worked with raptor rehabilitators, too. Tell us more about that?"

"When I was going through Stanford, I joined a raptor rehabilitation group near the campus. I've always loved the hawks and eagles. In my summers, I went to Scotland where they have an incredible wildlife center near Roslin. They cared for all animals, not just raptors." Cari smiled at the older woman. "Rehabilitation is a favorite of mine, and actually dovetails in with beekeeping."

"So," Mary said, pleased, "all things wild appeal to you?"

"Actually, yes. Over the years I continued to work with rehab groups here in the USA, wanting to establish some kind of foundation for them. In the United Kingdom, they're very advanced in that regard, and I wanted to bring that template or blueprint over to our country."

"That's interesting," Chase murmured, wiping his mouth with the white linen napkin, "because Mary hired a young woman named Jenny McClaren. Her family has created the Roslin Wildlife Center near Edinburgh. Might you have heard of her?"

Heart thudding once to underscore his question, her eyes widened. "Oh, yes, of course I know the McClaren family quite well." Excitement tinged her tone. "I visited their facility when I was nineteen, and I'd taken the summer off to suss out Scottish raptor and wildlife centers. They had the best template of all of them."

"Partly," Chase said, "because their family has had five generations to create that advanced wildlife center. Did you meet Jenny?"

"No, but I met her parents, Gavina and Rory, who were very kind with their time to show me the operation of their center. Jenny, their oldest daughter, was studying at Oxford in biology, if my memory serves. Her sister, Charlotte, who was two years younger, was there and I got to meet and work with her. They're a family-run operation and they were grooming both their daughters to someday take over."

Mary chuckled. "Well, you're in for a nice surprise, Cari. I flew over to Scotland to see them three years ago. I was able to convince Jenny to come over here and help us build a wildlife center on our ranch, based upon their blueprints for Roslin."

"Oh, my!" Cari said, suddenly excited. "I didn't know this!"

Chuckling, Chase said, "Mary has, over the years,

expanded our ranch in many directions, and all of them good. Jenny came over to supervise the building of our facility, Silver Creek Wildlife Center. She's quite well connected to the major raptor associations all over the world, and she knew good people who we could hire to staff our facility."

Mary reached out, patting Cari's hand. "So you never met Jenny?"

"No . . . I didn't. But this is amazing! Does she live here on the ranch?"

"Sure does," Chase said. "We built her a home near the facility. While we hired contractors, we also worked with her on the kind of home she'd like to have while she was here."

"Jenny has a five-year contract with us," Mary said, "and then she goes back to Scotland to help run her family's wildlife center. She has two more years on that contract. She's helped us get a wonderful small-animal vet whose specialty is wild animals, and another who is a bird expert. Our supervisory vet, Catherine Tavish, knew Jenny, had met her at many major international veterinary meetings over the years, and she persuaded her to move out here and be supervisor over the entire facility." Mary preened. "Our center has become the state of Wyoming's go-to place for all things having to do with injured wildlife or domestic animals. It took us a year to build the center and hire the right people."

"We have three vets at the center," Chase told Cari. "They work full time. In the summer, vet students from around North and South America come here to learn and help Catherine and her team. It's a win-win for everyone."

"This is incredible!" Cari said. "When can I meet Jenny?"

"How about tomorrow morning?" Chase asked. "The center is a mile away and is closest to the main highway through the valley."

"I'd love that!" Cari whispered, suddenly emotional. "You two have truly created a blueprint for multi-use of your land, this microclimate, and taking advantage of it in a very positive way."

Mary glowed. "Our family has always dreamed big and outside the box, Cari. We want to have wise use of our land, of the soil, the air, and the water. Chase isn't one to brag, but our ranch has, in a sense, become a template for other ranchers in this part of Wyoming. A lot of people have reduced their eating of meat, and many more are leaning toward being vegan, which has impacted cattle ranches in a huge way. They are all looking for other ways to sustain a lot of family ranches, and ours, as well as Logan Anderson's ranch, which is located next to ours. His family, by the way, has Scottish roots. We'll have to make sure you get introduced to him shortly. He's much like Chase from the standpoint that his family has always protected the earth as we do."

Chase rose after the dinner was done, collecting plates and taking them to the kitchen. They ate the bread pudding dessert. Afterward, he brought out the coffeepot and poured fresh coffee into the awaiting mugs. "Mary, we need to fill you in on some serious things that Cari let me know about shortly after she landed here."

Frowning, Mary said, "Oh?"

Cari felt her stomach squeeze in reaction. The elder had her silvery hair in a braid over her head. Though older, Mary Bishop was a world-class entrepreneur of the finest kind. She didn't hold much hope that the woman would want her to stay on the ranch, making her family a target of Dirk. Placing her hands beneath the table, palms damp, she tried to swallow her nervousness as Chase sat down and told his mother the story. As he finished, she saw Mary's face become sympathetic looking, not judgmental. Cari expected her to ask her to leave tomorrow morning. Who would want their family in danger? She knew she wouldn't.

Eyeing Chase, Mary said, "I'm glad to hear you're planning to touch base with Dan. He's our ace in the hole. He has eyes in the back of his head and he'll ensure the safety of everyone in this valley, not just our family and employees."

Cari tried to remain unresponsive to the woman's gruff reply. Part of her was relieved, but another part, scared to death for this wonderful family.

"Then," Chase said, "you're in agreement with me that we keep Cari here? I think part of her wants to leave in order to protect us from her stepbrother."

Mary nodded and gave Cari a sympathetic look. "Just about every family I know, with some exceptions, has a darkness that haunts them, of one sort or another, through a particular family member. Dan Seabert, our sheriff, is ex-military. Chase served his country, too, and my son knows how to protect his own. I'm sure if you go with him to see the sheriff tomorrow, Dan will come up with a plan of action." She tapped Cari's hand. "We need you here. And I know you don't want to stay long due to the threat from your stepbrother, but he hasn't found you. He may never find you here, Cari. That doesn't mean that

Chase and I, or the sheriff, won't be on the lookout for him. And who knows? Law enforcement in California may nab him, too. So, I think your abundance of caution, while warranted, is probably lessened because you've hidden out with us. And from what Chase said, your stepbrother has all his ties in California. It makes sense he'd stick around there and renew them. Criminals tend to know one another and have their own network."

Swallowing hard, Cari gave a slight nod. "I really think Sheriff Seabert needs to know. But so do the townspeople of this valley, too."

"Oh, no worries on that," Mary said, giving her another sly smile. "We've perfected the best communication among folks who live in this valley. Word will be passed. Silver Creek Valley is a place where people pull together as one when there's a crisis of any kind. We're neighbors and we help each other out. So, don't you worry about this. All right? I want our focus on saving our poor honeybees and then creating a plan for the future. I did my research on the best expert in the field of commercial honey operations, and you're at the top. No," she said, her voice turning gruff, "we want you here. You're going nowhere." She cracked a grin. "We'll have a meeting with our employees here on the ranch as well. I'm positive, once they hear everything, that they'll vote to keep you here at Three Bars, as well."

Feeling invisible tons of worry dissolving around her, Cari gave the elder a kind look of thanks. "I'll do everything in my power to give you a beautiful facility. That's a promise, Mary."

"I know you will. Now, I'm sure you're tired and stressed by the travel and worry, so why don't you call it a night? Chase will take you to the sheriff's office tomorrow and we'll get that piece in place. Then"—Mary raised her brows, giving Chase a merry look—"you might take her out to the wildlife center to meet Jenny. She needs a nice, positive lift and welcome to our valley. I'm sure after she spends some time at Jenny's amazing facility, that she will realize staying here is a good thing."

Chase nodded and said, "Sounds like a plan, Mary."

Cari excused herself and set the napkin on the table. "Well, you have made my day, week, month, and year," she whispered, her voice emotional and grateful. "You're right, Mary, I am absolutely exhausted."

"Then," Mary said, waving her toward the living room, "take a nice hot bath in your suite, and then hit the sack. A good night's sleep always makes the next day look positive and hopeful."

May 27

Cari sat stiffly in the chair in front of Sheriff Dan Seabert's office at nine a.m. the next morning. She told her story, gave him several photos of her stepbrother, and his prison information. She liked the man, who was in his early thirties, with reddish-brown hair that hinted he might have Irish or Scottish blood in him, his green eyes reminding her of a raptor's pinpointed, focused gaze. He was not a handsome man, his square face unreadable, his cheekbones wide, a hint of freckles faint shadows across his cheeks and nose, again hinting of Irish or Scottish bloodlines.

Chase and he were all business and they talked military jargon, alphabet soup that she was not familiar with, although they both would stop and explain to her what it meant. She liked being seen as part of the team, not some unimportant addendum to their planning session.

Dan had a large desktop computer and he would turn the screen toward her from time to time. And he gave her the latest information from law enforcement in California on their efforts to track down Dirk. She appreciated his care, even though he was gruff and his sentences short and to the point. He wore a tan uniform, the sheriff's badge above his left breast pocket, his hair military short. He was clean shaven and had many small scars across his long, strong-looking hands, as well as here and there on his face. He missed nothing. Truly, Seabert was an eagle in disguise and she felt some of her worry melt away.

"So, here's the plan, Cari," Seabert said, turning the desktop screen toward her. "I'll be actively, daily, in alignment and receiving any intel from California law enforcement in their efforts to locate your stepbrother. They'll be sending me a lot of photos of him, plus other smaller details. I'll work with our local television station, put out the word and show Dirk's face to the public. We'll do this every week to keep it fresh in the minds of our residents. No one will know you are here, and your name will never be mentioned. People will think that this is a county-wide alert on an escaped prisoner, but that's all. We're going to give you a fake identification, a different name, so while Dirk is loose, he won't be drawn here because he heard his stepsister's name through the convict communication grapevine that's in every state. He's part of a major regional drug ring coming out of California, and I'll be asking my assistant, Sergeant Pepper Warner, to set up deep-cover info to protect you. She was a forensic FBI agent and I worked with her when I was a SEAL over in Afghanistan. I recruited her once I left the military and became sheriff here in this county. She's the best of the best. You'll work with Pepper and she will be your contact from here on. Pepper will have a line into me about you anytime she needs it. She'll be your go-to person. Are you okay with that?" He drilled her with a sharp look.

"More than fine," she admitted. "I—I never expected this level of help . . ."

"Well," Seabert growled, moving the screen back toward him, "welcome to Silver Creek and my county. We take care of our own."

Those words sunk into the fear and anxiety that she always kept a lid on, deep inside herself. Her hands were clasped in her lap, damp, but now her tense fingers began to relax. "Should I color my hair a different color?"

"Won't hurt," Dan said, "if you're okay with that?"

"I'd feel better. My biggest worry is someone getting hurt because I'm here." She touched her long, black hair. "Maybe cut it shorter?" She saw Chase wince but he said nothing, avoiding her glance in his direction.

"Even better," Dan said.

"I'll do it."

On the way back to the ranch, Chase said, "I know this is none of my business, but you have beautiful, long hair halfway down your back. Couldn't you just dye it for now?"

"It's worth it, Chase. Hair grows back. I'll use a rinse

on my hair, not dye it. In fact, I'll use henna as a rinse. At least that is natural."

He smiled a little as he drove back to the ranch. The day was young, the sky a pale blue, clear, the sun warm and welcoming. "Just tell me when you're going to do it so I'm not shocked by the change," he teased, giving her an oblique look, one corner of his mouth lifting.

"I'll give you some warning. Are we going to the wildlife center now?"

He slowed the truck and turned into the huge gate of the ranch. "Sure are. I gave Jenny a call earlier this morning, that we were coming. She's excited to meet you."

Cari sat back, feeling less and less tense and worried. Maybe Dan Seabert was right: Dirk would stick to the drug turf he knew because he had all those connections he'd made over the past decade there. Maybe he would forget about her parents and her, as his whole world had always orbited around the drug and criminal culture.

Chase introduced Jenny to Cari and it sounded like old home week to him. The two women gravitated to one another like opposite ends of a magnet and he grinned to himself as he stood back, watching them hug one another. For the first time since Cari had landed, Chase saw her finally beginning to relax. She wore the set of jeans she had on yesterday, changed to an emerald-green long-sleeved top with a cream-colored vest over it that hung around her hips.

She had her long, black hair in a ponytail and he silently bemoaned the fate of all that beautiful, silky, gleaming black hair being cut off. That was a selfish desire on his part and he knew it. At age thirty, he was wise about sex, lust, and making love to a woman. Cari was the type of woman he'd met in his dreams but never in person. Not until now. Chase wasn't too eager to tell her that, either, because she was about to become his employee. That meant hands off and keeping his foot out of his mouth.

Since the #MeToo movement, and a lot of frank talks with his mother about it, Chase began to see how the male patriarchy had branded him with certain ways to see women. He'd gone through a couple of years after #MeToo, taking a hard look at what patriarchy had done to women and men. And he'd spent those years afterward—with the help of his mother, who was a very wise woman—cleaning out the branding of the patriarchy he'd unconsciously taken on, and replacing it with respect toward all women, treating them as equals and never as sex objects or seeing them as less than human. He saw a number of men around him doing the same thing. That movement had created a lot of deep, painful discussions between husbands and wives or partners. But it was worth it. He was glad his father had always treated his mother as fully his equal and with respect in every way.

"What a gift, Chase!" Jenny called to him, her blue eyes dancing with joy. "Thank you for bringing Cari into my life! I'd heard of her visit to my parents' facility in Roslin, but had never gotten to meet her in person!"

"Well, there's always second chances in life," he murmured, meeting her smile. "Why don't you and Cari spend an hour or so together? I just got a text from my manager, Tracy Hartimer, and have to take a drive over to see her. I'll pick Cari up after that?"

Cari smiled. "That would be wonderful. Then, we could go back to your office and look at that large-scale map so I can get to work on a proper bee plan for you."

He put his Stetson on his head. "Sounds good to me. Now"—he wagged a finger in their direction—"you two stay out of trouble. Huh?" He squelched a grin as he saw the women laugh and give each other a knowing look. "Later," he said, lifting his hand and leaving the office area.

"Oh," Jenny said, gripping Cari's hand, "when Chase let me know you were here, I was just over the moon about it!"

"I was just as giddy," Cari admitted, seeing how dark Jenny's freckles across her cheeks and nose became when she was happy. Jenny's hair was short and a pixie style. She knew a lot of falconers and eagle owners cut their hair so the strands wouldn't get swept up between the bird's feathers, causing issues. Either that or a woman working with raptors would always have her hair in a ponytail between her shoulder blades.

"What would you like to do first? Go see the raptors? Or see our veterinary area? Just tell me, because one hour isn't going to be enough to take in everything. We're a huge, busy facility."

"I know," Cari said. "Could we sit down in your office with a cup of coffee? There's some private things you need to know about me and what's going on." Instantly, she saw concern come to Jenny's sky-blue eyes. She had large, black pupils and in some ways, Cari was reminded that she looked very much like an attentive eagle. Often, she'd seen attributes or physical traits of the falconer or eagle owner mirror some traits of their raptor. And Jenny was no exception to this observation.

"Why, of course! But then, I must show you our raptors that we use for our weekly show here on the ranch, as well as our medical facility where we have birds and raptors of all kinds recovering from many types of injuries."

"Love to see it all," Cari said, following Jenny behind the huge L-shaped counter and to her rear office.

"So," Jenny said, leaning back in her black leather desk chair, frowning as Cari finished her story, "this is very serious business with your stepbrother."

"It is," she agreed, sitting out in front of the antique oak desk. "How are you feeling about it?"

Raising her thin, red eyebrows, Jenny said, "The fact that Chase is ex-military, and Dan Seabert is ex-SEAL, makes me feel very secure, even though this cloud is a terrible thing to be hanging over you and your parents, Cari. I don't know if I'd have as much strength as you do, if it was happening to me and my family. It must be a terrible burden for all of you to be carrying every minute of every day."

"It never goes away," Cari agreed quietly, "it just dials up or down in intensity. Having been with Sheriff Seabert this morning, hearing his plan of action, really helped dial down my anxiety and fear for the people here on the ranch, as well as in the valley."

"Well"—she sighed—"you couldn't have chosen a better place to hide than here in Silver Creek. It sort of reminds me of the movie *Lost Horizon*, where a British diplomat tries to protect some Europeans and help them leave a Southern Asia revolution. Their plane crash-lands in the Himalayas, and by accident, they stumble upon the Valley of the Blue Moon, and a place called Shangri-La."

"I believe you're talking about the original book that was written by James Hilton in 1933. I read that book as a child, many times, loving it. I thought the movie, which I saw much later, was not up to the book at all."

"Indeed," Jenny said. "But the idea of a Shangri-La truly fits Silver Creek Valley. I believe Mr. Hilton tapped into an archetypal dream that we all have about a place that gets along with everyone, regardless of gender, skin color, or religion. I think most people in the world ache for that kind of place." She lifted her hand. "And I think you'll find a lot of it here, in Silver Creek Valley. When they first started settling this area in the mid-1800s, it was wild and untamed. Everyone had to work together to survive, and then they thrived. It has been that way from one generation to the next. I just love being here."

"Then, you're not upset that Chase is hiring me? That I'm dragging in the threat of a stepbrother who wants to kill me?"

"Heavens, no, lass. I don't know what I'd do if my sister had it in for me! I admire your courage and survival sense. Even more, I relish your honesty and putting the lives of people who are around you, first, not last. That speaks to your quality."

"Good," Cari whispered, once again relieved by the openness and the care strangers were bestowing upon her. "Thank you, Jenny. Thank you for your support and understanding."

"Let's move on, then." She rose and placed her empty cup aside. "Come with me and we'll visit our raptor area first, since you have a background in it."

Cari openly admired that the complex reminded her vividly of Roslin Wildlife Center. The whole area was laid out in four different modules. One was raptors and birds of all kinds. The second was the veterinary surgery and recuperation area. The third was a vet area for all other injured animals, whether wild or domestic. The fourth was a huge conference and training facility for visiting veterinarians and students who worked there in the summers, supplementing their knowledge of animals.

Outside the facility, Jenny showed her the raptor area. It consisted of flat, hard-packed dirt ovals where raptors could fly and be trained if they couldn't overcome their injuries or be released into the wild. Here, they learned how to become a "made" raptor and they became part of a weekly show, and also part of the roving raptor program to schools around the county.

There was another training area for younger raptors to learn how to fly and hit a moving target that a falconer whirled above her or his head. The cages were huge for the eagles, fresh water in bowls, and every morning, a large plastic pan with tepid, clean water put into each unit, so the bird could take a bath, if they chose to do so. In another area was a lot made of fine sand, where birds could "dust" themselves to rid themselves of unseen mites, the sand removing them from their feathers. It was, for Cari, a Shangri-La for the raptors, clean, well-kept, and safety measures in place for the birds.

As they stood outside in the warming sunshine, Cari looked around and said, "I swear, this place is almost an exact copy of Roslin."

Tittering, Jenny said, "Aye, lass, it is."

"And you'll be here for two more years?" she asked. Jenny wore a set of brown coveralls, black rubber boots up to just below her knees, and a thick black nylon jacket that fell to her hips. On her head she wore a dark green baseball cap with the Three Bars logo on the front of it.

"Yes."

"Do you miss Scotland? Being home with your parents?"

"Very much, but when Mary and Chase handed me a dream come true, using Roslin as a template for the very best a wildlife center could be, and setting it here in the USA, I couldn't say no. Besides"—and she smiled fondly—"I go home for three months from November through January, every year."

"That's wonderful," Cari said.

"It's a dream job. What they allowed me to do here is a template that has already taken flight here in the United States. Did you know we are building facilities in Pensacola, Florida, Alexandria, Virginia, and Minneapolis, Minnesota, right now? I'm overseeing them, as well, so even though I'm here on the ranch, I'm frequently flying out and around the US, working with construction superintendents, the people who will be running it, and giving them information they need."

"You are really busy!" Cari said, admiring her even more. "Do you ever get time to fly your raptors?"

"Not as much as I'd like," Jenny admitted, walking

back into the protected raptor facility. "You said you held the same raptor licenses as I do. Right?"

"Yes, because I still service that part of the industry, and the other half of my life is beekeeping consulting."

"Good, then come with me." Jenny gestured for Cari to follow her down a wide path of cedar shavings between two huge eagle cages. They kept walking until they came to another area, which was closed off from the eagles, and this was their hawk and falcon facility. Jenny walked at Cari's shoulder. "Are you rusty at training a young bird to hunt?"

"A little," Cari admitted. "Why?"

"Well, we had a young female red-tailed hawk who was hit by a car when she was just a fledging. She was bruised up pretty badly, lost some of her flight feathers, and the driver pulled over to save her. They wrapped her in a shirt and brought her here, to our facility." Jenny opened a door and went inside a slightly warmer area. This was the bird hospital, as she called it. "Over here," she said, making a left down a white-tiled aisle that was spotless and clean.

Cari came to a halt in front of a large hawk enclosure. Inside was a beautiful red-tailed hawk. Next door to her was another hawk of the same species, so she had company. "She's beautiful and big!"

Jenny nodded and they halted in front of the airy cage. "We call her Wild Child, even though Valkyrie is her official name, because she's of a huntress temperament and she takes no prisoners. I've been the one training her, but in the next couple of weeks, I'll be gone. Valkyrie needs someone who knows what they're doing.

She's sharply intelligent, and doesn't put up with a handler who really doesn't know what he or she is doing."

"In other words," Cari said, studying the young hawk, "she doesn't tolerate beginners."

"No. She's a 'hot' hawk."

"Nervous? Anxious?" Cari asked.

"No, just fully intense like a laser-fired rocket, is impatient, wants her own way and is headstrong despite her youth." Chuckling, Jenny said, "And that's probably what got her into trouble, trying to fledge and fly before her body and wings were actually ready to do the duty."

"I've met raptors like that," Cari said drily. "They're always the ones that fall out of their nest or fly too early and land on the ground."

"Yep, Valkyrie is like that. She's a hot hawk in terms of being a totally relentless hunter, isn't afraid of anything or anyone, and she'll crash through trees and branches to get her prey, which is highly unusual. Most hawks that survive know you don't do that and get away with it. Usually, they end up with a broken wing, grounded, and then some predator will make a meal of 'em."

"Right you are. But how do you know she'll go through tree branches?"

Grimacing, Jenny said, "I had one of our older students work with her, and one day, Valkyrie decided to go to the nearby woods instead of work with the creance line. Pamela saw her fly above the trees, spot something, and then dive right down through the tree limbs. We put locators on their tails so we can find them, and when Pamela got to her, Valkyrie had a dead squirrel in her claws, mantling over it, making a meal out of it. After our Wild Child was done with her meal, the student put the jesses back into place on her legs and brought her back to the facility."

"Maybe she's half harpy eagle?" Cari asked with a sour grin. "They are a South American eagle who will literally dive into jungle trees after a monkey, leaves and twigs and branches exploding around them as they do it."

"Yes, well," Jenny said with a chuckle, "the harpy is about the only eagle whose wings can take that kind of punishment and not break a bone. They are a massive raptor, as you probably know."

"I've seen two in captivity, both in South America," Cari agreed. "They are a huge eagle. I wouldn't want to try and work with one."

"Makes two of us. So, maybe tomorrow? If you get an hour off? Drive over here and I'll see how you and Valkyrie get along. I need someone to pinch hit for me on this hawk for the next few weeks. By then, she'll be ready for release, unless she hits a tree branch that breaks one of her wings."

"I'd love to do that, Jenny. I'll ask Chase if he minds."

"Oh, he won't. I'm sure he'll keep you busy with bee work, but he's not a slave driver, either. Just text me if you can make it over at one p.m. tomorrow?"

A thrill went through Cari. "I promise, I will."

As they got back to the office, Chase was just walking up to the door, his hat coming off.

"Well?" he teased. "What do you think?"

Jenny gave him an evil look. "I'm stealing her from you, Chase, from time to time. She's gonna work with our famous Wild Child when I'm off on one of my trips."

"Ohhh . . . that hawk. I call her Trouble."

Cari laughed. "That's not very kind!"

"No," Chase grouched, "it isn't, but Valkyrie has a very stubborn mind of her own and she flies like she's got jet engines strapped to her wings."

Jenny joined in the laughter. "Aye, you're right about that!"

Chase gave Cari a look of respect. "Jenny wouldn't ask you to take on Trouble if she didn't think you could do the job. I'm impressed."

"Yeah, well, don't get *too* impressed," Cari warned him, walking toward the door. "Let's see if we can keep our problem child out of the forests and not busting through tree limbs and twigs first."

Rolling his eyes, Chase said, "Oh . . . that one . . . yeah . . . she has another nickname around here: Tree Buster . . ."

Chapter Five

June 1

Where was that bitch of a stepsister of his? Dirk Bannock sat inside a tent on a Los Angeles sidewalk, smoking a joint, waiting for one of his men to come and give him information on some coke and the deadly drug, fentanyl, coming up from the Mexican border near San Diego, California.

His mind churned over and over on Cari. To no avail. He'd tried calling her cell phone number. He'd had his men stake out the condo and they hadn't seen Cari's car, or her, in a two-week period. He'd had a friend of his hack into his parents' desktop and found nothing about Cari on it, or where she might be. The job she'd had, she'd quit, and no one knew where she'd gone.

Yeah, Cari knew he'd kill her the first opportunity he'd get. Right now, he was busy setting up his old drug network, taking down and killing those who thought they could replace him. Four men were dead at either his hand or his gang's hands. Now, he was on top again, as it should be. Until he could stabilize and renew his drug ties with

Mexico and Canada, Cari was an addendum to his life.
There would be a time when he was ready to hunt her down.
And once he did that, then he'd go after his stepmother.
First, he wanted Nalani to suffer when she found out her
daughter had been murdered. Of course, he wouldn't leave
any evidence he had been the cause of her death; he'd
be careful about that, but Nalani would know it was him.
He smiled, allowing the pleasure of that moment to flow
powerfully through him. That little bitch stepsister of his
always kept him in hot water, always tattled on him to
her mother. His father had allowed him to get away with
everything, but once his dad married Nalani, trouble
began in earnest for him. His hatred of women was well
in place, thanks to those two who had conspired and
worked against him every opportunity they'd gotten.
Yes, they'd both pay. With their lives.

The morning air was a mild temperature. Today would
turn hot, probably in the eighties. Outside, through an
opening in the front of the gray nylon tent, he could
see other homeless people walking past his place of resi-
dence on the sidewalk. He could smell breakfast cooking
in someone else's tent.

Yesterday, he'd gotten a call from Pablo Gonzalez,
a well-known drug lord from Guatemala. The forty-five-
year-old cartel king was a smart, careful player, wanting
to create drop zones and drug routes in Wyoming, with
an eye on taking the drops to Chicago, a main area
where drugs were wildly popular. Pablo's lieutenant told
him they'd run into a lot of problems in Wyoming, in a
place called Wind River Valley. He'd pulled out of there
and was now looking for a new valley to move quietly
into, without the fierce blowback from law enforcement

or the citizens, in his first foray into that state. Was Dirk interested? Hell yes, he was! Being able to expand his empire was always top in his mind. What he had to be careful of was that the Mexican drug lord didn't get wind of him working with the Guatemalan one. Usually, regional drug kingpins like himself played in one back-yard, not two. It could be costly to Dirk if one or the other found out. Drug lords, after all, demanded fealty and loyalty above everything else. And if he was caught double dealing? They'd send out a team to murder him. No, he had to be careful and look into Gonzalez's plans to try a second time to establish his drops and routes through Wyoming.

The sprawling city of LA was a good hideout for him, for now. Since escaping prison, he had dodged law en-forcement's efforts to find him. Hiding in plain sight in one of the largest homeless camps in LA was a wise move. He'd let his hair grow shaggy, with an unkempt beard to go with it. Purposely, he'd fitted in with the homeless population—for now.

Leaning back on the sleeping bag inside his gray nylon tent, he finished off the butt and flipped it out the door, clasping his hands behind his head and relaxing into the soft, thick folds of his bed. It was better than sleeping on hard concrete, that was for damned sure.

June 2

"These are very differently built hives than the others," Chase said to Cari. The shipment of thirty Flow Hive 2 types had arrived from Australia, from a company created by a father and son, who were beekeepers. It was nearly noon and Cari, with the help of Theresa Sandoval, had unpacked them and built them according to the clear, easy-to-understand booklet this morning.

"They are," Cari agreed, running her fingers across the peak of the rooftop of the first Flow Hive. "I'm interested in their outside-the-box, so to speak, technology. The Langstroth hives you have, are far more work intensive. You have to remove part of the hive to collect the honey. With the commercial Flow Hive 2, you don't have to, which is a huge time advantage to beekeepers and the bees. You don't have to use a smoker, no centrifugal extractors, and best of all, no back-breaking work of pulling the honey supers up and out of the Langstroth box." She leaned over and pointed to a metal lever. "Turn this and it opens the channel within the honeycomb and the honey drains via gravity, into the pipe at the back of the hive and directly into the container you've chosen to utilize. This way," she said, giving it a pleased look, "the bees are *not* disturbed, and you don't kill bees by removing and putting your honeycomb panel supers in and out of the hive boxes, which is more humane for our bee people."

"Seems like it's really a twenty-first-century leap into a better hive?" Chase guessed, looking it over and then comparing it to the five Langstroth hives that had survived.

"That's why I ordered thirty of them," Cari said. "Over the last couple of years, I've gotten a lot of positive feedback from beekeepers who are using them around the world. Now, no hive is perfect, and this Flow hive will need upkeep and care just like any other type of hive, but the fact your honey is going directly into a container, is a huge improvement."

The warmth of the sun beat down on his shoulders. The weather had gone from cranky in April and May to the longed-for summer temperatures. Today, he wore a blue denim shirt, the sleeves rolled up to just below his elbows. His pair of elk-skin gloves hung partially out of his rear pocket. Chase knelt down, gauging the metal stand that the Flow Hives had. "Seems very sturdy."

"And made out of lightweight aluminum," Cari agreed. "There's a lot of wonderful improvements in this Flow Hive, and Theresa and her children are super excited about them. In fact"—she turned, pointing in another direction—"she and her children are assembling the other Flow Hives in the three fields around your ranch right now. And the packets of bees are to arrive early next week so we can install them in all of the new hives. It's an exciting time."

Rising to his full height, he looked at the purple flowering heads just coming into season for his alfalfa field. "The alfalfa and clover fields will be blooming by next week," he said, nodding. "Your strategy to place the Flow Hives with the older box hives is a good idea. That way, you can tell which works better for the bees and their keepers."

Cari was wearing a ranch baseball cap along with her jeans, a pink top, and a light terry jacket. She had gone to Helen Dinkins at the Mariposa Hair Salon, a hairdresser in Silver Creek, and cut off her hair and gave it to Locks of Love, for women who had lost their hair during chemotherapy. And Helen had shown her how to use the henna, which was messy compared to the commercial rinses or dyes, but Cari wanted something natural. When she'd come back to the ranch, she saw how sad Chase looked at her cut hair, but he said nothing. Cari felt the loss, too. She loved her long, silky, straight hair. She'd grudgingly gotten used to her very short auburn-colored hair, sometimes still startled by it when she looked into her bathroom mirror. Now, she had a driver's license with her new disguise, several ranch credit cards with her fake name on them, and her identity change was complete. Every day that she worked outdoors with the bees, Theresa, and Theresa's children, the fear of Dirk was slowly beginning to dissolve.

Having Chase as her boss was heaven, and a special, growing hell for her. She'd never been drawn so instantly to a man, and that scared the bejesus out of her. There were few men in this world who treated a woman not only with respect, but as an equal. He was a rare find. The more she worked with Chase, the more her heart wanted a relationship with him. *Argh.*

"How's things going with our Wild Child over at the raptor training grounds?" he asked, giving her a grin.

"Valkyrie is truly a very unique character." Cari laughed. "Absolutely fearless and fierce. She's scared of *nothing*."

"I took Jenny to the airport the other morning and she was crowing about how *well* you and that young red-tailed hawk are getting along."

Snorting, Cari muttered, "Oh, our Wild Child is a handful and she knows it. She'd been good flying back and forth on the T-stands, so I thought I'd get her off the creance line. So I flew her out in the oval flight meadow the other day."

"Yeah, well, how'd that go?"

Scowling, she said, "Not well. The first place Valkyrie went was to fly over that grove of trees. She scared me to death! She dove into a tree at something, crashing through the treetops again, and when I found her by the radio receiver we had affixed to her tail feathers, she was on the forest floor with nothing to show for it." Laughing, she said, "Apparently she went after a squirrel or something and it beat her to its safe place. She was shrieking, flapping her wings, stomping around on the pine needles around the base of that pine tree, totally pissed off. I saw the squirrel looking out of its hole, which was dug between two of its roots. The squirrel was scolding loudly, *chut-chut-chutting* at the hawk, who was pacing back and forth in front of her hole—just taunting her. Serves Valkyrie right. She hopped up on my glove and I put the jesses between my fingers, fed her some mouse meat from my pouch, and she was a happy bird."

"That was a happy squirrel, too."

"Yes, but I was terrified that she'd fractured her wing with that darned dive. I swear, she thinks she's a peregrine falcon mated with a harpy eagle! She dove straight down into that treetop like it wasn't even there, her whole focus on that squirrel she saw beneath the leaf cover."

Chase walked her down to where the two ranch trucks were parked along the dirt road. "That's a pretty interesting visual, if you ask me."

She giggled. "Well, when I got back to the raptor module, I ran immediately to find Dr. Cathy. Valkyrie had skinned herself on that dive, and a bunch of small feathers around the front of her left wing were ripped off. Cathy took a look at her and said she was fine, just a bit of most probably a bruised ego, was all. She said to give Valkyrie a rest for about four days before taking her out again, and she suggested keeping her on the creance line. I agreed."

"That hawk has the nine lives of a cat," he muttered, shaking his head. They halted at the trucks. "Would you like to come with me into town? I know you want to stay on the ranch for fear of Dirk being around, but you need to get out of here every once in a while. We could have lunch, some pizza if you want? I have to go over to the bank to sign some papers, but that won't take long. Are you game?"

Tucking her lower lip between her teeth for a moment, Cari avoided the pleading look in Chase's gray eyes. The man knew how to make a woman melt.

"You've been here on the ranch since you arrived, Cari. Come on, this isn't going to hurt anything. I'll be watching for Dirk if he's around, which I don't think he is. Dan just talked to the sheriff in California and they said Dirk was spotted yesterday at a homeless tent area in Los Angeles. He got away. But they are looking for him, big-time now. So, I know he's not here in Wyoming. I'll keep you safe."

"They saw Dirk?" she whispered, her voice suddenly off-key. Her hand automatically went to her throat.

"Yes, a city cop spotted him. He walks a beat in one of the tent city areas and saw him at dusk. With things getting dark, Dirk slipped away into the night. Now they are handing out his picture to everyone in all the tent cities, letting them know he's an escaped convict. The reward for him is ten thousand dollars, and the sheriff said that anyone who spotted him trying to use the cover of a tent city would turn him in, in a heartbeat."

"That's good to know. So, he's in Los Angeles?"

"Yes. Why?"

"That's where he had his later connections. He's probably gathering up his group again."

"In one way," Chase said, giving her a sympathetic look, "you know where he is. I guess this is the first sighting they've had of him. Dan also called your parents on the burner phone he keeps at the office. He gives them a weekly update on you. They were relieved to hear where Dirk is located."

"I know they're frightened, too," she whispered, frowning, looking away and fighting back tears. How she missed her mother! They couldn't talk for fear Dirk, who was a gamer and a software code writer, would hack into a cell phone, or their desktop, to get information on where she might be. They had not been told where she was, to protect her and themselves.

"Hey," Chase called gently, placing his hand on her shoulder momentarily, "I hate to see you sad like this, Cari. I know it's hard on you. It would be on anyone. Since you know Dirk isn't in Wyoming, why not have a lunch with me in town? I'll do my bank business after that and then we'll come home."

"Okay," she whispered. "I do need to get out a little bit."

"Let's drive back to my office, pile in one truck, and take off."

Cari tried to hide her yearning for a more private and intimate relationship with Chase. She kept reminding herself that he was her employer, she knew office romances rarely worked out and if they did, someone had to leave the company. Not that she was sticking around long-term, which was now a painful jab into her heart, but she had a two-year contract she'd signed, to bring the family's honey business to fruition.

As they entered the town of Silver Creek, Chase began to point out businesses to her. She spotted the Mariposa Hair Salon, a pink two-story building a block away from the main drag. She liked that everyone seemed to recognize Chase, waved to him from the sidewalk or another vehicle. He waved to them in return. This was a productive town and it seemed very busy!

"Is the traffic always like this?" she wondered.

"No. We're into tourist season from June first through the end of October. There's a lot of cabin rentals around the valley and people stay in them. There's fishing, hiking, swimming in nearby lakes, and all kinds of things for people who love the outdoors to do around here."

"I'm surprised you don't have cabins for rent on your ranch."

"My family, right or wrong, wanted to maintain our privacy. Logan Anderson feels the same way. But some see it as a good source of income. So, a cottage industry of sorts took off. Some of the other ranchers have either added cottages or they've gone full-on with dude ranches for tourists. Which is fine, but it's just not our kind of fare."

"You'll make your money from more environmental businesses, rather than being impacted by huge numbers of human beings who come with their garbage in tow and leave it behind for your town to pick up."

"Well, we do have a weekly raptor show during tourist season on our ranch, but as you've seen, it's the closest facility to the entrance to Three Bars, and people aren't allowed beyond that parking area and flight facility."

"I'm sure kids and parents are thrilled with it. I know I still gasp with awe when I see a raptor fly, land, or take off. It's magical."

"Speaking of magic?" He gave a glance in her direction. "Theresa said you are truly a bee fairy come to live among us humans."

Laughing, Cari said, "Really?"

He slowed and turned into the Oldham Pizza Parlor and parked. "Yes. I first thought that when that group of bees flew from the hive and landed on your left shoulder. I've never seen anything like that."

"I have," she said. Climbing out, her stomach growled. It felt like she was free, the sun against her face, a soft breeze as she walked to the front of the truck. Chase held the door open for her and she thanked him.

Inside, the place was busy. What struck Cari was the soft background music they were playing. Chase pointed to a corner booth that had just emptied and she headed in that direction. Sliding into the red leather booth, Chase on the opposite side and taking off his Stetson, she sighed. "I've *never* heard classical music in such a place!"

"Oh . . . that . . . well, the owner used to be a violinist in a symphony orchestra back East before he retired and came out here." Chase lifted his hand to the owner, who was waving at him from behind the counter. "Henry Oldham was a violinist," he said. "He and his wife moved here when he was fifty-five years old, and started the pizza parlor. I remember the grand opening, walking in and hearing classical music. I felt kind of bad for Henry and his wife, Winifred, because I thought their choice of music would be a turnoff." He managed an apologetic smile. "Fortunately, I was wrong. I never realized how many folks in Silver Creek love and know about classical music."

"You weren't raised on it, I take it?"

Shaking his head, he said, "No, I was not. But over the years, Henry, who comes out and talks to all his patrons, started educating all of us about the music. I got so I really like some of it."

"Such as?"

He looked up at the ceiling, thinking. "'Ode to Joy' by Beethoven?"

"That's a beautiful piece. Who is your favorite composer?"

"I guess it would be Modest Mussorgsky or Richard Wagner," he admitted.

"Ohhhh," she teased, "'Night on Bald Mountain' and 'Ride of the Valkyries,' by any chance?"

Chuckling, he said, "How'd you guess? Maybe I like those songs the most because it reminds me of riding a horse in the middle of a thunderstorm."

"Plus the Valkyries were women on horseback taking the souls of the dead soldiers off the field of battle and back to Valhalla," she noted.

"You know your classics, don't you?"

"I try to keep that a secret. When I listen to classics with my Apple earbuds, I just relax so much. The music is always calming to me."

The waitress came and they put in their orders. Cari also wanted a salad. Folding his hands, Chase asked, "What do bees think of the classics?"

Tilting her head, she gave him a mysterious smile.

"How wonderful of you to think in those parameters. Do bees like music? Or not? If so, what kind?"

"What's the consensus of opinion?" he teased, drinking from the glass of ice water.

"I've tried several experiments, none of them scientific, just curiosity on part. One day, when I was in New Zealand, I had allowed my earbuds to hang across my neck as I worked with a beekeeper and her hives. At the time, I was listening to Brahms. The bees heard it, even though I had the volume very low, and they flew to the earbuds, and pretty soon? I had two balls of bees on each bud, and they seemed to love the music. When it was done playing, they went back to work and flew off. We all thought that it was rather an amazing moment. Who had thought of playing music for the bees?"

"Maybe the wind is their song?"

She smiled and wrapped her fingers around the beaded, damp glass of water. "Maybe it is. We know that bees see differently, but that they have many, many as yet undiscovered abilities and skills we know nothing about. The next day, the beekeeper and I decided to try another classical song in my earbuds. Not as many bees came. The third day, I tried Strauss's 'Emperor Waltz' and oh my! We had at least fifty or so bees on each earbud. When the waltz was over, they flew away to do their duties."

"Hmmm," Chase said, watching who came and went in the busy place, the volume of talking muting the music. "Do bees have likes and dislikes on music? Will the music help them produce more honey? Or less?"

"All great questions I can't answer. I later flew to Melbourne, Australia, to work with some beekeepers there, and I tried the different songs. This time, those bees much preferred Strauss to Brahms. And then I went to Tasmania to work with beekeepers, and we tried the same songs there. Those bees didn't care for either one! Instead, we played some aboriginal didgeridoo music and they loved it!" She shrugged. "In some ways, they are just like people, I think, with certain tastes in sounds, just as we humans do."

"Fascinating. You said those bee packets were coming from Louisiana. Maybe they prefer Cajun music?"

Laughing, Cari said, "It could be! We should try it sometime and see."

"You do know that Theresa sings to them when she's working with a hive, don't you?"

Eyes widening, Cari sat up. "No . . . I didn't. What does she sing to them?"

Shrugging, Chase said, "I don't know. I only know that she told me a few years ago that certain songs in Spanish were well loved by the bee people. She always hummed or sang those songs when she had to get into a hive to check out the brood box or the supers, to set the honey."

"Did she use smoke to calm them?"

"No. She said humming certain tunes calmed them just as much. I never saw her use a smoker, nor does she ever wear beekeeping gear, except for a hat."

"She is very magical, then," Cari whispered, awed and pleased.

"But so are you."

Giving him a questioning look, she said, "Tell me something. Did your parents read fairy tales to you growing up?"

"Sure did. One night my father would come in and sit next to my bed and read. The next night, my mother did."

"You believe in them?"

"What? Fairy folk? Sure. Who doesn't?"

Looking around, Cari said, "Oh, you're probably the only person in here who does, Chase. Nowadays? Children aren't raised the way you were. My parents surrounded me with classical music, myths, fairy tales, and all types of magical books like the Harry Potter series. For me, bees were magical. My mother always said that the little people were actually taking on the shape of a bee when they wanted to live in our world and not theirs. I guess I fell in love with them because of that connection."

Their pizza came, steaming hot, cut in front of them, plates and napkins served with it.

"Glad you like pineapple on your pizza," Chase said, sliding a piece to his plate.

"Glad you like it, too. With my mother coming from Hawaii, pineapple is used in just about every form of cooking and many desserts."

"You're a rare woman, Cari."

Smiling, she raised her brow. "And you're a rare man, Mr. Bishop."

"Is that a compliment?"

She could see him preening, so male and so easy to read. "Mostly." She saw some of the masculine puffing-up of his chest dissolve, and he frowned slightly.

"What does a rare man consist of in your eyes?" he wondered.

Wiping her lips, she said, "I strongly dislike males who are Neanderthals. They think they can own a woman, own her body, abuse her, disrespect her, keep a boot on her neck and never give her the support so she can make her dreams come true like he can."

"Good definition of a Neanderthal," he congratulated. "My mother was hell on wheels when I started budding some of those tendencies when I was in grade school. I'd come home mimicking other kids and I got it from both my parents. Stereo. They righted my rudder in a hurry. My mother, especially, trained me daily on how to respect women, and know they were my equal."

"Did your father agree?"

"Sure did. He always gave credit to Mary. She's actually the one, from the time she left high school, that has made this ranch bloom. Her ideas, her vision, have really made Three Bars a very special place, where environmental businesses can be showcased because they flourish here under her care, judgment, and intuition." He smiled fondly. "I don't profess to have my mother's big picture and entrepreneurial skills. My father wasn't an idea machine, either, so I guess I took after him."

"But you have wonderful management skills, Chase. You know how to make things work, how to build a team of women and men wranglers, and get the job done on time and right. I don't think you're any less important to the success of Three Bars than your mother is. It takes two, a team, to make it work."

He grimaced and started in on his second piece. "There's the rub and there's the prize."

"What do you mean?"

"Finding the right partner."

Her mouth twisted. "Oh, that. Yes, well, you are right. I've got a dismal track record." She bit into her pizza and then wiped the corners of her mouth with the napkin.

"I don't want to compare track records, but mine went bust, too."

"Thank God I never married," Cari said. "I was way too young, too green, and had no idea how men were. My father died when I was nine years old."

"I'm sorry, I didn't know that . . ."

"It's not something I tell everyone," she admitted. "He was the light of my life, he adored me and I adored him. He taught me from early on how boys should respect me as their equal. My mother and he were so much in love. That's where I learned what real love was, but I sure couldn't repeat it, it seems."

"I lost my father when he was forty-five years old," Chase admitted, "so we sort of have a similarity there. I do understand how much of a loss a father is to your world."

"That's so hard on children, even if you're an adult by that time. I always leaned on my father, and he had such a great sense of humor and such wisdom, plus patience, with everyone." She finished her second slice and wiped her hands and mouth. "That's why when my mother married Blake Bannock, two years after my dad died, I felt like I had been spun off into some other world, a very dark, horrible one. Dirk, his son, was twelve, and suddenly my wicked stepbrother. Dirk hated me on sight. I had done nothing to him, but he saw me as his enemy. I had this horrible feeling he wanted to kill me. It scared me so much that I was afraid to go to my mother about it because she was happily married to Blake. I couldn't tell anyone. Dirk has black eyes. They're probably dark brown, but to me, they looked black. And he'd give me this awful look, like he was going to come over and kill me, so I became a shadow in our household. I pretty much disappeared from their lives and had to stay a step ahead of Dirk. I lived in terror, Chase. I was so young, lost because of my father dying, and then my stepfather's evil son, a year older than me, came into my life. It was so jarring. I don't think I ever got over it."

"I'm sorry, Cari. It's tough to hear you say that and then to see how fey you are." Chase managed a one-sided smile. "Fey meaning fairylike, vulnerable, fragile, and otherworldly."

"My sun sign is Pisces and my mother always told me that I was the two fish, their tails tied together, each swimming in a different direction. And that I was highly creative, but that she saw me as an oyster without a shell and having to learn how to live down here on this Earth and survive without it. She always worried about my survival."

"So did you," he said, putting the last four slices of pizza into an awaiting box. "You had a stepbrother who saw you as competition, I'd guess. He didn't want you to be there. His kind likes to be the center of attention, and he didn't want to share it with anyone. Am I right?"

"So right," she admitted faintly. Looking out the window, watching the traffic, she added, "Eventually, I did tell my mother, but I was going off to college by that time, and I would be out of the house and finally escape Dirk. He was selling drugs in school at age twelve, and I knew it. If I told my mother? She'd have turned him in to law enforcement. I kept it a secret. Blake, his father, doted on him, spoiled him rotten, gave him all the money he wanted, and Dirk didn't have to lift a finger to earn it. I don't know why Blake didn't see what his son was doing."

"I don't either. This has been a rough childhood for you in many ways for a long, long time."

"It got much better when I was in college." She opened her hands. "This isn't very good table talk, but I've told you half the story about Dirk entering our lives, I might as well tell you the worst part." She saw him frown, a darkness in his eyes that looked like worry for her. Taking a deep breath, she lowered her voice so that only Chase could hear her speak. "When I was seventeen, I saw Dirk get into a fight with his girlfriend. He took a gun out and shot her in the head, instantly killing her. I screamed and ran. I was afraid he'd shoot me next. I ran to the bus that I knew would take me to the police station. I was so shaken up I couldn't phone 911 or anything. I just wanted to run as far away from Dirk as fast as I could. When I got to the police station, my knees were so weak that I was afraid I'd fall. Somehow, I made it to the sergeant at the desk. I think I half sobbed and half told him what had happened. They instantly sent out a cruiser."

"My God," he whispered. "What happened then?"

"I-I stayed at the station. It was the only place I felt safe. I called my mother at work and she called Blake. They came to the station. By that time? They'd found Dirk and took him down, cuffed him and read him his rights. He was taken to a jail cell long after my mother and Blake arrived at the station. We just waited there together. I told them what happened. The police confirmed through my eye-witness account, that Dirk had shot her." She took a deep breath and held his turbulent gray gaze, feeling such warmth and a sense of protection pouring off him and surrounding her. It gave her the courage to go on.

"Dirk was charged with second-degree murder and he got twenty-five years."

"Did you have to testify?"

Giving a jerky nod, she whispered, "Yes. I was terrified of having to do it, Chase. After I got out of the seat, done with my testimony against him, Dirk screamed out that he'd kill me sooner or later. Of course, the judge ordered him out of the courtroom and they dragged him out of there, cursing me and my mother, Nalani. To this day, I can see his insane face, those crazed, black eyes of his, and his voice . . . screeching at us like a madman."

Sitting back, Chase digested her quiet admission. "No wonder you wanted to be honest with me at the airport when we met."

"You and everyone here in Silver Creek deserve to know and be protected from him, Chase. He's a monster. He has no heart. No soul. His defense attorney tried to get him off on grounds of mental illness; that he was a sociopath, to which the psychiatrist agreed in testimony to the jury. But the jury saw something different. Worse. If they let him out of prison? He was insane, and would kill again. They were right."

She pressed her hand against her heart. "And I'm his next target."

"Not if we can help it," Chase growled, giving her a look that said so much, that he would protect her at any cost. Even at the expense of his own life, if it came to that. In that moment, he became excruciatingly aware that he was falling in love with her. Real love. Forever love. He was old enough now to know the difference. And yet, she was hunted. Well, Dirk Bannock had just met his match and then some, whether he knew it or not. He'd been a behind-the-lines sniper for months on end in enemy territory. He knew how to track and he knew how to live off his survival instincts and his knowledge of the land. He knew who his enemy was. Dirk Bannock was someone he was going to make an in-depth study of. He'd go to Dan and ask for his help in assessing Bannock, wanting to bone up on his profile. He knew the sheriff could get him information that only law enforcement was allowed to see. He'd sit in Dan's office and read it, absorb it, and remember it. Because he realized now, more than ever before, Dirk was going to hunt down Cari.

This time, he would make the difference. He'd stand between them. And he'd take that sick, twisted druggie down, just like he had his enemy combatants in Afghanistan. This time around? Cari was going to be protected, but he would never tell her what he planned to do or how he was going to find out everything possible on Dirk before her stepbrother could strike again and kill her.

Chapter Six

June 3

Chase wanted to say so much more to Cari, but he grimly realized the amount of pressure that she was under. As they walked around to the parking lot at the pizza parlor, he fished out the fob to the truck. Cari looked stressed by their talk and she had good reason to be. Her once flushed cheeks were now pale. She had her hands tucked in the pockets of her lightweight jacket. Her lips were pursed. He slowed as they got to the truck and he opened the door for her.

"Are you sorry you told me?" he asked quietly, holding her darkened gaze. "Just talking about it, I imagine it's all avalanching emotionally on you again."

"How could you know that?" she asked in a whisper, leaning against the truck, looking up at him.

He shrugged. "I was behind the lines in Afghanistan for five years as a sniper. I was always in harm's way. I had orders to take out certain Taliban or ISIS leaders and would be dropped in under cover of night. Sometimes it took me a month to locate my quarry, and all that time,

I was in enemy territory. There were never any clear lines of demarcation between safe and dangerous, Cari, between the Afghans who were pro-USA and those who sided with the Taliban and the ISIS terrorists groups."

She studied him. "I guess I never realized just how much danger you were in, Chase."

"Well," he teased, trying to lighten the mood, "you don't come from a military family. You probably aren't too up on military things."

"You're right. We really are from two very different worlds."

"And yet," he said, keeping his voice light in hopes of pulling her out of her dark, dangerous past, "we have a lot of things in common. We both love the Earth, we're ecologically and environmentally oriented, we like the animals and insects, and we're both working toward making the world a better place to live. Those are strong ties that we share."

She nodded, looking down at her feet and then lifting her chin. "You've killed men."

"And a man is trying to kill you." He saw her face change, sag, and that haunted look return to her eyes. "In my case? I was taking out the enemy who were murdering Afghan villagers—men, women, and children. They'd torch their villages, rape the women, murder the children. What I was doing was an act of protection, trying to give those villagers a chance to live and thrive."

"Did you like what you were doing?"

"No . . . never. But what do you do if evil is walking the land? Murdering innocents? Do you let them keep on doing it? Or do you put things in place to permanently stop them?"

"I never thought about it in those terms." She sighed. "I cry when a bee gets accidentally killed when I take out a super panel. I could never do what you have done."

"When evil stares me in the face, I'm not going to let it kill me. And not everyone has those kinds of reflexes built into them, or to do the right thing by confronting that evil, even if it haunts us for the rest of our lives." He saw her nod, sadness in her eyes, but he sensed it was for him, not for herself.

"I guess . . . well . . . my mother's Hawaiian family had warriors in it, and I grew up hearing how they fought for their king, to keep their land. My father was an airline pilot and before that, he'd been in the military and flew combat aircraft. Maybe I didn't get the gene on how to survive or protect myself?"

He stood about two feet from her, his hand resting on the open door. "I don't think you're helpless, Cari. Look what you did to hide and become invisible to Dirk. You took action. Granted, you didn't use a gun, but then, not every situation requires a gun to settle an issue, either. Sometimes just protesting with others, or using your voting rights, or making your voice heard to your political leaders in your town or state, is an act of defense or offense, depending upon what the situation is."

"My mother and stepfather refused to go into hiding. I tried to persuade them to do it."

"Dirk is after you, not them," he said gently. "You are his target. And you did take prudent action, Cari. Luckily"—he looked around and then held her unsure gaze—"you landed here, with us. This isn't the Wild West anymore, but ranchers and farmers tend to carry arms, have a rifle or a shotgun in their homes. We still get grizzly bears coming in from the nearby mountain range, but usually it's black bears. We work with the state wildlife department to get such dangerous animals away from our cattle and other livestock. We don't want to kill them, either. But in your case, our best defense is an offense, and that means the sheriff and Pepper Warner are contacting me weekly, and sometimes more often, on anything regarding Dirk. Until he's caught, you're not safe, and we all know that."

She looked around and crossed her arms. "I feel I've been so lucky to have come here. Guns scare me. Even more since I saw Dirk murder his girlfriend. I know what they can do." She halted, and frowned. "I just hate killing anything, Chase . . ."

"I know. Come on, climb in. Let's get those other errands done and we'll go back to the ranch. At least there you feel safe."

"Oh, a hundred percent," she assured him, getting into the truck. Strapping in, she turned as he started the engine on the truck. "I feel better by talking with you, Chase. I always do." She managed a slight smile. "Are you sure you aren't fey yourself?"

Laughing heartily, he drove the truck out of the parking lot and onto the street. "Mary used a lot of words to describe me growing up, but never used the word *fey*."

"Well, there are male fairies," she said. "You must have seen Legolas in a *Lord of the Rings* movie?"

"Yes, I did."

"You remind me of Legolas, just a tougher, cowboy version, is all," she said, watching him for reaction.

"I never had to swing a sword."

"No, but both of you rode horses and did battle, so there is some kind of connection."

"Very little." He touched his short hair. "Legolas had really long hair. I don't."

"But he was a protector, too, just like you."

He grinned and turned into the parking lot of the bank. "Don't you think it's sort of baked into male DNA to protect others? I'll be back in just a moment." He climbed out. "We'll continue the conversation when I get back."

Smiling, Cari sat back, watching the bustle of early afternoon traffic. Silver Creek looked as if it came straight out of the 1900s, the buildings all seemingly built around that time, but well cared for. It was a town thrown back in time, she decided. Catching a glance of Chase coming out of the bank, she admired how strong, tall, and confidently he walked. Unlike others, however, he looked around, was alert, and seemingly was still in sniper mode. Or, she thought, maybe he'd done that work for so long, it was a natural part of him now.

Chase climbed in, noting that there was a slight pinkness to her cheeks once more, and her beautiful, large, cinnamon-colored eyes had returned, the darkness no longer in them. Inwardly, he heaved a huge sigh of relief. He understood that it was good for her to get things off her chest, so to speak, to talk them out. His mother, Mary, hammered that into him, too . . . and forced him to talk about his feelings to her all the time. That, too, was baked into him, and this time her training was helping him to instinctually know where Cari was at, and the core of her fear was far more evident to him now than ever before. He really did need to initiate more deep, searching talks with her in the future.

Starting the truck engine, he twisted a look in her direction. "One more stop. They just built a Dunkin' Donuts in town. I'm hearing from everyone since it opened three weeks ago, that their donuts are really good. Want to find out?"

That boyish look made Cari's heart race. "I'm all in. Lead the way."

"So, you're a donut girl?"

"Absolutely. I love donuts. My mom made them for us at least once every couple of months and then taught me to make them. Dirk refused to learn how to cook from the moment he entered the household. My mother had some pretty intense talks with her new husband about this, and over time, she let it go."

"Mary taught me to cook starting at age nine, when my eyes were above the kitchen counter." He chuckled.

"My father loved cooking and he was an ace at using spices of all kinds. That's what he loved to do when he wasn't flying." Cari sighed fondly, closing her eyes over those memories. "He taught me how to use spices. He was always bringing back bottles of fresh spices from around the world, wherever he flew. Does Mary like spices?"

"Absolutely. When we get home? Check out the drawer next to where the flatware is kept. You'll see about thirty different jars. Mary likes to grow them here on the ranch. She's got a company and a manufacturing building, employing a number of people from Silver Creek, who take the fresh plants, dry them a particular way, and then grind them up. Have you seen her facility?"

"No, and I had no idea she had one like that." Cari clapped her hands. "Gosh, this is almost like having my father back. What wonderful memories I have of him putting just a pinch of a certain spice on the tip of my tongue to taste. And then? He'd use that spice and show me how much to use on either a fruit, vegetable, or meat." She sighed and smiled. "This is such a gift!"

His heart felt like it would burst out of his chest. The blazing, glistening look in her gold-brown eyes totaled him as a man who wanted nothing more than to hold her in that moment of sheer ecstasy. How much he missed his own father, understanding how much she loved hers. They had both experienced something no child wanted, but had happened. "Well," he said, "how about tomorrow morning at nine a.m., I drive you out to her facility?"

"Will Mary be there?"

"I can ask her to be there if she doesn't have something else that needs tending at her grocery store."

"That would be wonderful!"

"Then it's settled. Mary will love showing you her pride and joy. All the herb gardens were built around the facility. I think you'll like it, too." He turned into another parking lot. "Want to come in? You can choose your favorites and we'll get them boxed up for you."

She smiled. "Great. I can pay for my own, Chase . . ."

"Nah, you're part of the family, Cari. I was going to buy four dozen and have my manager dole them out to everyone when we return to the ranch."

"That's wonderful of you!" She gave him a look of awe

and wonderment. "An employer who buys hot, freshly made donuts for his crew. Wow!"

Chuckling, he parked. "Come on, let's go drool . . ."

The place was never empty, and today was no exception. They wandered over to the glass displays with so many different kinds and colors of donuts, including donut holes, and it was a secret pleasure to watch Cari's expressions. She leaned over, eyeing every type of donut, the different colors, the sprinkles, the sugared, glazed, and cake donut types. She had clasped her hands to her heart, leaning down, completely enraptured with the heady, tantalizing sweet smells, lost in the world of donuts. She was more a child in that moment, than the mature woman he knew. In a crazy thought, Chase wondered if she would be the same way with her young children, teaching them the wonders of the world so innocently and sweetly. Something told him Cari would. In some ways, he was reminded of his mother showing him something new when he was young. She would urge him to hold it, smell it, and if edible, to taste it. And then she'd tell him a story about it. If it was a fruit, what kind of tree it came from, what the fruit was used for and the kind for making pies, cakes, or homemade ice cream. He recalled sharply when he was three years old, just a toddler, when a thunderstorm had broken over the ranch. It had been a long, hot, dry summer. Mary had shrieked with delight, grabbed him up under her arm, settling his legs across her hip, and she hurried outside. The first drops of rain started to fall—huge, fat drops that when they hit the earth, looked like small explosions, sending up blasts of dirt in their wake.

"Do you smell that?" she asked him, taking him out to the edge of the porch as lightning zipped across the sky, followed by rolling thunder. "Chase! Do you smell that wonderful perfume in the air? Oh! Smell it! Take a breath into your nose. What do you smell?"

Chase recalled the scent of the first drops hitting dry earth. Years later, when he was nine years old, Mary sat down with a dictionary to teach him about that wonderful, life-giving smell. She always was adamant about expanding his vocabulary. "It's called petrichor, Chase." She'd open the dictionary to that page, put his finger on the word. "And what does it say? Read it aloud to me."

He took such teaching from his always enthusiastic, excited mother seriously. "It says, a pleasant smell." He looked up at her. "It is, Mom. It smells like perfume."

"Exactly!" Mary praised, giving him a proud look. "What else? You know that the words we use today come from ancient languages like Latin, Sanskrit, and Greek. What does it say about petrichor?"

"That Greeks said *petra*, meaning stone, and *ichor*, the fluid that flows from the veins of the gods, Mom." He twisted to glance up at her, a very pleased look in her expression. She'd given him lessons in Latin and Greek since he was eight years old, because they were the roots from which most languages came. He had a keen memory and loved all those words.

"Well!" Mary said, patting his head, "you're right. And this leads me into some Greek myths, stories that tell of the fluid that flowed through the veins of their gods."

"Wasn't that blood, Mom?"

"Excellent question, Chase. It was their form of blood,

not exactly like a human's blood, but it still gave them life."

Trying to grasp the concepts, he asked, "So? The rain hitting the ground smells like their kind of blood?"

"You could say that. The fluid in their veins gave life to whatever it touched, and because rain is vital to everyone's life, humans in Greece believed it to come from their gods and goddesses, who they worshipped."

Chase smiled to himself, recalling those times, relishing them, grateful he had a mother much like Cari did, who was more childlike, excitable, always seeing the wonder of the world around her and sharing it passionately with others.

"I think I made up my mind!" Cari said, straightening and giving him her order. She only wanted three, but he persuaded her to get a dozen for the employees out at the raptor facility, which she was delighted to do. For the next fifteen minutes, Chase simply indulged his fantasy about Cari, the way she gracefully pointed to a donut, her quick smile, her eyes gleaming with joy, all made him ache in a new and unfamiliar way. It felt as though his heart was widening by the moment, whether it was her breathless laughter with the woman behind the counter, the huskiness of her tone, or the way she became one-hundred percent immersed in the moment. He realized that Cari was one of these rare, unique people who literally *did* live in the moment. That was tough to do, but as a sniper, he'd learned how to do it; to shut everything else out except for his narrow focus on his quarry. For her, it was a narrow focus on that group of rainbow frosted donuts. A grin tugged at the corners of his mouth as he ordered four dozen donuts to go.

They carried the boxes of heavenly fragrant donuts, just made, out to the truck and set them between them, then climbed in, ready to take their surprise gifts back to the people who made the ranch what it was today. Chase cast a glance in her direction. "Tell me, where did you learn to live in the moment?"

Startled, she blinked. "What?"

"Several times now, when we're together, I've noticed that you live in the moment."

"Oh? I didn't know that. Is that bad?"

"Hardly. I had to teach myself how to do it as a sniper. It saved my life time after time."

"But . . . I'm not a sniper. What do you mean by 'living in the moment'?"

"A hundred percent of all your six senses are focused on one thing. Nothing else exists, before or after or around you, except what you're doing in that moment." He pointed a thumb toward the donut boxes. "For example? I felt a shift of energy around you when you started choosing donuts. Your focus was on the donuts and only them. You had no awareness of your surroundings, what someone else was saying or who was in there. You were a hundred percent *there* with those donuts. Nothing else existed in that moment except you with them."

"Oh," she murmured, placing her hand against the column of her long neck, considering his definition. "My mother is Hawaiian. She taught me how to do that when I was very, very young. To be, what she called, *present*."

"Zen Buddhists teach being in the moment, or present, as part of how to live our lives, too," he noted. "They spend a lifetime trying to do it. Watching you? It comes naturally to you. There's no effort. I felt a shift in you and saw you move into that space."

"Really?" She became flustered. "What do you mean a *shift*, Chase?"

He grimaced. "You'll probably laugh at me, but when I was a sniper, my instructor told me that as I hunted my quarry, and once I had him, I would automatically *shift* into this Zen-like state. Nothing existed outside of me and my quarry. My whole focus—body, heart, and soul—was enveloped in that moment. And as for the *shift*, my instructor told me everything is energy. Simply energy. Whether it's seen or unseen, it's still energy. When I lived in that moment, nothing else existed. My six senses were focused on him and only him."

"Oh, dear . . . well . . . my mother taught me it was natural for all children to be one with the Hawaiian goddesses and gods; that it was the world they lived in, and that I could practice going there."

"Interesting," he murmured, turning onto the highway that would lead back to the ranch. "My instructor called it the fourth dimension, and it's outside our third-dimensional reality. It's outside our conscious awareness. He made me aware that the *shift* was going from our normal three-dimensional world where we live, into this other dimension, the fourth one. There, I was one with everything; colors became brighter and more intense, sounds were amplified and my hearing was extraordinary. He said that I had that 4D awareness, which a sniper needs so no one can sneak up on him or her when ready to take out the target."

"Would another example of a fourth dimension be

like geese that fly in formation but never crash into one another?"

"I think that's third dimensional. Scientists called it murmuration. Have you heard the term?"

Shaking her head, she said, "No. What is it?"

"The ability for hundreds, even thousands of birds to move as one, never crash into one another, as though performing a dance that only they know and can perform in the sky. Scientists now think the magnetism in birds' brains give them that extrasensory knowing about their space and location of their flock mates. That's why they don't collide with one another during flight. It's as if they *sense* their closeness to one another and know how to stay a safe distance. And you know what is really interesting?"

"What?"

He tapped the back of his head. "Our instructors informed us that human brains have magnetite in them, especially in the brain stem and cerebellum, our old, ancient, first brain we had as humans. It's part of the limbic system, which is, in my opinion, our original 'animal' brain. This is the one that uses all its six senses to survive, to suss out a shadow that's really a predator stalking them, or a smell that's different from the normal scents of an area, things like that."

Her eyes widened. "That's incredible. I didn't know that."

"In sniper school, they had us do months of training in the subtleties of what animals see when they're out in fields, mountains, valleys, and pastures. We learned to refine our senses, hone them into being more animal than human. We were as much the hunted, as the hunter, just like every animal, unless you were the predator at the top. That predator doesn't have to worry about being hunted, but the rest of us do."

"Is that why you are so alert? Earlier today I noticed how you seemed to be scanning the area around you, almost as if you had radar on or something. I've seen you do that on the ranch, too."

"That's sniper stalking," he said. Slowing down, he made a turn into Three Bars. It was a mile down the well-cared-for dirt road to the main area of the ranch. "Sometimes snipers have to go into cities or crowded places. They have to sense or see their quarry and then fade back into the background and disappear."

"You aren't obvious about it, that's for sure."

"You're very good at sensing, too," he said. "I think because of your inborn sensitivity, your use of your senses in general, that you'd make a very good sniper."

She groaned. "That is not much of a compliment, Chase."

"It is a compliment. Sometimes I watch you from my truck when you're working around one of the hive areas. And if you're alone, I hear you speak to them in a very quiet, low voice. You walk very softly, you don't make any fast or sudden moves. It's almost as if you become a bee yourself when you are there with them."

She laughed a little. "Well! One of the first things we teach young beekeepers is to *never* make sharp, sudden movements around bees. They take that as an attack and threat. I used to follow my mother around the hives my grandfather had in Hawaii. She taught me to walk and move like she did, like a ballerina in slow motion. I remember she told me to pretend I was a warm, quiet breeze moving in and among the hives, that my arms were like slow, beautiful clouds, and that the bee people would love me for being the sky."

"Nice to put it that way," he murmured, looking around at the green pastures. In some, there were wranglers herding a group of cows. In others, there were sheep or goats. "She was teaching you to be one with the bees."

"Yes. But as a sniper you were melting into and becoming one with your environment. Right?"

"Exactly. Or to lie or sit for hours, camouflaged, unmoving. Snipers are very patient people."

"So are beekeepers," she said, smiling.

He drove over to the office and parked. "Let's unload these three boxes and give them to my forewoman, Tracy Hartimer. Then, we'll drop off a box at the raptor facility."

"I met Tracy once. She's hilarious! What a sense of humor. And she always wears a pistol on her hip."

"Tracy seems to be a magnet for trouble," Chase said with a sour grin, taking two of the boxes. Cari took the third box and they carried them to the front door of the office.

"OMG!" Tracy yelled, standing up behind her huge, messy desk. "I've died and gone to *heaven*! Chase, you rascal, you! I can smell those donuts clear over here!"

Cari laughed and set one box on her desk. "Chase said you'd distribute them."

Rolling her eyes, Tracy opened the box, snatching a chocolate-covered donut. "Well, pardner, don't believe *everything* he tells you."

Chuckling, Chase set the other two boxes on the desk.

"Figured on your next run around in the truck, you'd hand them out."

Tracy took a second chocolate donut. She held up her hands to Cari. "Did the boss warn you about a two-donut gun slinger?"

Giggling, Cari shook her head.

"Yeah, she'll shoot donut holes at you," Chase said, backing away from the desk as Tracy munched content-edly.

Cari couldn't stop laughing. This was the first time she'd seen these two together. "Oh! You two are a comedy team!"

"Naw, just donut-starved wranglers, Bee Queen."

Raising his brows, Chase looked over at her. "Is that Tracy's nickname for you? You know she gives everyone some kinda name, earned or not."

"Tracy and I met when I was working with Theresa. We'd just put the last of the Flow Hives in place and the bee packets had come in. She stayed in her truck because she said bees didn't like her."

"There's some truth to that," Chase admitted, winking over at Tracy, who had polished off the first donut and was working hard on the second one. His forewoman was tall, lean, and all hard muscle. Her father, Lance, had trained her well, over a twenty year period, for this job. He had died two years ago and she'd easily stepped into his boots.

Wiping her mouth with a tissue from the box on her desk, Tracy gave Chase a jaded look. "Actually, Bee Queen, it was a hornet's nest I ran into one day in one of the groves on the back forty. I accidentally sawed off some treetops and a falling limb hit the paper wasp nest, and then all hell broke loose and they blamed me for it."

"Oh," Cari said, raising her own brows, "how did you get out of that one? Wasps and hornets can be *very* aggressive."

"I ran for the truck, and luckily it was only about two hundred yards away. I made it in record time. Only ended up with three stings," she said, smiling proudly, pointing to her left arm.

"Did it destroy their nest?" Cari wondered, worried.

"No, the branch just grazed it, but they were shook up about it and then took it out on me. Of course, I was the one doing the tree topping, so I probably had it coming. To tell you the truth? I honestly did *not* see that wasp nest. I just didn't."

"You're not sniper material," Chase teased her.

"Clearly not." Tracy gobbled the last donut and closed the box, then picked up all three boxes.

Chase opened the door for her. "We're taking box number four down to the raptor area," he told her.

"Good to know. I'm sure everyone there, especially Jenny the red-haired Scot, would *love* to have a box. See you later, kids." She chortled, walking out the door.

"I guess you have a bunch of donut-holics here on the ranch?" Cari asked, smiling.

"Might say that. But hey, that's better than having smokers or drinkers, of which we have none. Mary believes what you put in your mouth or inhale either keeps you alive or takes years off your life, and she won't have it."

"I noticed that no one smokes," Cari said, following

him out. They waved to Tracy, who was already in the truck and zooming out of the parking lot at high speed.

"Tracy goes nowhere slowly," he said wryly.

"Was her father or mother a race car driver?"

He opened her door for her. "No, but you'd think she had the DNA of an Indy 500 driver, and then some."

Chase hungrily absorbed her laughter. Tracy was good for everyone. She was tough, fair, and had one helluva black sense of humor. But then, so had her dad, Lance. She ran Three Bars efficiently. Everyone loved her because beneath that tough cowgirl façade, she had a heart of gold and everyone knew it. Plus, Tracy always made people laugh, and that was a trait worth gold in itself and it wasn't something money could ever buy.

In the truck, Cari asked, "Would you, if you have time, teach me to look around like you do?"

Surprised, he glanced at her for a moment. "Sure. Any reason why?"

"Well, I can see I'm missing something. Look at Tracy. She didn't see that gray wasp nest. If I'm out with domesticated bees and their hives, I have a very intense focus on them. But I would like to be taught how to not only be focused, but also open up my senses or sight in a way that I was more aware of my surroundings. I think that's something worth learning. Don't you?"

"Well," he jested, "yes, if you're going to be a sniper." He saw she frowned, and then felt bad. "Sure, I can show you some of the tricks of our trade."

"Oh, good! I admire your alertness, Chase. I'd like to learn it, too, and be subtle about it, not obvious."

"Is this because Dirk is on the loose?" he asked her

quietly, pinning her with a searching look. Cari grimaced and clasped her hands in her lap.

"Yes, it is. Will you teach me? I promise, I'll try to be a good student."

His heart broke. He tried to lose his scowl and lightened his voice for her sake. "All right then, let's set up a schedule. Why don't you let me know on a weekly basis when you have an hour off here or there, and I'll begin to teach you what I know. Does that sound okay to you?" He gave her a quick, worried glance. Instantly, he saw her eyes light up and her face take on that glow of an excited ten-year-old. Anything to make her feel safe, he told himself. Whatever it took, he'd do it.

"Thank you for doing this, Chase. It will make me feel safer when I'm not on the ranch, because I really miss being out in the public, out shopping or just being with people."

"I understand," he said, the raptor enclosure coming up. "How about next Monday?"

"Perfect. I'll have a schedule. What should I wear?"

"Just your everyday clothes."

"Oh. Nothing special?"

"Not unless you want to wear greasepaint all over your face, neck, and hands," he teased.

She laughed.

His heart opened even further. He wanted this woman in his life. Forever.

Chapter Seven

Cari could hardly contain her excitement. Good as his word, Chase drove up and parked alongside the dirt road and climbed out. He was going to teach her how to walk quietly today; something she honestly had never thought about until now.

He was dressed in a dark green canvas type of shirt, well-worn blue Levi's, and his scuffed, scarred leather cowboy boots. The black Stetson he wore always signaled to her he was a man of deep knowledge and kept most of himself to himself. That had to change! In some ways, she was hungry to know Chase on a much more personal level. Yesterday, she'd stayed in her office and mapped out the rest of the business plan for their new honey company and had gone over it with him and Mary in the late afternoon. Everything had been signed off on, everyone happy. Now, she could play!

Chase walked up to where Cari stood just on the edge of the grove of oak trees. He smiled a hello. "Well, are you ready to walk differently?"

"Am I ever!" she said. Pointing down to her shoes, she asked, "Are these okay?"

He studied them. "Sure, any kind of shoe, with the exception of women's heels, will do."

"I hate heels. My mother never let me wear them, nor did I want to. Our next-door neighbor, who is in her seventies, one day showed me what wearing heels in her twenties did to her feet. Did you know she had huge bunions on each foot? So bad that her big toe has crossed over the next toe? I'd never seen that before!"

"Mary is death on them, too." He stood a few feet away from her, looking out over the flat plain where all the different pastures were located. It was a warm June morning, the heavy scent of grass in the air. He inhaled it deeply, a perfume to his senses. "Beautiful morning."

Sighing, Cari said, "It is. So? What do I do to walk without a sound?"

"Well," Chase murmured, turning toward the grove of oak trees that numbered over a hundred, of varying ages, "you need to study the ground first. What is the soil like? Is it hard packed? Gravelly? Soft packed so that your heel sinks down into it? Is it dry? Wet? Something in between? You have to assess what you're going to be traveling across, first."

She frowned. "Gosh, I never ever thought of it like that." She knelt down on one knee. The fallen leaves of last year were still visible. Pushing them away, she poked at the earth and cleared it enough to take a good look at it.

Chase knelt next to her, digging up a bit of the damp soil. "We live in what geologists call a sedimentary area. All this region was shallow ocean millions of years ago. In fact"—he looked up, silently gauging the silence of the oak grove—"if you do a little googling, you'll see that North America was actually in two halves, with this shallow ocean in between the landmasses. And when the two pieces eventually, because of tectonic plate action, cemented together, the ocean still remained all across what is now known as the Southwest and the Great Plains. Wyoming is a part of that landscape to this day." He sifted the soil through his fingers. "If you feel the earth? Right here, in this grove, it's a mixture of sand and clay. The top layer is sand, but about a foot down, it's clay. If you walk in sand, it will cushion your foot, but you will sink into it just a bit or a lot, depending upon the quality of the sand. And by the sand absorbing your weight and how fast or slow you are moving, it will quiet your walk."

"What about that clay?" she wondered, slipping her slender fingers through the light brown soil that had been hiding beneath the dried leaves that had fallen the year before.

"It's like concrete," he said. "Just the exact opposite of sand. But"—he smiled a little, glancing over at her— "clay is good because it's tough, sometimes, to track your footprints across it. It doesn't absorb anything. The problem with clay is when it's wet, it's slippery as hell. If you've driven your car on black ice? You don't see it, but you can skid a car in circles on it when the tires roll over it. Same goes when you walk across wet clay. It's the soil's version of highway black-ice conditions."

"I've lived in the San Francisco area most of my life and we don't get black ice or snow," she jested.

"There's a good patch of exposed clay soil in another part of the ranch. I'll take you out there one day, throw some water across it, and then you'll see just how slippery it really is."

"That's amazing information," she said, giving him a look of pride. "You learned all of this as a sniper?'

Shaking his head, he said, "My family instructed me about the different soils. My grandfather taught me how to track, starting when I was eight years old. He'd take me pheasant hunting with him, and later, deer hunting, when in season. That's where I learned most of my walking-without-being-heard skills."

"I would imagine the sniper instructors were happy to see you coming, then?"

"It's part of it," he said, losing his smile. He straightened to his full height and Cari followed him into the grove. "Now that we know the soil, the next thing you have to assess is what is lying on top of it. Chances are, whatever it is, there will be something that makes noise if you step on it, thereby alerting the enemy, or the animal you're tracking."

Frowning, she looked around. "Well, there's no spring grass on this ground, that's for sure."

Chase leaned down and picked up a couple of acorns and opened his palm. "That's because acorns have tannic acid in them and these scarlet oak leaves are acidic, and most grass doesn't grow well in shade, anyway. This is a grove that is almost entirely in shade due to the canopy of the trees themselves." He pointed upward, tiny slats of light dancing here and there through the canopy. "And these acorns, while edible, aren't tasty at all, except to animals. They're pretty bitter tasting to us humans."

"I've never heard of a scarlet oak tree."

"They're an eastern- and middle-America oak," he said, dropping the acorns to the ground. "My family planted several large groves of them for lumber purposes. They're a great oak for furniture. In fact, in your office, that big double-wide oak desk you work from? That was made from another grove east of here by my great-great-grandfather."

"That's such a wonderful family heirloom. I never knew that."

"Just about every piece of furniture you see in the ranch house came from one of the generations of my family," he said. "I like it because I grew up being taught by my parents about the history of every one of them, whether it was the kitchen table, a sofa, or a head- and footboard on a bed. Kind of gives me an appreciation for the hours and skill that went into making them in the first place. Most of our furniture comes from those scarlet oak groves."

"My mother has some of my grandmother's furniture, made of monkeypod, from Hawaii, that she had shipped over to the US. I loved hearing the stories about that beautiful wood. Nowadays, they use monkeypod for lovely wooden floors in the Islands. Our furniture has gorgeous streaks of red, brown, and gold in it. I never tire of looking at it."

"I've seen monkeypod," Chase said, "and I agree, it's beautiful, hardy, and can handle flooring. Did you know that it's a hardwood? And this tree also grows in Central America and tends to be a golden color, without the red or brown streaks in it."

"I had no idea." She gave him a humored look. "I can

see that my knowledge of my surroundings is really lacking."

Chase shrugged. "Your focus is on bee culture. I know you absorb natural-occurring information about where you want to place the hives. I've seen you study the soil, the trees, and surrounding bushes or grass, and how it might affect them. I don't think you're lacking at all."

"That's true," she agreed, "but my focus has been what makes an impact on bees and where they create a hive." She lifted her arm, looking around the grove, hearing the song of a western meadowlark. She'd often seen the yellow-breasted, large songster out on fence posts, singing their hearts out, their song melodic and beautiful. "How I wish you could grow monkeypod trees here."

Grinning, Chase said, "Me, too, but we're in the wrong climate. They'd never survive a winter here, much less the lower temps. Well? Are you ready to look at what makes noise and can give you away?"

"Absolutely."

"We have a floor consisting of old oak leaves that fell last autumn, sticks that have fallen off the oaks, and some branches here and there." He pointed to them beneath the cover. "If you're lucky and it has rained of late? Those leaves will absorb the water, and when you step on them, it won't make a loud, crackling sound. Same goes for small twigs or little branches that have fallen off the trees."

"But if it's dry?"

"Well," he said, lifting his Stetson for a moment and scratching his head, "then it's a whole other deal. The leaves will crunch good and loud. Even a small twig, if stepped on it a certain way, will make a snapping sound.

And if you step on a larger branch? It will make a very loud noise."

"Why couldn't you avoid this place, then?" she demanded. Pointing to the slight slope up from where they stood, that had rich, green grass growing, she added, "Why not walk out there?"

"If you're in enemy territory? You don't want to be seen, Cari. Walking in deep woods, away from the edge or boundary of it, especially, can hide you very well, instead of sticking out like a sore thumb out there"—he pointed toward the grassy slope—"saying 'shoot me.'" He chuckled and so did she.

"Point taken," she admitted. "If I was forced to go through this grove, how on earth would I ever get through it without being found? I'd be making all kinds of noise!"

"Depends," he said. "In the mountains of Afghanistan, you can climb a tree and hide in the upper foliage."

Wrinkling her nose, she stared at the oaks. "Ugh! I couldn't even get up the trunk to climb any of them!"

"That's a bail-out choice, climbing a tree," he said. "When all else fails and you have thick cover, then it's a choice. If you're quiet and they don't have a dog with them to smell a trail, you might get away with it. But it's not a first choice."

"What is, then?" she demanded, frustrated.

Chase placed his right leg outward on the dried leaves. "You need to walk this way: all your weight on one leg needs to be on the side of your shoe, and then you gently place your heel down after that. It's what we call the 'fox walk.' And,"—he pulled out a pair of leather moccasins from his back pocket—"you need the right footgear. You're wearing a fairly heavy boot, and that won't work. You need a very flexible shoe that will bend with your foot."

"Are you telling me you carried moccasins over in Afghanistan?" she asked, stunned.

"Sure I did." He handed her a pair. "Hope these fit. I bought them the other day, guessing your shoe size."

Giving him a humored look, she took them and sat down, quickly swapping out the boots for the more adaptable footwear. She noticed that he drew another pair of moccasins from his other pocket, sat down, pulled off his boots, and slipped them on. "Are those the same ones you used in Afghanistan?"

"No, but I wore a pair out about once a month. I'd finish a mission, get picked up and flown back to my base. Mary sent me fifty pairs of Indian-made moccasins and I kept them in my locker. Every time I went out on a new mission, I carried enough pairs, depending upon the geography of where I had to go." He knotted the laces of the last moccasin and stood up. He held out his hand to her, and she slipped her fingers into his and he eased her to her feet.

"How do they feel?" he asked, checking them out.

"Actually, you're pretty good," she said, a little awe in her voice. "They fit really well."

"Phew."

"Oh, come on! You're the most unassuming man I've ever run into, Chase. You never boast, crow, or shout out to the world how good you are. And you're good at many things." She put her hands on her hips, giving him a dark look. "The only way I find out about you is through observation and actually doing some job with you."

A one-cornered smile came to his mouth. "It's a need-to-know basis only."

Cari snorted. "Oh, don't give me that! You said the other day Mary made you be more communicative than most guys."

"She did," he agreed, settling the moccasin against his large foot until he was comfortable with it. "Isn't it more fun finding out what a person does or is made of, sort of like a treasure hunt?"

Another snort and Cari followed suit, making sure the bottom of her moccasins were flat against the soles of her feet. "The only problem with that is that you don't give me a treasure map to follow! I don't call that communication. I call that hiding."

Another chuckle.

She liked the silvery gleam in his eyes. Both of them enjoyed their repartee with one another. "You're like a bunch of nesting dolls from Russia," she accused lightly.

"I'm no doll," he said.

"Okay, then you're one of those Chinese boxes that frustrate me trying to find a way to open them up."

"That I'll say thank you to." He winked at her.

"You're such a tease," she accused, laughing.

"Okay, I'll try to be more open with you. Fair enough?"

"That would be nice," she agreed.

"Ready to do the fox walk?"

"Let's do it!"

"First, bend your knees slightly," he said. "Next, put all your weight on one foot, and once balanced, lift up the other foot. Then step forward. You'll note that as you extend your right leg forward that your left knee is bent and will act like a shock absorber, as well as helping keep your balance. As you bring that foot down, Cari? Land on the outside of it, then roll the weight back to the heel, and then settle the entire sole on the ground. Go ahead, try that."

Well! Cari muffed it time and again. She was having trouble flexing both knees fairly deeply, which, Chase explained, helped lower her center of gravity more toward the ground, therefore controlling how lightly the outside of her moccasin contacted the ground. She tried again and again.

"You're doing fine," Chase said, giving her a nod. "Keep working at it."

"Rome wasn't built in a day, you know," she huffed, her arms out to balance herself. "This is hard work!"

"At first," he said, sympathetic, "it is. But the more you do it? The easier it becomes."

"Did you walk this way in Afghanistan?"

"Many times."

"So?" she challenged, extending her left leg, trying to balance on one deeply flexed right leg. "How much of the time?"

"Depended upon the situation," he said.

"But it comes naturally to you now?"

"Yes. Okay. Stop. Take a breather and relax. Watch what I do . . ." He moved to the side where she could fully see the actions of his body and how he placed that foot on the ground.

"You don't even have to hold your arms out like windmills to balance yourself," she growled.

"Practice makes perfect," he said, slowing each movement down so that Cari could clearly see the steps taken to make that footfall silent once it contacted the ground.

"I'll never be able to do that!"

"Sure you will." He turned and walked back toward her. "It just takes practice. And patience."

"I thought I was a patient person," she groused, trying it again.

"Focus on your body, listen for when you place your foot on the side. See if you hear a sound."

To her surprise, she'd totally forgotten about the noise, instead wavering around like a three-bladed airplane propeller, completely out of balance.

"See?" he said, catching her glance. "No sound. That's good. You're doing it right. Now? All you have to do is get your body to move in a more fluid way. That will come with time, so be proud you are not making noise."

"Humph."

"You do get grumpy upon occasion, don't you?"

"You're an unmerciful tease, Chase Bishop."

He preened.

She snorted and gave him a chastising glare, her arms still out to keep herself balanced. "I'm just not used to being so low to the ground, keeping my shoulders in alignment, not bobbing up and down like we do in a natural walk. This is hard!"

"Didn't you think learning beekeeping was hard?" he wondered, walking silently beside her, keeping a distance between them as they moved deeper into the grove.

"Never."

"Do you remember trying to walk when you were a toddler?"

"No. I suppose you do?"

"Petulance will get you nowhere, Ms. Taylor."

Cari's barking laughter echoed around them. "Tell me.

Were you an instructor at the Marine Corps school, I wonder? You certainly behave like one."

"No, I was always a field operator. I didn't want to be an instructor."

"Coulda fooled me." Her arms went up and down as she lost her balance, breaking the rhythm of her fox walk. "Crap!"

"Focus, Cari. Focus on your body. You were doing fine."

Cari absorbed the low tenor of his tone; it was gentle yet supportive. "Okay . . ." she grumbled belligerently, "I'll try some more . . ."

"You're the one who wanted to do this, remember?" He couldn't help but give a dark chuckle. That earned him an equally dark, shooting look. "I like all your moods, Cari. One minute, you're a thunderstorm, shooting lightning bolts, and the next, a beautiful rainbow after a storm."

"I'm trying to concentrate . . . but thank you . . . If I didn't know better? You're a poet and didn't know it."

"Sounds like you're one, too. You can rhyme words, Ms. Taylor."

Another derisive snort. Chase had to give her credit: Cari was stubborn and kept trying. It took her about half an hour, but by that time, her knees were trembling, unused to such stress on them. "Hey," he said, "let's call it a day. You've done well. Tomorrow, do it for half an hour. Every day for about two weeks, and you'll be good to go."

"I'll probably turn into a fox," she muttered, giving him a one-eyebrow-raised look. She straightened and came back, sitting on the ground and taking off her moccasins and pulling on her work boots. Chase joined her.

"I'll pay you for the moccasins. How much were they?"

"Oh, no you won't. Just consider them a part of our business deal with the ranch."

She smiled, knotting the laces. "I wonder how many women have swooned over you, Chase. Not only are you a gentleman, but you also give out donuts and moccasins to your employees."

"Oh . . . women," he grunted, getting to his feet and stuffing the moccasins into his back pocket.

She stood up, dusting off her butt and then picking up her moccasins and placing them in her pocket. "What's wrong with women?"

"Nothing, believe me. It's just . . . well . . . I don't have a good track record with them. I'm going to the raptor training area. Do you want to come with me? Are you still working with our feisty red-tail, our Wild Child?"

Her truck was parked below, near his. Looking at her watch, she said, "Jenny wants me to keep working with Valkyrie."

"Do you?" he asked, grinning as they climbed into his truck.

"Very much so! I love all wildlife, but have a special love for raptors. She's so smart, Chase. She's scarily human to me."

"As long as she doesn't go after your bee brethren, right?" As he pulled out on the road, heading toward the raptor installation, he pointed to the small plastic box on her side of the floor. "If you're thirsty, there's cold soda and water in there."

Touched, she nodded. "Would you like one?"

"Sure, I'll take water."

"So will I." She opened one of the glass bottles and placed the screw top aside. "Why glass? Why not plastic?"

"Why kill all our wildlife and ocean animals with plastic?" he returned, taking the proffered bottle from her.

"I've tried to find glass instead of plastic. How did you do it? What company in the USA is doing this?"

"Mary," he said, taking a deep swig of the water. Wiping his mouth with the back of his hand, he said, "right here in Silver Creek. Mary is an entrepreneurial spirit and for real. She hated plastic everything when no one was making a peep about how bad it is for our environment. There were some glassblowers in town and she called them in for a conference. She gave them seed money to start making glass bottles of all types and kinds, for drinking water, baking, and cooking, to be sold in her grocery store. Pretty soon, word got out and a number of other, larger natural food grocery chains across the USA, bought into them, too. Pretty soon, our little town's glass bottling manufacturing plant grew to huge proportions. And since Americans and a lot of others around the world have realized how deadly plastic is in our lives, they're looking for glass containers of all kinds to replace them. Mary just gave the Silver Creek Glass Company a huge loan to expand, because the demand has skyrocketed and there's no sign it's going to stop."

"That's incredible. Sitting with her for dinner at night, you'd never tell how successful she really is."

"My mother," he drawled with a smile, "is a true force of nature. Everything she touches turns to gold."

"Or maybe, the goose that lays golden eggs?" Cari suggested, returning his smile.

"That, too. Or also." He pulled into the raptor parking lot. "Come on, I'll help you fly that bad girl of yours."

* * *

Cari wasn't surprised that Chase knew his way around raptors. Just a few days earlier, Jenny had told her he held a falcon and eagle's license in the US. That impressed her. It was good that he was familiar with all the different areas of his ranch that were making money for him. She was sure Mary was the driving force behind it, but her son truly liked the different mix of environmental businesses they worked hard to bring about.

Why wasn't this man married? Or have a partner? It made no sense to her.

She went to her locker to get her flight glove, then went to the refrigerator to pull out some mouse meat for her charge. Buckling up the pouch around her waist that would carry it, she walked out to the well-protected raptor housing area. When she turned the corner, she heard Valkyrie's shrill greeting. She began flying back and forth in her cage, lighting on the entrance/exit to her cage door, then flying back and forth once more.

Over time, Cari came to realize her hawk not only recognized her, but this was Valkyrie's way of showing her excitement and joy at seeing her once again. It was her "hawk greeting."

"Chase called you a bad girl," she told Valkyrie as the bird came and landed on the perch next to the door. Opening it, she gently placed the soft leather jesses around Valkyrie's thick yellow legs. The hawk leaned forward, and Cari double-checked to make sure those jesses were placed correctly. Valkyrie ruffled her beak through Cari's hair.

Giggling, Cari pulled back. "Val!" she said, "you're tickling my scalp!"

The hawk made soft little shrill sounds, much like a baby raptor would to its mother. It was a sound of "feed me." Pulling a small bit of mouse meat out of her pouch, she gave Valkyrie some. The hawk flapped her wings and gobbled it quickly, her yellow eyes shining with joy.

"Are you going to be a good girl today?" Cari asked drolly, threading the hanging leather from the jesses between her gloved fingers.

Instantly, the hawk leaped upon her glove, which was just below Cari's elbow. Carefully pulling her arm out of the door, hawk on board, she locked the cage and then turned around, picking up her green baseball cap. "Let's go, girl. Chase is out there waiting for us. You're gonna get your tail feathers flown off today. A real workout. And no creance line, so you'd better not fly off to that grove of trees!"

Once out on the flight oval, two metal landing T's at either end, Valkyrie began chutting excitedly. She saw Chase put a bit of meat up on the T. He moved away.

Cari unwound the jesses, which were much shorter than normal, for flight oval flying. Instantly, Valkyrie flapped and took to the air. The flight oval was half a mile in length, and a good place to train and strengthen an injured hawk like her, to return her to the wild.

Cari laughed as she saw the hawk make a beeline for that T, widening her wings, tail down, yellow legs straight out in front of her, those mighty talons of hers opened. The instant she landed, gone was the meat!

She saw Chase's expression, a big smile on his face as

the magnificent raptor landed and then shrieked. Instantly Valkyrie did a ballet move, facing Cari, watching her put meat up on her T. Off she went like an arrow shot out of a bow! Although she was a red-tail, she had the juvenile markings of a white breast with long, black vertical oval feathers and no red on her tail. Only mature red-tails, who were five years or older, got that gorgeous rust-red coloration that could be seen easily by everyone.

For the next twenty minutes, Valkyrie flew and snacked on mouse meat. It was a good workout for the hawk, who, Jenny said, would be released shortly. She had regained her proper weight and from all signals, Valkyrie would know how to hunt. Cari just hoped the silly, immature hawk with the hot temperament wouldn't continue her canopy-tree-crashing antics. That would kill her, at worst, and injure her out in the wild, most likely breaking her wing, rendering her unable to fly and she would eventually starve to death. Cari didn't want to think in those directions, but with wild things, she had to.

Chase rejoined her at the raptor facility after she let him know she was going to take Valkyrie inside. Cari had just placed a large rubber tub, about four inches high, filled with water, into the hawk's home, when he arrived at the cages. Once Cari left the cage, Valkyrie instantly leaped off one of her many perches, landed in the middle of the tub, and began giving herself a bath, water splashing in every direction. Cari smiled, watching the hawk. Chase came to her side.

"She's a hundred percent in whatever she does," he murmured, watching her dip her head into the water, rivulets streaming down her neck and across her back, her wings scattering hundreds of droplets all over the place.

"As I heard my father say, 'throttles to the firewall,' with her."

"That's a military term, for sure."

"Well, he was in the air force as a young man. I guess I grew up with a lot of his military slang in the household."

"Hmmm, I'm not gonna test you on that one. Our military slang and acronyms are infamous, so I'll stay away from some of the more embarrassing ones."

She snorted. "Oh, like FUBAR?"

Now it was his turn for his eyes to widen. "He told you that one? You were a small child."

"I was about eight when that came flying, pardon the pun, out of his mouth. My mother, Nalani, about came unglued when it happened. My father had been making a rocking horse for me and I was standing there, watching him. He slammed the hammer down on his thumb instead of the nail. That's when the acronym came flying out of his mouth."

Rubbing his chin, Chase nodded. "Yeah, well, I do a little cursing under my breath when I nail my fingers with a hammer, too."

"Did you pick that up from your father, too?" Cari prodded.

"My father put in four years in the Marine Corps. Believe me, I heard a whole bunch of salty language, but he was always careful not to say it when Mary was around. She would wash my mouth out with soap when I mimicked my father in front of her. I had no idea what they meant, of course. And then she'd go after my father and threaten to wash his mouth out with soap, too."

"That must have been a sight." Cari laughed. Valkyrie was done with her bath and flew up to a perch near where her favorite humans stood, and began to fluff and ruffle her feathers, preening with her beak and drying them. Opening the cage, Cari picked up what was left of the water in the tub. Chase kept the door closed until Cari was about to leave. Some hawks would take any opportunity to escape and fly out. Valkyrie seemed content to preen, not even lifting her head to see Cari remove the bathtub out of her home. Chase closed and locked the cage after Cari had cleared the doorway.

"That was a lot of fun," he said, washing the tub out with soap and water, rinsing it well and drying it with a nearby towel. He set it up on a wide shelf with several others.

"You don't get out here that often, do you?" Cari asked, drying off her hands.

"Not as much as I'd like. Before you came, I was sort of the stand-in volunteer to help Valkyrie back to flight status. But I'm glad you're here. You can tell she really loves you. Not all hawks get close to their handler in that way. It's a real compliment to you."

"She didn't exactly ignore you," Cari said, walking out of the premises and back into the sunlight. Settling her baseball cap on her head, she added, "Time for me to get back to work." Looking at her watch, she said, "Theresa and I are checking the Flow Hives today. Everything seems to be fine, but weekly checks are a must, just in case."

"And with all the clover and alfalfa fields in bloom,

I imagine those bees are busier than a one-armed paper hanger."

"Better believe it!" She reached out, placing her hand lightly on his forearm. "Thanks for a wonderful day. I learned so much!"

Chapter Eight

June 15

Dirk Bannock waited outside a warehouse in Silver Creek, Wyoming. The sky was cloudy, like it was going to rain at some point. He wore a black hoodie, hands tucked into the front pockets, shifting from one booted foot to another. This warehouse, old and dilapidated, obviously not in use any longer, sat three blocks off the main drag. A criminal named Brock Hauptman, a go-between for the Pablo Gonzalez drug team and his crew, was to meet him. It was the first such meeting after a lot of phone calls between them.

Dirk trusted no one. He wore a pistol in his belt, the hoodie covering the fact. He went nowhere without a gun. And he'd driven here himself, avoiding anyplace where he could be identified, have someone take a photo of his mug, and then potentially set law enforcement on his ass. He glanced at his watch. It was nearly noon and he was hungry as hell. He didn't know what Hauptman looked like, but that was fine with him. No email photos were sent, either. Criminals like himself wanted a very low profile, their faces left unidentified for good reason.

A black pickup drove up. A large man, at least six foot two, about forty years old, with a black-and-white scrub beard showing his age, climbed out. His dark brown gaze cut to Dirk and he sized him up. Hauptman wore a pair of jeans and a nondescript brown shirt that wouldn't draw much attention. He did, however, have a straw cowboy hat on his head and he wore a pair of well-worn cowboy boots. Probably trying to fit into this valley, Dirk thought, since it was mainly ranches of one sort or another.

Straightening, Dirk remained leaning against the corrugated aluminum wall near the locked front door. The man was tall, muscular, and meaty beneath his clothes. He found it humorous that Hauptman, who was coming around the front of his truck, his small brown eyes narrowed on him, was playing the part of a cowboy, when in reality, he was a white supremacist who hated anything other than white skin, and had been to prison several times. The scar on his left cheek was at least an inch long, Dirk guessed, and came out of some kind of fight. Probably in prison. Hauptman moved with the confidence of a man who knew exactly who he was.

"Bannock?" he snapped, coming to a halt six feet away, raking him up and down with his gaze.

"Yeah. Hauptman?"

"Yeah." He thrust his large, thick hand outward toward Bannock. "Let's go get somethin' to eat. We'll chat a little, fill our stomachs, and then we'll see what happens next."

Shaking his hand, Dirk said, "Fine with me."

"The place I'm taking you, Olive Oyle's, has good

food, all kinds of choices. Hop in." He gestured to the truck.

"I want to sit somewhere away from any cameras so I can't be ID'd," Dirk told him, climbing in. He noticed, on Hauptman, as his sleeve pulled up, a Nazi tattoo just above his thick, large wrist. Like himself, all of Dirk's tattoos where hidden beneath his garments.

"No worries. I don't come into Silver Creek too often, but there's a nice corner booth beneath the camera, so it won't be taking photos of us."

Slamming the door shut, Dirk said, "Suits me. Let's rock it out."

Cari had decided to use her newly acquired confidence and had driven into Silver Creek by herself to run a few errands. Her confidence was based upon several things. First, she practiced her walking silently every morning for at least half an hour. She found getting up at dawn and watching the sun rise was a wonderful time to practice. It didn't take anything out of her hectic, busy day, and that was good.

Every time she thought about Chase, her whole chest warmed up. During the past few weeks, he'd taught her more and more, so that she was beginning to build a new kind of confidence she'd never acquired before. For that, she was grateful. He was a wonderful teacher, patient, explaining everything, and today she was going to test it all out. She hoped he would be proud of her efforts.

Parking in the back lot of Olive Oyle's, her favorite restaurant, she hurried in the side door. Chase had taught her to never go in a front door if the place of business had a side exit. He told her terrorists always wanted two things: big, plateglass windows along with a front entrance. It was easy to kill people that way. Not that he thought that Silver Creek would be attacked by terrorists, but she should always know her entrance/exit points. So, today she was going to put all that teaching to use!

Feeling good, she settled the green baseball cap on her head. It was a bit coolish, with rain coming in by mid-afternoon, so she wore her lightweight green ranch jacket over her short-sleeved pale blue top. As usual, she wore her jeans and work boots, and a small backpack slung over her shoulder. She detested purses, and carried a small, dark gray canvas day pack on her shoulder, instead. That way, she could stuff it with everything she needed when out with her bees. It was large enough, very handy, and not that weighty.

Running her list of to-dos, as Chase referred to them, she pulled open the side door. It was noon and the place was packed, as usual. She had called ahead and reserved a very special booth: Chase had taught her to take a corner table or booth so that it was farthest away from any windows, close to a secondary exit door, or near the kitchen, which always had one or two swinging doors where the cooks and waiters had access to the kitchen. He'd told her to never move fast, but to try and be like a ghost that no one sees stand up or sit down. And since she'd have a booth near the kitchen, which gave her eighty-percent viewing across the restaurant, she could see who walked in, as well as who walked past the establishment. That was a lot to remember! He'd laughed and said that after a while, it got to be second nature.

She was grateful he realized that until Dirk was apprehended, she was on tenterhooks. By giving her these kinds of what he called "black ops" tools, her confidence was building daily. She didn't want to say she was falling in love with Chase, but she knew she was. It was as if he could peer deeply into her fear and make suggestions based upon experience to share with her in order to minimize her anxiety. Each piece of information made her feel stronger, more sure of herself, and no longer did she feel like a target.

Entering the restaurant, wearing her sunglasses, she was met with a combination of laughter, people chatting with one another, and the low bluegrass music playing in the background. She looked to her left. Sure enough, there was a RESERVED sign on the corner table next to the doors of the kitchen. Chase had taught her to keep her baseball cap on, lower the bill over her eyes. She could look around and not be seen gawking, which always got the attention of a terrorist. Ordinarily, she would take off her cap and set it on the table near her elbow. Not today.

She took the booth, removed her sunglasses, her back toward the corner walls so she had that wide-angled view of the patrons in the place, as well as people coming and going through the main entrance. Her confidence soared.

A waitress came over to take her order. Cari gave it: She was getting a to-go box for Chase and she ordered a grilled cheese sandwich and a salad to eat at the restaurant. Chase knew she was trying out all the tools of his trade today and asked for a hamburger and French fries.

She'd laughed and promised she'd bring it back to him. That was the least she could do!

Settling in at the table, she remembered to put her knapsack between herself and the wall, so she could grab and go, if necessary. Plus, Chase said that in his work, he always had a pistol in a hidden holster beneath his loose clothing, unseen, but handy if he needed it. Well! Cari wasn't going that far! She hated guns and violence for too many good reasons.

What she did do was take out her Apple iPhone and hold it in her hands in such a position that she could scan those in the restaurant without them realizing it. Chase had related that one of his missions had been to find an ISIS leader. He'd watched the enemy for a month, finding out where he ate, what establishments he visited in the village. Dressed like any Afghan man, Chase had waited in a fairly large restaurant, if it could be called that, and had sat at a corner table next to the cook's area. He'd taken the shot, killed his target, and escaped through the kitchen, out the back door to where his van was waiting, engine running. He'd memorized the layout of the village, knew escape routes, and disappeared before anyone could find, much less chase and capture, him.

The waitress brought over her glass of ice water and left. Sitting back, appearing more relaxed than she had in a long time, she raised her iPhone marginally just enough to scan the place. No one was taking any notice of her at all. She felt very smug and confident because Chase had told her to blend in, make no odd or fast movements, sit relaxed, and pretend to be scrolling through her cell phone. He told her that his cell phone, in certain cities where they could be used, was filled with identification recognition apps of the bad guys, so that as he took a photo of a face, he could run it on the spot to see if he had an ISIS leader or not. She, of course, didn't have that and didn't want it, although Chase had suggested that she put Dirk's face and prison photos on her phone with that app, but she resisted. She didn't want the energy of her stepbrother anywhere near her in any shape or form. Chase had said he understood.

Just as the waitress brought her meal, she saw two tall, large cowboys enter through the front entrance. A gasp tore from Cari. The waitress was still handing out her food and gave her an odd look.

"You okay?" she asked.

"Uh . . . yes, yes, I'm fine." She wanted the woman to leave. The two men came in, but the waitress was in her line of vision. Did she see what she thought she saw? No! Impossible! The one without the cowboy hat looked like Dirk! *Oh, God!* Her heart raced hard in her chest, and she stiffened, and then ordered herself to appear relaxed as the waitress left, giving her full view of the place.

Cari nearly choked as she slowly lifted her head, hopefully unseen and not making a weird move that would draw their attention. Over in the opposite corner of where she sat, the two men slid into a booth. She noted instantly that they sat below the video camera where they could not be photographed. Her stomach clenched. Hard and painful. It *was* Dirk! It was him! Oh, God, what was she going to do? Her mind raced over so many questions, adrenaline and cortisol flooding her bloodstream. She wanted to run! No! She couldn't! Chase had warned her about that. Any fast, quick movements would earn her unwanted attention by both those hard-looking men.

Eighty feet separated them from her. The bigger man kept his straw cowboy hat on. She lowered the bill of her cap just enough to hide her face from them. Would Dirk recognize her? She'd cut her hair off, dyed it henna red. He seemed to be completely attentive to the unknown cowboy with him. Who was that other guy? Chase had taught her to look for weapons. They didn't seem to have any on them.

What was Dirk doing *here*? She sat there, feeling like a scared rabbit with no defense except to run. Her palms were sweaty and cold. Her sandwich was growing cold in front of her. She had to eat. Taking a bite, she almost felt like throwing up!

EAT. EAT THIS! Pretend you're relaxed, just one of the patrons. Don't stand out. Blend in!

Her mind churned. What to do? All she wanted to do was escape!

The cowboy with Dirk was constantly looking around, just like Chase told her to do. If he was with Dirk, then this man was what? A convict? An escapee? Was he a druggie friend of Dirk's?

Every bite of the sandwich was foul tasting to her. She was so scared out of her mind that Dirk might identify her that all she wanted to do was escape. Chase had told her to take slow, deep breaths. Just pretend nothing was wrong. She had the bill of her cap such that no one could see her full face, and for that, she was grateful. He'd told her the baseball cap, where it was accepted as ordinary headgear, was one of his best disguises.

SLOW DOWN! Stop this! Dirk isn't looking at you. He's looking at that other guy!

Every cell in her body screamed: RUN!!!!

She had to think! She kept eating, the cheese sandwich like ping-pong balls being choked down her gullet. *Look normal. Act normal.* Oh, God, this was so hard! Her admiration for Chase's job as a sniper went up a thousand notches. Still, as she slid careful looks, she saw Dirk was fully immersed in the cowboy and whatever he was saying. A waitress walked over, taking their order. In a few minutes, she came back with two mugs of coffee for them and left again. Cari's heart was pounding like a sledgehammer in her chest. She felt shaky and so scared that she wanted to freeze, but knew she didn't dare.

What to do? What should she do? The longer she stayed in the restaurant, the better the chances that Dirk might identify her. And then what? Was he carrying a gun on him? Would he get up and come over and shoot her? Closing her eyes, the bill of her cap down as she woodenly chewed the sandwich, Cari saw the flashback of Dirk lifting his gun and without any hesitation, putting a bullet in his girlfriend's head. There was no remorse on his face. Nothing. Just a cold-blooded, heartless, soulless being.

Yes, he'd come across this restaurant and shoot her just as easily, and she knew it.

THINK, CARI! THINK! STOP PANICKING!

She knew if she did panic, it would definitely draw their attention because she'd jump up, slam through those double swinging doors, race through the kitchen to the rear entrance, and then run to her parked truck. Thank God, she had parked on the side of the building and near that rear exit!

Trying to calm her racing, scared-out-of-her-wits mind, she took a drink of the ice-cold water and then set the glass down. Dirk wasn't looking around. His only focus was that cowboy. They were in deep conversation.

"Here you go."

Cari jerked and looked up. The waitress had bought her to-go box in a sack.

"Oh," she said. "Let me pay you now?" She grabbed her knapsack, finding her billfold.

"Well," the woman said, "just go up to Trudy, who's at the cash register near the front door. She'll take care of you."

"No! Wait." Cari handed her a twenty-dollar bill. "Keep the change. Thanks . . ."

The waitress lifted her brows, took the bill. "Hey, thanks . . . that's mighty nice of you."

"You're welcome."

The waitress left.

Cari slid a glance across the room. The two men were now in deep conversation, heads together, their meals having just arrived. Neither was looking around. She moved to her cell phone, which was near her hand. Her heart started a heavy, staccato beat. If she could take one photo . . . just one . . . and if she could get out of here alive, she could take the photos to Dan Seabert. Could the sheriff, with this information, get here fast enough to capture Dirk? Could he? She didn't know. Taking what appeared to be a selfie, in reality the camera lens was focused on the two men in the corner. Snapping it, she slid it in her pocket.

It was now or never. She had to get up and turn and go into the rear, through the food prep and chefs, and out the back door. And she had to look casual doing it. Oh, God! Could she? Standing, her back to them, she gathered up the to-go order and her knapsack. Her mind spun, her knees felt so weak, she thought she'd fall. No, she couldn't!

The swinging doors flew open as a waitress sailed out with a large order. Instantly, Cari moved and slipped into the prep area. Two waitresses looked up, smiled and said nothing, gathering their orders. The cook was at the grill and ignored her. Quickly, Cari moved along one side of the area, spotted the back door, which had a screen on it, but it was open.

The urge to run nearly overwhelmed her, but she kept her leisurely, relaxed pace. In no time, she was outside on the restaurant's back steps, and into the warm June air. Gasping, she looked around. No one was there. She ran around the corner and then halted, spotting her truck. There was no one around, so she sprinted for it.

Jumping into the truck, she started it, kept her gaze on both doors of the restaurant. Had Dirk seen her leave? Her mouth was dry. Her hands shook as she backed out. Putting the truck in gear, she drove quickly to the highway. She grabbed her cell phone, calling 911. In stutters and stammers, she told the operator what had happened and to get the sheriff's dispatcher, fast.

She was heading to the other side of town where Dan's headquarters were located. The stoplights made her panic increase a hundredfold. She kept looking in the rearview mirror, the two side mirrors, afraid that Dirk was following her. She had to keep her cool!

At the sheriff's building, on a side street from the highway, Cari leaped out, running for the front door. She almost slammed into Dan, who was hurrying out, several of his deputies behind him.

"Dan!" she cried. "It's my stepbrother, Dirk Bannock! He's in Olive Oyle's with another man!"

Dan hauled her into the large waiting room. "Okay, did you get a photo of him?"

"Y-yes," she said, taking her iPhone out of her pocket. She quickly got to the photo, handing it to him, trembling.

"Let me run identification on both of them," he said. "Come with me. You're safe here, Cari. Everything's going to be all right."

"I need to call Chase."

"You can call him from my command center. Follow me."

She wanted to cry with relief. She'd escaped! Her knees felt so shaky that she grabbed at Dan's upper arm.

"I-I'm feeling weak, like I'm going to fall," she whispered raggedly, utterly embarrassed.

One of the other deputies, Pepper Warner, gripped her by the arm. "I got you, Ms. Taylor. Just lean on me. We need to get to the command room ASAP."

"Th-thanks," Cari whispered, leaning against the tall woman deputy who seemed as solid as a rock compared to her. Dan had trotted ahead and disappeared around a corner, down another hall. Pepper led Cari that way, to a door that had a number pad on it. After punching in the code, it clicked open.

Dan was standing over his computer operator, who was running the app on identification. He looked up. "Hang in there, Cari. Sit her down, Pepper, and get her some water, will you?"

"Sure thing," Pepper answered, giving Cari a gentle look as she guided her to a chair. "Just sit. I'll be right back. The worst is over . . ."

How she wanted to call Chase! But her phone was on the console of the computer, Dan leaning over his geek's shoulder, gaze riveted on the large computer screen.

"Bingo!" Dan crowed, giving Cari a look of admiration. "That's your stepbrother, Dirk Bannock, all right. The guy with him is a very well-known white supremacist who has been trying set up shop in the nearby mountain range outside of Silver Creek. His name is Brock Hauptman. Good work, Cari!"

She felt faint, covering her face with her hands and leaning back against the chair, a sob wanting to tear out of her, but she struggled to control it.

"Cari?" Pepper returned with the water, placing one hand on Cari's slumped shoulder. "You okay? Do you feel like you're going to faint?" Pepper placed the glass on a nearby table, both her hands resting on Cari's shoulders to steady her. "Look at me. Talk to me?"

Gulping, Cari squeezed her eyes shut and tried to control her surge of feelings. She felt Pepper's strong but firm hands on her shoulders holding her, in case she did faint. "I-I'll be okay . . . just give me a minute, Pepper?"

"No hurry," Pepper said, her voice husky with concern. "You're safe here. You know that, don't you?"

Opening her eyes, she saw Dan on his radio that was attached to his left shoulder, giving a lot of orders she couldn't hear. "Y-yes . . . just such a shock. I-I thought Dirk would recognize me . . . kill me like he killed his girlfriend."

Pepper groaned and sat on the chair next to hers, a hand still on her shoulder. "You poor thing. No wonder you're having this kind of a reaction. What can I get you?'

"My phone." She pointed to it. "Please? I have to call Chase. It's so important. What if he and any of his wranglers are coming into town? What is Dan going to do about this?"

Dan straightened and walked over, giving Cari her phone. "Pepper, stay with Cari. Keep her here. I'll be in touch." And he was gone.

"What is Dan going to do?" Cari asked the deputy.

"I'll be listening on my radio and keep you in the loop," she said, and tapped the earbud in her left ear.

"Is he going to shoot up the restaurant and arrest Dirk and that other guy? Won't people get killed?"

"Nah, Dan doesn't work that way. He knows if these two dudes are in there, he's not going in to arrest them. They've probably got weapons on them. Dan doesn't want collateral damage."

"What's that?"

Pepper smiled a little. "Friendly fire or killing innocent bystanders and civilians. He won't do that, Cari. Chances are, he's going to order our helicopter up, at an altitude of about seven thousand feet, so those two, when they do leave the premises, won't realize that we're tracking them. Did you see what kind of vehicle they came in?"

"N-no, I didn't. I just saw them coming in the door." She dialed Chase's phone, her fingers trembling badly.

"I'll talk to Chase when you're done, Cari," Pepper said.
"Good idea . . ."

Cari waited impatiently, the phone ringing and ringing.
"He's not answering," she squeaked, terrorized.

"Cell phone coverage isn't everywhere in the valley,"
Pepper said. "Let me try something else. Stay here. I'll
be right back."

Cari was going nowhere. Her legs felt like limp spaghetti
at best. Worried, she saw Pepper go over to the command
center console and make a radio call. To who, she didn't
know and she couldn't hear what the woman said. Pepper
Warner was nearly six feet tall, medium build, and seemed
so solid and confident to Cari. Her black hair was as short
as Cari's. She liked the woman's gray eyes because they
reminded her of an eagle's intense, focused gaze. She
was probably in her late twenties, Cari guessed, very
pretty, obviously an outdoors woman, a tan over her
hands and face. Pepper was on that call for a long time,
or it seemed like it.

"Okay," Pepper said, coming and sitting down next to
her, "here's what I've initiated. I've sent a deputy sheriff
to Chase's ranch. Chances are, Chase is out of cell phone
reach, but I told the forewoman, Tracy Hartimer, about
the situation. She said Chase was unreachable. I've asked
her to shut down the ranch, keep everyone on it, and
wait to hear from us before going anywhere. I told Tracy
you were fine, so Chase won't worry. I asked Tracy that
he call you on your phone as soon as he's in range. I'm
sure he will."

Relief flooded her and she placed her hand against
her chest. "Thank you . . . I was so worried. But what

about the townspeople, Pepper? Who is safe? How will they stay safe? They don't know that Dirk is a convict, that he's on the run."

"Dan will do nothing. He has an unmarked SUV, a green one, beat-up, and looks nothing like a police car. He'll stay out in the parking lot across the street and watch. He'll also put some of his plainclothes detectives at every angle outside that restaurant so they can identify the vehicle, and they'll get the plate number, as well. He wants this quiet, no fuss, and by doing it this way, everyone remains safe. Okay? So don't worry. We've got it covered."

Her heartbeat was beginning to slow. She gripped the glass of water, drinking in gulps. When she set it down, some of the water slopped out, her hand trembling badly. "I wish I could be calm, cool, and collected like you are, Pepper."

Patting Cari's shoulder, she smiled a little. "It's not my stepbrother who wants to kill me. If I were in your shoes? My adrenaline would be up and shooting like Fourth of July fireworks."

"B-but you're trained for this, too. Right? Chase told me that the first responders are different than most of us civilians. He said it was in their DNA to think clearly through dangerous situations."

Pepper shrugged. "He's right about that, Cari, but believe me, we have our let-down reactions afterward. And we're in the business of keeping a cool head in a crisis. We have to in order to do the right thing at the right time."

"I'm not built like that," she said wearily, suddenly

feeling exhausted emotionally, and all her strength dissolving.

"Look what you did," Pepper said, giving her an admiring look. "You kept your head, and you even got a photo of them. That's remarkable. Most civilians wouldn't think to do that. Your actions have helped us enormously. I hope Dan can get that helicopter up and going before those two leave the restaurant."

"Will Dan follow them in that beat-up SUV, then?"

"Yes, he will, but he'll keep his distance. He knows how to tail without being spotted. He'll also put out an all-points bulletin, so if they drive out of our county into another, he'll have alerted them, as well. We've got this . . ."

"I hope so badly they're able to apprehend Dirk. What about the other guy?"

Pepper shrugged. "Intel is that he was released from prison six months ago. Dan heard from two local lumber companies up in the mountains that a group of men with Nazi flags and other Hitler stuff were living off the land up there. Dan believes it's a white supremacist group, and he considers all of them domestic terrorists. Maybe this Hauptman guy is the leader and your stepbrother is trying to hook up with him?"

"I don't know," Cari admitted, gripping her phone in her hands. How she wanted to hear from Chase! Whatever mind games she'd been telling herself about Chase had now all been violently ripped away. She was falling in love with him. No longer would she lie to herself about it. More than anything, she wanted Chase's arms around her. Right or wrong, he made her feel safe.

Pepper patted her shoulder. "We've got puzzle pieces to start putting together. I know if Hauptman is connected with this group up in the mountains, Dan will call in the FBI pronto. They are hot on the heels of every white supremacist and white nationalist group in the USA. They want them all behind bars."

"That's good news," Cari whispered, touching her forehead. "I feel so weak and tired, Pepper."

"It's called an adrenaline crash." She gave her a sympathetic look. "It's a normal reaction. Anytime you have the fight-or-flight hormones plowing through your system at light speed? You feel threatened and your life is in danger? There's always a plummet afterward, and that's what you're experiencing right now."

"It's awful."

"Just rest. Keep drinking your water. You don't have to move or go anywhere, and I'll stay with you so you'll have company. I'll also hear what's going on out there because I'm hooked into Dan's main number." She tapped her radio on her left shoulder.

Leaning back, Cari closed her eyes, gripping her phone. Oh, just to hear Chase's low, soothing voice! What would he think, once Tracy got ahold of him? Would he be as rattled and shaken by this as she was?

What were the chances that Dirk would show up *here*? Had he somehow found out where she was? Was he enlisting a group of racist domestic terrorists to find her? Hunt her down? Her mind went wild with awful scenarios she'd never considered before. It left her feeling even more of a target, that her life was but mere minutes, or days, from being brutally taken away from her.

The radio went off on Pepper's shoulder and she listened intently.

Cari sat up, worried.

"Well," Pepper said, after the transmission was finished, "bad luck. Our helicopter at the airport has a mechanical issue. It can't take off and follow them. Damn."

"What does this mean, then?" Cari asked, her voice off-key. "Are they going to get away?"

"No," Pepper said grimly, frowning, "but it takes our best asset out of the picture. With it, we could have known exactly where they were going. Now, Dan is going to have to follow them the old-fashioned way once they come out of the restaurant."

"But won't that be good enough?" Cari asked, hopeful.

"Not necessarily. Depends on if they stay on the main highway or not."

"But . . . aren't satellites coming across this area? Couldn't they be used?"

Pepper gave her a softened look. "They're all military, Cari, not law enforcement. And even if we could get permission, it would have to be through the FBI and the military command. It's pretty tough asking a satellite to change its orbit."

"Ohhh," she whispered. "Well, this is bad."

"What I wish we could have is a Pred," she muttered.

"What's a Pred?"

"A large military drone known as the Predator. They could follow at ten thousand feet, never be seen, and we could have known their exact destination."

"Do you have a drone?"

"No. We have small ones, but nothing on the scale

I'm talking about. We'll just have to do old-fashioned gumshoe work here to track these two."

"But if they stay on the highway? You can know their location?"

"It's a start. These domestic terrorist groups usually shift around a lot, to keep their locations a secret. Let's wait and see what Dan can do or find. At least, we know two of the perps and we know they're in this area. That's two pieces of good luck you provided us." She smiled proudly over at Cari. "You're a real heroine. You know that? Most people wouldn't have thought to do what you did. Chase is going to be awfully proud of you, too. Everyone will be, although it will be kept quiet and known to only a select few."

"I don't feel heroic at all." Cari drank the rest of the water and then looked at the time on her iPhone. "It feels like time is passing so slowly," she murmured.

"Adrenaline crash. It feels like time is slowing down, but Dan has been gone twenty minutes already. I'm sure they've totally staked out the restaurant and are just waiting for the two perps to leave."

"I hope they leave the state," Cari muttered, scowling. When would Chase call her? She knew one couldn't drive forty, fifty, or sixty miles an hour on those dirt roads on the ranch, for fear of crashing. Everything was going to take time. How badly she wanted to see Chase! But even a phone call from him right now would be like heaven to her. Cari felt as if she'd been dropped into Hell. Literally. Chase was her guardian angel. If he hadn't schooled her on black-ops sniper skills, she'd never have gotten out of that situation in the restaurant alive. She'd have screamed, panicked, and tried to run. That would have put everyone in that restaurant in danger, too. No, Chase had taught her some fundamental operating procedures and today? They'd paid off. At least she hadn't gotten a lot of innocent people dead, including herself.

Chapter Nine

June 15

Chase was down on his hands and knees along with two of his other wranglers, beginning to remove a huge boulder that was standing in the way of the new pipeline fence. He saw a rooster cloud of dust coming their way on the dirt road. He was on the farthest part of the ranch and had come out to look at the efforts of his construction group of women and men, who were tackling an area of mid-sized boulders.

There were two bucket-type machines taking the boulders to a nearby dump truck. This was a huge undertaking, something he'd been avoiding since becoming the owner of the ranch. Yet, ten thousand acres were sitting empty simply because of the medium to large rocks in the soil. It would be one thing to get a couple of bulldozers with a hook in the rear to pull them up and out, but it still took a lot of sweat, human muscle, and due diligence to then take them to the dump trucks waiting in line to deposit them in one specific area so the soil could be tilled and utilized.

"Hey," Jake called, standing up. "Someone's comin' our way at high speed." He pointed behind Chase.

"We're out of cell phone range," Chase said, frowning, wiping the sweat off his brow and standing. Squinting against the sun, he pulled his Stetson down to shade his eyes. "I'll go to my truck and use our radio to call Tracy and ask what's going on."

"Good idea," Jake agreed.

Chase couldn't tell whose vehicle it was, the dust high and heavy and disappearing down a slope. It would take another mile for it to come up and out of the dust, and by that time, he might be able to identify it. The truck was half a mile away and he saw Jake jogging toward it.

Another of his hands, Merry, came up beside him. "Looks like someone has a fire lit under him. Must be important?" She looked up at Chase, a question in her expression.

"Yeah. Hope it isn't bad news."

"Maybe we should think about a different radio system when we're out this far," she said, her hands on her hips, her elk-skin gloves dusty.

Rubbing the back of his neck, Chase said, "You're probably right, Merry. When we finish up here I'll talk to Tracy and get something in motion on this. It's worried me for a long time when we're out at the edges of the ranch and there's no cell coverage. Merry, you take over the rock removal project. I'm going to my truck to find out what's happening. Keep me updated by truck radio or talk to Tracy if you need anything."

"If we break a leg out here, boss? Unless we can get to a truck radio, we're stuck."

She was right. "I hear you," he said. He trotted toward the truck. About the time that Jake reached his vehicle, he recognized the sheriff's black-and-white SUV. His gut tightened. Whatever it was, it wasn't good. Muttering a curse, he turned.

The deputy sheriff climbed out of the SUV upon spotting Chase standing by his truck. Chase recognized Ginger Harris, a blond-haired woman of forty, coming his way, a serious look on her face. What was going on? He looked toward the main area of the ranch, although he couldn't see it, but wondered if a fire had started in one of the main buildings. There was no black smoke staining the bright blue sky.

He met Ginger midway. "What's going on, Ginger?"

"Dan sent me out here to get you. No radio could reach you, even though we tried your truck radio."

"Yeah, I know. We were too far away to hear a call. What's up?"

Ginger said, "We need you back at the sheriff's office right now. Cari went into town on some business, stopped at Olive Oyle's Restaurant, when she saw her stepbrother come in with another gent."

His heart dropped and Chase opened his mouth, but Ginger held up her hand.

"She's okay. She's safe with us at the office, which is why I want you to come with me."

"What happened?" he demanded, his voice tight.

"Cari was in the restaurant, ordering a meal. She saw her stepbrother come in with another male. She was able to get a photo of them, slipped through the kitchen and out the back door. Luckily, she'd parked on the side of the restaurant where there were no windows. She called us on 911 and headed for our office. Dan listened to her story, took the photo and put it in our facial recognition app." Her voice turned dark. "Dirk Bannock is hooking up or running around with a white supremacist that's trying to hide in the mountains north of Silver Creek. His name is Brock Hauptman. Right now, Dan is tailing them in our unmarked green SUV. Our helicopter has a mechanical issue and can't get off the ground to follow them from the air, undetected. So, he's doing his best to tail them after they left the restaurant to try and find out where they're going."

Cursing softly, he said, "You're sure Cari's okay?"

"Shaken up, but okay."

"Was she recognized?"

"No, we don't think so. She can tell you the details. Do you want me to take you in or do you want to drive in with your truck?"

"I'll follow you in. Sorry you had to come out here, Ginger. Bad spot for communications, as you know."

"I understand," she said, moving to the door and opening it.

Shutting the door, Chase took a huge, deep breath, putting his truck into drive, turning around, following Ginger in the sheriff's vehicle. His heart was thrashing in his chest and he unconsciously rubbed that area before putting both hands on the steering wheel. They could only go so fast on this dirt road and Ginger was leading out, hightailing it as fast as she dared. He hung back a good half mile because the rooster tail of dust made it impossible for him to see the road. It was a long drive back, even halfway, to get cell service. He unsnapped his shirt pocket, pulling out his iPhone, setting it in a cup holder device and turning it on. As soon as it came within range, it would beep, alerting him.

His mind spun, wondering how Cari was doing and what she was going through. This was a shock! For him, her, and the valley in general. The look on Ginger's face had been grim. He'd known about the intrusion of the white supremacist gang moving into some timber-cutting areas. The two lumber companies had been given permission by the US Forest Service to thin the timber, not clear-cut it. They were up in the mountains, usually five- to nine thousand feet, still cutting roads into the area for the trucks to haul out the chosen timber. There had been rumblings about a gang of white males up in those regions. Sometimes, the companies would find some of their tools stolen, or a portable generator went missing.

Further, ranchers who owned pastures below this activity, were finding some of their cattle shot, skinned, and the meat taken, leaving the carcass in the field. It wasn't a good situation and now it was much worse.

No one had been able to find that racist gang of white males, but there had been plenty of sightings since mid-March, when the worst of the weather was gone for the season. The ranchers, who Chase knew, had called a valley-wide conference in late April about that gang, who were dressed in military cammo uniforms, and always carrying military weapons on them. The ranchers involved were damn well upset, losing cattle to these thieves, as well as convinced that these men were up to no good, and they feared for their families' lives. Chase wondered, as he drove, if Dan was now going to call in the FBI to start investigating, because white supremacists were considered domestic terrorists.

Cari . . . his heart and mind focused on her. He wanted to know what happened, how it happened. How was she doing? Of late, he'd seen her confidence blooming and it made him happy. He knew she had gone into town by herself this morning, a test, to see how she did. It had been Cari's idea, not his. He'd endorsed it, of course.

He pushed his fingers through his short, dark hair, aggravation flowing through him. With Dirk in the area? This had to pulverize Cari in so many ways, especially emotionally and psychologically. When someone witnessed a murder, as Cari had, one never forgot it. Ever. The shock of it was soul ripping as far as he was concerned. And for someone like Cari, being a witness to Dirk's murdering his girlfriend had devasted her in every possible way. Which told him Dirk was a sociopath and it wouldn't bother him at all to murder someone else. But for Cari? It had rocked and ripped her world apart. The fact Bannock had promised, in court, to find and kill her? That was enough to total any human being, because he meant every word he'd screamed at her.

When his cell beeped, he picked it up, pressing Cari's phone number. It rang and no one answered. Was she sleeping? Had her battery died? He didn't know, so he called the sheriff's office. The dispatcher, Sue Ramford, answered.

"Hey, Sue, this is Chase. Is Cari there?"

"Hi, Chase. Cari's asleep in the women's locker room right now. Pepper just came out to let me know."

"Is she all right?"

"Cari looked really drawn, pale, and she was exhausted. Pepper took her to the women's locker room and Cari fell asleep immediately."

"Is Pepper still around?"

"Sure. You want to speak to her?"

"Yes, thanks," Chase said.

"Pepper here. Hi, Chase."

"Hey, what can you tell me about what's going on? Is Cari all right?"

"She's in shock, Chase, which is to be expected, but I think getting to sleep will help her a lot. You'd be proud of her. She said that you had been teaching her some black ops stuff and she used all of it this morning when Bannock unexpectedly entered the restaurant. She even got a good photo of him and Hauptman, who is the white supremacist we think is heading up that gang up in the mountains north of our town. We had helo trouble and it's grounded, so Dan is in our unmarked SUV and tailing them. He's hanging way back, about half to three-quarters of a mile because it's across flat land, no hills or other landmass to discourage them from seeing him."

"What's Dan going to do?"

"Our office has already alerted the FBI, and an agent has just been assigned to it. That individual will be flying into our airport later this evening. Dan has asked one of us to pick him up when he lands."

"That's good news. We need the FBI's logistics and help on this."

"Better believe it."

"How's Dan doing?"

"He's twenty-five miles out and still on the main high-way, nearing the end of the valley where the mountains are located."

"Too bad about the helo."

"Isn't it, though? They're repairing it as I speak."

"We need a Pred."

She laughed heartily. "That's what I said, but I don't think the feds or military are gonna trust us with one."

"I've got miles to go before I get on the main highway, Pepper. If Cari wakes up before I get there, let her know I'm coming in?"

"You bet I will."

June 15

Cari suddenly woke up. Where was she? Her heart was pounding, a nightmare, a dark man stalking her with the intent to kill her, rattling her and shaking her awake in terror. A small light was on the wall, and she slowly real-ized as she pushed strands of hair away from her face, where she was.

Making a frustrated sound, she got up, her boots nearby. Hearing nothing, she pulled them on and laced them up, standing, looking around the silent, large room that had four beds in it. Grateful that Pepper allowed her to use the room, she wiped her eyes. There was a clock with radium dials above the door. It was 3:00 p.m.! She'd slept a lot!

Instantly, her heart focused on Chase. Where was he? Did he know what had happened? Trying to settle her emotions down, moving into that peaceful place she always went to when working with the bee people, she felt better. Calmer. That was good.

Opening the door, she stepped out into the empty women's locker room. It was quiet, unlike her world that had been turned upside down. Going to the bathroom, she washed her hands, dried them on several paper towels, and glanced into the mirror. She looked scared. Or maybe it was her imagination. She used her fingers to comb through her mussed hair, satisfied that it was in place in a coherent way.

Moving to the door, she pulled it open. Across the green tiled hall were a series of cubicles, each surrounded in glass. When she saw Chase sitting with Pepper in one of them, her heart thudded hard in her chest. The desire to run to him, cry out her terror, wanting his arms around her, coursed through Cari.

Thankfully, her mature side understood that it was up to her to handle herself and her emotions. No man was ever going to do that for her. Compressing her lips, she watched them for a moment, getting herself together. Two hours had passed since the incident had happened. Did Pepper know anything else? Had Dan been able to follow Dirk? Need to know drove her forward. As she passed the cubicle, she saw them both raise their heads in her direction at the same time. She gave them a weak smile and raised her hand, heading around the group of offices and coming in the open door where they sat.

Chase, upon spotting her, was on his feet instantly, and she saw his raw concern for her. There was no mistaking how he felt, but he remained where he was. Pepper also stood.

"Hey, you look a lot better," Pepper greeted her. "How are you feeling, Cari?"

Hesitating at the doorway, she croaked, "Better, I guess." She looked at Chase, feeling waves of emotion pouring off him even though he'd said nothing. "Have you found out anything else?" she asked the woman.

Pepper nodded. "Listen, why don't you sit down and Chase will fill you in. Can I get you anything? I need to go check in with the comms room."

"No . . . thanks," Cari said, heading for the chair. She didn't dare go to Chase, afraid she'd turn into a ball of anxiety and fear. She saw his gray eyes darken as she sat down.

"I can fill you in," Chase said, giving Pepper a nod. The deputy closed the door quietly behind her and left.

"How are you doing?" Chase asked, his voice low with concern.

"All right, I guess. I still can't believe I did just as you trained me to do."

He gave her a proud look. "You got a photo. That took a lot of courage, Cari. I imagine all you wanted to do was run?"

"And then some, but then I remembered what you said about looking relaxed, as if nothing was wrong, even if I was scared out of my mind."

"And you did it. Can you tell me what happened?"

Nodding, Cari filled him in, her hands clasped tightly in her lap. She wasn't more than six feet away from Chase, but she swore, she could feel an invisible warm blanket enclosing her, holding her, making her feel utterly safe. She knew it was coming from him. He was a strong, courageous marine, someone who had faced death many times, looked it in the eye, and didn't flinch. Right now, she hungrily absorbed his nearness and care. When she was finished, she asked, "Has Dan found out anything yet?"

"No. They turned off on a main logging road about twenty-eight miles west of Silver Creek. There's two main logging companies up in that area that have federal government contracts to thin the forest, and that's what they're doing. That one main logging road splits off into about seven different feeder dirt roads where the timber trucks are hauling out the chosen trees."

"Couldn't Dan have followed them?" she asked.

"No, because Dirk or Hauptman, his partner or whoever he is, would have immediately realized they were being tailed. It would have blown the whole thing. Dan stopped and turned around. He waited an hour, hidden on the opposite side of the highway, behind a thick grove of bushes, waiting for them to come back out, but they never did. He'll be returning here any time, now."

"What will Dan do?"

"An FBI agent is flying in tonight. Pepper's going to pick the agent up at the local airport and bring him here, to HQ. I'm sure they'll come up with some kind of plan."

"Will they go after them?"

"Most likely," he hedged, "but until we get details, I just can't say." He gave her a searching look. "I know this has upset you a lot."

"Understatement. The last thing I thought I'd ever see

in that restaurant was Dirk walking in." She took a deep, shaky breath, holding his sympathetic gaze. "I was so scared, Chase. So scared . . ."

"Anyone would be," he soothed. "But look what you did, Cari. You did everything right. Everything that I taught you about surveillance."

"I can't believe I did it, Chase. Internally? I just shake my head and wonder how I managed to do it. My fear has never been greater than in that moment."

"I believe you." He looked around the busy place. "What do you want to do?"

"Go home. Back to the ranch. Is that all right, Chase? I don't want Dirk to follow me there."

"He didn't recognize you, Cari," he said gently.

"Oh . . . well . . . yes, I guess you're right," and she touched her temple. "I'm just like a roiling nest of angry hornets right now. I know I'm not thinking clearly."

"By going to the ranch, you'll be safe," he promised. "Personally? I want you nowhere else but there, in that ranch home, with me until we have more intel and a plan of action from Dan and the FBI."

Cari gave him a painful look. "*Why* did Dirk show up *here* of all places? I'm in panic mode, Chase. Did he hack my parents' computer? Their cell phones? My parents do *not* have any information on me in either place. *How* did he know I was *here*?" She jabbed her index finger down at the floor, her voice filled with fear.

"I don't know, Cari. It could be nothing but bad luck; you were at the wrong place at the wrong time. It could be that simple of an explanation."

She snorted. "Dirk hates me. He's always hated me.

And he meant it when he said he was going to find me and kill me."

"I believe that. But let's wait until Dan and that FBI agent can put their heads together on a plan. Right now, we know for sure that Dirk is here, in our area. What that means? No one knows." He stood up, offering her his hand. "Come on, let's go home."

Without hesitation, she took his hand. His flesh was toughened with hard, constant outdoor work, hand broad, fingers long, the dark hair on the back of it reminding her how powerful and masculine he always seemed to her. As his fingers curled around hers, she leaned against his right shoulder.

"I want to hold you, Cari," he rasped.

"Yes . . ." She felt him enclose her gently, guiding her cheek against his shirt, feeling the firmness of his flesh beneath it, the scent of him as a man. Automatically, she leaned fully against him, hungry to have his arms coming around her shoulders. He stood there, unmoving, allowing her to be as close or as far away from him as she wanted to be, allowing her the choice, which was hers alone.

Closing her eyes, her head beneath his chin, which rested softly on her hair, she leaned fully against him, almost sagging, struggling to stand upright because her knees were still mushy feeling, even now.

Chase held her, feeling her tremble. She felt frail to him. Inhaling the sweet fragrance that was only her, he rasped against her hair, "It's going to be all right, Cari. We'll get through this together. We're a good team . . ."

Hot tears crowded instantly into her tightly shut eyes. Her arms went around his torso and she held him hard, never wanting this moment, or this sense of safety, to end.

Her emotions wrestled with her mind. Just having him standing like a giant Sequoia tree hardened by the elements for thousands of years, yet feeling his gentleness, the way his arms lightly enclosed her, not a gesture of unspoken possession, but letting her know she was truly protected, washed through her, erasing so much of her raw anxiety.

Forcing herself to stand, to release him, Cari looked up at him. His gray eyes were almost colorless, pupils huge and black, trained upon her and she felt nothing but that wonderful heat of protection that continued to blanket her. "I-I'll be okay," she managed, stepping away, her arms dropping from around his waist. "Thanks, Chase . . . I needed that . . ." But she needed so much more from him. They weren't innocent about life, about what happened between men and women when there was an attraction between them. And now, more than ever, Cari knew her attraction to Chase was serious. Even now, she worried Dirk might sneak onto the ranch, kill him, and then her. She did not want anyone else hurt because of her. And yet, there was no place else for her to go. She couldn't go home, couldn't go see her parents. They were all targets of Dirk's.

"So did I," he admitted hoarsely, picking up his Stetson. "Come on, let's go home."

"I think a long, hot bath sounds really good to me."

"And while you soak? I'll fix us dinner for tonight."

Cari walked out after he opened the door. "I'm not hungry at all, Chase."

"You need to eat something. We'll sort our way through this stuff later."

"Do you think Dan is back?" she asked as they walked toward the foyer of the building.

"I don't see him," Chase said, looking around. "He's pretty hard to miss." He gave her a wry smile, his hand coming to rest lightly against the small of her back. "He'll be in touch with us, I'm sure. Right now, let's concentrate on you." He halted near the foyer doors. "Have a seat near the wall," he directed.

She gave him a frown. "I thought we were walking out to your truck?"

"We're in surveillance mode now," he said, guiding her to the chair.

And then, Cari got it. "Do you think Dirk is out there, his gun trained on the doors? That he could shoot us?"

"No," he murmured, giving her a gentle look. "It's a precaution until we know for sure where he is, that's all. I don't expect him to be out there, although I'll take no chances. When you see me drive up? Come out and climb in. Okay?"

Shaken, she felt her fragile state of protection dissolving. "Yes . . . okay . . ." she whispered.

Chase caressed her hair. "It's going to be all right, Cari. Just relax. I'll be back in a few minutes."

Feeling foolish, Cari watched him leave. Shivering, she wrapped her arms around herself, not wanting anyone to see her in such a state. The women and men of the sheriff's department put their lives on the line every day. She didn't have the inner courage they did and she had always stood in admiration of it. Now, more than ever before.

And Chase . . . Her heart beat hard and she closed her eyes, feeling his arms go around her, allowing her to rest against him, to hear the slow, strong beating of his heart beneath her ear. How that sound grounded her emotionally! No man had ever touched her heart, her soul, as Chase did. And she'd said nothing about how she felt toward him.

Bitterness coated her mouth and she opened her eyes, watching for his truck to arrive. She'd been so much trouble to Chase. And it wasn't fair to him or to her. But now? With Dirk in the mix, her whole life as she saw it beautifully developing here in Silver Creek, was blown to smithereens. Cari didn't know what to do. What to say. Maybe she should run away, telling no one where she was going. Becoming lost in three hundred million people. Dirk wouldn't find her then, but his shadow, his threat, loomed over her like the sword of Damocles.

Chase pulled up in the ranch truck.

She quickly rose, pushed open the door and looked around, feeling like a scared victim of some unseen predator. Her mind was running wild with scenarios as she climbed into the truck and belted up.

"Okay?" he asked, putting it in gear.

"I wish I could shut off my mind, Chase. It's running wild."

"Normal reaction," he assured her gently, driving out of the area and onto the main highway that would lead to the ranch.

"When you were a sniper, were you ever scared?" she asked, looking around.

"All the time. Fear, if used properly, can be your best friend," he explained. "It keeps you alert, hyperalert, actually. It's a higher state of being, able to feel what's around you even if you can't see it or hear it."

Wrapping her arms around her torso, she leaned back, and staring up at the ceiling of the cab, she muttered, "How did you stand it, then? How could you? I feel like a sack of jelly inside myself, Chase."

"You haven't been trained for it, that's why," he told her quietly, sliding her a glance. "Don't be hard on yourself and don't compare yourself to me. That isn't fair to you."

"Because I'm a civilian. Right?"

He cut her a brief smile. "Right."

The sunlight coming into the cab warmed her. The air-conditioning was on, but on low, which she appreciated. "I'm a mess, Chase. I don't know if I should run, hide, stay here, or go somewhere else."

"Before you make any decisions? Let's wait to see what Dan and the FBI have in mind. That will help you sort out what you want to do and what our options are."

"I can't go home. That would be the first place Dirk would look. I don't want to be anywhere near my parents, because he could be watching them or having some of his gang watching them. I know he hates my mother and I know he wants her dead, too." Her voice cracked and she sat up, her hands in fists on her lap. "It's not right that someone can turn so many people's lives inside out, stalking us, scaring and threatening us twenty-four hours a day, every day."

He reached over, his hand covering one of her clenched fists. "We'll take this one step at a time, Cari. Right now"—he squeezed her hand and then released it—"let's get home. We'll do the small things, the everyday things that make you relax. Your life rhythm needs to be given back to you. And we can do that for you."

She sniffed. "My parents have to be told. Oh, God, Chase, what if Dirk goes after my mother?"

"I'm *sure*," he told her firmly, "that Dan will be in touch with not only the sheriff of the county where they live, but the FBI will be involved in this, also. We'll know who to contact and what they think should happen with your parents as the new plan plays out. They may have them go into hiding, which, in my opinion, is the worst-case scenario."

"We can't afford a bodyguard living there with them."

"No one can." He slowed the truck, making the turn into the ranch entrance.

Cari took a small breath and released it, fighting her own panic and anxiety. This midafternoon was a perfect summer day, something that everyone loved so much. Summer—ninety days of sun, warmth, and everything in bloom—felt like such a gift from Mother Nature. Her beloved bees were out gathering nearby pollen from alfalfa and clover fields that stretched like a lavender quilt across the ranchlands. It was so beautiful to look at. If not for Dirk, Cari could have appreciated the beauty of the ranch, the summer colors of life throughout it. If only this sense of safety would stay with her, but it came and went like an ocean tide.

"We're home," he murmured, guiding the truck into the gravel oval, parking in front of the family homestead.

Nothing had ever felt so good to Cari. It meant safety. And love . . . love for Chase that was blooming in her heart, something she'd ignored until now. "I always like hearing the sound of that," she whispered, giving him a warm look. "Home. It just sounds so fortifying, so solid . . . like a promise . . ."

Chase nodded and settled the Stetson on his head, climbing out. He came around and opened the door for her. Taking Cari's hand, he helped her down. "Why don't you go in, get that bath, soak, and come out when you feel ready."

"Yes," she said, reluctantly releasing his hand. "I'll do that . . ."

"I'm sure we'll hear from Dan by tonight," he said.

"Good. I hate this uncertainty."

"I guarantee you, everyone does," he said, shutting the truck door.

Cari reminded herself she wasn't the only one who was in danger. Everyone on this ranch could become Dirk's target as he hunted for her. And that wasn't right or fair. What was she going to do?

Chapter Ten

June 15

Cari had taken a long, soaking bath, much of her anxiety dissolving in the heat of the water that surrounded her. Washing her hair, getting clean, feeling safe within Chase's home, all allowed her to think more clearly. She changed into a set of pink linen trousers and a cream-colored, three-quarter length tee that felt soft and comforting to her skin.

Combing her hair, she looked at herself in the misty mirror. She was pale, very pale. Her eyes looked dark and frightened. Even her lips were pursed, pulled in pain or anxiety or both. Hands flat on the sink, she dragged in a deep breath. It was near suppertime, and although she wasn't hungry, she knew she had to eat. The amount of energy she'd used up earlier today needed to be replaced.

Opening the door, she smelled spaghetti, the garlic a nice scent on the air. Chase was busy in the kitchen, his broad back to her, chopping up vegetables. Walking across the living room, she made sure he could see her coming. Early on, he told her to never approach him silently from the rear. His automatic response was to assume it was the enemy, and he might accidentally harm her. The more she knew about Chase, the more she realized his years as a sniper in enemy territory were now a part of him, and she respected his request.

"That smells good," she said, moving into the kitchen, catching his glance.

"I figured some comfort food tonight was in order, nothing heavy on your stomach, and it just might taste good," he said, finishing up the tiny pieces of garlic. He tossed them into the sauce pan and stirred them in. He rinsed his hands in the sink and grabbed a towel, drying them off. "You look a lot better. How are you feeling?"

Cari fell into their routine. Chase would cook and she would set the table. "Better."

"I don't think we'll hear from Dan until tomorrow morning," Chase said. "They need to talk at length with that FBI agent who's flying in."

"Okay," she said, taking the blue-and-white plates over to the table. "The main thing I'm worried about is Dirk. Did he recognize me?"

Pulling open a drawer, he laid two dark blue linen napkins on the counter. "I don't think so, and I'll tell you why. If he had, why would he have stayed where he was? Don't you think he'd have done something? And when you turned from that corner booth and went into the kitchen, I'm pretty sure he'd have come after you. Why would he leave you where you were if he did recognize you?"

"You have a point," she said quietly, picking up the napkins. "I've asked myself that question, too."

"He's used to seeing his dark-haired sister with long

hair, not some woman with short red hair. Plus, you said you had the bill of the cap low enough so he couldn't really see your whole face. I think he's here for another reason. And that's why we're going to have to wait to find out from Dan what it might be."

She pulled the flatware from the drawer. "That still means he's in this area, Chase." She gave him a dark look. "And that's the real problem."

"I hear you," he said, pulling a large pot off the stove. "We don't have enough answers yet, Cari. Whether we want to or not, we're going to have to stand down, and wait until Dan gives us a call."

"Do you think he will?"

"Absolutely." He poured the steaming hot water that contained the pasta into an awaiting colander in the sink. "He's not going to leave us high and dry. Don't worry about that."

He placed the steaming spaghetti in a large bowl and handed it to her.

"Regardless, the chances of Dirk being around from now on is what really bothers me." She set the bowl on the table so they could both reach it.

"That's the big issue," he agreed, picking up another bowl with the fragrant, garlicky marinara sauce and placing it on the table.

Cari sat down and put the napkin across her lap, watching him sit down across from her. "You look so unaffected by this. How do you do that? Is that part of your military training?"

He scooted his chair up to the table, handing her the bowl of pasta, first. "I suppose. You can't be a sniper and get tangled up in your bubbling pot of emotions, that's for sure. Get emotional and you get shot. Emotions cloud decisions, Cari."

"Sure wish I had some of that DNA of yours," she grumped, taking the bowl.

"Oh, almost forgot the French bread in the oven." He quickly got up.

She smiled a little, setting the bowl near his plate. Maybe he was more affected than he realized? Or maybe he cared for her, was truly as upset as she was, but was hiding it better than she was? Men could be so taciturn. She watched as he transferred the fragrant garlic-and-butter-laden bread into an awaiting basket. That warm, fuzzy thought that he was as upset as she was, quieted her heart. Cari understood she was putting everyone at risk. *Everyone.*

Chase placed the basket of warm bread next to her plate and sat down. "You're looking stressed. What are you thinking about?"

"That if Dirk hangs around here or decides to live in this valley? That I have to leave, Chase." She saw him tense for a moment, his eyes narrowing upon her. "You know that and so do I. As long as Dirk is loose, even if he's not aware I'm here yet, he will, sooner or later. And once he finds out, he'll stop at nothing to kill anyone who gets between me and him." She spread some sauce across the very small amount of spaghetti she placed on her plate. Glancing up, she saw his brow wrinkle. "Neither of us can afford to pretend we don't know the truth here," she said in a low tone. Cari didn't feel like eating, but she forced herself.

"There's a long way before that might happen," he said, his voice low with feeling.

"And will any of us know that date or time?"

He placed the pasta on his plate and then the sauce over the top of it. "I believe we will. Getting FBI help means a lot more tools and vital intel at our disposal to find Dirk."

"Find him before he finds me?"

"That's about it. Come on, I want you to eat something, Cari . . ."

Chase grabbed the phone in his home office the moment it rang the next morning. It was ten a.m. and he was antsy inwardly, wanting to hear from Dan. Cari was still sleeping, and that was fine by him. It wasn't unusual for a person who had extreme trauma to sleep deeply many nights in a row. It was the body's way of healing from the shock it'd endured.

"Chase here."

"Dan," the sheriff said. "Can you and Cari come in this afternoon at one p.m.? Agent North, from the FBI, and I, have worked out a plan and you two need to be a part of it."

"Yes, we can. Anything you can tell me right now, though? Cari is on edge and so am I."

"Nothing happy," Dan said. "The FBI has been following Hauptman's white supremacist group for some time now. For the last month, Hauptman decided to make his camp up in the mountains, off that logging road that I tailed them to yesterday. We're going to get a drone in here, high altitude, with the help of the FBI and military, to find out more."

"What's Bannock doing there? Is he a white supremacist?"

"Not officially," Dan said, "but he's been rubbing elbows with different gangs and groups in Southern California who are part of his drug supply network that he's continuing to reinvigorate since he broke out of prison. That's how he got to Hauptman. But we don't have the reason why, unless Bannock wants to extend his empire from California and start moving eastward. He may be enlisting Hauptman to become a part of it. We just don't know yet. We have a lot more intel to share with you this afternoon. Tell Cari that we do not feel Bannock ID'd her. She's safe."

"For now."

"Yeah, that too. See you this afternoon, Chase."

Chase hung up the phone. He was torn between waking Cari to give her the information, or letting her sleep.

"Who was on the phone?"

Cari stood in the doorway, dressed in her pale pink fluffy robe that went to her ankles. She was barefoot and her hands rested on either side of the door frame as she looked at him.

Chase gestured for her to come in and he told her everything. She sat down, hands in her lap, frowning.

"Why can't law enforcement just go in, locate Dirk, and arrest him?'

"It's not that easy, Cari. White supremacist groups are heavy into military weapons. They're ready to start a war with the law or anyone else who crosses their path. We could lose a lot of people in a firefight, so it's not the smartest way to nab him if he's still up there with Hauptman."

She rubbed her face. "So? We see Dan this afternoon?"

"Yes."

Standing, she said, "I need to get focused on my beekeeping. I'll be out at the various hive locations with Theresa this morning."

"Good idea. I'm having Tracy buy you a radio so that no matter where you're at on the spread, you can always get ahold of me." He saw her face relax. How badly he wanted to protect her, drive around with her, but he knew she'd hate that, too. How to protect the woman he was falling in love with? There was no protection for his heart, which didn't care about the danger swirling around them.

"That's great. Thanks for doing that."

"Just stop by her office to pick it up on your way out to the hives?"

"I will. I'm off to get a quick shower."

"How about breakfast? I made a big omelet earlier. You could warm it up?"

"Yes, that's perfect. Thank you."

His office felt empty when she left. Chase knew she was putting on her best, confident face for him. No one else knew what was going on yet. He wanted to wait to hear what Dan and Agent North had to say before asking his employees to meet at Tracy's office to discuss the situation.

Cari was still shaken, but there was less darkness in those beautiful eyes of hers this morning. Sleep was magical, dissolving the shock, allowing her to focus on her daily rhythm, which would help her stabilize and focus. Chase knew only too well what shock did; he'd gone through it many times. A part of him grew angry over Bannock. That little twerp needed to be apprehended. Well, he'd find out more this afternoon, and it couldn't come soon enough.

June 16

Cari sat next to Chase at a long, blond oak table, in the planning room at the sheriff's office. She saw Dan come in the door, dressed in his usual tan uniform. He nodded to them and kept the door open for the FBI agent. He wasn't as tall as Dan, but middle-aged, somewhat overweight, and had the beginning of jowls, making him look like a bulldog of sorts. He was dressed in a dark blue business suit that didn't exactly fit him, and he certainly wasn't what she thought an FBI agent should look like. What did the agency do? Drag the bottom of the barrel and send this guy? Her heart sank. She glanced over at Chase, and saw his eyes narrow on the agent. Sensing he wasn't impressed, either, she tried to swallow her disappointment.

The door shut and Dan introduced Agent Henry North to them. They sat down on the opposite side of the table, facing them. Dan reached across and gave each of them a sheaf of papers. Agent North had a tape recorder of sorts and set it between them. Dan had pulled out his notebook along with the copies he'd distributed. North had declined the notes. Cari wondered why. She sensed there was irritation or something between the agent and

Dan, but if there was, it wasn't obvious. Just a feeling or intuition.

"I'm going to lead off," Dan said, giving a nod to Agent North. "I've had a chance to look at what the FBI is providing, and that's what you'll see in those handouts I gave you."

Cari removed the cover. What stared back at her was Dirk. It was his prison picture, and it made her stomach clench in terror just to see his dark, angry-looking eyes. Dan went through his prison record, and it wasn't anything Cari hadn't heard before. Agent North, who sat opposite her, seemed bored, looking out the window, where some of the long, black plastic curtains had been pulled aside, so he could see the sky and some green landscape outside.

"Cari? If you have any questions or comments, please speak up," Dan said. "No one knowns Bannock like you do."

"So far," she said, "everything you've spoken about, I already know. But I will chime in if I think something is important."

"Do," Agent North grumbled. "After all, you are his sister."

Sitting up, Cari glared at the slovenly, heavy-lidded agent. "I'm afraid you have the wrong facts," she snapped. "Dirk is my stepbrother. There is no blood shared between us, Agent North."

Giving a one-shouldered shrug, North said nothing and looked down at his papers in front of him.

Her heart was pounding in her chest, her adrenaline up once again. She expected an FBI agent to be sharp, crisp, well dressed, handle him- or herself professionally and be fully informed. Anger surged through her. And then a helpless feeling followed because she realized for whatever reason, Agent North was nothing like how the FBI was treated in TV series. He was practically the opposite! And along with that depressing realization was that North didn't really seem to care why he was here, and he certainly didn't seem at all worried about her life, or the fact Dirk could kill people around her, or Chase himself. Those last two thoughts seared her heart.

"Agent North has requested a large, military drone, an unarmed one, which will come from the nearest air force military base, and we can begin to have eyes on the group, plus videotape them, as well as single photos."

"So," Cari demanded, "does that mean Dirk is still up in the woods with that group?"

"As far as we can tell," Dan said. "We have the license number of the vehicle they drove back into the logging road. I've had a deputy hidden on the other side of that road, where she can't be seen, and so far, nothing has come out except logging trucks."

"He's still with them," Chase concluded.

"My best guess is yes," Dan said. He took a map at the end of the table and spread it out, turning it around so Cari and Chase could look at it. "You can see there are seven dirt roads that have been cut into that mountainside by the logging companies." He placed his thumb on the map. "This is the road they turned in on yesterday. Below that logging area? It's fenced ranchland and belongs to about four different families. There are no roads from the trees above, down to their ranchland. There's only one exit/entrance for the logging companies and Hauptman, and it's this one." He tapped it with his index finger.

"How soon can we get eyes on that area?" Chase asked, buttonholing North.

"Maybe tomorrow. I'm in touch with the base commander on our request. It takes some time," North said.

Dan sat down. "Until we can get a drone circling at ten thousand feet above the area, I'm keeping a deputy watching that road for in-and-out traffic. I don't want to have Bannock give us the slip. And, Chase, we'll let you know the details once the drone is taking off."

"Thank you. It's a good plan," Chase congratulated Dan.

"What's to say Dirk couldn't leave on foot? Hitch a ride?" Cari wondered.

"Well, we've thought of that, too, Cari. My deputy has a set of binoculars. My deputies are pulling eight-hour shifts out there, and they check out who's in the cab of every logging truck that goes out, or comes in. We want to make sure there's no one other than the driver in it. And if there is? It will be radioed in to us here at headquarters, and we'll send out a cruiser to check it out."

Some relief flowed through Cari. "Dan, I'm so glad you're here helping us."

The ex-SEAL gave her a slight smile. "We want Bannock, too. He's a murderer and we know he'll shoot first and ask questions later. I have our SWAT team on alert, too, because if we have to pull that logging-truck driver over, and Bannock is there? He'll try to shoot his way out, is my opinion."

Cari rubbed her face, forcing back tears. "Dirk is

heartless. He'll kill without thinking. I'm glad to hear you have a SWAT team."

Dan nodded, grim.

"Agent North," Chase said, "what do you see happening with this issue?"

Cari turned to Chase, hearing challenge in his low tone, the utter seriousness of his expression. She felt his protection.

"Well, this isn't a straightforward plan to grab Bannock. It would turn into a war of attrition, and we'd have to have military with the FBI, a small army, to go wade into Hauptman's gang to find him. That means a lot of potential loss of our people's lives, a lot of wounded, and we do not want to take that step. Yet. Perhaps if Bannock was in a city and not out on the slopes of this mountain range with thirty other domestic terrorists all proclaiming they are white supremacists, I would have a better plan than we do, currently. Until, and if, we can separate Bannock from this domestic terrorism group, we're going to have to do surveillance from the sky and on the ground, in order to see what our options really are."

"That's good to hear," Chase said. "Are you in touch with Cari's family in California? Do they know Bannock is out here in Wyoming?"

"Yes, we are working closely with the sheriff of their county, and her parents have not only been notified, but an FBI agent has been assigned to their case and they will be kept up on what is going on."

"Do they have protection?" Cari demanded, urgency in her tone, her gaze riveted on North.

"We've talked to them about a couple of options. The

county sheriff doesn't have that kind of person power to plant one of his deputies out in front of their house twenty-four hours a day. We suggested they leave and go somewhere unknown until Bannock is caught."

"Not much of a choice," Chase growled, scowling.

North shrugged. "They could go into witness protection. And so could Ms. Taylor."

"That's a radical step," Chase challenged strongly, giving Cari a concerned look.

Dan sat up in his chair. "Look, we need to surveil. That's the first step. Cari? I'd urge you to stay on Chase's ranch and not go anywhere near town until we can apprehend Bannock. And for sure, that is our goal. It's a game of patience. We don't know if this is just a visit with Hauptman and his group, or if he's cementing permanent ties and a relationship with them, and he's planning to remain in this area. Until we do"—he leveled a serious look at her—"we can't afford to have you identified. Neither myself nor Agent North believes your cover was broken. If you need something in town? I'm sure Chase will make it happen."

"I will," Chase agreed grimly.

Cari sat up, her heart beginning a rapid beat. "Dan? What if I left the area? What if I went somewhere else and hid out?"

Instantly, Chase said, "You have the best protection right here, Cari. With me. With the ranch. There's no way Bannock or any of these wannabe white male racists, are getting onto Three Bars. You are as safe as you can possibly be with us."

Her heart tugged in her chest. She heard the barely held

emotion in his gruff tone. Giving him a look of apology, she said, "These are questions I have to ask. I know you want me to stay, but by doing so, I'm putting you and all your employees, and your mother, Mary, in danger."

Dan gave her a sympathetic look. "At this point, no matter where you go to hide, Dirk might find you. We know he's an ace hacker, a black hat. Both Agent North and myself believe he's hacked into his parents' computers and cell phones. We believe he is looking for you. Frankly"—he opened his hand—"sometimes it's better to be under the enemy's nose than trying to hide from him. It's stressful as hell, and we all realize it. But for you to leave the ranch right now, when you have the entire employee population on your side, extra sets of eyes and ears, I believe you're as safe as you can be under the circumstances."

She sat back, feeling like a balloon that has just been popped and is deflating. "I don't want to put anyone at risk just because of me, Dan. I—I couldn't live with that."

"The only other option available to you," Agent North said, "is going into the witness protection program. And if you do that? You can never be in touch with your parents again. Your whole life changes. Completely and forever."

Stubbornly shaking her head, Cari said strongly, "I'll *never* give up my career. And I'll *never* cut ties with my mother."

Shrugging, North said, "Well, your options are limited, then."

Chase reached out, gripping her hand. "I want you on my ranch. I can protect you there. My wranglers, for the most part, are ex-military. They're vets. They know and understand warfare, especially asymmetrical warfare like this is with Bannock right now. Your best defense, Cari, is a strong offense, and you have it here at Three Bars." He released her hand, giving her a pleading look. "You have an army of people who have your back. If you leave, if you try to disappear and go somewhere else? We can't protect you."

"Right now," Dan rasped, holding her gaze, "we are your best course of action. If that changes, we'll be the first to let you know. Chase used to be a sniper, constantly working in enemy territory. He knows the drill. Right now, I think you need to take a couple of slow, deep breaths, settle in with the stress that I know is surrounding you, and trust the people who honestly do have your back."

Cari nodded, forcing away the tears in her eyes. She didn't want them to fall. She hated that most men thought a woman's tears were a sign of weakness, when they were not. "So, stick close to home," she said.

Dan nodded. "And let's say, if this thing drags on, because it all hinges on what that drone can photograph, and you have a toothache or something and need to go to the dentist in town? Chase or someone he asks to go with you, will be in order. You go nowhere alone when you're off his ranch. Okay?"

"Got it," she said.

"We'll be in touch," Dan told them, rising.

Cari was glad to be out of the headquarters. The sunlight was bright and warm and felt life-giving to her. Chase walked at her side as they went around the building to the large parking lot.

"Waiting is the worse part," she muttered, giving him a glance.

"Always is. That's where patience pays off, but that's also where your brain becomes a rat trap and finds all kinds of crazy thoughts to bring up to you while you wait."

"Ugh," she said, opening the door to the truck, "tell me about it!" She noticed that Chase was behaving a little differently. It was subtle, and if she didn't know him as well as she did, she probably wouldn't have given it a second thought. As she climbed in, she asked, "What are you doing?" She saw his eyes sparkle.

"Just sussing out the area," he said, shutting her door.

When he climbed in, she persisted. "Can you teach me what you're doing?"

He belted up and started the truck engine. "It takes years to be hyperalert. That's what you are sensing around me."

"I'm sensing something, but I can't quantify it," she admitted.

"Something like having eyes in the back of your head," he teased, giving her a quick glance before he pulled out onto the main highway.

"Oh . . . Well, you taught me how to walk silently. Why can't I learn to do what you do?"

"We'll try it. Maybe tomorrow? What's on your schedule?"

It felt good to Cari to be talking about normal business and work with Chase. It settled her, and her stress began to slowly ebb out of her. He had been right. A human's daily rhythm led to less stress, not more. It was a known quantity, familiar, and in her case, she felt very lucky that her job was something she loved so deeply: her beekeeping activities. "Theresa and I are meeting at nine a.m. and we're driving around to all four hive platforms for our weekly maintenance checks. I'll be making up a lunch and taking it out on the job with me."

"Be sure to take the ranch radio with you," he said.

"For sure." She looked out the window at how beautiful the world looked and how awful she felt inwardly. "I just want to keep busy, Chase. That will help me so much."

"I agree. Our daily rhythm is the best place to be when something as traumatic as this slams into your life. What can I do to help you?"

For a moment, Cari didn't know what to answer, afraid and yet wanting so badly to let Chase know how much . . . well . . . that she was falling in love with him. How would he take such an admission? She wasn't sure whether he felt the same way or not—or if he was like so many other males in her past who saw her only as a sex partner, and that was it. That's not what she wanted. Not at all. She'd made her mistakes, and she'd learned from them. Getting older gave her a level of experience that saved her from making them again, and also a maturity within herself of knowing what was really important to her, and what was not.

Turning, she studied his rugged profile as he drove. "That's something we both need to discuss, maybe me more than you."

"Want to talk about it when we get home? Or are you feeling exhausted and want to do it another time?"

"I feel okay, better actually. And yes, I'd like to talk once we get home." She changed topics, not wanting to pursue something so intimate and private with him in the truck. "I really like Dan. He's cool, calm, and collected, just like you. And he has that deep background in black ops, like you. I don't think I could get two better men to be at my side with this all happening."

"I saw the look on your face when North came in," he said, his mouth twitching. Slowing down, he turned into the ranch road.

"Oh . . . Well, I wish I wasn't so readable."

"It was subtle," he assured her with a chuckle. "What was your assessment of North?"

"On a scale of one to ten? With ten being he rocked it out of the park? I give him a four. I thought most FBI people were a decent weight because they had to run down suspects and things like that. I don't think North could do a fifty-yard dash in a minute. I was really disappointed, Chase, but maybe I know next to nothing about the FBI."

"You're right on all accounts. North has two months until he retires after thirty years with the FBI."

Her voice came out flat. "Oh. Well, that explains it." Brows dipping, her tone rough with emotion, she added, "Do Dan or you have any faith in this guy, then? Can you ask for him to be replaced? It's like he's just going through the motions. He seems somewhere else, not fully focused on us and my situation."

"Right on all accounts," Chase agreed. "But knowing Dan, who knows the military chain-of-command, which is very similar to the FBI, if North falls down on what he's promised to give us, like the drone, you can bet he's going to be calling North's supervisor and run it up their command structure until he gets what he wants."

"And if that fails?"

"Well, one thing you have to know about SEALs . . . they always have plan B, C, and D."

"Do you?"

"Absolutely. But we'll wait and see if North delivers. If he does? Then all the drone photography can be sent not only to the field office but directly into one of the sheriff's computers. We'll see that video at the same time. Dan is calling in the two logging company owners this afternoon to talk with them, and bring them in on the fact they've got thirty or so domestic terrorists in the area where they are logging. He can't leave them open to harm, either. And in doing this, Dan may get further information that will help us to find, first, Hauptman and his gang, but also find out whether Bannock is there with him still. Or not."

He parked in front of the ranch house. Unstrapping the seat belt, he looked over at her. "I don't know about you, but I could use a cup of good, hot coffee right now. Are you game?"

"Am I ever." She hesitated after opening the door. "Maybe then we could talk?"

"Sure. There's some leftover scones I made earlier. I'll pull out the cherry jam and we'll have some."

Smiling, Cari slipped down to the gravel. "You have such a sweet tooth, Chase."

"And that's just one more reason to like me?" he teased, grinning.

"I think we're about to find out," Cari said, her voice

low, but filled with hope. Did he love her? Was it all in her imagination? She loved him. Where was this talking going to go? The worst-case scenario for Cari was that to Chase, she was nothing more than an appreciated employee—and that was all. That would be devastating to her.

Chapter Eleven

June 16

Chase tried to rein in a sudden emotional crisis within himself. Finally, they were going to talk about a personal relationship with one another. Or was there really anything there?

He was making coffee for them and Cari was in her bedroom, changing clothes. Trying desperately to keep his expectations to little more than a friendship that Cari wanted, versus what he wanted, Chase could not tame his fears, or his anxiety over what she might say. This was so damned hard! He flicked on the switch, the coffee machine doing its thing. Glancing toward the hall where the bedrooms were located, he saw her door was still closed.

What was Cari feeling? Thinking? How much would she lay on the table between them? That one, long, heartfelt embrace he'd had with her stirred powerfully in his heart and mind, never allowing him to forget it. Hell, he didn't want to *ever* forget it! But, maybe she did. Maybe, in a moment of weakness, she'd capitulated to do something far more intimate with him because she simply needed human compassion and care, not something originating out of a growing love for him.

Rubbing his chest, he set the table with turquoise-blue placemats, a spoon, and the creamer and sugar bowl from the Willow Blue set. Plus, linen napkins of the same color. Mary had taught him well.

The air felt charged, electric, to Chase. He felt as if his entire focus was narrowing, like a sniper shot, into one of the most important moments of his life: How did Cari see him? Did she want more than an employee relationship with him? If so, then what? He saw so many hurdles that had to be jumped, if she did. She was her own woman and she was struggling with a nearly incomprehensible life-and-death situation. Warning himself that he shouldn't expect very much from her due to her present dire situation, he tried to dial back his own personal need for her. It wasn't fair to Cari to try and talk about such intimate things at a time like this. But he wasn't going to say no to it, either.

He heard the bedroom door open, and looked over. Cari had changed into her normal beekeeping attire. Understanding that her rhythm of daily life was helping her to stabilize, he studied her expression. Her cinnamon-colored eyes were darker than normal, but hell, after that meeting with Dan and North, why wouldn't they be? Nothing had been resolved, everything was murky and unsure. None of her angst and terror of Bannock coming after her, had been settled at all.

He pulled out her chair where she usually sat for dinner. "Have a seat," he invited. "I'll get the coffee. Would you like the scones?"

She shook her head, sitting down. "No, I'm not hungry."

"I don't know who would be after that meeting," he said, giving her an understanding look.

"It wasn't very helpful, but it's still a step in the right direction," she murmured, moving the linen napkin and opening it across her lap. "What did you think of it, Chase?"

He set the Blue Willow pattern cup and saucer in front of her and then sat down, opposite her. "It's a start." He hesitated. "Where do you want to begin, regarding us?" He was careful not to say *relationship* because she'd not defined it that way. Instantly, she closed her eyes, but then she lifted her chin, opened them, and fearlessly held his gaze.

"I don't know why the most important things to us, as human beings, are so hard to talk about."

He grimaced and nodded. "Because we're afraid of what the other person might say? Afraid of being rejected? Not agreeing with how we see something?"

"You should have been a therapist, Chase." She managed a thin smile, sipping her coffee, sliding her slender hands around the fragile cup.

"Blame my mother, Mary. She reinforced, from the time I can remember, to look into *why* a person said or did something, not to judge it, but try to understand the reasons behind the action or reaction."

"Right now? My heart is beating so hard in my chest with fear, that I think I'm going to die of a heart attack," she admitted.

"Mine's not exactly thumping slowly, either," he said, nodding. "Tell me what's on your mind . . ."

She hesitated, took a deep breath, and whispered,

"It's more about my heart, my feelings, Chase, than a mind thing."

He took a chance and said quietly, "So's mine, Cari. You're not a mind thing in my life, you're a heart thing, if you want to put it that way." Instantly he saw the tension in her face begin to melt away. Her eyes widened as she stared over at him, somewhat shocked.

"Truly?"

"I'll never lie to you," he said. "Never have and never will. Ever since I saw you at the airport, Cari, my heart was in the mix. At first, I told myself it was because you are such an incredibly beautiful human being, your kindness and understanding of life in general. The way you look at the bees under your care, your openness with not only me, but everyone. We have all flourished since you came here, whether you realized it or not."

"No . . . I didn't realize that."

"Probably because you've been running for your life, don't you think?"

She sipped her coffee. "Yes, it's overshadowed my whole life and being, since Dirk broke out of prison." Her voice changed and grew soft with emotion. "Except, when I met you at the airport, Chase, it was the first time I actually felt safe. Oh, I know there's this thing that women have to be protected, that they are helpless, and that is stupid patriarchal crap, but what I felt pouring off you was like a warm, stabilizing blanket around my being. As if you sensed or knew on some level of yourself that I was scared and running."

His heart began to slow its beat. "That's because, right or wrong, I did want to protect you. I don't know," he said wryly, "whether a man's response to protect is part of his

DNA or we all got brainwashed by the patriarchy male BS from birth onward." He saw something he'd glimpsed only a few times before in her large, wide, intelligent eyes: an emotion he couldn't name, but it sure felt damn good to see the *way* she was looking at him, softly holding his gaze. He forced himself to sip his coffee.

"You haven't tried to smother me, which is the experience I've had in the past with men in other relationships. By the time I was twenty-five, I was tired of it. Women can't do this, they can't do that, blah, blah, blah. This is a man's job. Only a man can do it." She snorted. "Please."

"My sense of protection toward you was because I sensed your being upset at the airport and I didn't know where it was coming from, or why."

"But you didn't try to do anything. I certainly didn't feel smothered by you."

He grimaced. "Whether I want to admit it or not, I've had some women in my life, from my past, that kicked my ass sideways about it. I've never married, but I had two serious relationships, both in the Marine Corps, which looking back on it, were bound to fail. I was out on missions in enemy territory probably seventy-five percent of my time in the Corps. That didn't leave room for any kind of relationship to grow."

"What did these two women teach you?" she asked. "I know the three relationships I had each taught me something; usually what I *didn't* want in a man."

"Well, my first serious relationship was with Hannah. She was one of the first women snipers in the Marine Corps. We met in Afghanistan, stationed at the same top secret installation in-country. She was fearless, damned intelligent, and I fell for her like fifty tons of rocks. I'd never been around a wholly independent, confident woman like her before."

"She was matriarchal, then?"

"Yes, at least by the present-day definition. That's how we met, at a cantina, going in to get a cold beer after coming in from different ops, and I saw her at the bar. She was utterly fearless. Completely, fiercely independent, and blew off guys like someone flicking an irritating fly buzzing around their head. I watched her in action with a number of men, mesmerized. She was sitting with another woman who was also in the Corps, but not a sniper. She ran Comms for our top-secret base, and they were the only two women on our small base. Thoughtless marines would approach both of them and they just blew them off. I found out later that the Comms officer was married and had two young children at home that her husband was taking care of."

"Hannah drew you because she was independent?"

He scratched his head. "Well . . . sort of. To me, she was like a star person, an alien female dropped in from another world into ours." He managed a wry glance. "I was fascinated with her. She didn't need anyone. She certainly didn't need a man. Or at least, the men who were, what she called, Neanderthals and patriarchal."

"Ah, so Hannah was completely matriarchal. If she was using that kind of language, she understood the difference, like I do."

"I'd never heard the word *patriarchy* before that. Hell, I had no idea what it meant. The only reason I heard it was one marine sergeant went over to hit on her and she let him have it, calling him a patriarchal Neanderthal. I had to go back to my room, go google the term in order to understand it. That sergeant didn't know what she was talking about, either."

"Of course he didn't."

"Is that why your relationships didn't work out?"

"Yes, all of them. After the third try, I just gave up. That was at twenty-five. I found my life just went better by avoiding males of the patriarchy, at least, on a personal footing. I had to work with them all the time in my career. After a while, it gets exhausting to deal with it day in and day out. That's when I decided to create my own beekeeping consulting firm. "

"Hannah taught me to put myself in a woman's place. God knows, we had a lot of hotheaded arguments about it, but in the end, I had to agree with her. Women do have it tough. They are suppressed by males. They are underpaid. Underacknowledged in every possible way. And often unsung, whether as artists, inventors, scientists . . . "

"Sounds like you had a pretty educational relationship with her," Cari noted.

"I did. Hannah didn't give an inch on her expecting me to treat her as an equal. She was, by the way, our *best* sniper in the Corps to date. She was good at her job. Even the Marine sniper school agrees that women make better snipers."

"Why did you break up?"

"Our jobs as snipers. We never had a chance to have backwater weeks to truly enjoy and do things together as a couple. We were both too good at what we did, so we were in constant demand."

"What about now?" Cari asked quietly.

"Hannah was killed in combat," he offered sadly, shaking his head. "I remember finding out about a month after my own mission in south Afghanistan was completed. We maintain radio silence with our base when we're out on an op. You know nothing about anything until you're coming in off that mission, Cari."

"That had to be a terrible jolt to you."

"It was," he admitted. "I really loved her and she loved me, but it was like putting two mismatched pieces together in a war-torn country where our lives were always on the line."

"I'm sorry."

"Thanks," he said, sitting back, studying her. "But let's get back to us. It was patriarchal men that turned you off?"

"Yes, totally. Women are taking back their power, Chase. We're not cute, cuddly sex toys for the boys anymore. We're intelligent, we're creative, we have a sense of ourselves, and we're assertive and going after what we want as in no other time."

"You are all of that," he agreed. "In some ways, you remind me of Hannah, but a softer version of her. She was in your face in a heartbeat." He smiled in remembrance. "She took no prisoners. You, on the other hand, seem very tolerant of the men around the ranch here."

"I think that's because of you, Chase."

"How do you mean?"

Opening her hands, she said, "I'm sure your father had a lot to do with how you saw yourself as a man, but your mother, Mary, sure sounds a lot like Hannah. She doesn't tolerate fools or the patriarchy, either."

He chuckled. "No, she never did. And it was my mother who did more to change my attitude toward women than my father. He still had patriarchy in his veins. Fortunately, he was smart enough to realize Mary was a self-made, confident, full-steam-ahead kind of woman and he made sure he didn't get in her way." Mouth quirking, he slid her a glance. "With you? I try to stay out of your way. And to be honest, a lot of what Hannah taught me when I was young and stupid, I use with you."

"That explains to me, at least, why half your wrangling crew consists of women."

"Right," he agreed. "I find women often pay more attention to details than men. It doesn't mean men can't learn that. They can. It's just that they have to work at it a long time to reach that bar that women so easily leap over. That's why Hannah was a superstar in the Marine Corps as a sniper. She paid attention to the details."

"How did she die, if you don't mind telling me?"

"A B-52 bomber dropped its load of bombs in the area where she was hiding to take out a HVT, high value target."

"Oh, no!" she whispered. Her hands pressed to her lips. "Oh, how awful!"

"Hannah was a friendly-fire casualty. It sickened me when I got back to base and was informed of her death. Everyone at the base was in shock over it."

"I can't imagine how you felt," she whispered, giving him a sympathetic look.

"Totally destroyed," he admitted. "Her body had already been flown stateside and she was buried with honors at Arlington National Cemetery in Washington, D.C. I drove to her parents' home in the Pocono Mountains of Pennsylvania, and they asked me to stay and I did. We spent a week together and I think what I shared about her and myself, helped them. Our missions are top secret, so we can never talk about them to anyone, Cari. I was able to give her grieving, devastated parents a side of Hannah they could know. Going there to see them was healing for all of us, especially me."

"I wish I'd known her," Cari said. "We women can use role models like Hannah who are staunchly matriarchal. She could have taught us so much about ourselves, how to conduct ourselves out in the world, and in personal relationships. She truly is missed."

He nodded, sipping his coffee. "I rebounded by getting into another relationship, and it was way too soon, I was still grieving, and it didn't go well or last long. If I'd been smarter, more mature, I suppose, I'd have waived off that relationship because I was simply not ready for it, whether I knew it or not."

"And you left the Marine Corps?"

"At twenty-six. My enlistment was up. I didn't want any more war. I came home. Mary was running the ranch by herself because my father had died at age forty-five of a heart attack. She was having problems handling a ranch and a huge grocery store in Silver Creek. For two years, she taught me the ropes of running Three Bars. At twenty-eight, she legally handed it over to me to run, and that's what I've been doing ever since, for the last two years. It's freed her up, and you can see her creative decisions are really good ones. I learn from her every day."

"Women's capacity to see overall patterns?"

"That's a good way of putting it," Chase agreed. "Mary is really good at seeing that, but so are you, Cari. You've got your own consulting firm. That takes a visionary with the ability to ground it and make it work."

"I got tired of men stepping into my path to try and control or direct me when I knew better," she said.

"That is one of the many things I like about you is your belief in yourself."

"My mother was instrumental in that, but so was my dad. When he died, my mother and I were devastated. He was ahead of his time, Chase, just like you. I think there is a very small percentage of males on this Earth who were raised matriarchal and taught to value and respect women just as they would any man. That's the way you treat me, and I've got to tell you, it's an aphrodisiac in some sense, to me."

He grinned.

She lifted her index finger. "Be careful, Chase. I'm not using the word *aphrodisiac* in a sexual way. Okay?"

He laughed and held up his hands. "Busted. Okay, so you're using the term to refer to something that gives you joy?"

"Ecstasy," she said.

"I won't go into the sexual meaning of that word, either," he said teasingly.

"As long as you realize the difference. I'm not flirting with you. I'm using words that mean something important to me, but all words, as you know, have layers and levels of meaning, depending upon the person and how they receive them."

"One of the many things that has drawn me to you, Cari," he admitted, his voice low. "I'm glad we're here, sitting down, talking about this . . . us . . . in an adult fashion. I'm scared inside, but I need to share how I feel about you. And I'm not sure if you'll be comfortable with it or not. I'm afraid of rejection, like anyone, but I'm more afraid by opening up to you, that you'll leave and never come back."

She sat up, her elbows on the table, watching him intently. "Like I said earlier, the hardest thing in the world for me is a personal relationship. And I'm feeling just as afraid as you are right now."

He sat back, frowning. "Why?"

"Before I saw Dirk come in that restaurant? I was constantly telling myself to stop being drawn to you, Chase. I didn't come here thinking about a relationship. My life was fine without a man in it until I met you."

"What was the draw, Cari?"

"How you treat me as an equal. You never placed your hand on me in a way that made me feel like I was being stalked or seen as a sexual object, or not being respected as a human being." She took a deep breath and looked away for a moment. Finally, she met his intent gaze. "This may sound totally bizarre to you, Chase, but I think I'm falling for you. It wasn't on purpose. It has happened little by little, every day in small, everyday things that showed me how much I looked forward to being around you." She turned and pointed down the hall. "I loved the thought of waking up and seeing you out here in the kitchen, making us breakfast in the morning. Or to be with you out at the hives, or talking over possibilities of other crops that the bee nation loves. You have so many good ideas and I always appreciate how you see the world, and how it touches you daily. Being with you makes me feel good. Even hopeful, despite Dirk being on the loose."

"Thanks for sharing that with me," he said, giving her a relieved look. "Ever since you came here, Cari, I've felt lighter and happier than I've ever been. At first, I didn't know why, but later, in quiet moments when I was alone, I began to ask myself why being with you did that to me. Over time, I realized I was falling for you in a serious way. At first, that shook the hell out of me because I was *not* looking for a relationship, either. I was involved in work, keeping the ranch in the black, and liking what I did." He gave her a look of awe. "You were like fog stealing into my world and you changed it, Cari. I know you weren't doing it on purpose. I know you were completely immersed in your job, and I liked that you loved your bees and cared for them so deeply. That drew my heart out and I began to see things, or try to, through your eyes. I wanted what you already had, that fey, mystical, otherworldly way of living and seeing life. It appealed so strongly to me, the connection you have with what is invisible, but is all around us. Mary calls it energy, and says that it's everywhere. I used to scoff at her as a kid, but later, as a sniper, I came to realize just how much I was connected to the unseen, becoming part of it, and surviving things I shouldn't have because I trusted it completely." He cleared his throat. "Just as I see you with your bees, who obviously adore you as much as you do them. That first time when I saw those bees fly to your shoulder, they seemed to be one with you. I fell for your magic then, Cari. Who *you* are. And no, I didn't want to change one thing about you. Rather, I wanted to be around you whenever I could, to learn about you, how you are a part of Nature, of that invisible yet very real energy Mary always talks about."

"I do live in that world, Chase. My mother is that way, too. Maybe it's our DNA. I don't know."

"Well, whatever it is, to me, I call that magic. And

you're magic to me." He touched his heart. "As scared as I am, I'll admit that I've never been more serious with a woman than you. You're like fog, disappearing under the sun's rays, but then you come back in the coolness of evening, the mist reminding me so much of the Earth magic that surrounds us."

"That's beautiful . . . I mean, how you see me. I guess I'm not aware of that, Chase, because I live in it." She smiled a little. "And as scared as I am? I'll admit that I'm powerfully drawn to you. I like your 'live and let live' attitude toward everyone. The people you employ respect you, like you, and I see it all the time. I'm afraid of relationships because I've chosen three patriarchal men three times now."

"But it sounds as if those men in your life didn't respect you, tried to remold you into the way they see all women. And you just wouldn't be put back into a box. Am I right?"

"I hadn't thought of it in those terms, but you're right. I was always in arguments with all of them, that a woman shouldn't do this or that. They wanted to shelter me, keep me as a pet on a leash. At least, that's how I felt."

"I hope I don't make you feel that way."

"No, not at all. You give me the freedom I need. I won't stay around a man anymore, even in business, if he won't treat me with respect and as an equal. Most of my clients are women, because I demand that fairness across the board."

"Did you feel like you were taking a chance with me? I was an unknown male."

"Yes, but remember? I had talked to Mary a number of times before. She spoke well of you and she is certainly fully matriarchal in every way. I found myself making the easy decision to choose your ranch because of that. I was hopeful that since you are Mary's son, that you were probably brought up to be more matriarchal than most men." She managed a one-cornered smile. "I was betting on it."

"Did the bet pay off?" he teased, grinning with her.

"Yes, it did. I'm feeling very rich right now. How about you?"

"The same." He sat up, clasping his hands and setting them on the table. "Where do you see us going, Cari?"

She raised her brows. "Oh, gosh, Chase, that's such a tough question to answer right now. Dirk is in the area. I had a near miss with him that still scares me every time I think about it." She opened her hands in frustration. "What I want and what is happening are diametric opposites. I have to focus on Dirk. I can't focus on you like I want."

"Hmmm, it's pretty much the same for me, Cari. Because I feel deeply for you, want to pursue a relationship with you on your time and needs, but Dirk is the issue I have to focus on instead."

"I understand," she answered, sadness in her tone. "Ever since he came into my life, he's always caused me trouble and fear. I thought that it would change when we got older. When they imprisoned him, I finally felt free for the first time in a long, long time. And then, he broke out of prison and I'm right back in this claustrophobic, hour-by-hour effort to live and not die."

"Not a good time for either of us to pursue a relationship," he agreed darkly, scowling. "But it seems to be growing between us, despite the circumstances. Wouldn't you agree?"

"Yes, despite what's going on, it certainly is."

He studied her, his voice low. "Cari, you walked into my life and you've been like sunlight coming into a darkness, a loneliness I've carried with me for a long time. I don't feel alone anymore. I feel like you see me, the human being. I find that so refreshing. You're something I've needed but I didn't know it until you walked into my life." He opened his hands, holding her glistening gaze. "I have *no* idea where we are going with one another. I didn't from the time I met you until today. It's a relief to know we're feeling similarly about one another, but our lives are in jeopardy and I'm not going to lie or shade that truth from you. Every day, I wake up scared that I'll lose you either to Dirk or because I've failed you or disappointed you."

She reached out, gripping his calloused, worn hand. "You have *never* disappointed me, Chase. Not *ever*. I've never been in a relationship with a man where I feel no pressure from him to be or do something for him that I don't want to do—until now. This is new to me, too." Her fingers tightened around his. "I'm just as scared as you are for the very same reasons. My imagination runs rampant and I have a tough time being mature and logical, but eventually, I calm down and I see things for what they are, not what I imagine them to be in a dark, threatening way. I worry more that something terrible will happen and you'll die and I'll be without you." She released his hand.

"Your fears are the same as mine. I find myself wanting to be overly protective of you, hide you away, keep you safe, but I also have to respect what you need to do, too."

"I listen closely to your ideas, Chase. I'm fine here on the ranch. I don't need to go into town. I feel safe here. You make me feel safe."

"Until we can get Dirk out of our lives or get him back into prison, we aren't going to have much of a life that we can concentrate on with one another, Cari."

"I realize that. I'm more scared of what I don't know than what I do."

"I wish you were a fortune teller," he teased gently, running his fingers down her lower arm and hooking her fingers with his. "But neither of us can predict the future. All we can do is work with Dan and this FBI agent. And take reasonable precautions." He squeezed her fingers. "Promise me one thing, though?"

"What?"

"Always tell me what you want or need from me, Cari. I'm not a mind reader. Sometimes I think I know what you're telling me with your eyes, the way you give me a certain look, but I'm never sure."

"Then ask me. Science says that our communication is seventy percent nonverbal and that only thirty percent is verbal. That's why the need to talk openly with one another is crucial."

Nodding, he said, "I'll try to be more open with you from now on."

"I know guys are drilled with being closemouthed about their emotions, but to allow our budding relationship to move forward, I need that from you, Chase. Never be afraid of asking me something or sharing something of yourself with me. I'm so thirsty for a man who can give-and-take in that way. I want you to be that man. It's like breathing clean air from my side of things."

"I know women have no problem telling their girlfriends about how they feel and that men avoid emotions like the plague with one another, never mind with the woman in their life. I'm not great at that, yet, but I'll get better. Just give me a chance, Cari?"

"You've got it." Her voice grew hoarse. "And you have my promise, I'll always be honest and up front with you, Chase . . ."

The wall phone rang.

Chapter Twelve

June 16

Chase gave Cari an apologetic look. "I have to get that. Usually if the wall phone rings, one of my wranglers needs something." He pushed the chair away. Reaching out, he brushed her cheek momentarily, and gave her a look he hoped she could interpret as his love for her. His chest felt like it might explode with unparalleled joy. Wrestling with his happiness, he forced himself to focus on the phone ringing.

"Chase here," he growled.

"Hey, it's Jenny, Chase. I just got a call from a raptor center in Southern California. They called and asked me if we had any young red-tailed hawks who were air worthy and if they could ask us to drive the raptor out to them. They are low on red-tailed hawks in their area and need an infusion of one or two young ones to take over the territory. Are you interested in doing this, Chase? I can't do it with my workload, but maybe you're free to take a trip over there with our Wild Child?" She laughed.

"Sure, we've done it before. When do they want Wild Child?"

"Well, sooner, not later. They said they have a male red-tail, but his mate was killed and they need a replacement."

"Call them back and ask when they'd like the hawk."

"Sure. Thanks!"

Chase hung up and turned, telling Cari about it. "What do you think? Would you like to drive over with me? Wild Child loves you. How about it?"

Raising her brows, Cari stood up, taking their empty china from the table. "Well . . . what about what's going on here? With Dirk?"

Shrugging, Chase said, "He doesn't know you're here. We can leave just before dawn, under cover of night, and take Wild Child to that center. It will be a week-long trip because we're going to have to find a raptor center along the way to put Wild Child up for the night and we'll find a nearby motel. It might take us a little longer because raptor places aren't exactly profuse in any state."

She set the cups in the sink and rinsed them out. "That sounds almost heavenly to me. Our honey collection is due at the end of June, but Theresa is fully capable of handling it if the supers are all filled in the hives. She and her family can do that." She turned, watching him walk toward her. "What about you? Can you be gone from the ranch that long?"

"Sure," he said, halting before her. "Tracy knows how to run the ranch without me. Besides, we'll always be in phone contact with one another if something serious happens."

"What about Dan? What if he calls and we're not here?"

"I'll give him our cell phone numbers. If anything happens, he'll be in touch with us, for sure. Plus, we'll give him the number to reach at the raptor center."

Compressing her lips, she closed her eyes for a moment, taking a ragged breath. Opening them, she gazed up at him. "This sounds like a wonderful vacation of sorts, just you and me."

"And don't forget Wild Child," he said, grinning. "She's a handful."

"Yes, our little Valkyrie, for sure," Cari said, managing a slight smile.

"Well? How about it? Maybe this is a heaven-sent break for you? Wouldn't you like to get away from where Dirk is presently at?"

She rested her hips against the counter, hands clasped in front of her. "Not only that, Chase, but what's the chances of us driving to visit my mother after delivering Valkyrie to the raptor center? I'd love nothing more than to see her in person."

He frowned, thinking about it for a moment. "I think it can be done, but that's going to take some prior planning because Dirk's drug gang is in that same area. Maybe we could arrange something where your mother leaves in the dark of night and drives to a place where we're staying. I can be your big, bad guard dog and your security while you're together. I don't trust druggies. I had plenty of run-ins with them in Afghanistan. In fact, about half of my kills were drug smugglers. Opium is big in that country and they are smuggling it across it to Pakistan, where it gets sold and sent to all points on the compass."

"That sounds even better," Cari said, suddenly hopeful and excited. "I can be with you, too."

"Yes, I was thinking about that. This could give us a chance to keep talking and not always having this dangerous situation hanging over us. I like the idea. We'll take Wild Child in a cage that we can put in the back seat of the truck. Then, we'll take breaks on the trip out, between you and me, fly her on a creance line, and feed her. She's used to flying every day. And if they're going to release her, then she really does need to keep up her daily flight schedule."

"We'll definitely keep her on a creance line between us," Cari said. "Because she's going to be in new territory, and if there's a raptor flying around, she might take off with him or they might get into a territorial flight, so I don't want her flying free."

"I agree," he said, feeling as if his whole world had lightened up. He smiled down at her. "Your mother doesn't know you've cut your hair and it's now a red color. You'd better prepare her, huh?"

Laughing, almost giddy, Cari said, "You're right! She's going to faint, Chase. She has beautiful black, shining hair like me, and it's down to her waist! I really should prepare her or she will go into shock."

"I think it will be good for both of you to see one another. We can find a secure location, and I'm sure the county sheriff will work with Dan, here in Silver Creek, and he'll get a plan set up where you two could safely meet."

She shook her head, giving him a look of awe. "All of a sudden, out of all this horrible darkness and threat comes good news. Wild Child gets her freedom. We get some wonderful time alone with one another and we don't have to be looking over our shoulders. And I get to see my mom!" Tears came to her eyes and she sniffed, wiping them away.

"Hey," he murmured, opening his arms, "it's okay to cry, Cari. You're under one helluva strain. Tears are good. Didn't you know?" He saw something in her glistening eyes as she came wordlessly into his arms, wrapping hers tightly around his torso. Groaning, he felt so good having her lean body against his, her cheek against his chest. Resting his chin lightly against the top of her silky hair, Chase murmured, "This is a real blessing. Someone's looking out for us, for sure."

Nodding, Cari closed her eyes, the tears continuing to leak beneath her lashes. "Just hearing your heart beat against my ear, makes my heart feel like it's going to burst, Chase . . ." She hugged him as tightly as she could.

"I like what we have, sweetheart." He pressed a kiss to her hair, inhaling the scent of her that filled him with such longing. How badly he wanted to consummate their relationship, but he knew he had to wait. Cari would let him know when that time had come. And more than anything, Chase wanted this relationship to go right, not wrong. Hannah had been a great guide to him emotionally and teaching him how to please a woman first, not himself. With Cari, now, he could share himself fully with her. That day would come . . .

He felt Cari's arms loosening and he opened his to allow her to step away from him. Her cheeks were glistening with spent tears and he reached for a box of tissues that was always on the kitchen counter. "Here," he rasped, handing her some.

"Th-thanks." She blotted her eyes.

"I hope the day comes," he told her quietly, holding

her gaze, "when it will be me kissing those tears away. You've been alone in this fight for a long time by yourself." He brushed a few red strands of hair away that had stuck to her temple. "I want to be the one who is there to protect you when it's needed, love you until you know how much you are a part of my heart, and then, we can face this world of ours together, stronger than ever . . ."

June 17

"Are you ready?" Chase asked Cari as they neared the ranch truck they would be driving to the Madre Tierra Raptor Center. She had worn her normal ranch outfit, her baseball cap on her head, a pair of sunglasses sitting on the front of her cap, and a short-sleeved dark green T-shirt with jeans. He was pretty much wearing the same type of clothing, although he always wore tough canvas long-sleeved cowboy shirts with the sleeves rolled up to just below his elbows.

It was cool at four in the morning, the stars twinkling above them in the darkened heavens. The weather was good, a front having passed through the area yesterday, giving them rain. He had put two jackets in the rear seat, just in case. Valkyrie was quiet in her travel cage, the specially made tarp covering all of it so she couldn't see out and get her feathers in a ruffle. She had drinking water in the cage, so she was set. Chase had put rubber ties to the bottom of the cage and anchored them so it wouldn't slide around, frightening the raptor unnecessarily.

He had transported raptors before, and Jenny had a special cage for just such events, made a long time ago.

All of the hawk's food—mouse and quail meat—were in a small ice chest, on the floor in the rear of the cab.

"Am I ever," Cari said, opening the door and climbing in. She shut the door quietly so as not to scare the raptor, and belted up. Chase slid in, also careful to shut the door quietly, as well. "This feels like I'm running away, but I don't care."

He nodded and started up the super cab. "Dan said the FBI is still collecting data from the military drone that went online yesterday and stayed on station for five hours above the area where they think Hauptman's gang is. We aren't going to know much for a while, so I'm glad we're leaving. Tracy will take care of the ranch and Mary is always there in case something happens. My mother will run the place until we return."

He eased the truck out of the gravel parking lot, the parking lights on, but not the headlights. At this time of morning, there was no traffic on the ranch at all and Chase was in security mode where Cari was concerned. If Dirk did know she was at the ranch, he would probably have someone, if not himself, watching the place for anyone coming or going from Three Bars. He'd told Cari what he was going to do and as they neared the main highway, she unbuckled and lay down on the seat. Chase had taught her that druggies often had infrared or other night-seeing devices that could pick up how many people were inside a vehicle. He wasn't taking chances. He had Cari lie down on the seat so it would appear that he was the only person in the truck. No one would suspect that Cari was in the truck, if they were being watched.

Once he made a turn to the right, heading out of town toward the interstate, he told her she could sit back up.

Glancing often into his rearview mirror for any headlights following him, the place remained dark behind them. That was good.

Cari turned in the seat, making sure that Valkyrie's crate was fine. The hawk was quiet, but she ran her fingers across the fabric to make sure. Everything was perfect. She turned around and sat down. "Oh!" she whispered, pointing upward, "I love looking at the stars through the sunroof."

"It's a pretty pre-dawn sky," he agreed, setting his cruise control.

Cari moved her feet around. "Tell me what these 'go-bags,' as you call them, really are."

"Why? Are they crowding your foot space?" he asked.

"No, they're fine. Just big and lumpy." They were two tan canvas knapsacks that Chase had filled last evening. She'd been busy packing her clothes in a small suitcase, which was in the rear of the truck beneath a canvas tarp, along with his. They were strapped down so they couldn't fly out.

"It's an old habit of anyone who has worked in intel or undercover," he told her, his one hand on the wheel, the other resting on the door arm. "You pack something small and leave it by your door so that in case there's a siren announcing a rocket or missile attack coming in, you grab it and go, running for the nearest safe place, like an underground shelter."

She reached down, feeling how lumpy the one closest to her booted ankle was. "What did you pack? Water and food?"

"There's a Glock 18 pistol in both of them, with plenty of ammunition," he warned her.

Instantly, Cari jerked her hand away and sat up. "Oh? But why would you pack two weapons, Chase? I thought we were safe. That Dirk is probably still behind us somewhere in that logging area in the mountains."

"Well," he said, glancing at her, the soft light from the dashboard showing her worried features, "we don't know *where* he is, Cari. And until we do? I'm not taking chances."

She sat back, feeling utterly deflated. "And I was so happy we were escaping . . . leaving him behind."

Reaching over, he gripped her hands, which were knotted in her lap. "It's just a safety measure, Cari. That's all. I can't have spent years of surviving out in the Sandbox of Afghanistan and not have learned something important from it." He released her hands. "I don't want you worrying. You don't have to. I'm in guard-dog mode from here on out. All I want you to do is be happy that Dirk is more than likely behind us and that we're heading west. We'll drop Valkyrie off at that raptor center and then we'll go meet your mother at the place where you'll be safe to see one another."

"You're right," she said, apology in her tone. "I guess . . . just having this window, this week with you, alone, without worrying about Dirk and what he's up to, is so important to me."

"The go-bags are just a part of my security training," he explained gently. "I do not expect any trouble. Okay?" He gave her a look he hoped soothed some of the anxiety he saw in her shadowed eyes.

"Yes . . . Okay . . . I just thought you took these things along because you *expected* Dirk to jump us, was all."

"No," he told her, shaking his head, "I don't. But you

have to understand, Cari, I was in enemy territory for years, and only safe, so to speak, behind the wire of our base, about six months of that five years, total. Old habits die hard. And they turned back up in volume when Dirk suddenly showed up. That's all."

"Are you worried about my mother? That she'll be attacked? Or she'll be followed to our safe place where we'll meet up?"

"That's why I packed my two Glock pistols. I know the sheriff is sending a deputy to take her to that location, and that he or she will be there with us, but I'm just not taking chances. Dirk's entire gang network is in that region. We have reason to be careful, sweetheart. That's all."

"I understand . . . now. So what else is packed in these go-bags?"

"Old sniper stuff. Syringes holding antibiotics. Ace bandages, gauze, dressings."

"In case you were hurt?"

"Yes. And the antibiotics can mean the difference between life and death if I ever contracted septicemia— blood poisoning—out on a mission. I normally couldn't be picked up for three or four days because there were too many enemy around to make a safe landing to get me."

"I just never realized," Cari whispered, giving him a worried look. "I'd seen a long scar on your left forearm. I wondered how you'd gotten it."

"I was running after my kill shot, and it was at night. I had on my NVGs, night vision goggles, full-out running, and I tripped. I fell over a five-foot cliff and landed on a dead tree. A limb was sticking up and it ripped my left arm open from my wrist to just below my elbow. I did almost bleed out, but managed to get a tourniquet on it above my elbow and keep on going. I got picked up five hours later and was flown into the Landstuhl, Germany, hospital and underwent surgery. That dead limb did a pretty good job on me. It took me four months to get back online again after that."

"I couldn't do that," she whispered, her eyes huge. "You have such courage . . . I had no idea, Chase."

"Does it bother you? Am I telling you upsetting things from my past? I can stop it. You've seen enough, and I don't want to contribute more to your nightmares."

"No . . . don't ever keep anything from me. I'm shaken emotionally by your courage under fire and amazed how calm you are under such dire threat of death. It doesn't scare me or upset me, otherwise."

"You were calm under threat back there at the restaurant when Dirk came in. Do you realize that?"

She managed a partial laugh. "No, not even!"

"If Bannock had ID'd you, your life would have been in real jeopardy. You knew that, but you kept your head, you thought through everything, and you didn't bolt or run. You're a lot more like me than you thought, Cari."

"I don't see it. I just remembered what you taught me, was all. And I was so grateful you did, believe me. Otherwise, I think I would have frozen, my mind blank."

"That's one of the strategies of staying alive for animals, too, so don't knock it," he told her wryly, turning onto I-80 and heading west toward Utah. At Salt Lake City they would turn south and head through Utah and into Arizona. From there, he'd get to I-10, and after passing into California, he'd pick up I-8, which would lead them to Old Highway 80, which would take them south, toward the border of Mexico. The raptor facility was located fifteen miles north of that border.

"You must have put water and food in your go-bags?"

"Well, there's two go-bags, one for each of us."

"Okay . . . what else is in them?"

"Water, protein bars, a sewing kit—"

"A sewing kit?" she asked, stunned. "In case you rip your clothes or something?"

He kept his face expressionless. "No, not that kind of sewing, Cari. If I got a cut or slit in my body, I could sew it up to try and keep infection out of it and also slow or halt the bleeding."

"Oh . . . did you have to go to medical school to learn how to do this?"

"No. There's an Army Special Forces school for people like myself who go there to learn how to handle bullet wounds or other types of injuries out in the field when instant pickup or medical help isn't possible." He wasn't about to tell her any more of the gory stuff. Chase wanted this to be a quiet time, a time where they could get to know one another without threats or violent details from his past life as a sniper.

"I see." She sighed and studied the horizon that was beginning to lighten up, announcing a coming dawn. "So you're handy to have around if I get hurt?" she teased, trying to lighten the conversation.

"You could say that," he murmured, smiling over at her. "Weren't you in the Brownies or Girl Scouts growing up?"

"I was, yes, but I didn't take any medical training. I was interested in bees, beekeeping, and agriculture."

"I see."

"I do know how to apply a Band-Aid, though," she joked, and they both laughed. "What else is in these bags?"

"A map of the area we're traveling through," he said. "And a good compass. If you don't have a map or compass, your senses and mind can play tricks on you and you won't go the direction that has water or help or bushes and trees to hide you."

"Wow . . . " she uttered. "I've never thought of that, Chase."

"They train you for this in the Marine Corps," he said, shrugging. "This is all part of becoming a sniper. They're spending about a quarter of a million dollars training us, so we're expensive assets and they don't want to lose us out on a mission."

"Seriously?" she gasped. "That much money?"

"Well, it costs a million dollars for each pilot in the military to learn to fly."

"I didn't realize any of this." She frowned, glancing down at the go-bags. "So, what else?"

"A good Swiss Army knife in each bag. Can't leave home without one. They are the most versatile tool on earth, as far as I'm concerned."

"I noticed earlier when we were in the house, that you put a leather sheath on your belt and it looked like a knife."

"It's my old military knife," he explained. "Just habit to bring it along."

"Sort of like a good friend?"

"Sort of," he said, but he didn't want to elaborate. He'd had a specially made CPM S90V blade made. It was super steel, consisting of steel with vanadium and carbon for the best wear resistance. "You use a knife for a lot of things, like chopping into bushes, cutting small limbs, and stuff like that."

"To hide in?" she wondered.

"Yes, that's one of many things. When you're out in the Sandbox, you want a knife blade that stays sharp because you don't have any way to sharpen it. The company, Crucible Industries, makes the best knife metal for the use that I needed it for. Crucible is legendary for their edge-retention on the blade, and a buddy of mine, another sniper who was retiring, told me to get one. He knew what he was talking about." He touched the nylon sheath. "This particular type of metal has three times the amount of vanadium and it makes knives corrosion resistant. There were times I had to swim across rivers, or get soaked in a storm, and I wanted a knife that could stand up to those rigors."

"Because rust will dull a knife blade?"

"Absolutely, it will. Plus weaken the blade itself over time. There's been instances when I had to cut through a limb as thick as my wrist, and I did it with this knife. It remained sharp after that chopping, and it sure sold me on it. The knife is just plain tough, no matter what I used it on. Once, there was an earthquake and I had to dig my way out of the back of a cave. It took me two days, but that knife was a champ and dug through some tough rocks and gravel in order for me to find another exit."

Cari stared at the knife and then up at him. "I'm not even going to bother asking you for more stories."

"Nah, just stick to the go-bag," he teased, chuckling.

"What else is in there?"

"Well, when out in the field I had identification that wasn't really me. If I was caught, they couldn't know my real name, where I was from, or anything else. There was always a small language book in Dari, the language most Afghan tribes knew, in there in case I needed it."

"Do you speak Dari?"

"Used to, quite a bit," he said, "but you lose it when you're not speaking it all the time. I knew enough in case I had to question someone I apprehended."

"So? No book in Spanish, since we're going to be close to the border with Mexico?"

Smiling, he said, "No, not on this trip. But there is a very important thing in there."

"What's that?"

"Toilet paper. Actually, wet wipes."

She giggled. "Geeze, Chase!"

"Well, hey, bodily functions and all that. They come and go on a twenty-four-hour cycle. Right?"

She nodded her head.

"I also have a portable cell phone charger in my bag. Where we're going? It's desert, low population, the Mexican border is roughly half a mile away from where we drive through Jacumba Hot Springs. That town is on Old Highway 80, where we need to go to get to the raptor place."

"That's close. I didn't realize that."

"Yes."

She frowned. "Wait. . . . isn't it dangerous to be driving in that area with drug smugglers always coming across the border?"

"It can be," he agreed, "but I checked and Border Patrol works out of that hot springs town, and they know all the routes smugglers take, so I think we'll be fine."

"Okay . . . whew. Anything else in these bags?"

"Actually, in mine is a first aid kit, which includes the sewing kit and syringes I spoke about earlier. And the usual stuff like a lighter, matches, cash, socks, flashlight, a space blanket for each of us, and water purification tablets. Are you impressed?"

Laughing, Cari said, "Only at the amount of stuff you can get in this small knapsack. It probably weighs a ton to carry it." She gave him a humored look, as dawn lightening the clear sky, chasing away some of the stars above them. "Seriously. Were you an Eagle Scout?"

"Yes, I was," he said proudly. "My father had been one, and I wanted to follow in his footsteps."

"Hopefully, we won't have to use these things you started training with so early in your life."

He grinned. "I don't think so. It's just a habit of mine; when I have to drive any distance, I always take a go-bag with me. It's just habit."

"I don't imagine you can get a go-bag like this on board a plane?"

"Wouldn't even try. But on a military cargo plane? They're well received."

"Chase, are you glad those days are behind you? Do you miss them? The excitement? The action?"

He liked her intelligence and insight. "No, to all of them."

"I was concerned you might have PTSD?"

It was his turn to give a snort. "Cari, there isn't anyone who has been in combat who doesn't have it, more or less. Unless you're a cold-blooded murderer who enjoys killing people, normal human beings aren't built that way. And when you pull a trigger that could end a life? It's going to affect you. No amount of mind games will stop it, either."

"Or drugs or drinking," she added, sadly.

"Yes, there's ways to escape it, but it's always temporary."

"What about you?" she wanted to know, her voice softening as she absorbed his strong, enduring profile in the morning dawn light. "How did you handle your PTSD?"

"The first year home was rough for me. It's great to have PTSD when you're in combat, and your life is on the line. But in civilian life? There are no threats. I came home jumpy, hyperalert, nightmares several times a week, an insomniac, and worst of all, flashbacks."

"Did you use anything, a medication or something, to help you with them?"

"Mary believed in chamomile tea, so I'd drink it, and darned if it wasn't calming. I was pretty amazed. It helped me a lot, bringing down the hyperalertness. I was so busy learning the ropes of the ranch that frankly, my focus was on the business, and I just pushed through a lot of the PTSD and kept on going. It worked for me, but I wouldn't say it would for everyone."

"But as a sniper," she pointed out, "you have an incredibly strong focus."

"Yes, and I believe that helped me enormously. I wouldn't let anything else bother whatever my focus was on. It's not that I didn't get the symptoms, I just wouldn't let them control me or my life, is all."

"And now?"

"I might have a bad dream once a week. I'm sleeping well, but when you run a ranch and your physical activity wears you out, you go to sleep at night. Mother Nature's best sleeping pill."

She smiled softly. "I feel so happy being here with you, Chase. You were right: This week is going to change our lives. I like having time like this to explore you, to find out all about you."

"I hope I haven't scared you off, have I?"

She laughed and reached out, placing her hand on his hard, thick thigh. "Not even! If anything, I feel more secure."

"Good." He placed his hand over hers. "I like what we have, Cari. I like where it's going."

She turned her hand over, lacing her fingers between his. "So do I, Chase. This is a dream I find myself in."

"I feel the same." And silently, he hoped like hell that it didn't turn into a nightmare with Bannock somewhere out there. Until he was caught, there was no such thing as having a life. And he wanted that more than anything else with Cari.

Chapter Thirteen

June 18

"This raptor compound is situated out in the middle of nowhere," Cari said, looking at the undulating hills, all yellow desert surrounding them. There were plenty of junipers, a hardy, tough, semi-desert tree that could survive with as little as seven inches or less of rain a year.

She looked at her cell phone, following the progress of Old Highway 80. At one time, the historical note said, this dirt road was the only way in and out of Southern California, below Los Angeles. San Diego was the largest city.

Chase kept his speed about thirty miles an hour unless the dirt road was rutted. "Be thankful that a road grader must come through here from San Diego County and take out all the potholes, ruts, and rocks. Could be worse. How's Valkyrie riding?"

Twisting her head, Cari saw the red-tail was alert, and looking around. They'd taken off the canvas that covered her crate in Utah, when the hawk remained quiet but attentive, getting used to the long drive. Some raptors would get anxious and keep flapping their wings, breaking off important flight feathers. "She's quiet and doing fine. I really think she knows she's going somewhere exciting. She's always been an adventurous hawk."

Chase grinned. "Yeah, tree bombing. Well, there are junipers out here, but I don't think she'll try them because their greenery is like a wire brush and the wood is thick and too strong for her to break off any of it, even small branches."

"Let's hope she's doesn't try it once, and find out the hard way," Cari muttered, turning around. They had made it to Page, Arizona, on the first day. A woman who was a raptor rehabber had invited them to put Valkyrie in her center while they took a nearby motel. Chase had made the reservation and he'd gotten two rooms. A part of her wanted one room. But was she ready for *that*? For actual, physical connection with Chase? Her heart instantly leaped into the fray and shouted, *Yes!* while her head warned her to continue at a pace comfortable for her. Was Chase feeling the same, needing her like she wanted him? Afraid to ask, she pointed toward the left. "There's a canyon coming up, the road is really close to the edge of it, so be careful."

"I see it," he murmured. "Don't worry, we won't slide over it."

"Better not! It's two thousand feet deep, Chase."

"A mini Grand Canyon. But this area has all kinds of weird geology. Look at those white limestone mountains rising up and out of that yellow soil." He hitched a thumb to her right. "And then you get lost in clumps or groves of juniper and probably some piñon thrown in, a few flat plains, and then a series of hills. All this used to be shallow ocean millions of years ago."

"It's desolate. I see absolutely no water. Dry as a bone."

"You don't have to live out here," he teased.

"But I wonder what Valkyrie can possibly find to hunt for?"

"Must be something, because there's a resident red-tail about twenty miles ahead of us. Right?"

"I suppose you're right. I just worry about her."

Laughing, Chase said, "That's rich. She's our Wild Child, the one that's *always* in hot water, danger, or in some kind of weird situation that hawks aren't supposed to get into at all. I think she'll do just fine out here in this desert area. There's plenty rodents out here. And snakes. Red Tails are big snake eaters. You know that."

"I do. I suppose I'm not looking at this area through her eyes," Cari grumped.

Chase frowned. "There's a vehicle . . . maybe two or three, coming up behind us at high speed."

She twisted around. They were on a flat piece of desert, the canyon on their left, less than ten feet away. "Who is it? I mean, who's speeding on this narrow, two-lane asphalt road?"

"I don't know," he growled, looking hard at the outside rearview mirror.

"Maybe Border Patrol?"

"I don't see any emergency lights flashing. The lead vehicle looks like some kind of army vehicle . . ."

Cari looked through the skylight, which they had open. The temperature at noontime was in the eighties, but the air was fresh and she preferred it over air-conditioning. Just as she reached forward to press the button on the dashboard to close it, hollow, thunking sounds struck their truck.

"GET DOWN!" Chase yelled, suddenly stomping on the accelerator. "Those are bullets!"

She wanted to scream as she ducked, putting her head to her knees, trying not to cry out in terror.

"Who?" she shouted.

The truck fishtailed, the speed so sudden that the rear wheels were sliding back and forth on the pavement.

"Don't know!"

The roar of the engine filled the cabin. Wind whipped in through the skylight.

THUNK, THUNK, THUNK.

"Why are they shooting at us?" Cari cried out, gripping her knees, burying her head between her knees. Chase could get shot. Killed!

Gritting his teeth, Chase held the wheel, moving up to ninety miles an hour, the canyon a blur on his left. There was no place to pull over. They were bracketed by a white limestone mountain on the right and the canyon on the left. He heard Valkyrie shrieking.

Escape! That's all he could think of.

The vehicles came upon them so swiftly, that he had no time to do anything but try and outrun them. He saw dark-skinned Hispanics in desert camouflage gear leaning out the windows with military rifles, firing wildly at them. They appeared to be drug runners. As they got closer and closer, they began firing constantly at them.

A bullet blew out the rear window, sparkling glass fragments showering through the cab. Then the front windshield blew out.

Valkyrie screamed, flapping madly around.

A bullet struck the front left tire. A huge *bang!* Suddenly, the truck lurched to the left.

Chase heard a second rear tire blow on his side of the truck.

NO! Gripping the wheel hard, he tried to stop the truck from sliding swiftly to the left.

Too late!

"HANG ON!" he yelled to Cari.

One moment, Cari heard the sounds of the road beneath them, the sound filling the cab. The next, the race of the big engine. They were floating! No, falling! She screamed when she realized they had slid off the road and were now heading downward into the canyon. Everything went into slow motion. She heard Chase grunt as another hail of bullets slammed broadside, into the truck. She felt a sting on her upper arm. Her eyes were tightly shut, her face pressed hard against her knees. They were falling!

Oh, God! They would all die!

Valkyrie shrieked over and over again, flapping wildly against the constraints of the cage.

The nose of the truck slowly came down . . . down . . . down . . .

They were going to die! Tears squeezed into Cari's eyes. Who had shot at them? *Why? Why?* Her hands ached as she clung to her knees, bent over, holding on. What about Chase? She didn't hear him! She was afraid to try and look up!

When would they hit bottom? How far would they fall?

And her stomach rolled with nausea as the truck began what felt like a slow motion turn. To her horror, they were now falling upside down!

The seat belt bit hard into her shoulder, feeling like a knife slicing into her as gravity pulled violently on her. She lost her grip on her knees, now held in place only by the seat belt. Without thinking, she jerked her arms around herself.

She had opened her eyes. The world was upside down. All she heard now was the engine, a sputtering, and the smell of smoke!

When would this end? When would they land? She knew she was going to die! There was no way to protect themselves. That canyon they'd just been forced into by those drug runners was two thousand feet deep!

Cari whimpered. She tried to call out Chase's name, but only a hoarse cry broke from her contorted lips.

Suddenly, the cab of the truck struck something. Cari screamed as the entire roof was ripped off! The sound of metal being sheared and torn off, hurt her ears.

The truck's nose suddenly dipped.

Cari's seat belt yanked at her. She was jerked hard, forward as the nose of the truck struck the cliff face, plowing into it. Dirt and rocks flew into the now opened truck. She shut her eyes, feeling sand, like thousands of tiny grains, slamming into her unprotected face and arms.

There was a groan and a rumble.

She shut her eyes, the jolt so powerful, she felt faint, as if her arms and legs were going to be ripped out of her body, from where the harness pinned her against the seat.

The truck flipped!

It felt to Cari as if they were going end over end. Every time the heavier part, the front of the truck, struck the cliff, there was more rending, tearing, and everything shook around her. Somewhere in all that sound, she heard Valkyrie shriek, but with her eyes closed, she didn't know if the hawk had been injured or killed.

Rocks and pebbles were flying like buckshot into the

cab, and it felt to Cari like they were inside a washing machine, going around and around. The smell of smoke choked her. The truck struck nose-first, again. The harness jerked her so hard that she lost consciousness.

Smoke! Fire! Chase forced his lids open. Everything was quiet. The truck was sitting upright, on an angle, the nose pointed downward. He snapped his head to the right. Cari was barely opening her eyes, her hand bloody as she reached up to touch her brow. They were covered with a fine film of sand. Shaking his head, he tried to clear it, having banged it hard against the door itself, almost knocked out by the impact. All the windows had been blown out. His mind shifted into military gear, and he reacted as if they were surrounded by an unknown enemy.

"Cari!" he croaked. "Are you okay? Talk to me?" and he reached out, gripping her shoulder, but not hard enough to hurt her, just to make her focus because she looked dazed. So was he. "Cari!"

"I . . . uh . . ."

"Are you able to move?" Terror worked through him. He counted at least three times the truck had gone end over end, and each time it hit the cliff, it had snapped the vehicle out into the air again, to fall another God knew how many more hundreds of feet downward until it plowed into the cliff once again. The fact they were alive shocked him. He thought they were dead. He repeated the question to her, his voice a harsh croak. Dirt was all across her short, red hair, dust on her cheek as she turned, looking at him, staring, as if not recognizing him. That scared him.

"We have to get out of here." He pointed at the engine. It was smoking. "Can you move?" he demanded sharply. His tone seemed to snap her back to reality.

"Chase . . . where are we? Are you all right?"

"I'm mobile. What about you?" He watched the first flames lick up from beneath the hood that was halfway torn open.

"Y-yes." She tried to sit up, slowly looking around.

"Get the go-bags," he commanded, pointing to them at her feet.

He tried to open her seat belt. It was jammed. So was his. Opening the nylon sheath, he pulled out his seven-inch military-grade knife. "Cari, lift your left arm now!"

She jerked it upward.

It took one, clean slice for the first harness and one for the second. She was free! Turning the knife, he quickly cut through his seat belt harness. Now, they were both free! Cari fumbled and grabbed the go-bags. She got one of them up on the dirt-filled seat, then the second one.

Chase took both of them, throwing them out of the window and as far away from the truck as he could. "Come on," he told her. He turned, getting enough room to try and open the driver's-side door. It was jammed shut. He cursed under his breath, twisted around, and with all his strength, he slammed his boots into it.

The door creaked open. Again, Chase hit it with another blow. Another foot widened up! There was enough room to squeeze through. "I'm going out," he told her. "Stay until I tell you to come this way."

Cari looked back and gasped. "Chase! Valkyrie is gone! The cage is totaled."

"Then she got free," he growled, straightening. The first thing he did was get to his go-bag. He hauled out the Glock 18, and slid the safety off as he scanned the top of the canyon. There was no one there. Yet. Had those drug runners moved on? He heard nothing. There was a breeze in the V-shaped canyon. He quickly studied the truck and where it sat, about a hundred feet from the bottom. It was in a precarious position. Leaning down, he looked in at Cari.

"Slide very slowly toward me," he ordered, holding out his hand in her direction. "Slow but sure. This truck isn't stable."

Nodding, she wiped her closed eyes with her forearm, opened them and then crawled toward him on her hands and knees.

The truck groaned and metal shrieked.

She gave a gasp, freezing.

"Come on," he urged her hoarsely. "Grab my hand!"

She made a lunge, both her hands gripping his.

The truck started to move away from Chase. With a grunt, he hauled Cari out. She cried once, because the space was narrow and her hips had jammed into it until she turned sideways. Cari flew toward Chase, slammed into him, knocking him backwards. He took the fall, a grunt coming out of him as they hit the earth together, Cari landing on top of him. Tensing, he held her to him so she didn't get hurt. He knew he was going to have a lot of bruises.

"Hold on," he rasped, slowly releasing her, guiding her to the downside of him so that he was between a possible enemy above them and the smoking truck. There was no way he was going to have Cari hurt any more than she already was.

"Stay down," he ordered, slowly rolling over, studying the cliff, looking for any sign of vehicles or drug runners. He saw nothing. His hearing was sharp and clear and all he heard was silence.

And then he heard an ominous *pop*.

Launching to his feet, he grabbed Cari, half dragging her, as far away from the truck as they could get, heading downward, rocks and pebbles like small avalanches, rolling downward around them. On the way, he grabbed the go-bags with the other hand, keeping himself between the truck and her.

The explosion that occurred knocked both of them off their feet. Chase never lost his grip on Cari's arm, holding her tight to his body as they were hit by a pressure wave that sent them tumbling. The crackle of fire, pieces of metal hailing down upon them, made him tuck himself around her to protect her. Smoke rolled by them, black, thick, and choking. He braced himself for the fall and once again took the brunt of it, grunting. They rolled at least ten feet, and suddenly stopped.

Sitting up, making sure Cari was okay, he looked up at what was left of their truck. It was as if a bomb had taken it apart. Chase was amazed they were still alive.

He got to his knees, leaning over her where she sat, her head against her drawn-up knees, her arms wrapped around them. "Hey," he rasped, his hands falling gently on her shoulders, "talk to me, Cari. We're okay. It looks like those drug runners moved on. Can you stand? Walk? There's a grove of trees down there and shade. I want to get us to them." He didn't add that he wanted to hide as soon as possible, in case those druggies came back looking for them. Hiding was his main plan.

"Yes, I think." She lifted her head. "I just feel like a puppet with no backbone."

He nodded. "We took a nine-hundred-foot fall." He studied where the truck had gone off the dirt road. He had no idea how they'd survived it. If the truck had raced off the cliff lip? It wouldn't have hit the cliff going down like they had. Instead, they would have nosedived in a long, large arc and he was sure, upon impact, it would have killed them instantly. Instead, the truck had slid off the road sideways at an angle, and it had saved them. He studied Cari, who alternately was in shock, and then clarity would come, and then she would go shocky again, her skin very pale looking, eyes dark with terror.

"What do we do now, Chase? Do you think those men will come back? Try to kill us?"

He turned his full attention to her. "No, I think they were racing to outrun Border Patrol that was probably behind them. I don't really know. I don't think they'll be back." At least not right away, but he kept that knowledge to himself. Cari was shaken up enough. He slid the safety on his Glock and pushed it down behind his waist. "I'm going to quickly check you out for broken bones."

"Okay." She looked at the truck, her lips parting, the vehicle utterly destroyed.

He started at her feet, squeezing here and there, gently manipulating joints to see if it caused pain. Nothing seemed broken. She had blood on her face from the windshield blowing in on them, and he was sure he had some himself. Her hands were bloody with scratches and so were his. "I think we have suffered whiplash of the neck and shoulders, plus we're going to have one hell of a collection of bruises. Let me check your head and eyes . . ." He found blood here and there on her scalp, picked out a couple of shards of glass as gently as he could, but nothing serious. Looking into her wide, cinnamon-colored eyes, the pupils contracted and expanded, much to his relief. If she had a head injury, the pupils would not open and close in response to light, as they were supposed to. He heaved an inner sigh of relief.

"Let me help you up." He slowly stood, offered her his hand, and gently brought her to her feet. Cari was dizzy and he placed one arm around her torso to steady her, bringing her against him.

"Aren't you dizzy, Chase?"

"No." Just hurting everywhere, but he was sure she was, too, so no sense in feeling any worse than they did already. "Let's get the go-bags and then we'll head down to that grove of trees at the bottom of the canyon."

"I'm so glad you have those go-bags," she said, stumbling and pitching every now and then.

"Makes two of us," he said, continuing to look around. He leaned over and hooked a strap from each bag around his left forearm and straightened. As they got on the flat yellow soil, sunbaked and hard, he felt Cari become more stable and sure of where her feet were in relation to her body. She was still shaken badly. He liked that her arm was around his waist. Absorbing her, feeling her strength and determination, he was so damned proud of her.

"What about Valkyrie?" she asked, looking around and searching the sky.

"I don't know. The cage top was ripped off. I think it

happened when the truck landed on its cab and it tore the whole roof off."

Giving him a horrifying look, she whispered, "Valkyrie could have died then. We could have been decapitated . . ."

"Yeah," he grunted, "but we kept our heads down and we had those seat belts, which saved our lives, keeping us in a fixed position. Let's hope Valkyrie was as lucky as we were, Cari."

"It happened so fast, Chase. One minute, it was like going for a Sunday drive, the next minute, those trucks raced up on us like they were racing in the Indy 500."

"I know." He led her into the grove of very old junipers, their thick trunks gnarled with age, their limbs skyward, providing wonderful shade. He guesstimated the grove was at least a thousand years old, perhaps more, because the trunks were three to six feet in width.

"Look!" she said, pointing ahead of them. "Water! It's a creek of some sort!"

"You're right," Chase said, sizing it up. "I think on the map we had, it showed a spring in this canyon. Maybe this is it."

"Water in the desert," she whispered. "Thank God." She pressed her hand to her heart over her dusty T-shirt.

Chase decided to take them to the green, grassy bank of the stream that was about four feet wide. The water was about knee deep, clear, and looked good to him. It would be a place to bathe and wash the grime and grit off them. "How's this for a place to sit for a bit? You have a nice old grandmother juniper to lean your back against and you can stretch out your legs in the green grass toward the stream."

"It looks wonderful," Cari choked fervently, sitting down, his hand guiding her. "Thanks."

He knelt down beside her, opening the go-bag. "We're in shock and have to drink water, Cari." He pulled out the bottle of water and opened the top of it, handing it to her. "Drink all of it. Sip it if you want. We need to rest and just be for a bit."

Nodding, she took it and thanked him, looking around. "This is so beautiful! And it's so arid everywhere else around us."

"Sort of like a Kalahari Desert oasis," he agreed, opening the second go-bag. He slugged down a quart of water in no time. He found the purification tablets and dropped one into it, moving to the stream and filling it with the cold stream water. "I'll bet this stream is coming from somewhere, but where? Do you remember seeing it on your cell phone map?"

"It just said 'spring,' but there was no thin blue line to indicate a stream was there."

Nodding, he capped the plastic bottle and shook it. "Could be an artesian well up there somewhere in the grove, which is really good."

"That means there's an underground aquifer," Cari said, patting the cool, soft grass. She looked up at him. "What are we going to do? I don't have a cell phone on me. Do you?"

Shaking his head, he grumbled, "Both of them blew up when that fire hit the gasoline tank. We're on our own. We're about twenty miles away from the raptor center. If we're up to it, we can walk it."

"But, what if those druggies are around, Chase?"

He touched her dusty cheek. "We'd only travel at night,

so don't worry. Right now? We need to rest and let the shock wear off. When you're like this, your mind isn't thinking clearly." He looked at his watch. It was one p.m. "It's starting to get hot. In June it says this area reaches a hundred degrees Fahrenheit. We're not putting ourselves out in that kind of heat and conditions."

"I want so badly to get out of these clothes, wash the dirt off."

"Why don't you do that?" He gave her a teasing look, touching strands of her hair. "I'd like to stay around, but I want to reconnoiter and understand where we're at." He put one go-bag at her side. "Everything you need is in there. There's a washcloth in there and soap, too."

"You never told me that!" She smiled a little.

His heart widened. Fifteen minutes ago, he was afraid Cari wasn't going to survive. Now, that sweet, honest smile of hers just axed him like nothing else ever would. "There's even a small towel in there. Don't you feel like we're at a five-star resort?" He gave a low laugh.

She reached up, catching his hand, kissing the back of it. "Total five stars, Chase. How long are you going to be gone?"

"Probably half an hour. I need to scout around. Make sure we're in a safe place. I think we are, but I want eyes on it. Okay?" He reluctantly released her long, slender fingers, hurting for her because they were blood-encrusted and dirty. He didn't like that Cari was in pain and suffering. He'd do anything he could not to have had this happen to them. And she was so damned brave, rallying, not helpless at all. She was a lot stronger than she looked, and he was proud of her spunk.

"Okay. I'm just going to sit here, rest, and let this

shock leave me. I feel better already." She held up the
bottle, half the water gone from it.

"Good. Drink up, sweetheart. I'll be back. You get your
Nature bath while I'm gone."

She managed a partial smile. "I will. You can take one
when you get back."

He winked at her, slinging the go-bag across his shoulder. "You can watch if you want . . ." he teased, and turned
to follow the stream.

This wasn't the first time she imagined what Chase
would look like without clothes.

It hurt to move. Every joint in her body ached like fire
itself. But they were alive. Looking up through the wiry
green fronds of the juniper, the sky was a light blue with
gathering clouds, and they seemed to be coming up from
the south, from Mexico. Was there a storm coming in?
Sighing, she looked at her hands and arms. So much
blood, most of it dried now, and how dirty she was! Tears
jammed into her eyes. They could have died. The thought
hit her so hard, she suddenly burst into tears and Cari
covered her hands across her mouth, sobbing.

For the next five minutes, she cried, her head buried
against her knees, shaking and trembling. *Death.* Chase
could have died. And so could she. And Valkyrie was
gone. Her heart ached for all of them. Finally, the tears
trailed off and she tried to wipe her eyes, only to see dust
turned to mud. Opening the go-bag, she dumped everything out beside her to see what, exactly, Chase had packed
in there. The Glock she carefully laid aside, next to the
trunk of the tree, more afraid of it than anything else.

Little by little, feeling like a child that had been given
gifts at Christmastime, she realized the go-bag was like

a hardware store in miniature. She found in one ziplock bag a bar of scentless white soap, a dark green wash cloth, and a towel of the same color, the size of a large hand towel, to dry her off fairly well. There was antiseptic ointment, which she laid out, also, to salve all her cuts and gouges. There was a homeopathic ointment in a small tube called Arnica montana, good for bruises on uncut skin, too. Even better, there were some packets of scentless shampoo, soda powder, and a toothbrush with floss. Right now, these items seemed to be like the greatest treasure she'd ever found. Chase had thought of everything.

The burbling, singing of the creek over the graveled yellow, brown, and cream-colored smooth stones was like a balm to her shock right now. There seemed to be a pleasant breeze that wound through this deep grove. Cari guessed the grove had sprung up because of the water flowing through the bottom of the canyon.

She drank the rest of her water, got to her hands and knees, and pushed to her feet. Taking a purification tablet, she dropped it in and mimicked what Chase had done. Capping the bottle, she shook it and then set it against the trunk of the tree.

Looking around, she saw little birds flitting here and there. Other than that, the place was silent. She heard nothing but the sounds of Nature, and maybe that was good. She reminded herself that Chase had lived like this in enemy territory for five years, alone, without immediate help, and risking his life.

Pulling off her T-shirt, she dropped it and her bra on the bank. Sitting down, she unlaced her boots, pulled off her socks, and then stood, shimmying out of her jeans and cotton panties. Placing the soap, wash cloth, shampoo, and towel in a line, she eagerly stepped into the water, testing it. Surprisingly, it was very cold compared to the high temperature around them. It felt glorious! The soles of her feet were tender, but most of the stones were flat, well worn, and she felt as if she were walking on a lumpy tiled surface. The water came halfway up to her thighs out in the middle, and that was where she sat down, holding her breath and going under, scrubbing the dirt out of her hair.

Gasping for air, she stood up, water running in rivulets across her body. For the next ten minutes she washed, scrubbed, and cleaned out her ears, hair, and every part of her body. By the time she was done, the water ran sleekly down her flesh. She was clean! Wading back to the bank, she got out, leaning down to pick up the small towel. There were so many scratches and deep-pitted injuries—from the glass, she supposed—on her neck, shoulders, and arms. So glad she'd protected her head and eyes against her knees, Cari realized it was entirely possible she could have lost her sight. That scared her, too.

Next, she got down on her hands and knees, washing every article of clothing in the water. Wringing each of them out, she shrugged into them, even though the material clung to her body. They would have to dry on her. It felt heavenly to be clean, and she began to explore the area after putting her boots back on. She stayed in sight of the one, large juniper that held her go-bag and that weapon. Cari didn't stray far, but on the other side, near what appeared to be the end of the grove, the water seemed to go underground again. How long was this stream? Blinking, she looked around. Everything was so quiet. Straining her eyes, she thought she saw on the other side of the stream and grove, a dirt road. Was she seeing things? Maybe so.

Feeling suddenly exhausted, she walked back to the tree and sat down, her back against it. What would Dan Seabert think? He promised to call them daily with updates on what was going on in his neck of the woods. What would he do if Chase didn't answer his phone? What would he think? Would he suspect something had happened to them? He had the phone number of the raptor facility. Would he call there? And what if they told him they hadn't arrived? What would he do then? She had so many questions, and no answers.

The material of her T-shirt was almost dry. She had decided not to put the bra back on, instead, hanging it up to dry. The humidity was so low in the desert, that everything she wore was drying swiftly. There was no comb in the go-bag, so she ran her fingers through her hair to tame it back into place. Putting the antibiotic ointment on her scratches and gouges, she felt halfway decent. Now she was so tired. Almost feeling drugged, the allure of the soft, fragrant green grass was too much for her to resist. She wiped off the go-bag, towel dried it, and then used it as a pillow and promptly fell into a deep, healing sleep.

Chapter Fourteen

June 18

Chase found Cari sleeping deeply when he returned an hour later. The heat of the day was oppressive, nearing a hundred degrees. He walked silently into the area. She had bathed and he smiled a little as he walked past her, heading down toward the other end of the grove, still checking the area out. Of most importance was the question of the truck. Were the drug runners coming back? Had they moved on? He wasn't sure and took no chances. He wore his Glock in a nylon holster, the safety strap off it, the safety off as well in case he had to draw it swiftly. He didn't trust druggies. These might be from Southern California or from Mexico, and not Afghanistan, but it didn't matter. They shot first and didn't bother asking questions later.

Satisfied that all was quiet where Cari was sleeping, he headed back, keeping to the thickest part of the grove, wanting to remain unseen. When he came back thirty minutes later, he saw Cari standing up, rubbing her drowsy features.

"Hey," he called softly, not wanting to startle her.

"Chase! Where have you been? I was scared you'd been hurt or captured."

He came up to her, wanting to hold her, but he was filthy and sweaty. "This grove is two miles long. It curves around a limestone hill." He pointed in a westerly direction. "There's a lot of caves all around the base of it. I've estimated the raptor center is roughly twenty miles from where we're at right now. This country is like Afghanistan: desolate, and hardly anyone lives here at all." He went over to the tree and shucked out his go-bag.

"We're going to a cave?" she asked, frowning and yawning.

"Yes. It's a good place to hole up for tonight. It's too hot to try and make that trek. And I don't want to travel in broad daylight and be seen by druggies. Besides," he said, opening his go-bag, "we're still coming out of shock, and I want to get some sleep tonight, get rested up, and we'll leave about an hour before dawn when it's a little bit light. If we maintain a hiking pace, twenty-minute miles? We can cover three miles in an hour. I figure, with rests in between, we'll make that raptor place in about eight hours. If we start before dawn, it's cooler and we're less likely to be spotted. That means leaving around four a.m., and if all goes well, we should be at the raptor place by noon. We'd be avoiding the worst of the heat, which is around four p.m. How does that sound?"

She came over and sat down near him. "Why couldn't we just walk at night?"

"Because drug running is active then. The night is dark, we've got a new moon, so no light to see the ground. We could fall into a hole and sprain an ankle, or worse, break a leg. I wish I had night vision goggles on me, but I don't. Night travel isn't an option."

"Why couldn't we just stay here, Chase? It's so beautiful, shaded, and we have water."

He grimaced. "There's a well-used road on the other side of this stream," he said, pointing across it. "I think the drug runners come in here quite often. I found a lot of plastic bottles, food wrappers, and stuff like that at certain places where I think they might make camp during daylight hours. We can't afford to stay here much longer, Cari."

Frowning, she asked, "Do they stay in caves on that hill?"

Shaking his head, he gathered up his toiletry articles and stood. "There's no sign of them, and I checked it out for evidence of any type of human activity, as well as tire treads of vehicles, or footprints. There's nothing." He looked up at the cliff above them, about half a mile away from where they escaped the wrecked truck. "We'll be a lot safer in one of those caves, Cari. I know it doesn't sound like a good place to go, but it is."

"Okay," she said, giving him a worried look.

"I want you to keep watch," he said, gesturing to the cliff. "Keep eyes and ears on it while I get out of these filthy clothes and take a bath in that stream like you did earlier."

"Oh, it was wonderful! I felt so dirty!"

"Go sit on the other side of this juniper. If you see or hear anything? Come and get me, don't shout or call me. Sound carries very easily in a canyon like this." He gave her a teasing look. "Or, you can stay here and watch me get naked and go into the water?"

She grinned and waved her index finger in his direction. "What a tease you are!"

"You might like what you see, huh?"

Rolling her eyes, she laughed softly. "I've *always* liked what I've seen of you, Chase."

"I like hearing the truth."

"Thanks for giving me the space and privacy to bathe. I loved getting clean."

He nodded. "I was tempted not to reconnoiter, but rather just sit somewhere and watch you undress and get into this water."

"Now the truth really comes out." She grinned and picked up her go-bag and headed to the juniper. "Let me know when you're done, huh?"

"It's going to take about half an hour," he warned her. "I have to wash all my clothes, too."

"That's okay. I'll stand watch."

"Okay," Chase said, walking up to her where she sat on the opposite side of the juniper, "I'm clean, and so are my clothes."

She looked up and smiled, drowning in the longing she saw in his gray eyes. "The only thing missing is your Stetson."

He made a mournful sound. "Yeah, it burned up in that crash. At least I have my baseball cap. We need to have something on our heads to protect them from the heat of the sun." He held his hand down to her. "Hear or see anything?"

"No, it was quiet." She slid her hand into his, cool and

damp from being in the stream. He eased her to her feet, inches between them. "Are you as stiff and sore as I am?"

"Yes." He didn't want to let go of her hand, but forced himself to do it. "Ready to go?"

She put on her go-bag, pulling it so the straps settled comfortably against her shoulders. She settled her base-ball cap on her head. "What about water?"

"We have two quarts on each of us," he said, walking around the tree and heading out of the area. "I found some plastic bottles and gathered them up at the end of the grove. We'll fill them with water, put purification tablets in them, and then they'll be our hydration for tonight, as well as tomorrow's hike."

She walked at his side. "I wonder if Dan or anyone is worried about us, Chase? Is he concerned because, you know, he calls us every day to report on anything about Dirk or that gang in the logging area."

"When he can't get ahold of us, at first he may just leave us a message. And if we don't answer in a couple of hours, he'll probably call a second time."

"Thinking we might be out of reach or something? No cell towers in this area?"

"Right. And if we still don't answer after that, I'm sure he'll call the raptor facility, asking if we're there."

"What if they tell him we haven't shown up?"

"Then," Chase said, "I think he'll contact that sheriff of San Diego County and get a deputy sent out to this area along Highway 80 to see if they can locate us."

"But that probably wouldn't happen until tomorrow," Cari said, matching his quick, long stride.

"Correct." Chase continued to look around, keep them in the thicker parts of the grove, not wanting to be out in the open by following the banks of the stream. "How are you doing, Cari? Am I walking too fast for you?"

She reached out, grabbing his hand. "My joints are stiff and painful, but by walking like this, I feel less pain."

"Walking increases circulation," he said, squeezing her hand. There was so much he wanted to say to her. Cari was game. Her core strength was coming out and Chase was relieved. He knew tomorrow's hike was going to be a miserable, hard sonofabitch for her. He was used to places like this and knew how to handle the landscape, but she didn't.

"Did you see? There's a lot of dark clouds off to the west."

"I did. We may get rain tonight. We're in a weather phenomenon called the monsoon season that comes up from Mexico every June through September in the Southwest. There can be violent thunderstorms day or night, but this is when areas like this get their rain for half of the year." He pointed a finger up through the tree canopy at the growing dark and swirling clouds above them. "Rain isn't our enemy," he told her. "When we start out tomorrow morning? If it's raining, that's a good thing."

"Why?"

"Because it acts like camouflage, hiding us from the prying eyes of drug runners that I'm sure are in this area."

"Oh . . . I didn't think of that."

He liked that she squeezed his fingers in return. "That's okay," he told her, holding her gaze. "Each of us has strengths and weaknesses. A good team, a good partnership, always works off one another's strengths."

"I like that about you, Chase," she said, looking into his eyes, her voice serious.

"I like everything about you," he rasped, slowing, leaning over and kissing the back of her hand. Her eyes went soft and he felt her longing. "We'll get through this together, Cari. That, I promise."

"Home for tonight," Chase told her as they squeezed between two large juniper trees that hid the entrance to the cave he'd chosen to hole up in. He guesstimated it was around five p.m., the sun starting a slow decline toward the western horizon.

Holding up one hand to protect her face, Cari followed him, getting whacked by the tough juniper leaves. She held tightly to his hand as he led her into a small, white limestone cave entrance. Ducking, she followed him inside. The light from outside filtered in through the junipers and inside she was able to straighten and look around. Chase released her hand.

"Follow me, Cari. Watch the cave sides, that limestone is sharp and it will cut into you."

Nodding, she remained close. The outer chamber of the cave was small, about seven feet high, the whiteness reflecting the light, making it easy to see. The cave turned into a three-foot-wide tunnel, the incline growing steeper as they went farther into the gloom. It was almost pitch-black when she saw a milky, low light up ahead. "Where are we going?"

"Second floor of this cave," he said, keeping his voice low. "We're almost there . . ."

Cari suddenly found herself in nearly a perfect circle of a second chamber, a quarter of its roof caved in, limestone rubble on one side of the room. The sand was soft beneath her feet and felt good to her aching joints. Looking up, she said, "Where are we?"

Chase led her over to near the avalanche, where part of the roof had fallen in a long time ago. "I wanted to find a cave that had entrance/exit points. You never go into a cave that has only one way out."

"Especially if drug runners decide to use the cave we chose?" she asked, studying the blue sky and sunlight above from the hole that was large enough for a truck to drive through.

He gave her a look of praise. "Smart woman," he said, releasing her hand. "If something happens? Then we have this as an escape route. When I found this earlier, I followed it up and out over there." He pointed to the right. "It comes out on the side of this hill, far away from the original entrance. If someone does come in here? We quietly climb up there, leave, and we're out of harm's way."

She shook her head. "I've never looked at caves this way . . ."

"This is a dry one. Come on, let's set up camp over there, opposite this exit hole. We've got plenty of water on us now, and we need to eat. We have to keep up our strength."

"Good idea," she agreed, looking around. The light from above showed smooth limestone walls where Chase had chosen to set up. He took the space blankets out and opened them up, setting them across the sand floor. In no time, he had a bottle of water and several protein bars laid out for them.

"You ready to sit down and rest?" he said, gesturing for her to come to the blankets.

Groaning, she sat down. "My joints ache like fire."

"We'll put some arnica cream on them after we eat," he said.

She took a protein bar from him. "Is this how you lived in Afghanistan?"

"Pretty much. Makes me feel like I'm back in the Sandbox, not here, stateside," he said mirthfully, opening the wrapper on his protein bar.

"Does it bother you?"

"Yes and no. Now? I'm grateful for the experience since we're in this mess. I know what to do to keep us safe, so we can make a run for that raptor facility at dawn."

"I would never have guessed these caves were here," she uttered, shaking her head, appreciating the protein bar, her stomach growling and hungry. Frowning, she changed topics. "Chase? In my head, I keep thinking that somehow, Dirk is a part of this, but I don't know how."

Becoming serious, his voice low, he said, "Remember, Bannock's drug network is in Southern California. I'm sure he uses the cartel in this area, their drug runners, to get the goods he's ordered across this border. "

"But"—she hesitated, frowning—"is he behind this attack on us?"

"I don't know. He could be," Chase said, giving her a sympathetic look because she looked stressed and emotional, her eyes glistening with unshed tears. "We won't know, Cari. Bannock has a large enough gang that it could be possible."

"But," she choked, finishing off the bar, "how could he know we were coming out here?"

"Maybe he or that gang figured out you were at Three Bars."

"But he didn't recognize me in the restaurant," she whispered in a strained tone.

Chase put the empty wrappers back into his go-bag and zipped it shut. He pulled her into his arms, resting his back against the knobby wall of limestone. She came easily, wanting his arms around her. Cari snuggled into his embrace, resting her cheek on his shoulder, looking up at him.

"What if he *did* recognize me, Chase? What if he pretended otherwise?"

He moved his hand in a soothing motion down her arm, well aware of all her cuts and gouges. "Anything's possible, Cari. The only way, if that's true, is that someone, maybe him, found out you are staying at Three Bars. They could have sent someone from Hauptman's gang to watch the comings and goings of the ranch trucks."

"I just have this horrible feeling," she whispered, pressing her brow against his jaw, "that he knows. I feel it in my bones. I think he arranged that crash."

"Well," Chase murmured, pressing a kiss to her hair, "if that's the case? No one has come back to double-check on whether we lived or died. I would think if he paid off this cartel to do this to us, that they'd damn well check for bodies, because they don't get paid otherwise."

"Maybe they're waiting for nightfall to check?" she wondered, her arm going around his waist. His clothes were still damp, but she didn't care.

"And that's why I wanted to move us out of that area."

"So," she said, pulling away, looking up into his eyes, "that's why you did that? You suspected the same thing?"

He kissed her wrinkled brow. "Sweetheart, I'm used to covering all possibilities. If you say you feel Bannock around? I believe you. Then it makes my decision to move us, to put us in a much safer place, that much better. He will probably not even think of looking for us here."

With a low sigh, she closed her eyes, nestling as close as she could in his arms. "You make me feel so safe in this unsafe world of ours, Chase."

"I always want to do that for you, Cari."

"Why can't you feel safe with me?"

He gave a low chuckle. "You do make me feel that way because I rely just as much on your intelligence, your awareness, your hearing and sensing things, as you do for me. We're a team." He hugged her gently, understanding how sore and bruised she was. "Okay? Does that make you feel better now?"

"Much. I'm not helpless," she muttered.

"No, you certainly are not. Women are much stronger than any man. My mother taught me that in a hundred different ways. You're not the weaker sex. We men are."

Laughing with him, keeping it low so that sound wouldn't echo anywhere else, Cari squeezed him with all her strength. His returning embrace made her melt with hot yearning for him and only him.

Silence settled into the cave. Cari absorbed his tall, hard body, how he seemed to surround her. She moved her hand slowly up and down his back. "I have a confession," she whispered against the strong column of his neck, inhaling his male scent.

"What?" he asked, continuing to slide his hand across her shoulders.

"This crash, Chase, has ripped away everything I felt

for you . . . I mean—" She took a deep breath, pulling back, fearlessly meeting his gaze. "Oh, I know we talked about how we felt about one another at the ranch a few days ago, but I wasn't being completely honest with you. What I didn't say and what this crash, this awful thing we're caught in, makes me want to tell you, is that not only have I been falling in love with you, but that I want to live with you, love you, I want to explore what we have and our dreams . . ." She saw his eyes suddenly remind her of a raptor spotting its quarry, but the burning quality flowed through her, making her feel bolder, more confident of herself with him. "I want to love you right now. Here. I don't care if it's a cave, Chase. What if something happens to us tonight? Or tomorrow? What if we're killed?" Her voice grew hoarse. "I want this night with you and only you, in every way that I can show and tell you of the love I hold in my heart for you alone . . ."

Chase remained very still, holding her gaze, clinging to it, her husky, tear-filled voice touching his heart and soul. "I love you for so many reasons," he rasped, kissing her brow, holding her close. "You're so much braver than I am."

"I would never think that," she whispered.

"I feel the same toward you, Cari, but I was so damned afraid to tell you, for fear you'd reject me or think that I was after you just for sex, and I'm not. In fact"—he looked up and then drowned in her gaze—"I felt like I was always in a minefield with you. There were so many times I wanted to touch you, let you know I was there for you, but I was afraid you'd interpret it as a sexual advance, when it wasn't."

"That's too rich," she murmured, shaking her head,

"because there were so many times I wanted to reach out to you, touch you, let you know that I applauded who you are, but like you? I was afraid you'd think me wanting to touch you would be misread and you'd think I was flirting with you, or coming on to you."

"Well," he grumbled wryly, one corner of his mouth lifting, "we're a pair, aren't we?"

"Maybe we had to go through that period, Chase. There's so much confusion over a touch or a look that can be misinterpreted by both parties. I'm not blaming anyone, but I was just as hobbled by it as you were."

"Until now."

"Yes . . . until now. I thought I was going to die earlier today. I'm still dealing with it. I was so afraid I'd never be able to kiss you, touch you, love you and have you love me in return. I know sex is a part of love, but it's certainly not the most important part of a partnership. I've seen that with my parents and I'm sure you did with your father and mother."

"I did. They taught me loving someone was more than just a toss in bed."

"Well," she said, leaning back and straightening, his arm loosening to allow her to do that, "I want you, Chase Bishop. I want to touch your heart, become one with your soul . . . and I want you to love me just as deeply."

"That's a tall order, Cari," he said, holding her yearning look. "But I'll do the best I can. Maybe if we have no expectation of the other?"

"Yes. It's the expectation, I've found, that's sets me up for disappointment." She reached out, beginning to unsnap the front of his damp shirt. "My senses, my heart tells me we will not ever disappoint one another."

"Well," he said, glorying in her assertiveness, "if it happens, I'd like to think we'll talk it out and learn how to fix it, to make it better for the other partner. Don't you?"

"Always," she said, smoothing her palms against his darkly haired chest, easing the canvas fabric away, delighting in the feel of his hard flesh tightening where she moved her hands, her fingers tingling as she slid them through the wiry hair across the breadth of him. His groan sent a shaft of heat straight to her core and she closed her eyes, simply absorbing the feel of him, the tautness of his skin, his calloused hands sliding gently to either side of her face, tilting her chin upward. Just the bare, feathery touch of his strong mouth against her parting lips created a keening moan that moved through her. Their first kiss was nothing like she imagined. Chase kissed her mouth tenderly, so worshipful, so sacred, as if she were some fragile, beautiful being, more goddess than human. All of that was communicated in the first brush of his lips introducing himself to her. How different Chase was from other men, who blundered on a first kiss, thrusting their tongue into her mouth, making her yelp and jerk away, angered by such an unwarranted assault upon her as a person.

She drowned in his mouth, taking his with her woman's sensing, more firm, sliding, giving, taking until she trembled, feeling utterly adored, worshipped, and desired. As big a man, as muscular and powerful as he was physically, none of that was communicated in his mouth sipping at hers, kissing each corner, sealing and cajoling, spinning her deeper into raw desire.

Moaning, she withdrew, pushing the shirt off his broad, capable shoulders, seeing the thick line of bruises where the seat belt had laid diagonally across his chest. Hers looked the same, but for her, she saw the warrior in him, perhaps battered, cut, and bruised, but he was no less in sync with her as she was with him, regardless of any pain he or she might be experiencing. Instead, feeling so attuned to him, their breathing heightening, their hands moving across one another in gentle introduction, articles of clothing falling away, released to the blanket in small heaps here and there, until finally, they were naked and looking at one another with a need that humbled Cari as nothing before.

Whatever her awful moments with other males who took, grabbed, pinched, and bit at her body, Chase was just the opposite. The softened, tender look in his eyes made tears well up in her own, and she swallowed convulsively as he lay down on the blankets, the long, hard curve of his desire obvious. And all hers. And she was all his. Already, her core was soaked, aching and wanting. As he cupped her shoulders, drawing her on top of him, her thighs opening, settling on each side of his narrow hips, Cari closed her eyes as she met him for the first time.

Chase closed his hands over her rounded hips, drawing her slowly forward, her wetness hot, gliding and caressing him. He groaned, arching up against her, the feeling electric, powerful and needy. Her hands rested like butterfly wings against his chest as she began to rock and slide back and forth on top of him, giving him equal pleasure, allowing it to sink in, like rippling, heated water pooling where they touched, sending out heated rivulets of utter pleasure. He gloried in her boldness, suspending them in those minutes of introduction, appreciation, and deepening the hunger both of them felt equally for one another.

Time dissolved. The world rotated only around them, right here, right now. For Cari, this moment was magical, precious, and would never be felt quite the same way ever again because their love was finally unfolding to one another fully, joyfully, and without reservation or fear. Absorbing the shudders through his body, his hands opening and closing against her hips, she could feel him monitoring her satiation, her enjoyment, clearly wanting her to revel in it as much as he was.

She leaned down, her hard nipples grazing the field of silky dark hair, finding his mouth, sealing it with her own, their breathing becoming ragged and fast. She took his lips swiftly, as if claiming him for her own, and lifted her hips just enough to meet, touch, and then allow him to thrust slowly into her. The moment was sublime, making her feel as if she were drifting into a beautiful universe of sparkling stars that were hotly spinning around her, floating with Chase, each making the other his or her own. And when he moved fully into her, widening her, triggering all those sweet spots within her, she suddenly froze, feeling the volcanic eruption of her own juices exploding from within her, bathing him, flinging her into galaxies of color, lights, and utter pleasure.

It was the first of five orgasms that he would cajole and urge out of her ripe, hungry body, and all she could do was continue to absorb the inner joy mated with his, the thrusts designed to tease her into coming, over and over again.

Finally, spent, she lay upon his body, her brow against his jaw, breathing raggedly, lips parted, and sliding her arms around his neck, holding him close, wanting him forever. Then, and only then, did he claim her as the man he was to her woman. And as he froze, growling, gripping her hips, grinding against her, Cari's heart burst open, so euphoric and profound, that she nearly felt faint. And afterward, she lay atop him, joined, his roughened hands moving slowly across the slickness of her back and hips, feeling utterly fulfilled as never before.

Tiredness swept through her even though she tried to fight it. As if Chase sensed her state, he eased out of her, guiding her to her left side, bringing her close and then taking the blanket and pulling it over them to keep them from getting chilled. As she laid her head on his upper arm, feeling the flex of his biceps, his continued tenderness toward her brought her to her knees in another way. No man had treated her so wonderfully as Chase just had. Her whole body felt like an overheated vessel, and she continued to feel those wonderful rippling sensations that were still alive and vibrating through her lower body. His other arm came around her shoulders and back, drawing her next to him, sharing his warmth with her. It was impossible to open her eyes. Cari continued to float, to focus on only Chase and herself. There was such an unspoken luxury that they'd shared between them.

She felt his mouth against her temple, kissing her lightly, as if urging her to just surrender to the sleep that so desperately wanted to pull her under into that warm, cossetting darkness behind her eyelids. Love for him welled up within her, consuming her, and she wanted nothing more than this moment out of time to be with him. Cari would never forget this one act of loving between them. Ever.

"Sleep, sweetheart," he rasped, kissing the top of her ear, "sleep with the angels, because you are one. I'll be here and I'll hold you safe . . ."

Those were the last low, rasping words Cari remembered hearing, the strength of Chase's arms holding her, his one hand against her hips, pressed against his hips, feeling as if they had melted fully into one another forever. And her last fragment of a thought was that she wanted *forever* with this man of Nature, who was as rough and rugged as the land he had tamed, and yet, with her, the most tender and thoughtful of lovers that she'd ever had.

It didn't matter how much danger swirled around them anymore. No matter what happened, Cari would hold this sacred moment in her hands and heart. Every second, every touch, every breath, was remembered and sealed not only into the memory of her heart, but a part of her soul. No one could take that from her. Not even Dirk. What she had just experienced and shared with Chase was beyond anything she could have imagined or expected. The act of loving her had been him unselfishly making her first, the priority, giving her the pleasure that she not only deserved, but that he wanted to tease out of her willing body, and give back to her. How many men were there like him on this Earth? Not many, from Cari's experience, and certainly her girlfriends all had bad experiences just like her. No, Chase Bishop was a rare find. He treated her like a human, not a sex object, not something to be used, hurt, abused, and then thrown away without care, with the selfish intent of not sharing anything with her.

He was a model of a twenty-first-century man who valued his woman as an equal, and with deep, abiding respect for who she was. Her man, Chase Bishop, was a dream come true, and that was the last thing Cari remembered, cossetted in his arms, warm, well-loved and adored as an equal.

Chapter Fifteen

June 19

"Are you ready?" Chase asked Cari in a low voice. They had awakened and reluctantly left one another's arms. To have her warmth, the softness of her breath as she slept against his neck, made him feel like he was in heaven. A heaven he'd never experienced before and he wanted so damned much more of it, too. Forever, with Cari.

"Getting there," she muttered sleepily, sitting on the floor, pulling on her second boot and lacing it up. She looked up, seeing bare dawn light out of the hole in the ceiling of the cave.

"Still sore and stiff?" he asked, zipping up his go-bag.

She groaned. "Worse this morning."

"Me, too. It will be a week before it all leaves. Getting out and walking twenty miles will definitely ease the soreness because of the blood circulation." He grinned, even though he was pretty sure Cari couldn't see it. The light in the cave was barely there in the pre-dawn hours.

"Are your feet and knees feeling strong and good?" he

asked, standing, pulling his knapsack over his shoulders and buckling up.

"I'm fine," Cari said. She stood, dusting off her butt, the sand fine, like sugar granules, poofing and floating to the floor of the cave.

"Let me help you," he said, opening the straps to her go-bag, easing it across her shoulders. Luckily, they had worn clothes in layers. They didn't have a jacket between them, but in the coolish cave air, they'd had one another to keep warm during the night.

"Thanks," she said, sliding her arms through the openings. Chase handed her the baseball cap and she put it on. "I'm ready."

He picked up her hand, placing it against the nylon belt of the go-bag. "I'm going to walk slowly. You hang on here and we'll thread that narrow passage to the cave below us. Remember how I taught you to walk silently?"

"Yes, I do."

"Let's employ it until we get out of this cave complex. All right?"

"I'll do that. Do you think anyone is down there?"

Hearing the trepidation in her low tone, he said, "Nothing . . . so far . . ."

"This is scary," she muttered, slipping her fingers beneath his belt.

"We'll be all right," he soothed. "Let's go . . ." Chase wasn't going to tell her that most of the night, he'd remained awake, listening with his keen sense of hearing. It had been a moonless night, the darkness complete. Several times, he heard packs of coyotes calling to one another outside the cave opening. Another time, an owl hooting to its mate. Luckily, no sounds of truck engines or men speaking in Spanish. It had been quiet. But quiet didn't mean safe, and he knew that better than most. Cari wouldn't have a clue, and that was fine by him. She worried under general circumstances, never mind what they found themselves in right now.

He halted near the end of the path, listening. Cari stood behind him, unmoving. His Glock was in his nylon holster, strapped low on his right leg, the strap that held it in unfastened. Earlier, he'd placed the magazine in the chamber and clicked off the safety. In Afghanistan that was normal procedure. If he got jumped, there would be no time to snap off the safety, load the chamber, and then fire. He'd be dead before he could get a shot off.

Scanning the silent lower cave, his eyes adjusted to the pre-dawn light, and he could see the outlines and the shadows. Lifting his chin, he sniffed the air. Often, in Afghanistan, he would hunt at night and sleep in a cave during the day. At night, people made campfires to heat their tea and he could follow the scent of the smoke to where they were located. It wasn't any different now. He was sure that drug runners used these caves and would start a fire to warm their food or coffee. He smelled nothing but a slight dampness to the night air.

He lifted his left hand and gave Cari's hand a squeeze, then released it, moving forward, staying close to the wall. They would not go out in the middle of the cave, where they would be a good target; they silently made their way around it.

He was proud of Cari; she was walking as silently as he was. Love flowed through him for this brave woman. She was completely out of her element, but she wasn't rattled, no drama, just quiet, common sense and listening closely to what he asked of her. How much he loved her! Chase wanted to do anything but leave the cave after they'd consummated their love for one another. He wanted to talk and share with her, and he wanted to know what was in her heart and mind, as well. But that wasn't going to happen. At least, not right now.

As he approached the entrance, he again halted, listened, and smelled the air. The astringent scent of the juniper trees filled his nostrils. The pre-dawn light was slowly growing and his gaze moved from right to left. The two junipers that stood guard at the entrance were good cover, and he slowly moved forward, his right hand on the butt of his Glock, in case he needed to use it.

Off in the distance, he heard that same owl hooting. From the direction of the sound, Chase thought the nocturnal hunter was in the grove behind them. Halting at the edge of the juniper, he again surveyed the area.

Everything was silent. He would ordinarily love this time of morning, watching the stars along the eastern horizon begin to fade and disappear beneath the coming light of the sun, but not this morning. Yesterday, he'd burned into his memory the trail that had led him to this cave. It was somewhat less rocky than the surrounding area, so he took it. The trail wasn't too steep, and he continued to aggressively sweep the area.

Within five minutes, they were on the flat of the land that stretched out before them. He pulled out the compass, the dials a pale green of radium, showing where west was. And that's the direction they needed to move. The horizon was a thin reddish line, and he hoped that wasn't symbolic of someone's blood. He turned, his voice low.

"We can walk normally, now. Give me your hand. Once we get a feel for the soil conditions, we can walk faster. If I get going too fast for you, squeeze my hand?"

She squeezed his hand in return.

He smiled into her eyes, able to see her features now. Leaning down, he kissed her brow and he turned and started their walk. Earlier, he'd asked Cari not to speak when they were traveling, especially during the first hour or so. If the drug runners were camped somewhere unseen, but heard them talking, it would make them targets.

As the sun rose, Chase could see the uneven ground even better. Cari was a trooper, keeping up with his twenty-minute-mile stride. He'd always relied on his cell phone for the time, not wearing a watch. Now, he wished he had one, but he could mentally figure out how many miles there were. Lesson learned.

The soil was dusty, peppered with lots of pebbles, a few larger rocks, a struggling cactus here and there, so he always had to watch for them and avoid them at all costs. Today was not the day to get a cactus spine through their boot or into their ankle or lower leg. They hurt like hell for hours on end, even if they were pulled out with a pair of pliers.

By the time the sun rose, around five a.m., the first rays shooting silently across the desert, Chase discovered a wash. He led Cari down into it. At the bottom of it, he brought her to one side, against the wall, and halted. Looking both directions in the gulch, the way was straight for nearly a mile on either side of them. He released her hand.

"Let's take a break," he said, shrugging out of his pack

and pulling out a quart of water. He unscrewed the cap and handed it to her. "Drink at least half of it. We have to stay hydrated."

Nodding, she took it.

Cari handed it back to him and he chugged down the other half, setting the plastic bottle on the ground and covering it completely with dirt, hiding evidence that they'd been here. Straightening, he turned, wanting to make sure she was all right.

"How are you doing?" he asked.

"Fine." Cari smiled a little, touching his bristly jaw. "I sure lost a lot of the soreness and stiffness."

"We've walked about three miles, in my estimation, that's why. Is my speed too fast for you?"

"No." She looked around. The wash was about eight feet tall. "Isn't this a good place to walk? It's going due west." She pointed down the wash.

"You'd have made a good tracker," he congratulated her. "Yes, this is ideal. The sides of this wash, if they remain taller than us, hide us from anyone or anything that might be looking for us." He melted inwardly over her sudden smile, drinking in that sparkle from her eyes. He couldn't resist, leaned over, sliding his hand behind her neck, gently drawing her to his mouth. He kissed her with longing, with love, and he heard her moan as she stepped up against him, her arms coming around his shoulders. It was the sweetness of her mouth, the way their lips slid against one another, her moist, warm breath against his cheek, that conspired to make him want to make love to her right then and there. Easing from her glistening lips, he grinned.

"If we were anywhere but here . . ."

"Yes?"

"You and I would be making love with one another on the spot."

Stepping back, she gave him a wicked, alluring look. "I'm game, Bishop."

Laughing in a low tone, he released her. "I like your spunkiness."

"I kinda like yours, too." She pointed to the bulge at his crotch.

Chase felt his cheeks grow warm and he was sure in the low light, that Cari wouldn't have seen him blush. "Am I seeing a whole new side to you, Ms. Taylor?" He saw her eyes glint, more the hunter than the hunted.

"Indeed, you are, Mr. Bishop. Shall we go? I'd like to get home, be back at your ranch, and be in bed with you."

He grazed her cheek, leaning close, holding her dancing gaze. "*Our* ranch, sweetheart, if I have anything to say about it." That made her brows rise and she blinked once, owlishly, studying him. His grin widened. Yeah, she got the message loud and clear, and if he didn't know better, liked it a whole helluva lot. So did he.

Chase dropped his hand from her cheek. "Yes, that means what you think it does, Cari. I want the rest of my life with you and nothing less . . . What about you? How do you feel about that?"

Cari lost her smile, becoming serious. She reached up, grazing his jaw. "I like the sound of it, Chase."

"Good. Come on, we have some miles to walk . . ." His heart lifted so high he barely felt his feet touching the ground. Cari's words, the emotional look in her eyes, the soft quaver of it, plunged Chase into a euphoria he had never dared envision, much less think, could happen. They were meant for one another, that's all there was to it. She was the queen of bees, he a king of ranching, and together, their castle, the Three Bars, would flourish, just as their love for one another was doing right now. He could barely keep his head screwed on straight, forcing himself to return to the sniper behind the lines in order to keep them safe, hidden, and hopefully, making that raptor facility by noon.

The heat began to build rapidly as the sun rose. Chase kept up the pace, Cari uncomplaining, keeping up with him. Not many people, even younger people, could do twenty miles in eight hours under normal circumstances. Sweat was running down his face and hours earlier, they had unclasped hands, which were wet with sweat. To his surprise and pleasure, the wash continued in a westerly direction with a few curves here and there. The air was sweltering, heat waves beginning around ten a.m., from his estimation. Slowly, the walls of the wash began to diminish, little by little. Their safety was eroded away as it did so. Still, it was much easier walking on a sandy floor than one with pebbles, cacti, and rocks that one could trip over. There were trade-offs.

Always, Chase kept his ear keyed to hear anything that was out of place. What he dreaded the most was the sound of trucks, truck engines, and anything having to do with human movement out here. At one point, around nine a.m., he'd climbed the slanted wall of the wash, lying on his belly, looking around. The area was flat except for small nobs and sloped hills here and there, some greenery with hardy junipers that had found an underground water source in order to survive. And those long, undulating heat waves surrounded them in every direction. Old Highway 8 was no longer in view, the whole region more or less flat.

He tried to find any dark, rectangular or square shapes on the horizon, hoping to see a building of some sort, but there was none. He'd slid down into the wash again on his belly. Cari was sitting, drinking water, resting in the shade of the wall.

"I don't see anything," he told her, kneeling down, taking the bottle she'd offered him.

"No buildings? No roads?"

Shaking his head, he drank deeply, finishing off the last of the water in the bottle, burying it nearby. Taking off his cap, he wiped the sweat from his brow with the back of his forearm and then settled it back on his head, the bill shading his eyes from the brightness of the sun. They had no sunglasses, as they had been in the truck. "I'm trying to remember that GPS map on the cell phone," he told her. "I remember a road. It actually had a name on it: Pitcairn."

She laughed, hugging the shade of the wash wall, her back against it. "Pitcairn as in the sailors who anchored on that island, mutinied from the *Bounty* and then went ashore to live there?"

He gave her a humored look. "Well, don't you think anyone living out in a godforsaken place like this has pretty much mutinied against society? That they want to be left alone on this desert island of sorts?"

Cari nodded, giving him a returning grin. "I'd say that was about right. As a matter of fact? Whoever named this probably has read *Mutiny on the Bounty*. Don't you think?"

"Yeah, I do," he said, absorbing her sparkling eyes that were filled with such love for him. His chest swelled with such emotion that Chase wished they were anywhere but where they were. How badly he wanted to sweep Cari into his arms, kiss her breathless, love her until they both fainted from mutual pleasure.

"That raptor facility was on another dirt road," Cari said with a chuckle. "The name of it is Bounty."

He chuckled. "Yeah, I think someone definitely read that book."

"That book was published in 1932," Cari said. "The authors, both men, were Hall and Nordhoff."

"Well," he said, "maybe their descendants live out here? And that's how the names came about?"

"I hope we find out pretty soon, don't you?" Cari giggled.

"By my recollection, we've got about two more hours to go, and then we should be close to where that raptor place is located."

"It would be nice to find a road that went west," she said, slowly standing.

"If it does," he chuckled, "it might be named Bligh, after the lieutenant who made the crew mutiny on the *Bounty*."

They laughed together. Cari leaned up, kissing him swiftly on his mouth. She gripped his upper arms. "I want this every day moving forward, Chase. I love to laugh with you. I love that we are on the same wavelength."

He kissed her cheek and straightened. "I guess if two

people in today's world have read *Mutiny on the Bounty*, there's gotta be something good between them. Ready?"

"Lead on," she said. "I'm right on your heels."

The wash continued to have shorter walls as another hour passed. Chase had stopped and looked to the west, searching for any sign of a building in between the wavering horizontal lines of heat. They were down to four quarts of water left between them. And they were drinking one an hour, the temperature still climbing and in the high eighties now, from his estimate. Cari stood next to him and they both searched the western horizon.

"Wait," Cari said, excitement rising in her voice. "Look there, Chase." She pointed to the southwest. "I think I see black blobs . . . are those buildings? I can't tell. The mirage is really messing up my vision."

He moved his gaze, looking at where she was pointing. They were standing in what little shade was left on the eastern wall of the wash. "Yes . . . I see something . . ."

"Did they teach you in sniper school to be able to read mirages and heat waves?"

He grunted. "Not exactly."

"But you see them? There's like two blobs. They dance around . . . I can't tell what they are . . . maybe buildings?"

He studied them. "I think you're right. That appears to be solid. It's not moving right or left."

"Then, maybe it's not a mirage, but a real building?"

He heard the hope rise in her voice. "Yeah, it could be."

"Is that the right direction?"

Again, he didn't want to worry her. "It's in the right direction." And it was the only thing on the horizon, so he was fervently hoping it was the raptor facility. There wasn't anything else out here. Cari's face was getting red. He was sure his was, too, but he was far more acclimated to desert heat than she because of his five years in the Sandbox. Her cheeks were rosy, face glistening with sweat, but those wonderful lips of hers were compressed, and he could see the dogged stubbornness in her expression that she was going to keep up with him, no matter what. He wanted to tell her that she was surprising him. At the ranch, she appeared fey, almost fragile. But when push came to shove, this other side to her, the tough woman warrior who was his equal, came out of nowhere.

He was going to spend the rest of his life uncovering the many layers of Cari, and it was going to be an investigation of pure delight on his part. He had always known she was a complex being, but now, he was seeing the fighter side of her rise to the challenge they were in, and he sure as hell reveled in her backbone, her unstoppable spirit and can-do attitude. In some ways, Cari was just like Hannah, but Cari hid it very well from most people until she needed to call on that reserve.

"You know," he said, gesturing for her to leave the shade and start the walk again, "you are one tough customer, Cari Taylor. I love the hell out of you for your strength and courage." He saw her eyes grow light, an impish grin on her face.

"Chase, I have never told you about my global trips, hiking in the Pyrenees, the mountains of Turkey, to reach beekeepers and help them. I did a *lot* of hiking, sometimes a whole day, to reach an out-of-the-way place where I could consult with the owners who wanted to establish a beekeeping company." She laughed and shook her head. "We have a lot to talk about and discover about one another, Mr. Bishop."

Chuckling, he nodded. "Guilty as charged, Ms. Taylor. Let's hoof it . . ."

Cari pushed herself hard. She'd never hiked twenty miles in her life. Her legs were tired and stressed. The stiffness was certainly gone, but now, her knees were beginning to ache and she was sure it was from the grueling hiking speed under a very hot, unrelenting sun. Chase seemed like a robot, tireless, in comparison. His flesh was sweaty, his mouth tight, and she could see what had made him the combat sniper he'd become. Under any other circumstances, she would not have realized it, but now she did, and she was so proud of him, of the kind of hardships he'd survived for five years. They had to survive this journey, as well. Would they?

"Wait!" Chase grabbed her, pressing her against the four-foot wall of the wash.

Gasping, Cari's gaze flew upward. She heard a noise!

"What?" she squeaked, her voice suddenly tight. Chase had placed her between the wall and his tall, hard body.

"I hear an engine. One vehicle. It's coming our way." He peered over the wall of the wash. "Whoever it is, they're hightailing it, high rooster tails of dust. I can't make out who it is, yet."

She felt his hands holding her firm against the wall. "Is there a nearby road, maybe?" she rasped, her throat tight, her heart starting to pound in her chest.

"I don't know," he answered gruffly, eyes squinted against the sun, watching, waiting . . .

"Who else could it be, Chase? Maybe it's the Border Patrol? They're out in this area, too."

"That's what I'm hoping. They're coming straight toward us. Unless there's a road I don't know about, that is just desert country. That doesn't make sense. We saw a number of dirt roads over this entire area and I'm sure Border Patrol uses them all the time when they make their rounds. They wouldn't go cross country like this . . ." He pulled away, releasing her. Looking toward the wash to the west, there were three juniper trees in the center of it. "Let's get to those trees. Run!"

She ran, digging the toes of her boots into the sand, her breath tearing out of her mouth. If it was Border Patrol? That would be wonderful! The toes of her boots dug into the sand, a filmy spray behind her as she worked to keep up with Chase, who ran like a gazelle compared to her. The trees were a welcome sight. They had run into two or three clumps of them on their hike through the wash, and they had welcomed shade and protection from the sun when they could rest for a bit beneath their branches. They were very old junipers, their trunks with silvered bark, anywhere between three to five feet wide.

Just as they reached the trees, Chase cursed. He whirled around, grabbing Cari by the shoulder, forcing her down to her knees between two trunks of the old, gnarled junipers that had grown together, forming a massive wall of wood in front of them.

"It's a civilian ATV! Not Border Patrol. They've got weapons."

Gasping for air, her lungs burning, she gave a low cry and scrambled back to her feet as Chase lodged himself between two of the trees with her behind him. "What? Maybe it's from the raptor facility? Someone out for a ride in the desert?"

Chase pulled his Glock. "No way. I see two men, and the one on the back of the ATV is carrying what looks like military style rifle, an AR-15."

"Oh, no! Drug runners?"

"Yeah," he growled. "And maybe we just have bad luck, Cari. Maybe this is a way they come because they're heading straight for the border, which isn't more than five miles away to the south of us. I want you to stay down. Curl into a ball behind me, put your hands over your head and lay as close to the ground as you can. Whatever you do? DON'T MOVE. You're protected where you're at."

Closing her eyes, sobbing for breath, she wanted to cry. She heard the engine loudly now. Men with rifles! Military rifles! Did they see her and Chase? Maybe they wouldn't! Chase's body was between her and the juniper trunks. She had curled up into a ball, her back against his long, powerful legs and his boots. Who were these men? *Drug runners*, her mind screamed.

The ATV growled louder and louder.

Her breath came in spurts. Her heart crashed in her chest. Hands over her head, a tight ball, Cari felt horribly vulnerable. Chase could be killed! She could be killed!

Chase gritted his teeth, placing the Glock against the rough bark of the juniper to steady his aim. His pistol would only be good at seventy-five feet. Those two men in the ATV drew closer, less than one-tenth of a mile away from them, now. He braced himself, left palm beneath the butt of the Glock, aiming at the man in the rear who was raising that military rifle—right at them. He sucked air slowly between his teeth, his entire focus, his life, in that bead he had drawn on the male with a weapon. He looked dark skinned, wearing a bright red bandanna across his forehead, bearded, desert camouflage clothing, telling Chase that he wasn't some tourist out for just a ride in the desert. No, they were speeding toward them like Hell itself was on their tail.

His mind whirled with questions. How had they tracked them? And then, he cursed beneath his breath. *A drone.* Druggies always had drones, flying at high altitude, checking to see if any Border Patrol might be in the region. Had these two drug runners been monitoring them with a drone? Too high for him to pick up the sound? It was entirely possible. In the seat next to the man armed with the rifle was a huge, tan, plastic box strapped down. It was big enough to have been carrying a drone in it. Sonofabitch!

So, the druggies that pushed them off the cliff and into the canyon were *still* after them! Sweat dribbled down in his eyes, making them sting. He blinked rapidly, the sound of the growling ATV hurtling straight toward them, the roar vibrating around them. It was as if these druggies knew exactly where they were hiding.

Before Chase could think further, he saw the yellow flashing from the muzzle of the AR-15. Bracing himself against the protection of the thick, wide trunk of the juniper, he yelled to Cari, "They're firing at us! DO NOT MOVE!"

The first bullets struck and whined through the grove of the three junipers. Wood chips and smaller branches cracked, snapped, flying like projectiles all around them.

He still wasn't in range yet! An AR-15 had a half a mile range where bullet accuracy was guaranteed. His puny Glock had seventy-five feet accuracy. The bullets kept exploding into the grove, more bark and chips of wood detonating around them. He heard Cari scream once. There was nothing he could do. She *had to stay put*! He knew how scared she was.

God, don't let her move. Make her stay exactly where she is!

The ATV began slowing, the closer it got to the grove. His breathing was slow and steady. How many times had he hunted bad guys just like these where there was no backup? They had none right now, either. The only thing that changed was that the woman he loved was huddled against his back legs, shaking. If only Cari weren't here! Chase would have done things differently, but more than anything, she had to be protected at all costs. He'd give his life for her. No question.

The bark exploded, slivers screaming in every direction. Chase prayed the thick, old wood of the trunks, which was shaking and trembling with every hit of an AR bullet, would hold up. He knew the wood on this type of tree was thick, hard, and nearly impenetrable.

The ATV slowed more.

Chase got a look at the driver.

Sonofabitch, it was Dirk Bannock! He was wearing a red bandanna around his head, sunglasses, camo gear, and a beard. And the bastard was smiling.

His mind whirled with shock. How had Bannock found them?

There was no time to think. The ATV was slowing and was within a hundred feet of him. Chase knew the shooter was Bannock—pointing his weapon after ejecting the empty cartridge and slamming another one into the weapon with the butt of his palm. The barrel lifted in their direction. The man stood up as the ATV came to a halt. He pulled back on the trigger, bullets pouring into where he was standing. Above everything, he could *not* move! He had to have a steady bead on him!

Wincing, more wood being torn out of the tree by the AR that was now on full automatic, Chase focused. The shooter was swinging the weapon wildly. He pulled back on the trigger of the Glock. It was a long shot. They were a hundred feet away. This weapon was only good for seventy-five feet. *Dammit!*

He caressed the trigger, the Glock roaring, bucking in his hand. The sound was like a clap of thunder around him.

There was a scream. The man standing up behind Bannock got slammed backward, knocked out of the ATV, the AR-15 flying, flipping end over end in the air and landing ten feet away from the machine.

The man landed flat on his back, about three feet from the ATV, a shocked look on his face. He struggled to get up, get to the AR-15 lying nearby.

Chase fired again.

The soldier, who was getting to his knees, was hit again.

Satisfaction soared through Chase as his bullet found center mass. If the soldier was wearing a Kevlar vest, it didn't show. The second bullet went right through his chest, slamming him backwards.

Dirk cursed loudly, grabbed his rifle leaning nearby, yanking it upward. He realized he was exposed now that his unmoving friend was dead. He leaped out of the ATV that was idling noisily in park.

"You're dead!" he screamed, coming around the front of the machine. Now less than fifty feet away, he started to lift the rifle.

Just as Chase was going to fire, he heard a screech above him.

In the next second a red-tail hawk attacked Bannock, her long, yellow legs straight out in front of her, talons extended.

Chase watched in disbelief as the hawk, who he was sure was Valkyrie, struck Bannock directly in the face.

Bannock screamed, dropping the rifle, the hawk's talons sinking deeply into his face, blood flying everywhere. He struck wildly at the hawk, trying to tear her off his face, whirling around, stumbling.

Chase grunted and charged forward. Bannock was now unarmed.

Valkyrie continued to shriek, her high-pitched cry filled with rage, her large wingspan of five feet slapping at Bannock as he fell backward, off balance, arms flailing.

The hawk released him, flapping away.

Chase landed on Bannock, fist cocked, slamming it into the man's badly lacerated, bloodied face. With one hard blow, Bannock crumpled, knocked unconscious. Breathing hard, Chase got up, kicking the AR out from anyone's reach. He made sure Bannock was knocked out and then he checked out the ATV. There was some rope in the bottom on the passenger side. Grabbing it, he jerked Bannock over on his belly, slamming him into the dirt, hauling his hands in back of him and making damn sure he wouldn't get his hands free ever again.

"Chase!"

Jerking his head up, he saw Cari's white face, her eyes huge, watching him from the safety of the tree.

"Cari! Come here! Grab these two rifles! Carry them to the ATV. Be careful, don't touch the trigger mechanisms!"

He pushed Bannock on his back, satisfied. Valkyrie shrieked above them, flapping toward the juniper and then landing, watching them intently. Even from where he stood, he could see the hawk's eyes filled with fury. Valkyrie had saved them.

Chase saw Cari pick up the rifles. He pulled the Glock out of his holster as he approached the other smuggler. Leaning down, he felt along his carotid artery on the side of his neck. No pulse. He straightened and saw Cari carefully lay the two military weapons in the back on the floor of the ATV.

He walked swiftly over to her, his gaze raking her body. She had blood on her face and arms. It was from the projectile splinters caused by the bullets slamming into those mighty junipers that had protected them.

"Cari," he rasped, gripping her arm, pulling her into him, holding her hard. He heard her say his name, her voice muffled against his chest, her arms going around his torso. He heard her sob. Had she seen Bannock? The hawk attacking him in the face?

Sweat rolled off his hard features as he held her tightly against him, his heart aching for her. They were safe. Or were they? He scanned the horizon, looking for more ATVs carrying smugglers. He saw nothing. But that didn't mean there weren't more and he just didn't see them yet. They, too, could have a drone, and he looked skyward, squinting, trying to see if he could spot one. He could not.

The late morning air was hot and stifling. He eased her away from him. "Cari? Are you all right? Talk to me?"

She shakily wiped the tears from her face. "Y-yes . . . just a lot of wood splinters . . .

"Bannock . . . you saw him?" he growled, turning his attention to Cari's unmoving relative.

"I-I saw everything." She sniffed, looking up at the juniper. "Valkyrie . . . she was around. I-I didn't know that . . . my God, she attacked Dirk just as he was going to shoot us . . ."

Giving her a mirthless look, he kept his gaze on Bannock. Anytime now, he'd regain consciousness. *The bastard.* "Listen, we need to do several things," he rasped. "I'm going to search Bannock for a cell phone or radio. I'm going to drag that dead soldier into the grove, as well. Maybe we can get help. I don't know. But at least now we have wheels. We have that ATV. We can quickly find that raptor facility, get to them, and get Dan on the line, as well as make an immediate call to Border Patrol. They're going to have a lot of questions for us."

She wiped her face and a stream of blood that came from her upper arm. "It all happened so fast. How could Dirk know where we were?"

Grimly, he released her, guiding her to sit down on the front passenger seat of the ATV. "My guess is that they had a drone watching us all along. They were probably looking for us after the crash, but the grove of junipers at that spring hid us. Only when we went out into that gulch and walked, did they spot us." He dragged the dead soldier between the trees. He turned, seeing Cari staring at Bannock, her hand against her lips. He wanted to protect her from all of this, but Chase knew he couldn't.

Leaning over Bannock, he searched and found a cell phone. He smiled grimly. The man's eyelids were fluttering. Soon enough, he'd start to become conscious. He held up the cell phone so that Cari could see it.

"Bingo," he told her. He instantly dialed Dan Seabert's phone number and walked over to where Cari sat. She was suddenly looking pale and shocky. She wasn't used to combat like he was. He could tamp down his emotions so he could think clearly and coolly. As soon as Dan answered the phone, Chase told him everything. He placed an arm around Cari's slumped shoulders and she leaned into him, closing her eyes. It was over. They were alive . . .

Chapter Sixteen

June 19

"You BITCH!" Bannock screamed as the Border Patrol took him into custody at the raptor facility.

Chase stood with his arm around Cari's shoulders, feeling her tremble as her stepbrother's voice echoed around the room at the visitors' center. He glared at her as he was taken away by two male Border Patrol agents, handcuffed. Chase had put Bannock on the back seat of the ATV, ropes around him so he couldn't do anything but lie on the seat. He also put a gag in his mouth to make sure he wouldn't curse at Cari. Thanks to the cell phone, he'd put in the coordinates for the raptor facility and driven two miles to it.

He felt Cari tremble, but she stood straight and tall, fearlessly glaring back at Dirk. Chase loved her for her courage under the circumstances. If it hadn't been for Valkyrie and the Glock with him, they would probably be dead right now. They'd be burying both of them instead of Bannock being hauled away. The FBI would meet them and take him off the Border Patrol's hands once they drove him back to their main headquarters at the hot springs.

When the main door closed, Cari looked up at him. "He'd have killed both of us."

Nodding, Chase didn't want to contribute to how she already felt, seeing deep sadness and exhaustion in her eyes. "But it didn't turn out that way."

"You saved us. Your go-bags saved us. And so did Valkyrie."

He smiled a little. "We also saved ourselves. You contributed just as much as I did. And Valkyrie?" He twisted his head to the left where a large group of raptor cages were sitting, half of them outdoors beneath a long roof to protect them from the overhead sun.

The red-tail had followed them to the facility, shrieking every once in a while, gliding about a thousand feet above them. When Cari climbed out of the ATV, the hawk had landed on her arm, never hurting her skin at all. Two of the owners, a husband and wife, had come out and coaxed Valkyrie to a glove with some mouse meat. From there, they had given her a large tub to take a bath in her new, large cage. She had a huge area to fly in, and was now on a large wooden perch, preening herself. She was full, clean, and happy.

Cari sighed, watching Valkyrie in her new, temporary home. "She had been watching over us all the time, Chase. I wasn't sure she'd survived the crash, but she had. I looked for her, but I never saw her."

"Neither did I. That cage had its top ripped off. I didn't know where she was. We had to survive ourselves." He squeezed her shoulders gently. "She's a little worse for wear, but the people here will let her heal up, and then they'll release her to the wild, to meet her mate who's waiting somewhere out there for her. She'll have a good life here, Cari. No question she helped save our lives. By Valkyrie attacking Bannock in the face? He couldn't fire at us. I've never seen anything like that."

Nodding, Cari looked relieved and gazed around the enclosure. "She knew we were in terrible danger. And she put herself in danger to save us." The two people who ran the raptor facility had offered them a shower, which they would take shortly. The FBI had already been in touch with them, and they would talk with them once they returned to Silver Creek. In the meantime, after cleaning up they would be driven to Jacumba Hot Springs in a Border Patrol SUV that was waiting for them outside the facility.

At the hot springs, they would rent a car, buy some clean clothes, and grab a bite at a local restaurant. The next morning, they'd give their story to the Border Patrol. Chase had killed a man, and they wanted all the details. Plus a report on Bannock. Lastly, they'd leave for Silver Creek in their rental car.

"How about that shower?" he asked, giving her a slight smile, rubbing her shoulder gently.

"That sounds wonderful. Wish it could be with you," she said, giving him a slight smile.

"I don't think that would work here. But maybe at a later time? Right now, you're in shock and honestly, so am I."

"I feel as if someone pulled the plug on my energy," she confessed, following him across the room to another door.

"Makes two of us. I can hardly wait to get home. How about you?" Because Chase knew the coming weeks were going to be hard on both of them for different reasons. As a sniper, he never felt sorry he had to take a life, and he didn't now, either. But it left an emotional mark on him that he would pay for later. It didn't matter the drug runner was intent on murdering both of them; Chase knew the toll on himself from taking another human being's life. He leaned over, pressing a kiss to Cari's hair. *A step at a time. An hour at a time.* Cari looked worn, emotionally drained, but so was he. He just didn't show it as outwardly as she did. How he looked forward to Silver Creek and their ranch . . .

June 23

"Helluva journey to California, wasn't it?" Dan Seabert greeted Chase and Cari as they entered his office at sheriff's headquarters. He shook their hands and invited them to sit down.

Chase shut the door behind them. "We're just glad to be home, Dan."

"I'm sure you are. Coffee?"

"Not for me," Cari said, sitting down. "We just had breakfast."

"Me either," Chase agreed, sitting next to her.

"Well, I'm getting my third cup. It's been a busy morning." He poured a cup and brought it over to his desk, sitting down. "How did the interview with the FBI go?"

"Exhausting," Cari murmured, giving Chase a sympathetic look. "They treated Chase like he'd done something wrong by killing that drug runner."

Chase reached out, squeezing her hand where it rested on the chair. "It's their job," he said. "They didn't arrest me, that's the important thing, but they do have to get all the sordid details."

"Well, they grilled me for over an hour," Cari said sourly, "two of them, a man and a woman."

"They always do that," Dan soothed. "They want separate interviews to see if your stories match up or not."

"They did," Chase said. "My interviewer said we were free to go and that if they had any more questions, they'd call us."

"That's a get-out-of-jail-free card," Dan said, pleased. He took a sip of his coffee. "You two underwent a grueling trial. The day the crash happened, I'd called you on your cell that evening. When I didn't get a response, I got worried."

"We were hiding out in a grove of junipers next to a spring," Cari said. "Glad to be alive."

"The FBI sent me photos." Dan shook his head. "I don't know how you survived that fall."

"Sheer luck," Chase agreed.

"You two look pretty banged up from it," he noted, making a gesture toward Cari's bruised forearm.

Cari looked at both her arms, a lot of scratches on them, too. "I feel like we went through a war, Dan."

"We did," Chase said. "But we survived. That's the good news."

Dan gave Cari a gentle look. "You're not like Chase and me. We were military, trained for combat, and you were not. It makes a huge difference on how you handle your head and emotions afterward. You need to talk to Chase when you're feeling odd or funny or over-emotional, Cari. Talking is good."

"Wow, all this coming from a man. I'm impressed, Dan.

Usually men are zipped up tighter than a drum and *never* talk about what they're feeling."

"I'm working at it," Dan said wryly, giving Chase a knowing look. "You women have us beat by a mile on dumping your emotions, working through them and releasing them."

"Where did you get so wise?" Chase asked, grinning.

Dan shook his head, rummaging around and finding a gray file hidden beneath a number of other items on his desk. "My sister is my main teacher," he acknowledged, opening the file, smoothing out the papers in it.

Chase glanced at Cari. "Her name is Raven," he told her.

"My *older* sister," Dan corrected. "She's two years ahead of me in just about every way. She's the one that broke down some of my walls and started me talking about my time as a Navy SEAL. It's been good for me. I owe her a lot."

"I wish," Cari said sadly, "that Dirk had been a positive force in my life, like Raven is in yours."

"Well," Dan murmured sympathetically, "they say that blood runs thicker than water, but that doesn't guarantee that siblings are going to always get along and save one another's hides."

"It sure as hell doesn't," Chase growled. "Bannock was the way he was long before he came into your family, Cari. And he was jealous of you, always in competition with you. I know his type: He was envious of you and your mother."

"Good psychology," Dan congratulated him. "I thought the same thing. But most stepchildren don't turn out like Bannock did. There's plenty of second-family situations, and the kids learn to adjust and get along. Thank God most don't end up like Bannock did."

"What's going to happen to him?" Cari asked in a low tone, her hands clasped tightly in her lap. "I know my mother and her husband have been contacted by the FBI."

"Yes, and that's what this file is all about, Cari." Dan lifted up the gray file. "The FBI just sent me a copy of it yesterday evening, which is why I called and asked both of you to meet me here this morning."

"What's happening to him?"

"Right now? He's back in his old prison in California. He's got a lawyer and he's going to court, charged with attempted first-degree murder of the two of you, as well as escaping from prison and all sorts of other things." Dan tapped the thick sheaf of papers in the file. "Bannock isn't talking to us. He won't tell us how or when he knew you were here. Or how he tracked you to California. We may never know, but maybe it will come out in the trial. And of course, you will be part of his trial, and so will Chase. I'm sure any jury in the world will find him guilty as the evidence, the facts, show his intent toward both of you."

"He was a drug lord in Southern California," Chase said. "Somehow, he knew Hauptman, but I'm not as clear on that connection."

"Hauptman uses drones, just like all of the cartels do now," Dan said, tapping the file. "They've been using them to carry drugs across the Mexico border to the US for years. Here's my guess on all of this," Dan said, leaning back in his chair, looking at them. "I'm just wondering when I went driving past them, following them at a good distance, if Hauptman didn't order one of his men who handles their drones to get one up in the air. If they did, which is entirely possible, that drone would have followed me back into Silver Creek. And if that drone had a camera attached to it? They'd have gotten photos of all of us. I'm sure if that happened, your stepbrother would have recognized you, even if he hadn't in the restaurant. The drug runners have highly advanced and expensive drones that can be at six or seven thousand feet, easily, and be following you around, Cari. Bannock would have known you were at Three Bars Ranch. And the morning you left? Who's to say they weren't keeping eyes in the sky on you and as a matter of course, followed your truck out. Some of those drones have infrared capability, and can see through the darkness. If that's so, it's possible they tailed you at a distance. And once they knew you were going to be in one of the desolate, isolated desert areas we have in the US, it would be easy for Bannock to fly out there, get picked up by one of his men and brought out to where you were on that last day, heading for that raptor facility."

Shivering, Cari moved her hands slowly up and down her upper arms. "God, this is creepy!"

"That's how druggies work," Dan said. "They have the money to buy the latest, most expensive gear and weaponry that they want. Whether Bannock comes clean and tells us how he found and tailed you, is another story. But from my experience with drug runners and cartels, which are active in our state as never before, I think I'm pretty close to what actually happened."

"It makes logical sense to me," Chase growled. "So, we'll be called to Bannock's trial to testify for the prosecution against him, right?"

"At some point, yes. Right now the attorney general

for the state of California is still gathering evidence. They won't go to trial until they have what they need to convict Bannock. And I'm sure they will."

"Will they put him away for good this time, Dan? Do you know?"

He shrugged. "I don't know, but I'm hoping so. The fact that he tried to murder both of you will probably put him in the slammer for the rest of his life."

"Without chance of parole," Chase growled.

"I'm sure the prosecutors will want that as part of the deal."

"If he ever gets out," Cari whispered, "he'll come after me and my mom again."

"When the prosecutors call you and ask you to come, and they question you at length, you can tell them exactly that. The fact that Bannock broke out of prison is really the nail in his coffin, as far as I'm concerned. I believe they're going to put him inside for the rest of his sorry-ass life, where his type belongs."

"Do you think he'll run his gangs from prison?" Chase asked.

"Possible, but instead of control belonging to Bannock, although he does have a strong cartel in Southern California, it will most likely pass to the next strong leader who isn't in prison. Eventually, Bannock will lose his clout, his ability to hold that cartel together."

"And if that's so," Cari said, hope in her tone, "that means he can't send a hit squad after me or my mother?"

"Right. Because a drug cartel doesn't like going off in directions that don't make them money. They really don't want law enforcement snooping around. They want to be underground and sell their drugs. They don't gain anything by sending a hit team after you or your mother. It just opens them up instantly to more scrutiny by the FBI and law enforcement. It's the last thing they want to happen."

"Good to know," Cari breathed, giving Chase a look. He reached out, squeezing her hand, giving her a reassuring smile.

"Well, from the looks of it," Dan teased, smiling a little, "it seems, Cari, that you are going to be around for a long, long time with this cowpuncher here. He's the meanest dude in the county. You just don't mess with a military-trained sniper. You just don't, and Bannock found that out the hard way. You'll always be safe here with us, in Silver Creek. So? Go home with your cowboy, Cari, and take the time to decompress together over what's just happened to the two of you. Okay? If anything else comes up, I'll call you."

October 25

Cari was at the first of her four Flow Hive platforms, making a weekly check on all of them. The last of the season's honey had been collected weeks earlier. The warmth of the sun drove away the chill on her shoulders as she carefully inspected each hive.

There was white frost on the grass around the hill, some of the grass already having turned yellow from the freezing nights. Chase had told her snow would start falling in late November, and then in earnest, in December. She wore a dark green nylon jacket that dropped to her hips, and it kept her warm. Her hair, now back to its natural black color, was growing and she was thrilled about that.

There were still some wildflowers, the five-foot borders around each of the large clover and alfalfa fields, in late fall bloom. The bees were flying and making their last honey for the year. Cari left half the honey in each hive, taking only half for commercial purposes. This time, no hive would starve for lack of honey.

Since returning from California, her whole life had changed in so many ways. Her body tingled in memory of earlier this morning, waking up, turning over and sliding into Chase's arms, kissing him awake, exploring his hard, magnificent body naked against hers. Just thinking about it made her want him all over again.

She heard the crunch of gravel and looked up. There was a part of her still on guard, even though Dirk was now in prison once more, in solitary confinement twenty-three hours a day, with one hour out in the yard for exercise. She had been able to visit her mother a month later after the crash, spending a week with her. It had been a tearful, happy reunion. Her stepfather had apologized profusely for Dirk's behavior, and she took the apology graciously. Sometimes, there were souls who were born into this world, she thought, that were damaged beyond repair when they came in. Her stepfather was as kind as her real father had been, clearly in love with her mother. Cari knew he'd suffered just as much as they had in a different way. No parent likes to think they created a murderer. It was a load he would carry until the day he died, although to Cari's mind, he wasn't the one who made Dirk the way he was. His real mother had been a drug addict all her life, and she wondered if Dirk hadn't taken a great deal of abuse from her.

Life, to her, was always an ongoing mystery, a Pandora's box of good and bad, sweet and sour. Right now, her life was sweet as honey and filled with nonstop happiness.

Straightening, she saw a ranch pickup parking behind hers on the dirt road below. A slight breeze made some of the last leaves on the deciduous trees take off and fly like birds for a moment. She enjoyed watching them dance and twirl on the invisible currents.

Lifting her hand as Chase placed his black Stetson on his head, he waved to her and he climbed the slight knoll toward her.

"Is anything wrong?" she asked, wondering why he was out here at this time of day. Generally, he was in his office all morning and it was in the afternoon that he made his trips by truck around the huge ranch. She thought how darkly tanned he'd become throughout the summer. And he had a blue chambray shirt on, sleeves rolled up to below his elbows, a pair of elk-skin gloves sticking out of his back pocket.

"No," he said, coming up beside her, sliding his arm around her waist, dropping a kiss on her smiling lips. "I just wanted to see you, is all," he murmured against them, and then released her.

"It was a very nice way to wake up this morning," she said, moving to the next hive to check it out. Theresa and her family had winterized them in the past three weeks. He followed her. "Did you get lonely?" she teased, kneeling down, checking the cedar on the concrete, making sure there was no wood rot, and there wasn't.

"Oh, sort of," he said.

She stood up, giving him a quizzical look. "You're up to something, Chase Bishop. What is it?" She put her hands on her hips. She swore she saw his cheeks redden, but couldn't be sure because she was facing the sun.

"Busted," he groused, and then gave her a shy, boyish look.

She saw him pull something out of the pocket of his chambray shirt pocket and frowned, waiting to see what was in his hand.

He cleared his throat a little nervously and held a dark blue box in the palm of his left hand. Meeting and holding her questioning gaze, he rasped, "I know it hasn't been long, but I thought . . . well . . . maybe this was a good time," and he fumbled with the box, his fingers large and not adapted well to small, delicate jobs such as prying open the top of the tiny blue box.

Cari stared down as he opened the box. There, nestled in blue velvet, were two gold rings. One had an etching on it that she couldn't quite make out. The other intrigued her. It was a series of channel-set, transparent yellow stones with horizontal black inlay between them. "What on earth," she said, reaching for them.

"I hope you like them," he said, worry in his tone. "I want your hand in marriage, Cari. I had these specially made for you . . ."

Gasping, her fingers froze above the wedding ring set and her eyes widened. "Marriage?" Everyone she knew lived together and didn't get married. Her generation thought marriage was old-fashioned.

He moved, uncomfortable, still holding out his palm with the box in it. "Cari, I love you. I'll never stop loving you," he rasped thickly, "but I want what we have to mean something a lot more than just cohabiting together. Any two people can live together. But to get married? That's a commitment. I don't know if you agree with me on it or not, but I think what we have is worth getting married for."

Touched to the point of tears, her smile watery, she took the box, looking at the rings. "They're beautiful, Chase. And yes, our love has certainly stood some tests. Really stressful ones."

"Do you love me enough? See me as a forever partner with you, Cari? Because that's how I see us."

She felt sorry for Chase. He was shifting from one cowboy boot to another, totally unlike him. She closed the box and threw her arms up around his powerful shoulders. Pushing up on her toes, she whispered into his ear, "Yes, I'll marry you. Now will you stop moving around like a mustang who wants to escape?" and she laughed, meeting his eyes, which held relief in them.

His hands fell on her shoulders and he grinned bashfully. "Then you'll marry me? Really? You're not doing this just because I want it, are you? I need to know you feel as strongly about this as I do."

"I do, Chase," she whispered, her voice breaking. Cari closed her eyes when he leaned down, kissing her lips with such tenderness that tears ran silently down her cheeks, the liquid flowing to where their mouths clung to one another, as if to seal their overflowing love.

Reluctantly, Chase eased from her mouth, setting her down on the ground. "You need to look at those rings, Cari. I don't know if you'll like what I've done. I need to explain them to you. Okay?"

He was precious, more the shy, nervous little boy than the heroic and courageous man who had saved her life. She opened the box and he stood to the left of her, watching.

"Take out the engagement ring?" he asked, and pointed at the yellow and black gemstones that lay flat against the surface so they couldn't snag and be pulled out of the setting.

Cari pried it out. She laughed with delight as she looked at it more closely. There were five faceted rectangular yellow stones with four black stones, like a stripe, in between them. "You know," she told him, sliding him a wicked look, "if I didn't know better, I'd say this looks like the abdomen of a honeybee." She grinned widely. "Well? Am I right?" Her heart melted as the largest smile she'd ever seen, pulled at his mouth, his gray eyes dancing with sheer joy.

"Yes," he said, amazed. "Yes, I had a woman jeweler in Silver Creek make it specifically for you. I didn't know if you'd recognize it or not, but you did. I feel pretty good about that."

"It's hard to miss, Chase." Cari was deeply touched by his thoughtfulness. "What are the stones?"

"They're very rare topaz. Yellow is rare anymore, the real yellow topaz. And the black stones are black tourmaline, and it's set in eighteen-carat gold from Alaska. I figured they have bees up there. Right?" He gave her a searching look.

Laughing, she nodded. "Bees all over the world, Chase. Will you slide it on my finger?" She handed it to him and presented her left hand.

He placed his hand beneath hers. "This is the best

thing that's ever happened to me: you." He slid the ring on her finger. It fit perfectly. Cari lifted her hand, studying it and watching it glint in the sunlight.

"This is beautiful, Chase . . . thank you." She threw her arms around his thick torso, squeezing him with all her might. She felt such love for him. What other man would possibly have an engagement ring made from scratch to emulate the honeybees she loved so much? She felt his arms loosen around her.

"You have to look at the wedding ring, Cari. I hope you like it." He peered down at her, worry banked in his gaze.

She took the thick, wide gold ring out of the box and looked at it closely. "Oh, my," she whispered, awed. "Chase! Those are honeybees etched in the metal! They're so beautiful!" She just looked at him in disbelief that he would do something like this, something that meant the world to her, and have it created just for her.

"You like it, then?" he asked, sounding worried.

"Oh! This is truly a work of art! And there's four honeybees on it! I just *love this*!" And once again, she threw her arms around his shoulders, hugging him for all she was worth. He held her tightly against him, their heads next to one another. "This is just the best, happiest day of my life, Chase Bishop! You are so thoughtful! I'm sure no other woman in the world has a honeybee wedding ring set!" She laughed, stepping away from him, meeting his relieved smile. In some ways, men were so fragile, and that is what made her love this man even more.

"There's only one of you, Cari," he began, becoming

serious. "I . . . well, I wanted something special for you because truly, I've never met a woman like you."

"What? You call me fey, like I'm more myth than real." She laughed, shaking her head, absorbing the beauty of the engagement ring, how much it meant to her.

"Well," he stumbled, "you're not a myth, but you are magical to me. Sometimes, when I look at you, I wonder if I'm making you up. Or, if you're really a fairy in disguise, and someday will disappear and go back home, leaving me alone."

"Ohhhh," Cari said, cupping his cheek, kissing him swiftly, "I'm not magical . . . well . . . the bees share their magic with me, but I can assure you, I'm going nowhere. I love it here, Chase." She looked around at the beauty, inhaling the woodsy scent of the fallen leaves, the sweetness of green grass and the clean, pure air of the valley.

He came and placed his arm around her shoulders, drawing her against him as he looked out over the land cared for by generations of his family. "We're the next generation for this land we're standing on," he rasped, kissing her mussed, shining black hair. "And I can't think of any other woman than you, standing at my side with me, to caretake it."

She looked up, seeing the love of the land reflected in his softened features. "It will be our children, someday, that inherit it from us, Chase. And what a wonderful gift that we'll work hard to give them." She felt his hand tighten around her shoulder, saw the tears glistening in his eyes, realizing just how deeply this moment was touching him . . . and touching her.

"Family," he managed, rasping, "means everything to me. It always has."

"To me, also." She sighed, resting against his tall, strong body. "I love you for a thousand reasons, Chase. Every day since we almost died out in that California desert, I think of one of those reasons why I do." Her voice softened, and she gave him a tender look. "Can you imagine two or three children helping me and you when we're out here on the land? How much fun it's going to be to show them how beautiful Mother Earth really is, how to love her and respect her in return?"

Nodding, he swallowed hard. "Lately, I've had some dreams I've never had before, Cari."

"Oh? What kind?" She knew that about once a week he'd have a nightmare from his time spent in the Sandbox. He'd wake up sweating, shaking, and she would, once he was awake, ask him if he wanted to be held by her. He always said yes. And then, as she held him with her woman's strength and love, the shaking and trembling would stop, and eventually, Chase would fall asleep on her shoulder, holding her and she, holding him. "Not another nightmare?"

"No . . . no, nothing like that. I've never had dreams like this before . . ."

"Tell me about them?"

"I'd dream of babies, and little kids, running around with us. We were laughing and having lots of fun."

"Hmmm, are you given to precognitive dreams, I wonder?" she teased him gently.

"My mother does have those kinds of dreams and they always come true."

Her eyes twinkled. "Well, they say psychic abilities pass down through the family."

"Do those dreams bother you?"

She shook her head, and looked at the sparkle of the sunlight through the gold topaz on her ring. "I dream of beehives, bees, and there isn't a more family-oriented group in the world."

"Good," he said, relieved. "When would you like to tell Mary and the rest of the crew here on the ranch?"

"Why not invite Mary over for dinner tomorrow night? We can make it a family celebration of sorts."

"I like that." He rolled his eyes. "But I have to warn you, my mother has been after me, ever since I came home, to get married. She says she's getting old and she wants grandchildren sooner, not later."

Laughing, Cari said, "Well, we'll just have to see what we can do about that."

"When would you like to get married?"

Sobering, she became serious. "Chase, I honestly thought I was going to die out there, huddled at your feet, hiding behind that huge juniper tree. All I could think of were the things I loved, like you, my mother and step-father, and how I hadn't told them how deeply they have been a rudder in my life, thanking them for all the thousands of hours they spent preparing me to become an adult." She reached out, gripping his hand. "I hope this doesn't shock you, but how about a December wedding?"

His brows raised marginally. "Okay by me."

"Then, let's make it early December and a Saturday, so everyone who wants to come, can attend."

"That's doable."

"Mary knows we're living together, so I don't think she's going to raise any fuss, otherwise."

"No." He sighed, shaking his head. "Because she'd do damn near anything to have a grandchild."

"Are you ready to become a father?"

"It's scary, I have to admit, Cari, but with your help and guidance, I think we'll muddle through Parenting 101 okay."

"You change the diapers, Bishop. *Not* on my to-do list."

His cheeks reddened and he shot her a sly look. "You are one wicked woman, you know that? But I love the hell out of you. We'll tackle this stuff side by side, and yes, I'll learn how to change diapers."

"And I'm going to breastfeed," she said firmly.

"All for it."

"Good, then it's settled."

He pulled her into his arms, kissing her long and deeply. As they parted, he rasped, "I'm going to love you forever, sweetheart."

Don't miss the next book in
Lindsay McKenna's
exciting SILVER CREEK series

STRENGTH UNDER FIRE

Due out in October 2021
Turn the page for a sneak peek!

Chapter One

"This is my new home . . . a new chapter in my life . . ." Dana Scott whispered to herself, sounding unsure about her life-changing decision. She had just bought a broken-down old log cabin and a hundred acres with the only money she had left in the world. This was her dream home.

She stood there, at ten a.m. in the cool morning, a range of Wyoming mountains behind and east of the cabin, rising out of the Silver Creek Valley. Fifty acres of land was composed of timber on the slopes covered with conifers. The rest of the land was on flat Wyoming valley that was an agricultural paradise. A slight breeze ruffled her loose red hair that lay against her shoulder blades. Pulling her denim jacket a little tighter around her, she felt panic rising and wrestled it down, like she always did. No stranger to fear, it had been a good friend the last few years of her life.

Drawing in a shaky breath, Dana had spent what her

parents had left her, and the last of it was in a bank in Silver Creek. She had no job—yet. She was farm raised, but there wasn't much of a call for a woman who had farm skills nowadays.

Looking up at the sky, it was a pale blue, the morning air clean, and the cheerful call of birds getting ready to nest was music that lifted her battered spirit.

Had she done the right thing? Spending money on this land and this broken cabin? Like the coward she was, she had run away from her traumatic past. Looking to make a break and start over, she'd left the Willamette Valley, rich winery and agricultural country in Oregon, and headed to Wyoming. Having taken a master gardener course earlier in her life, she'd used her knowledge and checked out the pH of the soil here in this valley, and it was perfect. Of all the places she'd potentially chosen in four different states, this valley had the richest soil with the right mix of pH, consisting of alluvial silt from old rivers now disappeared, and loamy clay. It was just the right formula for growing vegetables and fruit trees.

Her mother, Cathy, had a green thumb that she'd passed on to Dana, and she had plans for a huge garden. Once more, Dana reminded herself that this was her dream home, no matter how dilapidated and barren-looking the cabin was, and the wintered land just starting to come alive in mid-April.

A new start. A new life.

Despite all these changes, she felt a void and emptiness within her heart that nothing, not even buying the Wildflower Ranch, could fill. This ranch had been established in 1900 by a German husband and wife. Gazing left to right, she could see the winter had tamped down anything that had been growing wild here for several decades. There was a creek out back, perfect as an irrigation source for her plans for that garden and small orchard she'd envisioned.

She'd made an appointment with Mary Bishop, owner of Mama's Store, the most popular place in town to buy anything, and she'd filled out an employment form earlier in the week. Today, she'd find out if she had a job or not. Mary sold only organic, non-GMO fruits, vegetables, and meat. Although she had not met Mary in person, everyone spoke highly of her, and Dana had an appointment in less than an hour to speak with her. Her stomach clenched in anxiety. She had to have a job!

Dana knew she had to have income or she wouldn't be able to make the payments on her ranch property and bring her dreams to reality. There was a lot of fear gnawing at her. Could she pull this off? Had she just wasted her deceased parents' hard-earned money?

Feeling anything but happy, she walked slowly around the log cabin. Behind her, the main highway leading to Silver Creek was a quarter of a mile away. The dirt road into her property was deeply rutted and lacked grading, and would need a lot of care on a timely, ongoing basis. What was odd to her was that there had been a lot of vehicle traffic on it, and she could see where the flat land had a road of sorts plowed through it, heading to the slope of the mountain, disappearing into the thick, dark pines. Maybe it was locals who were hunting? She didn't know, but now that she had bought it, the first thing she was going to erect was a stout gate to stop unwanted visitors.

Her dark green Toyota pickup, more than ten years old, had handled the rutted dirt road easily. Turning on the heel of her work boot, she stared at the two twenty-foot tall timbers standing upright at the entrance to the place. Over time, and with lack of maintenance, the carved wooden sign that had once rested across them to create a wonderful entrance, had toppled off those two stout timbers, thanks to the seasonal winds that scoured the valley during the winter. It lay in two broken five-foot pieces, near the entrance. Etched into the battered, weathered oak sign were the words: WILDFLOWER RANCH. Whoever had been commissioned to create it had been a wonderful wood-sculpture artist because the words were carved into it, as well. It had lost its varnish a long time ago, the wood roughened by the winters. Still, she wanted to do something with it, get it fixed and lifted back into place where it had been for the family who had loved this place.

Dana wondered if the German wife, Hilda, had been responsible for that sign, or one of her offspring had it created? She would never know because the family had died out in 2000, with no one else to pass the ranch on to in their family. Since then, the land had lain dormant, unused, the cabin's upkeep gone, leaving it and the land to the ravages of time and weather. No one, the Realtor had told her a week ago, would buy the ranch because of the small family log cabin. It would have to be razed and a new home built on the property. From his point of view, the land was worth something, but the log cabin was a total loss. She almost said her life was a total loss, too, but she bit back the remark. She had to rebuild her life, just like this cabin needed loving care and attention to come back to life, as well.

Dana didn't want to destroy the cabin built in 1900 because, in part, it symbolized how she'd felt for the last several years. Destroying the log cabin, to her, was like symbolically destroying herself. She wasn't anywhere near healed from her experience, but saw the cabin as a reflection of where she was presently. Determined to save the cabin, and in doing so save herself, she'd bought the place. Her mother had always said life was unfair, but the way her entire world got upended, it was more than unfair. It was a daily hell on earth for her.

Glancing at her wristwatch, she saw that the appointment with Mary Bishop was thirty minutes away. Time to get a move on. Mary was considered the maven, the queen of Silver Creek, she'd discovered. The lively woman, everyone warned her, didn't act her age at all. She was spunky, driven, full of great ideas and easily excited over new projects. Dana thought, from talking to several people over at the Silver Creek food bank and kitchen where she volunteered on one of the days of the weekend, that maybe the word *passion* best suited go-getter Mary Bishop. She was a woman on a mission and she took it seriously.

Dana wanted this appointment with Queen Mary—and she meant that label in kind terms—to go well. Queens could rule with grace, responsibility, and in her idealistic world, a queen would have a great love of her people. Mary sounded like such a person, and that's all Dana could ask for.

Mama's Store was bustling with townspeople, lots of children, and some people with service dogs mixed among the crowded aisles. It was a huge place, far larger than she imagined from seeing it from the highway. A woman clerk led her back to Mary's office. Everyone was happy here, she noted. There were smiles, lots of laughter and neighborly chatting amongst those who pushed the grocery carts around the store.

Stomach tight with fear of rejection, Dana followed, trying to keep her face looking normal, not fearful or anxious. Pulse pounding with stress, she pushed through the crowd, following the clerk through the loading dock area and to a small glass-enclosed office. Inside, she could see a petite woman with short, silver hair working at her large, messy-looking desk.

"Go on in," the clerk invited, opening the door. "Mary, here's Dana Scott. She has an appointment with you?"

Taking a deep breath, Dana moved forward, spotting a chair in front of the desk.

"Yep, she does. Come in, Dana," Mary invited, lifting her head, waving her into the office.

Instantly, Dana could feel the elder's piercing scrutiny. Her stomach clenched, the door closing quietly behind her. Would Mary have a job for her? "Yes, ma'am," she said, standing, hands clasped in front of her.

"Sit, sit," Mary murmured, and gestured toward the chair. She put down her pen and moved some papers to one side, grabbing a blank piece of paper and placing it in front of her. "It's nice to meet you. Are you new to Silver Creek?"

Sitting, Dana murmured, "Yes, ma'am, I am. I've been here for two weeks."

Squinting her eyes, Mary said, "I hear from Judy, over

at the food bank, that you've signed up to work a day on weekends over there."

Dana tried to keep the surprise off her face, but didn't exceed. "Well . . . yes, yes, I did."

"Why?"

This was supposed to be an employment interview. Thrown off by Mary's gaze fixed on her, making her feel as if she were being checked out, Dana tried to relax. Opening her hands, she said, "Because I was raised to give back to others who didn't have as much as we did."

Giving a nod, Mary said, "That's commendable. We need folks like you in our valley. Here"—she looked around at the busy loading dock area where boxes of goods were being off-loaded from the semitruck—"we're all one big, messy family."

"The Realtor said the same thing," she said, nodding.

"How's that sit with you?"

"Fine. I grew up on a large farm in the Willamette Valley of Oregon, and everyone knew everyone else. We were like a large family, too, of sorts."

"Good to know." She pulled an employment form from another stack of papers, looking down, frowning and studying it. "So? Why on earth would you leave your farm in Oregon to come here?" She looked up at Dana.

Uncomfortably, Dana moved in the chair. "Life changed," was all Dana would say. "I needed to find something close to what we had in the Willamette Valley and start over."

"Hmmm," Mary said, giving her another searching look. "We buy organic produce from that valley. I'm very well aware of how important it is to Oregon. The

Willamette is a north-south valley, one hundred and fifty miles long. Very rich soil there, and a wonderful place to grow any crop. Wine owners love that area, too. Silver Creek Valley has very similar soil conditions."

"Yes, that's why I chose to come and put down roots here. I just bought the Wildflower Ranch."

"Ah," Mary said, sitting back in her chair. "Did you now?"

Dana wasn't sure it was a smart thing to admit to Mary, who reminded her of an eagle, missing nothing. Her face was wrinkled, but that didn't take away from the authority or power she had. "I know it's run-down . . ."

"We all have times in our lives when we're run-down, too. Even ranches here go through that up-and-down cycle. What do you think of the place?"

"It has possibilities. The soil is an excellent mix of al-luvial and loamy clay; perfect for plants and fruit trees."

"So?" she said, rocking back in her chair. "Tell me what your plan is for it."

Dana wanted a job, not to discuss the broken ranch. Still, Mary's interest was there and her voice was kinder once she found out she'd bought the place. Dana said, "I want to repair the cabin, use the fifty acres on the flat of the valley to grow organic vegetable crops and put in a small orchard of about thirty trees."

"It has a nice, year-round spring behind that cabin," Mary said, nodding thoughtfully. "So, you're going to farm it? Any animals you gonna raise on it?"

Shaking her head, she said, "I'm vegan. I don't eat meat. I can't stand to see animals slaughtered. I plan to raise vegetables, have a small herb garden, and plant fruit trees."

"Of course," she said, sitting up. "So? We're right at the beginning of our gardening and farming season in about a month. You got a tractor and plow? That soil needs to be turned, aerated, before you can plant anything."

Dana loved Mary's intelligence. "You're right about that. The soil doesn't look like it's been turned over for decades. I don't have a tractor."

"Want one?"

Taken aback, Dana stared at her. "What?"

"My son, Chase Bishop, has an old, antique farm tractor that's not all electronic with wazoo doodads and computers in it. He was looking to sell it to someone who might have a use for it."

"That sounds good, Mrs. Bishop—"

"Call me Mary."

"Yes, ma'am."

"Cut the politeness, too. I admire your respect, but remember what I said earlier, we're all family. You don't refer to family in those terms. Right?"

A sliver of a grin pulled at the corners of her mouth. "Okay, Mary, I can do that."

A quick nod. "You're wanting a job here because?"

"I need money to restore the cabin and rent or lease some farm equipment so I can realize my dream of bringing the Wildflower back to life."

"You're not afraid of hard work, are you? Or really tough challenges. But then, you're a farm girl and have been working every day of your life on your parents' farm."

"That's true," Dana admitted.

Mary scribbled a note on another piece of paper. "I'm gonna call my son, Chase, owner of the Three Bars Ranch.

I'm gonna ask him to loan you that old John Deere tractor and have it brought over there by flatbed truck, so you can start using it. What else do you need?"

Taken aback, Dana's head spun with confusion. "I . . . well . . . Mary, I'm looking for a job."

"And you're volunteering a full day at our food bank once a week, giving back to the community. Right?"

" . . . er . . . yes . . ."

"Remember? We're family?" She poked an index finger toward her. "Family works together as a team. You don't have the money to rent a tractor. Chase is gonna loan you his old antique so you can get going turning that soil and getting ready for planting."

Stunned, Dana blinked, unable to speak.

"And," Mary went on, making another note, "I'll make sure he brings over the disc and other plowing equipment that you'll need, as well as tools that go with farming. That place of yours needs a barn, you know? You have to have one to store your equipment, work on it, and keep it protected from the elements."

"Yes," Dana whispered, stunned, "I know that. It's in my plans."

"Good, good," she praised. "You also need a wrangler. Can you afford one?"

"Yes, I think I can. Part of my plan is to hire someone to help me. I can't do it alone and I know that."

"I got just the gent for you. His name is Colin Gallagher. He's a real loner, ex-military, has a lot of bad PTSD symptoms. He's working for my son as a wrangler over at the Three Bars Ranch, but wants to work on a smaller property. Colin is a hard worker, takes direction well, and won't disappoint you."

Dana didn't know what to do or say. "I—uh . . . Mary, this is . . . well . . . amazing . . . thank you."

Here's my plan for you, young lady," she said, scribbling a third note. "I've been looking for a local valley farm to provide me with certain vegetables and fruits in season. I'm needing a good, responsible farmer to fill in because the person who was doing this, recently died. I need a new individual whom I can work with. If you're amenable to that plan, I will pay you to do this, twenty-five dollars an hour, five days a week, eight hours a day. Fair enough?" She lifted her chin, eyes crinkling as she gazed at Dana.

Stunned by the offer, Dana whispered off-key, "You'd do this?"

"Well, of course I would! I believe in synchronicity. Pete, my dear old friend who used to provide my store for the last thirty years, passed on this last winter. I was looking for a replacement and here you are!"

Her mind whirled with the implications, the help she was going to magically receive.

"And," Mary said, "Chase will continue to pay Colin Gallagher. He's going to be 'on loan' to help you do the work that needs to be done around there. Your first priority, of course, is tilling the soil and getting the crops planted." She pulled another paper from another stack, handing it to her. "Here's a list of what I need, vegetable-wise. You look it over and let me know if you're interested in raising these particular crops. With fifty acres of flat valley at your disposal, I'm roughly calculating that you can supply my grocery store with what it needs nicely. We'll work out the details after you read up on my needs and we'll have several future meetings on your ideas for the land, planting, and so on."

"You're paying me to raise crops you need?"

"Yep."

"Do you expect me to give you those crops for free, even though you're paying me to do it?"

Mary laughed and rocked in her chair. "I don't do sharecropping. You'll be paid fair market price for all your produce. I believe in treating everyone fairly and like family. There's a lot of hard work involved in this farming, and because you grew up on a farm, you understand that better than most."

"I do." Dana was relieved that she would be paid for the produce; otherwise, she was a sharecropper slave and didn't want to be used like that.

"For me, you're a very valuable resource for our valley and my grocery store. But I want you to sign a contract with me, agreeing that no chemical fertilizers, herbicides, pesticides, or GMO seeds will ever be used."

"I'm right there with you," Dana said, trying to take in all of this unexpected good news and digest it.

"I figured you were, but we'll put that in writing because the people who come to my grocery store trust me. I'm not gonna let them down. Also, I'm assuming you're aware of companion planting and utilizing certain flowers, like marigolds, among others, to plant along with the crops. They're natural pesticides from Nature, and that's all you can use."

"Yes, my parents never used anything other than what

you're talking about. They produced alfalfa for cube manufacturers and they wanted 'clean,' non-GMO alfalfa for the animals that would eat it. My mother always used alfalfa cubes in her garden as mulch, because it's a wonderful source of natural nitrogen for garden plants."

"Good to know! I'm pleased." Mary stood up and offered her long, thin hand across the desk to Dana. "Let's shake on it. Around here, in most cases, a person's word is her or his bond."

Dana stood, smiled a little unsurely, still dizzied by what had just happened, and gently closed her hand around Mary's. "You've got a deal, Mary. Thank you for this opportunity. I won't let you down. I promise." She released the woman's hand. Mary beamed, her eyes sparkling, as she sat back down.

"Take my business card there," she said, pointing toward it. "My personal cell phone number is on there. The people who work to make my grocery store what it is, can call me any time they want. Welcome to our family."

Colin Gallagher felt a huge, dark load lift off his shoulders as he double-checked his flatbed load. The antique John Deere tractor was on board, and the disc and other plows, plus a metal box filled with farm tools that this woman, Dana Scott, would need.

Chase had come and got him out of one of the barns and told him his wish had been granted: He was assigning him to a small valley farm that had just been bought by a woman, which would be low stress compared to being around Three Bars. Mary had hired her to become her produce resource for the grocery store, and she asked that he assign a wrangler to help her. Colin jumped at the chance. He hated waking up at night, screaming, and then startling the other wranglers awake, as well. His PTSD was severe, and he was desperate to stop what was happening, but he couldn't. Fortunately, Chase had been in the military and understood. They were working on ten houses that would start to be built for the single wranglers and the families. Until then, the single male wranglers all slept in the bunkhouse. The women wranglers had a separate bunkhouse. He had been ready to quit because he was causing major sleep deprivation for the rest of the hands. And then Chase had come by with this new assignment.

It felt as if life were being breathed back into him as he slowly walked around the flatbed, checking the chains one more time that held the tractor in place, as well as the wide, thick nylon straps across the other items.

"Colin," Chase said, coming out of his office to see him. "My mother says there is no livable place on that ranch."

Frowning, Colin said, "You mean to tell me I have to come back here every night and sleep in the bunkhouse?" It was the *last* thing he wanted to do. He saw Bishop grin a little. Their military background had fused them closely, like brothers, to one another.

"No, I have a fix for it. Mary is buying a double-wide mobile home to be put on the place. I guess Dana, the owner, knows nothing about this yet, so you can break the news to her. You'll both have a bedroom, one at each end of it, so you'll have full privacy. It has two bathrooms, as well."

Relief poured through Colin. "That's mighty nice of Mary to do that for this woman, Dana."

"Dana Scott is her name. Mary likes her a lot. She's a farm girl from the Willamette Valley in Oregon, and that's all I know about her. She's agreed to raise produce that Mary needs for the store, but don't be shocked by how run-down the Wildflower Ranch is. There's a small log cabin there that should probably be torn down and a new house built, instead. Mary counseled one step at a time, here. You okay sharing a trailer with her? It's large enough to give you both privacy and you can meet in the middle where the kitchen and dining room are located."

"I'll make it work."

Chase clapped him on the back as they walked toward the front of the truck. "I know you've been worried about waking everyone at night."

"Yeah," he muttered, pulling his black Stetson down a little to shade his eyes from the rising sun.

"Well, these modern-day mobile homes are pretty air-tight and soundproof, so as long as you close your bedroom door at night, I'm sure Dana won't hear you."

"That's a big relief."

"This mobile home has four bedrooms. Mary's converting them into an office for each of you with two computer terminals, something you're going to need. And she's arranging for a wide-screen TV for the living room."

"I don't watch much TV," Colin admitted, halting and opening the door to the truck.

"You also have my permission to come back here for any tools or other machinery you need. Mary wants to make this as easy as possible on Dana, so she can make the planting this season, on June first. Just leave a list of items you need in my office, and I'll take care of it and have someone drive it out to the Wildflower Ranch for you."

Nodding, Colin climbed into the cab after pulling on his elk-skin gloves. "Sounds good, boss. I'll let her know."

"And get me her cell phone number, will you? Mary's already called the utility companies to put in electric and telephone, and another construction contractor is coming out to dig out a septic tank for the mobile home. She's got a plumber and an electrician already set up to put it in what's necessary before it arrives. Mary says about a week. It's going to be busy and hectic the first week or two, Colin."

"I guess so," he said, shutting the door and rolling down the window. "I'll be in touch. As soon as I unload all this gear and machinery, I'm going to assess what else she needs out there and I'll talk it over with you by cell."

Chase raised his hand. "Sounds good. Adios, compadre."

Relief flowed sweetly through Colin as he turned on the ignition, the massive truck engine coming to life. As a wrangler, there wasn't anything he couldn't do around this ranch, but he was well-known for his mechanical knowledge of engines, heavy equipment operation, and carpentry. As the truck rolled out of the driveway, he headed out toward the entrance, making a left turn, having to take this load through Silver Creek. He knew where the Wildflower Ranch was. Often, last summer, he'd hiked the mountains at the back of it. When his PTSD got bad, going into the woods, working with plants and trees, calmed his anxiety and his stress levels lowered. He recalled the small ranch's history, aware of a family claiming it in the 1900s. Now, this woman, Dana Scott, had bought it.

Who was she? Hold old was she? Did she have a husband and children? Knowing nothing about her made him curious. He hoped she was someone who was easy to get along with. Chase hadn't said anything about her personality to him. Still, he knew Mary Bishop well enough that she had an eye for good, loyal people who worked hard, were honest and easygoing.

He mentally crossed his fingers, turning onto the main road with his load. The sun was bright and he pulled down the visor, not having his dark glasses with him. Pulling the brim of his Stetson a little lower, he pressed down on the accelerator, heading out for his new job. What would it be like? Could he do it? Always worrying that his PTSD symptoms might interfere, he had no idea if Dana Scott was aware of his unseen wounds.

There was plenty for Colin to worry about as he drove slowly through downtown Silver Creek on a Monday morning at eight a.m. Mary had hired Dana Scott yesterday morning. Less than twenty-four hours later, he was bringing her all the farm equipment she could handle. The question he had was: How much did she really know about farming? Because of his PTSD, Colin was a loner. He didn't do well in groups of people and especially not a crowd. He was fairly good with one-on-ones, but if this woman hadn't a clue about farming, he saw that as a hurdle he wasn't sure he could leap.

As he left the busy morning commute into Silver Creek by those who worked in the busy, industrious little town, Colin pressed down on the accelerator. The ranch was eight miles west of the town on a two-lane asphalt highway. Not that far. He wiped his upper lip with the back of his elk-skin-gloved hand. Feeling anxious, he recognized all the symptoms starting to accumulate in him, making his stomach seize up, and his heart pound a little harder in his chest. He was going to have a woman for a boss, not a man. That was going to take some adjustment, because most of his life he had been around and worked only with men. Trying to tell himself that he'd met Mary many times and genuinely respected her type A personality. He always liked the devilry he saw dancing in her eyes, that quick smile and the way she would pat a person's shoulder, as if they were a well-loved family member. And no one was more generous than Mary was. Colin had seen her fund a number of start-up small businesses for owners right here in the valley. She wasn't afraid to invest in people, and believe in them heart and soul.

Was there any possibility that Dana Scott was like that?

Connect with  U s

Visit us online at
KensingtonBooks.com
to read more from your favorite authors, see books
by series, view reading group guides, and more.

Join us on social media

for sneak peeks, chances to win books and prize packs,
and to share your thoughts with other readers.

facebook.com/kensingtonpublishing
twitter.com/kensingtonbooks

Tell us what you think!

To share your thoughts, submit a review,
or sign up for our eNewsletters, please visit:
KensingtonBooks.com/TellUs.